Leonora

The Buried Story of Guadeloupe

Leonora
The Buried Story of
Guadeloupe

by DANY BÉBEL-GISLER

Translated by Andrea Leskes

Afterword by Vera M. Kutzinski and Cynthia Mesh-Ferguson

CARAF BOOKS

University Press of Virginia

CHARLOTTESVILLE AND LONDON

This is a title in the CARAF BOOKS series

THE UNIVERSITY PRESS OF VIRGINIA

Leonora: The Buried Story of Guadeloupe was originally
published as *Léonora: L'histoire enfouie de la Guadeloupe*
© Editions Seghers, Paris, 1985

First published 1994

Publication assisted by the French Ministry of Culture

Library of Congress Cataloging-in-Publication Data

Bébel-Gisler, Dany.
[Léonora. English]
Leonora : the buried story of Guadeloupe / by Dany Bébel-Gisler ;
translated by Andrea Leskes ; afterword by Vera M. Kutzinski and
Cynthia Mesh-Ferguson.
p.   cm. — (CARAF books)
Includes index.
ISBN 0-8139-1515-5.—ISBN 0-8139-1518-X (pbk.)
1. Léonora. 2. Guadeloupe—Biography. 3. Christian biography—
Guadeloupe. 4. Guadeloupe—Social life and customs. I. Title.
II. Series.
CT354.8.L46B4313 1994
972.97'6—dc20   94-26127
[B]   CIP

Printed in the United States of America

Contents

Leonora

The Buried Story of Guadeloupe

Of lives whose space is history

Sété léstravay.
It was the time of slavery.
White men then were so cruel. The things they did to black folks![1]
Grab the men from their homes, throw them in chains, carry them across the ocean, bring them here, to work.
To work without any clue, without saying things should be done this way or that. . . .
Isn't that real cruelty?
And if a black man didn't do well . . . A stake planted in the ground, the man attached. And then the whip . . .
That's how whites treated blacks then.
At Bréfort, just before the town of Lamentin,[2] a path goes down to the right near a large apricot tree. Blacks were put into barrels lined with nails and were rolled down to the bottom of the ravine, sprayed with kerosene, and set alight. The apricot tree fell down, but the stump remained. There's a hole in that stump. That's where the blacks were burned.
Oh, how the whites burned black folks in those days!
One day, at Lamoisse, they nabbed a big black man. A stake was pounded into the ground in front of the overseer's house, a large house with top and bottom floors. The white man's wife stood on her balcony, upstairs. They tied the black man to the stake to be whipped. Each time they raised the whip to him, the woman up above caught the blow. She shrieked, cried for help, suffered lashes and lacerations, was covered in blood. And the man down below stayed untouched.
Ah, what things those Africans knew.

Lè détoua vouè sa konsa yo di:	Some people, having seen these atrocities, cried out:
"Oh. . . Oh! Yo tiré nou an péyi an nou.	"Oh, oh! They carried us away from our homeland.
Yo anchenné nou.	They threw us in chains.
Yo mènné nou isi.	They dragged us here.

Leonora: The Buried Story of Guadeloupe

Yo fè nou travay.	They forced us to work.
Yo pa èspliké nou ka pou nou fè.	They don't tell us how to do things.
Yo ka enki asasiné nou akoud-fwèt	They kill us with their lashes.
Yo ka piké nou, yo ka brilé nou."	They sting us, they burn us."
Sòsyé la di yo:	The sorcerer replied:
"Ében yo ké vouè. Préparé zòt, i lè pou nou alé."	"They will see. Get ready, we are leaving, the time has come."
"Kamen nou ké fè?"	"How will we manage?"
"Toutalè an ké di zòt. Zòt tout paré zòt."	"I am telling you, get yourselves ready."
"Nou pé ké jen woutouné an Afrik.	"We can never return to Africa.
Sé an batiman nou vini.	We came by boat.
Apa asi lanmè nou ké maché. Pyé annou, sé pou alé an la-bou."	We cannot walk across the sea on our feet made for the mud."
"Toutalè an ké vin. Paré zòt."	"Get ready. I will return soon."
Nèg la anni alé an poulayé a poul a Blan la.	The black man entered the white man's hen house.
I wouvè poulayé la. I pwan dé zé.	He opened the hen house. He took two eggs.
"I di yo: an nou alé."	"I am telling you, let us be off."
An pati rèté, an pati alé.	Some followed him and others remained.
Yo alé anhòo pon Boukan la moun té ka pwan piwòg pou alé Lapwent.	They went to Moko Bridge, at La Boucan, where the boats leave for La Pointe.
"Apa èvè pyé annou nou ké alé asi lanmé."	"We cannot walk across the sea on our feet."
Afriken la té sav zafè a-i.	But the African knew how.
Lè yo rivé anba pon la, i fè sòsyé a-i èvè zé la.	They went under the bridge. He used his magic to break the two eggs.
On batiman parèt, flap!	A large ship appeared.
Yo pati, yo alé an Afrik.	They left and returned Africa.[3]

Anmann[4]
Peasant woman from Guadeloupe, Ninety-eight years old.

Of lives whose space is history

Mwen sé Gwadloupéyen
Mwen sé timoun enkyèt a on li-
  lèt inkyèt.
On ti lilèt ki vwè parèt é diparèt

—syèk dèyè syèk—
disparèt é parèt
fanm é nonm zòt senné kon ban
  pisyèt

fanm é nonm zòt dékatyé fanmi
  a yo
fanm é nonm zòt vann anba
  laplas a lankan kon bèsyo
fanm é nonm zòt maké kon bèsyo
fanm é nonm ki trimé kon bèt
  anba fwèt a zòt Mèt.

Sé fòs a bwa a yo ki mòfwazé
  gran bwa an jaden—ba zòt
  Mèt—
E zòt fè fòs a yo sèvi-yo foséyè
  pou yo-menm, Mèt!

Apré sa
kijan fè ou vlé fè mwen kwè
mwen sé vou
vou sé mwen?
Mwen tala!

I am Guadeloupean
I am a troubled child from a
  small troubled island.
A small island that has seen
  appear and disappear
—century after century—
disappear and appear
women and men that you caught
  in your net as if they were a
  school of fish,
women and men whose families
  you ripped apart,
women and men you sold on the
  square, at auction, like cattle,
women and men you branded
  like cattle, chained like cattle,
women and men who, like animals, slaved away under your
  whip, Master.
Their strength transformed the
  forest into gardens—for you,
  Master—
And with their own strength you
  had them dig their graves, Master!
After that
how can you make me believe
that I am you,
that you are me?
I, that child!

Sonny Rupaire

1

Antanlontan, timoun té timoun,

granmoun té granmoun

Long ago, children were children

and grown-ups were grown-ups

The coconut palm my parents planted is by now quite tall, the one they planted on the spot where my umbilical cord is buried, in the hamlet of Carangaise, in the parish of Capesterre-Belle-Eau, in Guadeloupe. That's where I spent my childhood with my brothers and sisters, five boys and four girls.

Papa hadn't much education, but he was a good worker. He raised us the way a man of his time was expected to bring up children, teaching us order, discipline, and respect for our ancestors and our elders. He worked on the Longueteau plantation[5] cutting sugarcane, and he planted all kinds of vegetables in his garden: *malangas, madères,* yams, manioc, Angolan peas, dittany, etc. We grew up on that plantation, raising chickens and pigs, helping Mamma grind the manioc flour she sold in town—in Pointe-à-Pitre[6]—and helping Papa harvest cane from the fields he sharecropped.

At the time of my birth, Mamma didn't lead a very pleasant life. My father returned from that business of World War I. He'd gotten a good dose of poison gas. He started drinking. Just then, right after the war, I was born. My mother wasn't happy, she had no time to sit down and talk with us. And when my father had drunk his fill of rum, he certainly didn't spend time chatting with us either. Quite the opposite; he purposely needled us, and we were better off keeping out of his way.

The atmosphere at home wasn't cheerful. I didn't have a happy family life. The mother is the mainstay, the *poto-mitan* of a family. Even in misfortune, she still loves and cares for her children. We were brought up together, our bellies kept full, we went to school, but our home wasn't merry, and Mamma didn't share her problems with us.

My father disliked any kind of fuss. He forbade us to fight with the other children. And they, knowing how strict and brutish he was, picked quarrels with us. We couldn't sock 'em one back. They'd rip up their notebooks on purpose and then come to my father and say:

Long ago, children were children and grown-ups were grown-ups

"Look what your kids did to us."

"Okay, here's twenty-five cents. Go buy some new notebooks—and scram!"

Those traitors got the money, and we got the beating. And no use protesting; you'd receive twice the dose.

At that time in Guadeloupe, children were children and grown-ups were grown-ups. When Mamma and Papa talked together, we children didn't know what they discussed. Only if it was serious did we have any inkling. But the children would never have dared interfere by saying, for example, "Mamma, stop!" or "Papa, stop!" We didn't have the right. We kept to our little corner, and even in the midst of a real fight, we had no right to separate them. So we just huddled together in the corner.

That's the way it was in our home. I don't know about other families, all I can say is that my father didn't find it one bit amusing when we disobeyed his orders.

Since we lived right near the school, he insisted that I stay in the house till the last bell rang and that I come straight home, especially in the evening. So I could never have fun and play in the schoolyard like my friends, who were sometimes there as early as seven in the morning. I made up for it during recess. I played *pichine* (knuckle-bones), *passe-palet* (leapfrog), circle games, and lots of others things. For fun, we made up our own games. Even if Papa didn't let me play certain games, once at school I followed the other kids.

One evening after school, I joined a group that headed off to knock down mangos with stones and gather, along the roadside, the fallen fruit—the *kabanné* mangos—that ripened at the foot of the trees, hidden by the leaves. I arrived home at six when it was already dark. As my punishment, my father sent me to gather fodder for the pigs. At six in the evening! I'll always remember it. I've forgotten many things, but not that, never. I trembled with fear. Our house, a wooden cabin with several rooms, sat alongside a road, far, far away from the cane fields where the rich grasses grew that I needed to gather. I was afraid. Impossible not to be afraid since it was already dark. First I passed three houses. Still okay there. Next I had to follow a path, leave behind the gardens, and enter the woods. I panicked. My head rang with the words, "Children, don't go out at night! The spirits will grab you, the *Nègres marrons*[7] will carry you away."

I trembled from head to toe. I might meet up with the she-devil or *Man* Ibè's Beast.[8] They could lead me astray and take me off with them. I began to run, to slither down the hill, shutting my eyes so as not to see the immense silk-cotton tree, home of spirits and the dead. Luckily, at the bottom of the hill, I met a woman I knew. If I hadn't recognized her, anything at all might have happened to me, I would have taken her for a spirit.

My father was strict with us. Most fathers were, then. Now, some mothers can't stand by and see children shaken too harshly by their fathers. But in those days, the father was in charge of everything. The mother had authority in the father's absence, but if a child misbehaved, the father was told about it when he arrived and took over. Papa gave us good thrashings. Mamma had her own methods. We could escape from her, run and hide, but she waited till we came back and were in bed; then she used a liana she'd hidden away, and we'd awaken to the sting of her lashes.

Just yesterday, a woman confided in me that she couldn't stand today's children because, in her time, when she brought up her own children, they obeyed without a whimper. I answered that we had to keep up with the times and change, had to understand that we can't raise children today the way we did yesterday. She wasn't too pleased, but I know that I, who brought up my first children well, now have a thirteen-year-old boy who may be the death of me. It's not that his upbringing has necessarily been worse, but his behavior is totally different from what theirs was. For example, they'd never have jumped around all the time the way he does. In fact, in my parents' home, no question of just telling them, "I'm going over to so-and-so's house," "I'm off to see what's-his-name." We had to stay together, crawl into our shells.

No question, either, of forgetting to greet a grown-up, even if our mother was angry with her. Saying hello is very important in Guadeloupe.

I often greet people, even young children I meet along the road. But people don't like to greet one another much anymore, though I'm not sure why. It used to be that when you went out with your mother, if she said hello to someone, you were expected to say hello too. Now, what a fuss! My daughter Emilienne, who lives in France, came to Guadeloupe for her vacation. I took her to see relatives. In Carangaise, the houses are lined up along the road, from one end of the hamlet to the other. That's where I was brought up so I know everyone, in all the houses. Since Emilienne accompanied me, I just said a quick hello without stopping at each cabin. But it's quite a distance from the bus stop to my parents' place. My daughter was beside herself! Since then, when I travel with her, I take a taxi that drops me off at my sister's door. If necessary, I go over afterward and say hello to the neighbors, to those right next door. I let them know I'm around.

I don't quite know what saying hello means to today's children, but I sense their discomfort. In Guadeloupe, people who don't say hello

Long ago, children were children and grown-ups were grown-ups

are considered snobs. This label is easily earned. Not saying hello to everyone doesn't necessarily mean you're a snob, but everyone knows the importance of a friendly greeting. When I used to go to Mass at Prise-d'Eau, all along the way it was, "Hello!" to this one and "Hello!" to that one. My children were upset. They got all worked up: "Mamma loves to say hello. Mamma says hello to everyone she meets!"

That's the way I brought them up, but I've already noticed that they don't like to greet people. As soon as my parents hinted that I should say hello, I obeyed. I would have to force it on my own children. And I don't, because why should people have to see me making them say "Hello, sir! Hello, madame!" And as for a kiss! Well, they do embrace and kiss their friends, but they certainly won't hug someone just to make you happy. Today's children aren't very eager to please!

It used to be that when your mother had a falling out with someone, you weren't allowed to be angry with that person yourself. Adults' quarrels weren't children's business. At least in principle, that is, because, of course, children would hear their parents saying things about a neighbor and be afraid to play in front of her house. I won't chase away a child simply because I'm on the outs with his or her mother. But some adults will.

There'll always be people who rear their children badly. Some give them a good upbringing at home, within the family circle, but the children still behave badly on the outside, night and day. As far as I'm concerned, well-brought-up children act the way their family taught them, don't talk back when scolded, and greet and respect older people. I'm amazed at how children today talk back! As a child I couldn't keep my mouth shut. I was beaten and I protested anyway. But I never would have talked back to my mother the way my youngest daughter did to me.

I asked her to wash her dishes. She answered: "I'll wash *the* dishes. But they're not *mine* and this isn't *my* house."

A friend visiting at the time was shocked. "No one would dare speak to me like that in my house. If I were you, I'd give her a good slap!"

"I know, I know, she reacted badly."

But it's true, she doesn't yet have her own home, the dishes aren't hers. She knows she must wash them but doesn't want us to speak of the dishes as belonging to *her*. I can't beat her for that, she didn't "disrespect" me.

Disobeying adults, cursing in front of them, shows a lack of respect. Children these days say whatever they choose to adults. As soon as they see you, they let loose their dirty tongues. A child may curse with his friends, but I feel he shouldn't do it when he sees an adult coming. If a lady is present, I don't use dirty words: that's what respect means.

Everyone talks about "good manners" this, "good manners" that. But heavens, it's a question of the child. No matter how hard you try to bring them up well these days—I'm not talking about in my youth— they generally don't respect adults. They must know how to respect their parents at home if they're to show respect for grown-ups in the street.

These days, people judge if you were brought up well by the way you eat. When I was young, both children and adults ate in whatever way they chose. It wasn't a question of the spoon in the right hand and the fork in the left, like this and that. If that's the meaning of good manners, we didn't have any at all. The only "manners" we were taught was respect for adults, respect for the family, control over one's words.

At our house we only sat down to eat at the table for special occasions,[9] and not even always then! Mostly we all picked up our plates and went to sit wherever we chose. My mother, always on the same step in front of the door, balanced her plate on her knees and took her time sucking and chewing each fish bone. She ate with her fingers. I think our parents were freer with their bodies and wanted us to be comfortable and eat the way we wanted to. Now you're told: "Your child should learn proper table manners just in case one day he finds himself in polite company."

So I've gotten used to it. I don't know where I learned, but my children know how to behave in the world.

Like allowing children under ten to run around completely naked; it's not done anymore. When we went to bathe in the river, mother took off all our clothes. We played in the river naked, fished for crayfish naked, did everything naked. At home we undressed in front of our mothers, but I never saw my mother undress, I never saw her naked. Bare-breasted, yes, but never all naked.

On Thursdays, by the banks of the river, she undressed us, took our clothes, washed them, and laid them out to dry. They needed to be dry by the time we went back so we could wear them that afternoon to religion class and to school on Friday.

Up till the age of ten or eleven, girls and boys bathed together nude, with their parents there or even alone, just with friends. Bathing suits were unknown. When the girls started to mature and their breasts began to swell, they were given a "bottom," a pair of panties to wear. After their period came, they had to cover themselves up. When a girl bathed with an old dress on, everyone knew she was no longer a child.

That's when your mother would take you aside and explain that you were no longer a child, that you could become pregnant and have a baby. I didn't get my period till very late, at seventeen. I don't know if it was because of an illness or if someone had cast a spell on me. I had

Long ago, children were children and grown-ups were grown-ups

trouble breathing, I was so fat. Although I was seventeen, I didn't ask any questions, not even how women got pregnant. Children didn't dare ask questions. I don't mean they didn't talk with their parents, but there wasn't an exchange of ideas, not a real dialogue. Only recently have parents really started talking with their children. And still, not all of them, so many children have never had a real conversation with their mothers.

I have three daughters. I never said a word to them about men. Even when they got their periods, I didn't say anything. It's true, I didn't tell them a thing. Young people learn everything from their friends these days. They know what it means to get your period. The oldest got hers quite late. It hadn't come, and then, one day, she called me: "Mamma. I have blood in my underpants."

"Well, you've gotten your period." And I gave her what she needed.

My second daughter is rather lazy. She never really knew how to wash out her own underpants. So when she got her period, I flew into a rage. She was eleven years old, and I asked myself: How could such a dirty child care for her cloth rags? (Disposable sanitary napkins didn't exist then.) A neighbor who had heard the whole exchange took me to task: "What are you saying? All mothers have one wish—to see their daughters get their period. And you're complaining! Aren't you ashamed?" I was so angry I didn't even bother to answer.

I'm not like some mothers who check on the regularity of their daughters' periods. Only one of my daughters was something of a problem: she was seeing a young man and missed her period one month. But it wasn't anything, only a month late. People advised me to prepare an infusion of *doudou* flowers. Supposedly it helps "bring it on" and can also produce a miscarriage. Had she caught a chill washing clothes at the river? Since I didn't know, I worried. I didn't think she was pregnant, so I said nothing. I kept my anxiety to myself. Finally her period came, and up till the time of her marriage, she never had another problem.

I can tell when my youngest daughter has her period because her panties run in the wash; but I don't really keep track of it with my girls. They've never been particularly loose. If they'd wanted to, they could've taken advantage of my trust since I never bothered them much about it and don't think about it all the time. The children could've fooled me, but that's the way I am. I often say to them: the one who gets in trouble knows why because, in these enlightened times, people generally don't let themselves, let their *kò*, go adrift.[10]

One of my neighbors already keeps an eye on her daughter, who hasn't even gotten her period yet. She's been watching her for a long time, and closely. She doesn't give a damn about her sons. The boys get the girls pregnant, and their mothers are proud of it. But the girls bring their babies home.

My daughter undoubtedly has a different view of things, but my own comes directly from my mother's generation. Nowadays, and I'm not kidding you, they even go so far as to teach sex education at school! Were we told what goes on between a man and a woman? When a young woman got married or set up housekeeping with a man, what did she know? The old ones were very secretive. They thought their morals were correct. But they weren't quite because, with their secrecy, they sent us out to get in trouble. We could've slept with a guy without knowing there was a chance of his getting us pregnant. We heard nothing, knew nothing. Some young friends, looser than we were, carried on their little affairs, but what did you really and truly know?

In addition, you didn't have the right to look an adult straight in the eye or to stand in front of women when they were busy making something special: *carapate* oil that keeps our frizzy hair from getting too dry.

One of my aunts was a real expert at making it, but once we children had helped her shell the beans, she chased us away. She feared we'd divulge her secret method, tell how she made it. She didn't want us to watch her. But how could she stop us when the kitchen was only screened off by bamboo slats? I hid and carefully watched the whole procedure. Since I already knew how to shell the beans, why not learn how to make the oil?

After I'd watched for several months, I asked my mother to let me make some, just to try a *poban,* a little bottleful.

"Why? So you can ruin my oil? No! Where have you learned how to make oil?"

"You learned from auntie. So did I, Mamma."

"What a nervy child! If you want to try, okay by me. But if you ruin my oil, watch out! You'll get as many lashes with the liana as there are husks in this pile of *carapate* beans!"

I was used to shelling the beans, removing the kernels, and mashing them with a pestle. But I didn't know the secret of when exactly in the cooking to remove the foam and then cool everything down. I had carefully observed that my aunt would add a bit of soap at a certain moment and then the oil would separate out cleanly. But at what point? When the mixture started to boil and turn white, I cried out: "Look at the oil!" My mother began to argue: I was going to ruin the oil. Forgetting all respect due an adult, I raised my voice and pushed her away.

Long ago, children were children and grown-ups were grown-ups

"Let me do it. I'll manage."

All excited, I didn't take my eyes off the pot. I added the bit of soap, cooled the mixture, and the oil separated out. I had succeeded, and in making a whole liter! My mother didn't believe her eyes when she saw so much. From then on, she had me make the oil. For the rest of her life, she never again made it herself.

I had stood up to my mother, I hadn't been afraid, but, in general, fear was what guided us.

Of course, we had a great deal of respect for our parents, but thinking back, I remember mostly fear and that we, as children, weren't respected. There is a way to get children to respect you but I don't think it should be through fear. Certain parents terrorize their children; that's why one sees so many who can't express themselves. It's true, even today they still can't speak out. Neither could we.

When we returned home from school, we first did our chores before sitting down to study. We were organized like a line of mice, from the biggest to the smallest, boys and girls, each responsible for a specific task. The girls did the dishes, prepared the meals, washed the clothes in the river, and tidied up the smallest children. The boys helped in the garden, swept the packed earth in front of the house, and took care of the pig.

Our most difficult job was fetching water—every morning before school and every evening. At least by going in a group, we made the task somewhat more bearable. In the morning, we went to *Man* Yoyo's spring; in the evening to Monsieur Léonil's, at the bottom of the hill. What a circus when it rained! With the buckets balanced on our heads, our toes had to grip the slippery mud as we carefully watched every step, and sometimes we'd get to the top, slip, and give back all the water to the earth! Nothing for it but to start again. No question of returning home with an empty bucket. Each of us had a system for avoiding this slippery hill. One, on his way to work in the morning, would cut holes in the slope to help secure his footing; another would try to make a path through the bushes. . . . It was hard but we were used to it, and what's more, it was our job and we never thought of refusing.

Certain Thursdays, my mother took me with her to help prepare the manioc.[11] From the age of six, I helped her grate while the older children harvested the roots. They brought sacks of roots and began the peeling and washing. Then the roots were *gragé*[12] and squeezed to expel all the poisonous juice. Meanwhile, others had lit the fire under the cooking platter and piled on dry wood. It really heated up well. The very finely grated manioc was spread out on the burning hot platter.

With a large wooden spatula, the *mèt a mannyok,* the manioc was stirred and stirred, first a twist to the left, then a twist to the right. That was the most difficult part and the most unpleasant too. Standing there in the heat, watching as the flour dried to make sure it didn't burn. It takes a certain knack. Afterward, we used the fire to cook *cassaves.* What remained on the platter, the *kakapanyol,* was for us children.

When the time came to harvest the sugarcane, the entire family—men, women, and children—were mobilized to help Papa. From our field we had to carry the bundles of cane up the hill to the side of the road. The bundles were heavy, the slope steep, the red ants bit our necks, but we helped willingly since we were working our own land. Papa never asked for our help when he worked for the white man.

Our upbringing was a never-ending hardship. I call it a hardship, but it wasn't really as bad as all that. My parents brought us up according to the customs of my grandparents, the old folks. I, too, raised my first children the way I was raised. There were strict rules of conduct which Papa followed to the letter.

I never saw him wash any dishes. That wasn't done.

His responsibility included earning a living by working on the white man's plantation, in the sugarcane fields, from six in the morning to 1 P.M. Once back home, he'd find his meal ready, then rest and go off to work in his own garden in the afternoon. Like all the other women, my mother was responsible for the house. Preparing the meals, washing, ironing—that was the work of women and girls. Asking a man for help would have been unthinkable! The women did it all.

My father was such a strict and authoritarian man that the other children in the area feared him and didn't come play outside our house. Luckily, we could meet them every day at evening prayers, since my father allowed us to go.

An old gentleman said the prayers. His name was Papa Yen. He gathered all the children together at six o'clock. I don't remember the prayers he taught us, but I do recall our joy. What happiness to go out in the evenings, to be with Papa Yen, and to play after prayers!

I can picture myself, a little later when I must have been somewhat older, part of a circle in the moonlight. I don't know if my father had sent me there, or my mother, or if I went without permission, but there I was, in the circle with my sister and all the others. Each moonlit night, Monsieur Fistibal assembled the girls and boys, and parents too, under the large mango tree near *Man* Leonille's place. We made a large circle, sang, listened to tales, and played *boutou.*[13]

Armed with a *boutou* made from two shawls of brightly colored

Long ago, children were children and grown-ups were grown-ups

Madras cotton tightly braided in the shape of a baton, Papa Yen would plant himself in the middle of the large circle and chant:

"Man Fiyolé, au bord de la rivi-
ère Séré sa, é sa, séré sa . . . "

"*Man* Fiyolé by the riverside,
hide this for me, and this, hide
this for me . . . "

Whack, the *boutou* hit you. In you'd go, into the center, and the chant would continue:

"Madanm la ka vini, séré sa douvan kon déyé, séré sa . . . "

"Madame is coming, hide this in
front, behind, hide this . . . "

Oh, it was wonderful! The only real freedom I remember having as a child. I never missed a single one of those moonlight gatherings. I was all ears and eyes so as not to lose a word of Monsieur Fistibal's stories. I can still hear him telling *Persillette* as clearly as if it were happening today.

"*Tim tim!*"

"*Bwa sék!*"

"Everyone, old and young, parents and children, and you too, roosters, chickens, pigs, dogs: silence! Come and be seated, open your ears, close your mouths, listen to the story of Persillette's troubles, Persillette, the brave little girl."

"*Yé krik!*"

"*Yé krak!*"

"On the edge of the hamlet of La Plaine, in the parish of Trois-Rivières, behind Savon Hill, lived *Man* Didine and her husband *Pè* Jofrèt, with their pig, three goats, and seven chickens.

"A little farther along, a large silk-cotton tree hid the cabin of an old woman. She never went out, never visited anyone, no one came to see her, and no one knew her name. She was called simply 'the old woman.' If you had the misfortune to meet her on the road, you quickly turned your head away. She had the eyes of a sorceress, which burned into you.

"*Man* Didine was heavy with child. One evening, she yearned for a bowl of fish soup. *Pè* Jofrèt's brother, a fisherman, had just brought them a beautiful fresh pink snapper. Why wait till tomorrow?

"*Man* Didine scaled the fish, prepared the garlic, onions, hot peppers, chives. . . Damn! No parsley. You know how pregnant women are. She not only pictured the fish soup in her mind, she could already taste it in her mouth. Fish soup without parsley wasn't soup at all. She must have parsley.

"*Man* Didine, with her natural woman's curiosity, had already taken a turn around the old woman's house when she was out. She'd seen lots of parsley in the vegetable garden.

"*Man* Didine feared but also yearned. She decided to go and knock at her neighbor's door. She tapped gently,

"Knock! Knock! Knock!

"She tapped harder,

"Knock! Knock! Knock!

"She called out:

"'Is anybody home?'

"No answer.

"'Anyone here?'

"Night began to fall; *Man* Didine was hungry. She said to herself: 'Perhaps my neighbor is asleep already. I don't want to bother her. I'll just gather three sprigs of parsley.'

"And *Man* Didine entered the vegetable garden. She pulled up three sprigs of parsley and, since she was good and honest, left a coin in their place as payment.

"Just as she was getting up, she saw the old woman standing before her, straight as a rail, arms crossed on her pale dress, jaw set, and eyes shining with fire.

"'What are you doing in my garden? You've come to steal.'

"*Man* Didine felt her baby turn over in her womb. She trembled like an acacia leaf.

"'I haven't taken anything, only three sprigs of parsley for my soup. And I left five cents for it.'

"'I don't want your money. You've come onto my property, you've pulled up my parsley. You'll pay me for it.'

"*Man* Didine was very frightened. She said, yes, yes.

"'What I want is the child you're carrying. I'll be its godmother. So you remember always what you did tonight, you'll call her Persillette.[14] And now, away with you.'

"*Man* Didine hurried off. Her desire for fish soup was gone. She returned home in tears.

"That's how the true story of Persillette began. She hadn't even left her mother's womb, poor thing, before misfortune befell her.

"Is the audience sleeping? *Yé krik!*"

"*Yé krak!*"

"No, the audience isn't asleep.

"*Man* Didine gave birth to a girl child. The day of her baptism—

Long ago, children were children and grown-ups were grown-ups

zip!—the old woman appeared to name the child. She slipped her hand under Persillette's head and said:

"'Seven days after the seventh year of this child's life, she must cross my threshold and come to live with me. You, her mother, have made me a promise. You're all bound by this vow.'

"And she returned home, disappearing behind the cottonwood tree.

"*Man* Didine and *Pè* Jofrèt had prepared all sorts of good things to celebrate the baptism: juices, liqueurs, and especially *chodos,* and a tall, tall seven-layer cake. . . .

"But no one felt like laughing any longer, no one wanted to have fun, or even to eat or drink. Who were the only happy ones? The children. They ate and drank everything themselves, enough to make their stomachs burst.

"Persillette grew up and became a beautiful little girl. Each morning, she was held between her mother's knees while her well-combed-out hair was plaited into two long braids. *Man* Didine never spoke to Persillette of what had occurred before her birth, but every day she thought about it. She kept turning the question over in her mind: How could she escape the old woman?

"Persillette's seventh birthday approached. She started school. The schoolhouse was far away, down one hill, up another, and visible only once you passed through the forest.

"On her first day, *Pè* Jofrèt accompanied Persillette. He carried a small basket containing the lunch *Man* Didine had prepared for her: two green bananas, a piece of fish, and a *grossetorange.*

"'This evening,' said *Pè* Jofrèt, 'you'll return home with Noémie who lives near us. Don't dawdle along the way. Be careful that night doesn't fall while you're still in the forest!'

"When they arrived at school, Persillette was a little afraid to leave her father; it was the first time she'd seen so many children together, and the teacher didn't look very friendly. . . .

"Oh, Persillette, that's nothing! If you only knew what was in store for you!

"*Yé krik!*"

"*Yé krak!*"

"As it turned out, the teacher wasn't so frightening, and, by the end of the day, Persillette could already recognize "0" and "1".

"She started off on the way back home with Noémie. At the top of the hill, in the forest, they stopped briefly to catch their breath. Persillette sat down on the root of a large mango tree. Just beside her she saw a hole in the trunk of the tree. Without thinking, and talking all the while, she stuck her hand into it and then her arm. At the very bottom of the hole, her fingers felt something. With the natural curiosity of a little girl, Persillette tugged, pushed, tugged again, and finally pulled a box out of the hole, a locked golden box.

"Noémie cried out: 'Put that back in the hole, right away!'

"And off she ran.

"Persillette didn't understand a thing, but she didn't want to be left behind. She replaced the box in the hole, and then she too ran. A little farther on, Noémie was waiting for her. She was out of breath, her heart beat rapidly: bum, badum! bum badum!

"'Persillette, never pick up things you find in the forest or on the paths. They belong to sorcerers and devils. Especially gold. And don't tell anyone or you'll have bad luck.'

"Persillette promised. When she arrived home, she told her parents all about her day at school but breathed not a word of the golden box.

"Soon her seventh birthday arrived. Her parents didn't know how to tell her the news.

"'Persillette, my daughter, you know how much we love you.'

"'Oh yes, Mamma. I love you too.'

"'My little girl, we must part.'

"'Oh no, Mamma! No, I don't want to!'

"'Alas, little one, I've made a promise . . .'

"And *Man* Didine told Persillette how she got her name, the story of the parsley, about her godmother, everything. . . . Persillette cried. She didn't want to leave her beloved parents. The only times she had seen her godmother, the old woman had looked intently at her with those red eyes. Persillette had felt a chill run through her whole body.

"*Man* Didine cried.

"*Pè* Jofrèt cried.

"Persillette was the first to dry her eyes.

"'Mamma, Papa. Don't cry anymore. I'll go to my godmother's house, but don't worry, I'll be back, I'll find a way.'

"The seventh day after her seventh birthday arrived. Persillette, brave little Persillette, gathered up her three dresses—the one for Mass, the one for school, and the one for home—her nightgown, and her little underpants. She tied them all together in one of *Man* Didine's large, colored cotton squares. She kissed her parents lovingly and headed off down the path.

"She hadn't even arrived at the silk-cotton tree when she smelled a terrible odor. Like that of a dead dog lying alongside the road. She approached the cabin holding her nose. There the old woman stood, straight as an arrow.

"'I've been waiting for you Persillette. Why are you holding your nose? Don't you like the aroma of your dinner? Come, let's go in!'

Long ago, children were children and grown-ups were grown-ups

"She ushered Persillette in. The cabin was very dark and sweltering under the hot tin roof with the doors all closed. It smelled of rotten leaves, incense, candles. . . . From the beams hung dead birds, dried frogs, a large iguana. . . . In a corner, a skull leered at her. Persillette wanted to run away. Her godmother pushed her toward a box filled with dirty rags.

"'Here's your bed. Now, go out and fetch me ten buckets of water from the spring. You'll eat afterward.'

"While she carried the buckets of water, Persillette thought: 'This godmother is really strange. I must find a way of getting away from here without causing problems for Mamma.'

"After the tenth bucket had been filled, Persillette was tired and hungry. The old woman dipped an enormous ladle in the *canari* that sat on three hearthstones behind the cabin. She filled a *coui* to the brim with a mixture that smelled very, very strong, and she served it to Persillette.

"The poor creature sat down on a stone in front of the door. Her stomach turned over. How could she possible eat it?

"'Godmother, what's in my *coui*? Meat or fish?'

"'It's meat, my girl, good meat to make you strong.'

(It was rat and bat meat.)

"'Godmother, are these yams or *malangas* with the meat?'

"'They're good root vegetables, my dear, to fatten you up.'

(They were leftovers from the pig's meal.)

"As soon as her godmother went into the cabin, Persillette emptied her *coui* in the bushes and went off into the forest. She was hungry and looked around. She found some *zikak,* some rose apples, and two guavas. Her stomach stopped grumbling, and she returned to the cabin. She undressed, washed herself well, put on her nightgown, and went outside to sit on the doorstep alongside her godmother to take in the cool night air.

"'Persillette, aren't you sleepy?'

"'No, godmother, I just want a little fresh air.'

"'Persillette, don't you want to go to sleep?'

"'No, godmother, it's too hot in the cabin.'

"Her godmother had some special things to do. She wanted Persillette to fall asleep. She started to sing: 'Persillette, go to sleep! Persillette, go to sleep!'

"Persillette sang back: 'No godmother, I'm not going to sleep. . . .'

"I look up, I look down, I don't see anyone.

"'Persillette, go to sleep! Persillette, go to sleep!'

"Persillette's eyes began to close. She went into the cabin, lay down on the pile of rags in her box, and fell asleep. Suddenly she sat up, awakened by a noise. The old woman stood there, filling a *poban* with a red liquid. She waved her hands about, pronounced some words, drank the liquid, and fell on the floor, bam!

"Persillette pretended to sleep. Hidden behind her rags, she trembled but wanted to see everything. Strange things were happening on the floor. The old woman's dress became all shapeless, her skin separated from her body and remained there on the ground. A ball of fire rose up, swirled around, and took off into the sky, passing through a crack in the door.

"Persillette, completely terrorized, was unable to sleep. What would happen next?

"At about three in the morning, the ball of fire returned. It landed gently on the floor, rolled toward the skin on the ground, extinguished itself, and soon Persillette saw her godmother rise up. Then, totally exhausted, Persillette fell asleep.

"The next morning at school all the children were speaking about a *soukounyan*.[15]

"'I saw it, I saw it, a large ball of fire!'

"'It's going to suck blood, bite people. . . .'

"'But what is it? How can it do that?'

"'Papa told me about it, it's a person who's made a pact with the Devil and agrees to bring him a child's heart.'

"'It's been a long time since a child died in town.'

"'Maybe the *soukounyan* promised to give it to the Devil later. . . .'

"Persillette didn't say a word. Her blood froze in her veins. She had just understood who the *soukounyan* was and who the child. That day, she didn't concentrate much at school. She tried to figure out how to get away from her godmother. On the road home she questioned Noémie:

"'Tell me, this story of the *soukounyan,* isn't there any way to trap it?'

"'Yes, of course, but you must know how. My uncle told me about a man he knew who had managed to do it a long time ago.'

"'What did he do?'

"'He hid outside at night to keep watch at the crossroads. The *soukounyan* passed by over his head. He spoke certain words, traced a cross on the ground, and planted a pair of scissors in the exact middle. When the sun came up, the *soukounyan* fell down. All that was found was a pile of burned flesh.'

"'What words did he say?'

"'Ah, that's the secret. The words the *soukounyan* says when it transforms itself. No one knows them. . . . Persillette, I'm afraid. What if it comes to steal our hearts?'

Long ago, children were children and grown-ups were grown-ups

"When she returned to her godmother's house, Persillette did her chores as if nothing had happened. She fetched water, fed the pig, swept the doorstep. . . . She ate a small bit of dry bread that Noémie had given her. The meal prepared by the old woman smelled even worse than that of the day before, so she threw it out and went to lie down.

"That evening she didn't want to fall asleep. She waited, firmly determined not to let her heart be taken. The old woman stayed outside a long, long time. . . . Persillette's eyes started to close. She fell asleep. Watch out, Persillette! Wake up!

"*Yé krik!*"

"*Yé krak!*"

"Clink, sounded the bottle as it knocked against the *poban*. Persillette heard it. She opened one eye. Her godmother lifted up the *poban*, swallowed the contents, and recited:

"'Wadika! Wadiko! The Evil One's claw is the Villain's paw. Wadika! Wadiko! Fly, fly, let me fly!'

"She fell to the ground, slipped out of her dress, lost her skin, transformed herself into a ball of fire, and took off into the sky.

"Persillette had listened well, understood, and remembered. She jumped out of her box and searched the cabin. It had only one room and wasn't large, but it contained so many jars, boxes, bottles, and barrels. . . . She rummaged through lotions, powders—yellow, green, red, and violet—through dried leaves, and bones. . . . Persillette looked and looked. Finally, under the mattress, all the way in the back, she found a small roll of paper tied with a ribbon. She opened the knot, and on a yellow parchment she saw black letters with two signatures at the bottom, red as blood. Persillette wished she could understand the writing but she couldn't read.

"So you see, you little lazy ones, why you should study hard at school!

"*Yé krik!*"

"*Yé krak!*"

"Persillette thought for a while and then made up her mind: she'd ask her parents to read the mysterious writing for her. If she hurried, she'd have time to get back before her godmother returned.

"Flip, flop! She was outside, barefoot and in her nightgown, running with the roll of paper in her fist.

"Knock, knock! Open up!

"'Who's knocking like that at this hour? Who is it?'

"'It's me.'

"'Who's me?'

"'Me, Persillette, your daughter. Open up!'

"'My Lord God Virgin Mary Joseph Saint Anne! Persillette! Has something happened?'

"'Don't be afraid, Mamma. It's just a piece of paper I found at godmother's house. I want to know what it says.'

"'A piece of paper? What paper? First of all, its not paper. It looks like human skin. Don't get involved in what you don't understand, my daughter!'

"*Pè* Jofrèt had already put on his eyeglasses. He read:

> On the third day of the full moon in the month of November, the undersigned agrees to sacrifice a young girl, remove her heart, and offer it to Beelzebub, prince of the shadows. In exchange, the undersigned will receive, now and henceforth, upon signature of the present pact, the fifth power of the forces of hell, the power of vampirism.

"Hardly had this last word left his lips, when a strong wind began to blow, the whole cabin trembled, the tin roof shook, and a devil, completely naked and all black, appeared at the door.

"*Man* Didine didn't hesitate an instant. She grabbed her bottle of holy water, made the sign of the cross, and sprinkled the Devil as she cried out:

"'Off with you, Satan, to the eternal fires!'

"The Devil disappeared. He had come because he'd heard his name called out. Everyone at *Man* Didine's trembled. Holding his head in his hands, *Pè* Jofrèt slumped down on his bed. Persillette huddled against her mother. But the time had come for her to leave; it was almost midnight. She rolled up the parchment with its ribbon and went out into the night.

"Near the silk-cotton tree, she saw someone right in the middle of the path. Upon approaching closer, she realized that her companion wasn't a living Christian soul: a human doesn't have the cloven hooves of an ass, a human isn't tall as a coconut palm, a human doesn't have eyes as red as embers, a human doesn't have the horns of a bull.

"It was the Devil awaiting her. Persillette pretended not to see him and tried to slip by. But the Devil blocked the whole width of the path.

"'Mister Devil, please let me pass. I must return to my godmother's house.'

"'Give me that parchment.'

"'It isn't mine.'

"'If you don't give it to me, I won't let you by.'

"And a wall of fire rose up in front of Persillette. The poor little thing fell back. The Devil made a move to grab the rolled-up parchment.

Long ago, children were children and grown-ups were grown-ups

Persillette wanted to run. Fire surrounded her. She threw the contract into the flames. The fire, the Devil, everything disappeared.

"Uh oh! Persillette, what have you done? What will happen to you now?

"*Yé krik!*"

"*Yé krak!*"

"Finally, Persillette could pass by the silk-cotton tree. And then, what did she see? Rotten luck! In front of the cabin, very much upright and awake, the old woman was waiting for her.

"Persillette thought, 'I'm lost. How can I get out of this mess?' She approached her godmother.

"'Good evening, godmother!'

"The old woman caught her by her hair, yank!

"'Where have you been at this hour? You've rifled under my bed. You've taken my contract. Where have you hidden it, you miserable wretch? I'm going to kill you right now. I'll preserve your heart in a jar of frog's blood and offer it up to the Devil at the full moon.'

"She threw Persillette on the table and raised her large knife. Persillette didn't agree at all. She wasn't going to let herself be killed like that. She twisted and turned and finally freed herself, though leaving some hair in the old woman's fist, grabbed the knife, slipped off the table, landed on her feet, dashed out the door, and disappeared into the forest.

"Run, Persillette, run! Hide! The *soukounyan's* vengeance is terrible!

"All of a sudden Persillette saw a light, a red light moving right toward her. It was the ball of fire! Persillette stopped. Running wouldn't help. She'd have to fight it out.

"She traced a cross on the ground, planted the knife right in the middle, and cried out:

"'Wadika! Wadiko! *Soukounyan,* I am your master. Fall, fall, you must fall down!'

"And there was the *soukounyan* circling about her head with the noise of a cyclone. The whole forest shook, the bamboo clattered, the gum trees groaned, the acacias quivered. . . . Persillette could hardly breathe, her throat was blocked, her bowels knotted up, she was going to die! A small voice whispered to her: 'Pull out the knife! Pull out the knife!'

"It was true. Persillette felt that if she pulled out the knife, she wouldn't suffocate any longer, the forest would calm down.

"Where did the voice come from? Wasn't it the *soukounyan* who wanted to trick her? Once the knife was pulled out, wouldn't the *soukounyan* descend on her to drink her blood and rip out her heart?

"Persillette resisted. Her whole body hurt more and more. 'What the hell!' she thought. She moved her hand toward the knife. Shusht! All the noises stopped.

"No, Persillette, no!

"Persillette drew back. The *soukounyan* howled, the forest rumbled, everything started up again.

"The earth cracked open. Persillette was thrown into an abyss. She fell, head over heels; over and over she turned. 'Lord God Virgin Mary!'

"She couldn't stand it any longer. Again she moved her hand toward the knife. Her head stopped turning. Persillette responded:

"'Nothing doing, *soukounyan*. You won't get me!'

"The *soukounyan* shrieked with rage. Then it turned into an enormous bright light, and the beast with seven heads appeared. It was right there, right next to Persillette, spitting fire from its seven mouths, and behind it came the monsters, dragons, devils. . . . The forest crawled with devils, like mongooses in an abandoned cane field. Persillette was burned, stung, pinched, bitten; she was suffocating, her eyes ran, her body felt as if it was being rubbed with hot pepper. . . . All the time she heard: 'Pull out the knife! Pull out the knife!'

"She dug in her heels and stood straight as a post, determined to fight to the finish. The *soukounyan* circled around her, close, closer, closer still. Fast, faster, faster still. Persillette was lifted off the ground. Soon the flight of the *soukounyan* slowed. It moved away from Persillette, flying lopsided like a man full of rum. To the right, to the left, up, down. It fell, got up, fell again, and, blip!—went out.

"The devils, dragons, and monsters disappeared, and the forest became quiet again. The sun lit up the treetops.

"Daylight had arrived! Persillette was exhausted, her whole body ached. She got up and walked over to where the *soukounyan* had fallen. Only a pile of burned, blackened, smelly flesh remained. Now she could pull out the knife. She had won the battle.

"The skin of the old woman, abandoned like a dirty dress, was found on the floor of her godmother's cabin. Persillette returned to the home of her parents, *Man* Didine and *Pè* Jofrèt. And well she deserved it, the valiant little black girl."[16]

That wasn't the end of the story. To vanquish the Devil, Persillette had to destroy its nest, which she found in the trunk of the same mango tree where she had discovered the golden box. For a second night she fought—this time against the spirits, against *Man* Ibè's beast. Finally, Persillette set fire to the Devil's lair and was delivered from him forever.

2

Asi chimen zékolyé

On the road to school

The strange thing is not that Guadeloupean children draw
houses with smoke curling from the chimneys, but that they
draw faces in profile with long straight noses, small lips, and
pointed chins.

Gérard Lauriette,
Philosophie de l'enseignement des écoles A.G.E.P.

Nineteen twenty eight, the year of the terrible cyclone that ravaged
Guadeloupe, the year I started school.

The sheet-metal roof of our house, a large four-room cabin with balcony, had been blown off. We were lucky, most of the village houses
lay completely demolished. Ours, made of strong "northern wood"
and protected by shingles, withstood the wind. Devastation marked
the countryside. Even the coconut palms and the breadfruit trees were
uprooted. Fallen trees blocked the paths, banana plants hugged the
ground like sweet potato creepers, breadfruit, mangos, and custard
apples littered the ground. The sugarcane had lost its *zanma* (leaves),
and only the stalks remained standing. The children, who filled their
stomachs in this forest of sticks, thought it a blessing.

For the first few days, the breadfruit, bananas, all the fruit knocked
down by the squall fed us. But it quickly rotted, leaving provisions
in short supply. The mayor organized food lines. Each family had an
allotment of rice, oil, and cod. We'd go into town with a coupon.
Mother, having left at 5 A.M., might return at 6 P.M. without so much
as a piece of fish or a grain of rice, with only her torn dress bearing
witness to the fight.

Little by little, life returned to normal. People rebuilt their houses
and replanted their fields. Soon after the cyclone, at age nine, I
started school.

The trunk of a large hog plum tree[17] alongside the road marked the
old wooden building rented by the town in order to open this school,
my first school. A small, ordinary cabin, with two doors in the front
and two in the back, one on each side, and with a sheet-metal roof
that the sun heated up like an oven and the rain pounded like a drum,

pounded so hard it kept us from hearing the teacher even when she shouted. The inside dividing wall had been removed to make one large room from two smaller ones. A narrow aisle separated the younger children from the older ones, and the teacher stood in the middle, handling the two levels. Children from all the surrounding area came to this school in the Upper Carangaise. My parents lived right nearby, so I didn't have far to walk.

The following year, a new, much larger school was built down below, with slats in the windows. I went there to study for my certificate of elementary studies. Other students, also born in 1919, stayed up in the old school. They became jealous and began to dislike me. Why had I been chosen? Was it simply a question of the month of my birth? I'd turn fourteen in November.[18]

My memories of school are hazy. When you begin late—and age nine isn't exactly early—and don't stay long, school can't leave very clear images. You can't have sucked dry its juice nor shared a sense of comradeship with your peers. To really live your school experience intensely, your older brothers and sisters must show an interest in it; as a young child, you must breathe in the smell of learning at home. My family wanted to send me earlier, but because of the school's small size, I had to wait till someone else left or got too old for the class and was sent away. And while you're waiting, your age catches up with you. . . .

Neither my father nor mother had gone to school. When they were young, parents weren't very eager for their children to get an education. They couldn't afford the cost and preferred to have the help at home. They themselves had known only sugarcane, manioc, and poverty. Besides, there were few schools in the countryside and not many children in those schools. So what if you were absent? You went to school or you didn't go, it made no difference. When your mother needed you to work the fields or watch a younger brother, you just dropped out of school. She'd go tell the teacher: "You won't see the little one anymore, she'll be helping me now." That's all there was to it. No one made a fuss the way they do today.

Many people of my age now reproach their parents: "I don't know how to read or write, and it's all your fault. You wanted me to clean the house or take care of the younger kids rather than go to school."

In 1930 things began to change. The teachers told the parents of bright children: "It's a shame, Madame, and it upsets me, Isidore's a capable student and could do well; don't keep him home with you, send him to school, he'll become a gentleman." Some parents understood that education could serve a purpose by helping their children move up in the world, get a good job, develop.

On the road to school

When, as a young child, I was first learning to read, I still couldn't evade the call to household chores. Later, my homework became more important, and my mother would say: "Let Leonora study her lessons in peace. Lise, can you please take her place?"

Did my mother have something in mind? Did she understand the importance of school? She needed to come to my defense because my sister Lise didn't always gracefully accept doing my chores while I studied.

"Leonora's lazy. She only pretends to work. She takes advantage of me because I'm sick and don't go to school."

Actually, I did hide my laziness by pretending to study, while Lise, in poor health, often missed school. I was the only one of all my brothers and sisters to advance very far in school. I, the youngest. None of them attended for more than a year or two.

When only two months remained before the exam for my certificate, there was no longer any question of my fetching water from the spring or putting the meal on to cook. In addition to the weak coffee I drank every morning, with some *cassaves,* my mother gave me a large bowl of milk. And on Sundays, I got the beef marrow, the second best cut of meat after my father's. I had to build up my strength, "nourish my brain" with snails, crayfish, *chodo,* and all sorts of good things normally reserved for special occasions like marriages, communions, and baptisms.

Class started at 7:30. As the hands of the clock approached 8, you'd be kept out, as punishment, and were forced to stay in the sun because, before leaving home, you had to fetch water and to finish all your chores. I never arrived late, and luckily too, because the whip rained down on those who did, and kneeling in the sun all morning was awful.

During my school days, the teachers—both men and women—were real dictators who terrorized us. We had to ask their permission for everything. To go to the toilet, you'd have to wait your turn. Only one child was allowed out at a time. Sometimes, if the kid before you took too long, you couldn't hold it in any longer, and to your horror, you wet your pants. Then you'd feel the blows!

The first year I wasn't much interested in what went on in the classroom. The teacher didn't speak my language, Creole, and I couldn't say anything, discuss anything, do anything. And I was afraid, afraid of the blows. Mademoiselle Clarion had a reputation for having invented the following correctional method: one blow to the palm or the closed fist for each error. And no question of complaining to your parents. They were the ones who brought us to school and handed us over to the teacher saying: "Here's my child. If he doesn't obey you or learn properly, beat him. If he protests, tell me, and I'll give him more of the same."

In the evening, no one wanted to confess that he or she had been beaten that day. Now things have changed: parents come to school and insult the teacher if he so much as lays a hand on their child. In my day, a mother might also separate two fighting children by giving each, hers and the other one, a smack or a lash with a leather belt. Everyone took it for granted and congratulated her. The other day, I watched a quarrel between a father, who had stopped a fight this way, and the mother of the second child. She screamed: "Aren't you ashamed to hit a child who isn't yours, you big bully? You can't do that. I'll take you to court, just wait and see, you'll get what's coming to you. No one has the right to touch my child, no one!"

And similar scenes occur nowadays at the schoolroom door! During the time I attended school, I never heard anyone criticize a teacher or even ask for an explanation. It was a quick "Hello, sir!" or "Hello, miss!" when they passed on the road. No conversation, but better not forget the greeting. It seems to me there was a certain respect, a feeling that the teacher was somehow different, larger, of another species. As a child I used to wonder whether any of them—teachers, priests, nuns, policemen—peed or crapped, if they ate the same things we did and had people to bathe them. They always acted superior to us and to the people we knew. The arrival of a priest or a nun in the village made for big news. We had to behave: no running, crying, or laughing, just a sweet smile for them. With their great black robes, their white hoods framing their faces and falling onto their shoulders, they looked like God himself approaching.

Today, lots of white folk teach school but not then. Yet our teachers weren't really dark-skinned blacks either. My first teacher was a mulatto, Mademoiselle Clairon, then I had a *chabine*[19] as fair as one of our little *Blancs-pays*.[20] She was called "the cat," and she spoke in a tiny, tiny voice that emerged like a fine trickle of water. After the mulatto woman and the *chabine,* I had a fat-bellied mulatto man, Monsieur Petibas. They were my only teachers. The teachers didn't change often then. Now it's an endless stream.

To enter the classroom, to go outside for recess, or to leave, we had to form lines and sing. One, two, one, two, the barefoot company advanced. In the school up on the hill, only an occasional pair of shoes was to be seen. There were more in the upper grades. Those parents who could, bought an inexpensive pair. We only wore shoes to school on the first day. After that, they were put away and only taken down for special occasions: Mass on Sunday, funerals, and village festivals. They had to remain new-looking, clean, and shiny as long as possible.

On the road to school

No chance of buying two pairs, and, of course, the same pair couldn't very well be used for school too. Even when we went to Mass, all of us, big and little, carried our shoes or hung them over our shoulders, the laces tied together, one dangling in front and the other behind. When we reached the spring of Pérou, near the church, we each picked out a corner and washed our feet before putting on the shoes. If well cared for, a single pair could last a year or two. Of course, those shoes were better made than the shoddy ones of today. Yet children can't attend school barefoot now. I don't know whether the school makes the rule or parents feel pressured, but you must find something to cover all the feet in the family. My children have worn every possible type of foot gear: shoes, sandals, *mika, pépa.* Even if you haven't a cent, you can at least get *pépa,* the very cheapest sandals, for your children. The word *pépa* comes from the Creole, *pé pa,* and French, *je ne peux pas* (I can't), buy real shoes.

You shoe and clothe your children according to your means. The dress is tailored to match the client's purse! At least in principle, because nowadays the children do the ordering. No matter that I say to my daughter who is in tenth grade: "Save that best dress of yours for going to Mass."

"No, Mamma. What a silly idea, to keep clothes for special occasions! Mass, school, they're all the same. I want to look nice when I feel like it."

She overdoes it. One dress in the morning and another in the afternoon! And as for shoes! Children decide which styles they'll wear. They want this one and not that one. It's up to you to find the money. The children's revolution. And the parents let it happen, go along. Children ask, parents give and don't know how to refuse. Just seeing these young girls run off to school, all made up in their new dresses and high heels, makes you wonder what their parents expect them to get, an education or a man. Maybe they don't think about anything besides showing off their attractive, clean children. Or maybe, these young girls like to parade around in front of their friends and show by their clothes that they're from a higher class, can change dresses three or four times a week, and go to places the others can't. It makes an impression on the youngsters with only two or three dresses for the entire year, who wash, mend, and iron them carefully. Their parents are either poorer or stricter: I can give you this much and this is what I will give you. I agree that girls should always try to look their most beautiful and pay attention to their grooming, but it shouldn't be overdone or used to humiliate others who haven't the means.

Among my classmates, only three came to school with shoes on. One little, ladylike mulatto girl and two Indians from the Upper Carangaise.[21] They were brought up that way, wearing shoes all the time. On Thursdays, we went down into town for religious instruction, barefoot as was the rule. Our Indian friends and Florinette, the mulatto, had to comply. They removed their shoes, hid them in a sugarcane field, and then picked them up on the way back so as to return home just as they'd left.

On our way back, we gathered all sorts of fruit along the roadside: guavas, surette apples, malaca apples. We ate sugarcane and apricots. At the top of Manbo Hill lived a spotlessly clean old woman. I don't remember her name but can still visualize her bed, raised off the floor and covered with sheets made from flour sacks stamped "Product of France." Her cookware gleamed like the sun. We'd stop at her place for a drink of water before returning home, our stomachs all *doudoumso,* skin stretched tight as a drum's.[22]

There was no cafeteria in the school. At noon, the students heated up their lunches. Florinette, somewhat snobbish, didn't like to be seen with a lunch box. She'd ask one of us to carry it for her saying: "Stay here with me. I'll share it with you."

From her big lunch box she'd remove yams with meat sauce and cabbage salad. When crayfish were available, her mother would put aside three or four big *rois-sous* for her with yellow bananas. Never breadfruit, which cooled down too quickly, but *malangas, madères, adò.* . . .

Our parents could only give us a small portion of weak coffee in the morning before we left with a *cassave,* and for lunch, bread with oil and a piece of roasted breadfruit. Florinette would give us her lunch box. She said she'd eaten so much meat she was sick of it. She wanted bread with a spoonful of oil in the center, like the rest of us. She'd run over to a small *lolo*[23] near school to buy some.

Before leaving for school, she'd already had bread and milk, she told us. She and her sister could buy whatever they wanted in several stores where their father had opened a charge account. They took advantage of the opportunity and bought all sorts of delicacies. Florinette shared them with us: ham, sausage, things our parent's couldn't give us. She nibbled a mouthful here, a mouthful there but was always full, had already eaten too much at home.

My Indian friends didn't belong to the class of poor, despised Indians who lived on the plantations. Their father was a manager, their mother ran a shop, and the children helped us all benefit from it. Almost every day they brought us "French food": cheese, white butter spread on thick bread, and also sweets—*pipilit,* tapioca candies, *doucelettes,* coconut sugar candies, breadfruit *popotes,* and especially mint- or lemon-flavored candies. . . . They cleaned out the shop to stuff their friends. And made lots of friends that way, too. We always went looking for them, we children of agricultural workers who had nothing. I don't mean to say that by feeding our faces they staved off the normal mistreatment of Indians, because we really liked them anyway.

In general, Indians were poorly esteemed in the community, but this family lived up on the heights with the black *gwokyap* (the rich blacks), like the Bolo family. They got along well and often saw each other socially. The real disenfranchised Indians, called *kouli Malaba* or *Teïta,* worked and lived on the plantations at Cambrefort and Changi. Wherever they assembled in large groups, trouble always followed.

The Indians invited everyone, without regard to skin color, to their great religious festival, the Maliémen,[24] to share the goat curry served up on banana leaves. When the festival of All Saint's approached, the Indians organized dances on the plantations. I found them beautiful and comical at the same time, like Mardi Gras. Weeks before, they hung their flag in a mango tree near the manager's house. When the day itself arrived, Indians came from all over, crowds and crowds of them, as if for a public demonstration. All the blacks who wanted to come were also welcome. Food galore, enough for everyone: goat curry, *moltani,* huge piles of rice, everything spiced with chili peppers. Oh, Mamma! Fire! They danced all night long. I loved to watch them in their magnificent multicolored costumes that sparkled. They looked like radiant suns with their enormous round headdresses full of tiny bits of mirror. At midnight, Maldévilen appeared.[25] Maldévilen, a man who'd stayed inside for an entire week without seeing a soul or eating anything. Singers, drums, and cymbals fell silent. People whispered, "Maldévilen's coming." He advanced, illuminated by torchbearers. His costume gleamed. He entered the circle and danced, swirling around and around. At a certain point, someone brought him a white rooster. He lifted the animal to his mouth and with a sharp bite, severed its neck and drank the blood. I didn't much care for that part.

One day I entered my friends' home. A sister of theirs had died in childbirth. People crowded around the dead woman. I was very taken aback. I didn't understand the lamentations; I couldn't tell if the mother cried, sang, or laughed.

"Viktorin, pitit an mwen! Han, han, ay manman!"	"Victorine, my child! Heh, heh, Mamma!"

She rocked back and forth.
"Heh, Mamma, heh, Mamma!"
But not a tear fell from her eyes.

"You are dead, you'll be happy where you're going, I don't have to worry about you now. . . . "

She was talking, talking while singing. Hysterical laughter seized me, and I had to leave the house.

Afterward, it was explained to me that the Indians celebrate death by laughing. And they cry at a birth: a newborn child, one more mouth to feed.

Our three friends were just about the only ones in our class to speak French at home. In addition to Daniel Feltan, that is, a little *palo* (pale and wan) mulatto whose father was a baker and mother, a teacher. A somewhat spineless boy, pampered and overprotected, he was nice to everybody. We made him speak Creole. Another child, the little lady-like Billon girl, was different. With lips pursed and her haughty air she'd claim: "I don't understand Creole."

One evening, for some reason or other, she was punished. Her mother came, bringing water, bread, cookies, all sorts of good things. The teachers made her return home with her basket.

When we started school, most of us didn't know a single word of French. But only French was allowed in their schools; Creole was forbidden. You had to speak French, well or poorly, forcing your mouth to open and close if necessary, but you had to speak it. In the classroom, that is, because outside during recess hardly a word of French could be heard in the air.

In the beginning, you didn't understand anything the teacher said. Little by little, you learned to read and write French, and learned the grammar. You could complete a dictation without mistakes. But to explain the words, that was something else! For instance, I made hardly any errors and was told I read well, but did I understand anything in the text? Often I recited passages without knowing the meaning of what I was saying. Bravo! Perfect score, 10! I had learned the words by heart, helter-skelter. At school you're taught proper grammatical French: relative pronouns, subordinate clauses, the indicative, the subjunctive, the Devil and his horns . . . but just try to speak and you don't know where to put the words, when to use the formal *vous* or the familiar *tu,* a total mishmash.

We'd speak "French" with our friends, and act so haughty about it. But a French all our own! I wonder what kind of language it really was! We weren't comfortable with the grammar or the language. Of course not, because we didn't speak it regularly or naturally, but only when required to in addressing the teacher. No one was around to correct our mistakes. Only the teachers, priests, nuns, the "proper folks" used French. As a child, I don't remember knowing a single adult who spoke French. The language was much less widespread than it is today.

On the road to school

On Thursdays, no school. The day was ours. First, of course, our chores at home: water detail, fetching water from the spring. The trips it took to fill the barrels and cauldrons! And wood detail: gathering enough wood to cook the day's food. Kudos for the one who carried back the largest load, but the quality also counted. We needed good wood, wood that burned slowly, not like the "Negress wood" or charred sugarcane stalks, which flared brightly but burned out too quickly.

After sweeping up, we could go out and have fun wherever we chose, but, when the hour of our father's return approached, it was in our best interest to run home. Often the boys went off in one direction and the girls in another. We weren't interested in the same things. The boys ran after their "wheels." They'd filch the iron circles from the barrels of salted meat or cookies they found. A bit of iron wire twisted together to guide the wheel and off they'd go, down the road in a clatter of metal. The boys were always willing to run errands to the store. On the way, they'd meet friends, organize races, stop to play *kristal* (marbles),[26] and all this time their mothers waited for them to return with the groceries.

Playing tops wasn't a girls' game either. There were champions, both in carving the tops and in spinning them. The tops were sculpted with a knife out of very hard wood, quite round with a small head. The boys scraped them, polished them with a piece of broken bottle, often leaving a bloody finger along the way. Finally, they'd attach a round-headed nail right in the middle of the point and painstakingly wind the string around the neck. Everyone waited expectantly: Would the top spin well and long? Be properly balanced? It was best to keep a good distance back from the thrower, it could be dangerous! If he missed his aim, the top could catch you on the nose or a whip of the string bite into your calves.

The girls preferred quieter games: jumping rope using *mahault* lianas, playing with *popotes*. We didn't have store-bought dolls even at Christmas. We made our "children" ourselves, out of rags, and dressed them: shoes out of woven rush, dresses sewn from leftover scraps of material we found under the table, hats of *bakoua* straw, handkerchiefs knotted round their heads.

One of our friends, a spoiled child, made her mother buy dolls from France, dolls with beautiful hair and blue eyes. They were our "babies." Our black rag dolls were matrons. They represented the grandmothers. Each doll had its own bed, mostly built by an older brother from slivers of cane stalks. We made the mattresses, sheets, and pillows.

For the big game of playing house, girls and boys joined forces. Near a cousin's cabin, we found abandoned an enormous iron basin, which had been used to prepare manioc flour. We transformed this into a house. A branch of the guava tree planted behind held up the "walls" of woven coconut leaves. We were well protected inside with our little household: round cookie box for a table, cut bamboo for chairs.

I liked to be "mamma" and give orders: "Suzelle, Gilberte! Run to the store and get me a half pound of cod, a half liter each of rice and black-eyed peas, a *roki* of rum, a *poban* of oil. Don't forget bread— two loaves." "Gerard! Go fetch water from the spring. And don't play around sliding down the hill!"

The girls returned, arms laden: breadfruit *popotes* for the bread, mango leaves for the cod, *graines-l'église* for the beans, sand for the sugar. Ground hibiscus leaves served as oil. The ravenala tree retains rain between its branches; we collected it into cornucopias of *madère* leaves, and it stayed nice and cool.

During the long vacations, my cousins came up to Carangaise from the city with everything needed to cook a real meal. I'd never seen anything like it: pots, bowls, red pottery plates like our parents had, but in miniature. Their mother had also sewn tiny jute sacks full of rice, sugar, lentils, and red beans. Together with the things we found around the place—guavas, bananas, cane beans, birds trapped with lime or killed by the boys' sling shots, land crabs unearthed from their holes—we prepared feasts!

And fishing for crayfish! What a process! First gather *niches à poul-boua* (termites' nests) and scatter them along a good kilometer of river. Then wait almost an hour and, in the cool of the day, the beaters would move downstream, beating the water with branches and making a racket. Other kids waited down below, baskets between their knees, trying not to let a single crayfish escape as, in their panic, they rushed right toward us. Of course many got away, but we always caught enough to cook and have some left over to take home.

We caught crabs with a *boulèt*. Once we found the crabs' holes, we'd place above them a large flat stone, held balanced by a small piece of wood. Near the wood was some bait: a piece of bitter orange, some orange squash, breadfruit, sugarcane. The crab came out of its hole and, as it tried to get the food, would jiggle the bit of wood. Plop! The rock fell, trapping the crab's legs or covering the hole and preventing it from retreating into its home. All you had to do then was pass around with a basket. You simply waited, comfortably installed in a guava tree. The crabs you didn't eat right away were left in a barrel to fatten up. They loved sweet potatoes, sugarcane, and chili peppers. I'm talking about the white land crabs and not the black, bearded ones whose legs are all hairy and are said to be better for your health.

On the road to school

We had everything on hand, not just for eating but for dressing up: bird feathers, shells, gourds, coconuts, leaves. . . . Mango leaves held together with the *touches* of coconut leaves, made magnificent garments. For our chic hats, we used large, round leaves from the grape trees. No need for store-bought toys. We were all children of poor families and relied on our imagination. During vacations, all came together—cousins, neighbors, friends. Each group selected a tree, a big mango tree with solid branches, for a house. Early in the morning we'd climb up into our houses and ask each other:

"Ka ou fè, lavouazin, ou byen dòmi?"

"Maché, mapòv, apa ti gaz ti dènyé bouden la ban mwen! Sété fèmé on zyé, wouvé lòt. Timoun la soufè èvè dan tout lannuit."

"Ou pa téni luil karapat alò? Vouazin machè, on mamman pa douèt jen manké sa."
"Ki jan lavi la yé jòdi la konpè? Ou tris kon fès a moun mò. Ka ki rivé-ou? Ou néyé an ronm yè soua. Konpè, fo pa lésé ronm vin mèt a kò a-ou."

"How are you, neighbor? Did you sleep well?"

"My dear, my youngest was so much trouble. No sooner had I closed one eye than I had to open the other. He was bothered by teething all night long."

"Don't you have any carapate oil? My dear, a mother should never be without it."
"How are things, brother? You're as sad as a corpse's behind. What happened to you? Did you drown in last night's rum? Friend, you shouldn't let rum get control over you."

What a crew we were! We loved to play at being parents, speaking like them, but not showing any disrespect.

Of course we also played school. One of us was chosen as teacher. The others sat down properly, a banana leaf for a notebook, a small white stick to write with. The teacher gave us problems, dictations, and beatings for our mistakes. We ended with songs, songs we learned to sing in a round at school:

Little daddy. Today's your birthday . . .
At my lovely chateau, ma tanti reli relo . . .

or during religious instruction:

I'll return to Normandy
The country where I was born.

Leonora: The Buried Story of Guadeloupe

and the ones Father Birnbaum made us repeat:

> *Oh, Alsace, my country fair,*
> *with valleys green and sweet,*
> *summer's bounty ripens there,*
> *grapes, hops, and wheat*
> *Yo, heh! grapes, hops, and wheat.*

Which sounded somewhat like this when he wanted us to sing it in his language.

> Dos Alsos manayditchen
> mé hèvè feutch unnbandèl
> unlèt mixennotgèn
> Yuhé, unlèt mixennotgèn.

God, how nasty Father Birnbaum was! He made us all tremble in our boots. He'd assign half a catechism, and if you hadn't learned it: a whipping! For their first communion, at age ten, many children who knew all the pages of the catechism failed, paralyzed by a fear of the whip. They'd start to tremble and shake, forget the correct answers, and fail to receive communion.

The following year, Father Leroux replaced Father Whipster. It was like night and day. He was very nice, took us to his house, fed us. . . . He liked Florinette so much that he sat her on his knees and fed her from his plate.

First communion was an important event for the families and the village. Florinette's father lent his wagon to the neighbors so they could ride to town. Those families without relatives in town rented a room or stopped at a boardinghouse for the nine-day retreat. Mothers who couldn't afford to rent by themselves teamed up and shared a room. They brought mattresses, beds, tables, all the necessities.

On the day after the ninth day of the retreat, following absolution and confession, came communion. To receive absolution, we dressed all in white, in a long-sleeved dress with a wide lace collar. The following day, for our first communion, a still more beautiful dress of embroidered organdy. A crown of silk flowers, like a bride's, held the veil. The first communion meal was served in the rented room or at the boardinghouse. Crayfish, roast chicken, white bread, *chodo,* champagne, coconut rum punch, and, for dessert, a layer cake, with four, five, even as many as ten layers, depending on the size of a family's purse. The cake had been presented at the church door by a *mabonne.* These women, wearing their best *matador* dresses,[27] would line up on either side of the portal, each with a cake carried upright on her head, the wooden tray steadied by a pad of Madras cotton. The communicants filed past between the two rows of cakes, the proudest child, of course, being the one whose *mabonne* carried the tallest cake.

On Monday, the family would clean up the room, and then, on Tuesday, would return home. The simpler meal on Tuesday was more like our normal fare.

At age fourteen, I left school. I'd been a good student, one the teacher expected to earn the certificate of studies. It was a real certificate at that time, a diploma. I failed the exam. And then completely gave up school. I hadn't failed by much—too bad for me—but my friend, Florinette, who spoiled me so, had her way blocked by the teacher, Monsieur Petibas, who persecuted her. She put up with so much at school. I remember it well. The other day, at Pointe-à-Pitre, I met one of my old schoolmates. We reminisced about the past and especially the dreadful things Monsieur Petibas inflicted on Florinette. It left a strong impression on us. With her intelligence, Florinette should have gone far in her studies.

Florinette was the only mulatto girl in our class. Her mother sewed beautiful dresses for her, pinafores that buttoned all the way down the back. She wore her hair either in one braid or in two, one on each side, tied with pretty bows. We envied her straight hair and enjoyed taking out the braids and then doing them up again. Her father, a very light-skinned mulatto, had married a beautiful *câpresse*. He was well known and liked in the village. A true gentleman. He could read and write and took part in politics. People said he was liberal and didn't fear the priests. When you met him, he'd always give you a lift in his wagon and dispense a bit of advice: "Have you studied hard, children? Don't forget, education is the shining light."

He helped everyone. He'd pick up those he found alongside the road, all those in need, and take them to a shelter or leave them in his kitchen for his wife, while he went to buy them clothes. Florinette's mother had more than her share of dressing wounds, washing stinking sores, and sewing clothes. She grumbled angrily: "Gilbert will end up causing me grief with all these broken rosaries, all these misfits he brings home."

He was a man who wore his heart on his sleeve, so different from my father, who frightened children. He treated his two girls royally. They said he brought them up not in slavery but in freedom.

He and Monsieur Petibas didn't share the same political views. They kept up a running argument, but Petibas took out his anger on Florinette, his student, picking on her endlessly. He became her tormentor. But, of course, he hadn't the right to mix politics in with his teaching!

Leonora: The Buried Story of Guadeloupe

In class, I always scored first in dictation and reading, Florinette first in arithmetic. With arithmetic, she'd say, you had to think in order to find the answer, whereas in spelling, you only had to remember. Right up to the end of her studies, she had trouble in reading, but proved herself a champion in math. Though not strong in French, her perfect grades in arithmetic helped her keep up. She should have taken the exam for her certificate, but Petibas refused to send her. After the exam, we gave her the questions to answer; she would have passed.

Petibas was very strict! "Student X, stand up and recite your lesson." His words fell heavily in the silent room. . . . You didn't know, you stammered. His "kneel down behind the blackboard" was not long in coming. No explanation, you'd just be punished and kept after school. You could be given as many as two or four weeks of punishment, kept in detention till 8 P.M. And while, in the classroom, you copied a rule of grammar or math one hundred or two hundred times, Monsieur Petibas would be running after the lady teacher out behind the school building. Spelling mistakes in composition brought on a rain of blows. Using all his strength, the teacher would strike the backs or the palms of our hands with a leather whip. An atmosphere of barbarity permeated the school. Isn't it barbaric to lift the dress of a child and whip her buttocks, leaving marks on her body? Complaining at home was useless. "The teacher beat you? Well, he must have had his reasons."

Some children, capable of succeeding, were so terrorized that even if they knew their lessons, they didn't raise their hands, fearing punishment for the slightest mistake. Petibas went so far as to kick the students. One boy took revenge. Carrying a sack full of stones, he climbed into a mango tree alongside the road. When the teacher passed underneath, he almost knocked him senseless and then disappeared from school.

Petibas really had it in for Florinette. He only partially corrected her homework: he'd give her a ten instead of a twenty. She was always first to raise her hand to answer mental arithmetic problems, but he never called on her. He knew, however, her weakness: reading. "Dorval, your turn. Let's listen to Dorval with her charming voice. . . . "

He poked fun at Florinette. All her efforts were in vain. The more she tried, the more he teased, making her lose her place or stutter at the end of a sentence. If, by luck, she managed to read a passage correctly, he made her repeat the words that were difficult to pronounce, those with double letters to articulate, the r's to roll or keep silent. If she hesitated, he'd pounce on her: "Mademoiselle, why the sighing? Mademoiselle, go on. Mademoiselle, we're waiting. . . . Mademoiselle, you're not saying Mass. Why these 'so-be-its' at the end of each sentence? Mademoiselle . . . Mademoiselle . . . "

On the road to school

"What an awful period of my life I spent with that teacher," Florinette confided to me the other day.

And reading aloud, what a trial for our little mulatto! For instance, *Little Palaemon*. No matter what tone of voice she used, it was never the right one. No sooner had she begun:

> *Little Palaemon, barely eight years old,*
> *Snatched away by the billy goat, strong and bold . . .*

"Mademoiselle, it's not a prayer."

She tried to master her fear and anger and continued in a stronger voice:

> *Across the garden and sharply drew up . . .*

"Mademoiselle, start again. You aren't reading, you're shouting."

She began to crack, her voice trembled.

"Start again. I don't understand anything you say."

Tears rolled down her cheeks. She pulled herself together:

> *Little Palaemon, barely eight years old . . .*

I thought it was almost right. But he harried her still more, and she broke down in tears.

"School's not a vale of tears, mademoiselle. On your knees behind the blackboard, and don't let me hear a sound out of you!"

How well she knew that corner behind the blackboard! She might spend an entire morning there, listening to all the lessons. One day, during arithmetic, no one managed to solve the problem. From her row, the row of students not preparing to take the exam, Florinette raised her hand: "Sir, I have the answer."

"You're bothering me, mademoiselle. Get up on the bench."

Up on the bench, she continued to raise her hand.

"On your knees!"

Her father had taught her to always raise her hand when she knew the answer. No other student had yet solved the problem. She waved her notebook. "Sir, sir!"

Furious, he grabbed her notebook. The answer was right. There was no correction he could make. He had to give her a perfect grade, 20 out of 20. He checked the notebooks of the students who hadn't found the answer and boxed the ears of those in the first row so hard that all the others shrank into their shells.

"Aren't you ashamed to let this Dorval do better than you? Go on, mademoiselle, up to the board and solve the two problems." She wrote the answer in a single line. He hollered: "I don't understand your reasoning. Go through the steps."

She went through it in three lines. No. She went through it again in six lines.

"You'll all be punished for two weeks. As for you—outside on your knees in the sun!"

God was watching over her that day. No sooner had she kneeled down in the courtyard than the bell rang for recess. Another teacher went over and asked what she was doing there. She explained: she'd been the only one to solve a problem. The teacher told the others and they all were furious with Petibas. "That mulatto's too pretentious for his own good. He acts like the cock of the walk but has nothing more than a primary-school education."

But they didn't say anything to him. They feared Petibas, who also served as principal, as much as we did. One morning, in the middle of the schoolyard, he wanted to punish a student. He whipped off his belt so furiously that his pants fell down, and there he stood, in his underwear. I assure you, no one laughed, neither teachers nor students.

That Petibas marked Florinette for life. He thwarted her progress, and all for political reasons.

3

Pli bèl moman an viv, tan a véyé

My favorite celebrations,

the vigils for the dead

> Know, too, that in these countries the dead are watched over
> during festivals, which are enlivened by the voluptuous and virile
> words of the drum, at which friends of the deceased honor him
> with an oration that merges the pain of death with the merry fer-
> vor of rum, dancing, and revelry. I love this relationship with
> death in which pleasure and joy aren't meant to blot out its
> abominable invincibility but rather where pleasure and joy
> bloom in direct sight of death: the festival and the funeral feast
> occur right in front of the corpse.
>
> Pierre Goldman,
> *L'ordinaire mésaventure d'Archibald Rapoport*

In the past, people stayed put more than they do today. Each family's
history was well known. The mistakes of so-and-so and the jokes of
such-and-such, both long gone, were passed down from one generation
to the next. Even as a child, I knew that the grandfather of the seamstress *Man* Honoré became crippled because he bathed on Good Friday, a day for staying home, relaxing, and doing nothing; that *Gueule-
Pointue* (Pointy-Face) owed that last name of his to his way of speaking French; that Mademoiselle Isidore, a withered old maid, went to
buy a brassiere in Pointe-à-Pitre and asked for a "tit hammock"; that
yet another, wanting to speak French, worked his jaw so hard that he
was left with a half-mouth twitch.

At every funeral, your store of knowledge increased. Thanks to the
vigils for the dead, each person's story endured.

In the village, the wake was the largest get-together, the biggest
event, the most elaborate party.

Word spread quickly when someone died. The conch-shell horn was
blown to announce the news to the neighboring villages. The town
crier then passed through the village itself, calling out: "Wake up!
So-and-so's dead! Come quickly, everyone! If you've a donkey, mount

him; if you've a horse, mount him; if you've neither donkey nor horse, mount your mother! Come, all of you, come!"

Everyone who could stand up attended the wake in the evening. One person would bring a bottle of rum, another candles, yet another two planks of wood. In my childhood, we didn't buy coffins, the carpenters came and made them on the spot. The dead person was carried on a bier and we all walked behind. No cars for the ride to church. We accompanied the corpse, leaving from the house of the dead person's "master"[28] and walking to the church and the cemetery. No matter what the weather, even in a thunderstorm, people went off to bury their dead. Men rolled up their pants, women gathered their dresses up to their calves. Sometimes we'd walk all the way to the church in town and then return to the village for the burial.

In front of the house of the dead person, storytellers, singers, and musicians would gather, some from distant places, from Baie-Mahault, from Morne-à-l'eau, and even from Anse-Bertrand—where, people say, dogs bark from their tails. Famous singers and well-known *léwoz*[29] dancers came to match themselves against the very best: those from Capesterre. The drums beat, stories of all sorts were told: tales of Brer Rabbit and Brer Zamba, tales of zombis and the she-devil, obscene tales and, finally, the ones I liked best, amusing tales peppered with jokes, riddles, and word games.

I adored the word games, made some up myself, and still today, when I'm at a wake, I'm the first to begin the round. "One day, my father and I were on a trip. We walked and walked till we came to a place where two points of land faced one another. We stopped there, at the point where the lands faced each other, and ate flesh which had not been born. Can you tell me where we were and what we ate?"

Then everyone thought and thought. When they answered incorrectly, others insulted them. "That's wrong, you bearded frog, you belted lizard, scaly legs, runny nose. . . . "

I don't mock people that way. Word games are too delightful, too interesting to be sullied by insults. Here, at Grosse-Montagne, I'm one of the few women who play word games at the wakes. In Carangaise, all the young girls took part in word games and riddles, but it must not have been so here.

To enter the game you must say: "I'd like a turn." The onlookers respond: "Okay." You tell the riddle. Everyone thinks, tries to answer. If it's wrong, you say: "That's not part of my game." Then they shout: "Don't keep us guessing; others want a turn!" But you let them keep trying and finally tell them the answer. "Unborn flesh is an egg. Points of land that face each other: I was on Gabarre Bridge between Grande-Terre and Guadeloupe proper."[30]

My favorite celebrations, the vigils for the dead

I like word games but don't ask for a turn at every wake. Before joining, I size up the mood; if only men are playing, it depends on their behavior. Some attend wakes just to tell dirty jokes. I don't like that. I won't take part unless the tone is right, especially if I'm the only woman.

I remember Monsieur Nibolot, a great storyteller, who made up word games based on history or on the Bible. He'd say to us: "Listen, this is from mythology, that's from such-and-such, that's from so-and-so. . . . " Perhaps he didn't know himself what it all meant. He spoke to us of 'Tila the Hun, of the French kings, asked questions about the Bible, about Moses. Complicated puzzles, not just little riddles like:

"Dlo pann? Koko."   "Hanging water? A coconut."
"Dlo doubout? Kann."   "Standing water? Sugarcane."

Or those well known to everyone:

"Tabliyé dèyè do? Zong."   "Apron behind the back? Finger-
                              nail."

   "I'm neither king nor queen; I make men tremble?"
"Rum."

We had to say them in French. It was hard work to make them up, remember them, and be able to explain them in Creole.

This tradition hasn't been lost. Last month, in Lamentin, I heard someone as talented as Monsieur Nibolot: a specialist in mythology, how he loves words, speech; what pleasure he takes in turning a beautiful phrase! And how easily he enters a game, either to guess or to ask:

   "What's my name? When going up or down the musical scale you'll find my first syllable. Crisscrossing the mother country, at the very top, you'll find my second. I was the bird beloved by poets and gods, the emblem of Napoleon I, I can't bend my head. Who am I?"

Turns out he was Simon Laigle.[31]

   "I was born in the cradle of mythology, my mother gave birth to me in the halls of mythology, I was raised with Hercules, Jason, all the gods and demigods. They're the ones who sent me to you this evening to tell you of their prowess, of the admirable exploits of the heroes of old, of the poets. Open up your ears and eyes wide! Krik . . . "

   "Krak . . . "

   "Have you heard of the Golden Fleece? Well, then, listen! The Golden Fleece was a ram from Boeotia. He escaped to Colchis with two children on his back. One, a boy, named Phryxus; the other, a girl, called Helle. Helle fell into the Red Sea and drowned. Phryxus was saved by the ram and put down in Colchis. Then the ram died. To commemorate this loyal deed, the gods transformed the head of the ram into a golden fleece, which was guarded in the sacred woods of Colchis by a seven-headed dragon. Now, King Menelaus was king of Diolcos. Okay. The centaur Chiron knew that the head of the ram that had been transformed into gold was at Diolcos. Chiron reared men, strong men, by feeding them on marrow from the bones of lions. He raised Hercules, Jason, the sorceress Medea, and the twin brothers Castor and Pollux and sent them out on a ship called the *Argo* on a quest for the Golden Fleece. The passengers were called the Argonauts. When they arrived in Diolcos, at the sacred woods of Colchis, they managed to enter the land where the ram's head lay. Hercules shouldered his weapons and arrows, which had been dipped in the blood of the Hydra from Lerna. He wounded the dragon, but it was so powerful that, although it fell, it didn't die. Then Medea's turn came, and she threw the contents of a flask into the dragon's mouth. Orpheus, the greatest musician of the ancient world, set his lyre singing. And, the story goes, the trees in the forest pulled up their roots and came to dance at his feet when he sang. So Jason won the Golden Fleece. And this same dragon was the one who caused the Trojan War, the Trojan War sung of by Muse, the Trojan War that saw the sons of Peleus and of Agamemnon divided. Sons who got involved. Why? Because Paris carried off Helen from King Menelaus. Then Agamemnon assembled all the Greeks to combat the Trojans at the ramparts of Troy. He succeeded in capturing Troy thanks to Ulysses, the craftiest of all the Greeks, who built a wooden horse. Ulysses was the son of Laertes, the husband of Penelope, and the father of Telemachus. He became the last Greek survivor of the Trojan War. For twenty years he roamed the seas. Upon returning home, he found a flock of "intendants" ready to marry his wife. His old dog and his son, Telemachus, recognized him when he arrived at the door. After he managed to repulse all his wife's intendants, he said, 'My departure was a cause for celebration, and now I return to a house in mourning.' Ulysses had killed so many suitors that the house was filled with blood. That's the story.

"I've spoken at length. Now let's take a rest. I'm not a poet, but poetry pours forth, flows from my heart like an inexhaustible spring. I've known no education but life and sunsets. Like Job I can say: 'Naked came I out of my mother's womb, and naked shall I return thither. The Lord gave, and the Lord hath taken away; blessed be the name of the Lord.'

"Now that's poetry! It's beautiful, melodious, and it fills me with happiness.

My favorite celebrations, the vigils for the dead

"The greatest poet of all times was *Vitorigo* (Victor Hugo). I love the line when he lost his daughter Léopoldine 'at sea during a voyage.' He had left France to take refuge in Jersey and Guernsey. He contemplated nature; he contemplated the sea. One day he saw an old shepherd bringing in his flock as the sun was setting. Something awakened within him. He gave it voice, and we can still read it today. This is what he said: 'The old man looking at the sun that sets, And the sun looking on the man who dies. Night follows day.'"

Oh yes, the fellow's gifted! He really enjoys himself. Once he's off, no way of stopping him, even if others ask for a turn. Every storyteller has a particular way of asking questions, of starting your mind working, of waking up the company when it falls asleep. Simon Laigle teases, without malice, but with well-chosen rhymes for incorrect answers:

"That's wrong! Have Kate make the cakes when she wakes!"

"Wrong! Number one son of Tartanson at Colson."

"Wrong! Out of my sight, you thief, you beggar. Without me, you're nothing but a heap of worms. Stay as you are. Go hide behind the cows!"

And he's off again:

"Who can tell me the name of the great king who was the scourge of God and who proclaimed: 'The grass shall never grow where my horse has walked?' Quite simply, it's 'Tila the Hun. The first thing king 'Tila did: he made his two sons fight each other. He gave each of them a knife. He was really a villain to do that. He continued his atrocities. Went out to kill his brother. His brother said to him: 'King 'Tila, you want to kill me to please your people, but always remember, King 'Tila, that the blood of the innocent can never be washed away, the blood of the innocent leaves its mark, King 'Tila.'

"And yet there was a man . . . a man . . . Wake up, clever storyteller, and continue the tale. A man who turned back King 'Tila in 1417. Yes, vanquished him on the Catalonian plains and gave his name to the first race of Merovingians. Merowig was the one, the conqueror of 'Tila.

"Krik . . . "   "Open your eyes, open your
"Krak . . . "   ears."
"Wouvè zyé, wouvè zorèy."   "Let those who are able to under-
"Sa ki konprann, konprann."   stand, understand."

"And listen, now, to the story of Dioudji, the slave beloved of his master. A man bought Dioudji. Finding him gentle and patient, he kept him well, and one day he said to himself that the poor fellow could no longer remain a slave and so decided to let him go. Dioudji wouldn't hear of such a thing and said to his master: 'Sir, I want to stay with you.' 'No, Dioudji. Go back to your own people, go back to the desert that calls to you. I won't hold you here any longer. In vain have I tried to make you understand that you're no longer a slave. I want you to know that everything belonging to me will be yours.' 'No, master,' replied Dioudji again, 'I'll stay at your side.' 'Go away, I say, desert bird. You're my favorite bird, but I'm giving you freedom. Go!' Dioudji left but returned in tears because his master was good to him and even considered him a son. Wrong, Dioudji, my boy! You always ate your fill, your master treated you kindly, but you lived in a gilded cage. And a bird, even in the most exquisite gilded cage, can never forget the trees and the forest. The poet put these words into the master's mouth: 'The desert calls you, return to the desert, Dioudji.'

"This slave story," continued Simon Laigle, "calls to mind that of Delgrès,[32] the black man who, in 1802, became a colonel in the French army and was blown up at Matouba with three hundred men. History tells us there were three hundred men plus two women. I've forgotten all their names, but both women were expecting babies. The one called Léonine was pregnant up to the chin by Delgrès. Delgrès knew the fort would be blown up. He used his sweetest words to convince the two women to leave. 'No,' they both answered, 'we'll stay at the fort.' And those two brave women died with Delgrès. Three hundred and two people were blown up at Matouba that way.

"Listen, too, to the words of that great man who delivered us from slavery, Victor Schoelcher: 'Where are you going?' his wife asked as he was leaving for Guadeloupe. 'I have a mission to accomplish,' Schoelcher answered, 'and nothing will keep me from it.'"

The stories, tales, riddles, and word games can continue like that till dawn. They keep the dead person and his family company. It's impossible for us to sit vigil and remain silent. The silence of death must be broken. We can't be together and keep from singing, laughing, telling jokes, and applauding the achievements of the wrestlers and dancers. Of course, at the beginning of the wake, we gather together and say prayers. But once the prayers are finished, life takes over, the life of the dead person, which we celebrate with song, drums, food, and drink.

I was the prayer queen in my village. Not everyone can do it; you must be chosen. Before dying, some say: "I want so-and-so to lead my prayers." Usually it's someone who knows how to read well. That person is called from house to house, asked to read prayers all the time. I was often requested, and I was obliged to go lead the prayers. But if it's always the same one who reads them, the others don't grow. Little by little, we started passing the book around so others could get involved. Capesterre is a progressive community, many people have gone to school and know how to read French.

Alas, people don't stay at a wake till daybreak any more. We used to spend the whole night and then, the following morning instead of going to work, we'd remain with the dead person's master to help clean the house, to cook, etc. Those were true relatives, members of one large family. Nowadays, the relatives are often the first to leave. It's one example of how families are smaller than they used to be. Father, mother, brother, sister, children—that's all. If your family is broken up like that, you must gather your strength.

On several occasions, I've been upset by seeing only two or three relatives stay on while all the others leave the wake before two in the morning to go to sleep. On the one hand, when I think about it, I know that people work and can't just announce to their boss: "I was at a wake," unless it's for a close relative. They know their boss could punish them. That's all true, yet, on the other hand, people today have laziness in their blood. There's no sharing of life and death the way there used to be. We too, after having been up the whole night, would often go to work. So it's not simply the bosses' fault for pressuring their workers; it also reflects the changed mentality of the people. They always want to sleep, they've become more selfish.

I think we live in a time when death is no longer one's own, and for two reasons. First, even if a close relative dies, you're caught in a bind since, if you go to school or work in an office, you can't spend the night at the wake and then stay home the next day. Second, if you live far away, you need money for the trip. That's all part of it, but I wonder if people are still the same when faced with death. I don't know the answer but think we have to try to explain these changes. In the countryside, the tradition of great wakes still continues. Sometimes the relatives don't agree. They say they don't want anything disorderly in front of their houses. Around me, I hear: "If I die tomorrow, I don't want any fuss. No singing, no drums—I only want word games. Word games and talking all night long won't bother me because they're sedate, things that 'well brought-up people' do."

In my mind that's racist. That kind of racism exists in our culture, the racism of people who have money, who're at the top of society, in the upper class. Some are in the lower class but, through some relative or other, have a foot in the upper class. They want to be snobs, and when they say: "No wake in front of my house," we can't have a wake.

In Petit-Canal, the church refused to bury people whose death had been celebrated by a wake with songs, drums, and dancers fighting with sticks. At Capesterre, the church didn't react that way. Here at

Grosse-Montagne, we congregation members are trying to revive the link between life and death. It's not as strong as it used to be, but it's coming along slowly because our way of looking at death hasn't really changed that much. Of course, just as the anolis that changes color still remains an anolis, death is always death. It's our way of reacting to it that changes.

Death used to be a great calamity, a disaster, for everyone. People shrieked, fainted, cried their eyes out! They were revived with ether or rather with leaves from the custard-apple tree, their feet rubbed with salt. The dead person's master was no longer in charge of the house. All the village people invaded it, took over, led by family members who were keeping themselves busy. Death was considered a great loss for the village as well as for the family. Everyone was upset, relatives and neighbors. It was a true catastrophe for all. Slowly, that has changed till now you no longer see all the signs of grief. You might say that some people want to cry like the white folks do, with small handkerchiefs, sitting straight upright, and stiff as boards.

It's our custom to jest with death and at the expense of the dead person's master. When fetching water you might hear: "The dead person's master cries so hard because he doesn't know where he'll find enough money to buy wood for the coffin." And the whole community joins in. One neighbor brings coffee, another rum, candles, or food. The house is cleaned, beds made, floors scoured; everything must be spotless. Some houses are straightened up only at the time of a death. In others, not much has to be done except fetching water to fill the barrels. I'm talking about in the country, not in town, where it's now in fashion to have running water and electricity.

All the children would scramble down the hill, my mother calling to us: "Run and fetch water!" Another urging her children: "Run and fetch water!"

We were all sent out to work carrying water. Oh how much water it took to bathe the corpse! The body was laid out on a sack on the ground and respectfully undressed. Whether man or woman, the private parts were covered. We joked while bathing the body: "Wash his nostrils well, and his teeth, so he doesn't come to you at night and pucker up. Wipe every corner with basil leaves, he must be clean to go and meet God. . . . "

I wash dead bodies too, but have learned that what counts is the cleanliness inside. Even washing the body ten thousand times with all sorts of plants won't make the inside clean. But it's a rite. We always saw the elders do it and so we continue to wash the dead, powder, and dress them. You love your body, take care of it, even if you're off to the bowels of the earth. True, you're heading underground, but you must be carried out of your house clean, you can't go dirty, with worn-out shoes and an old dress. Only during cholera epidemics are such things permitted. How embarrassing if the corpse reeks of sickness, or if the blood has congealed and the body gives off putrid liquid.

We Guadeloupeans are a clean people. It comes from our ancestors and even from Africa. People who didn't have all the conveniences and yet were still always clean. Even if a woman had only one dress, she always kept it clean. She'd wash it in the evening, dry it near the fire, and smooth it out in the morning with an iron heated on a charcoal fire. Nowadays, people don't iron clothes much anymore. Our grand-mothers ironed everything, even the old dresses they wore for sleeping. They always did. And if they didn't have time to leave the clothes out-side all day in the sun to bleach, they'd boil them up to eliminate the dirty smell. Our forebears were born with a love of cleanliness, a love of their bodies.

Once the dead person was washed and tidied up, the bathwater and leaves were placed under the bed. After the removal of the body, the water was poured out in a special corner of the garden and the leaves were buried. Nowadays, the water of the dead must be discarded im-mediately because, apparently, people steal it for use in magic and sor-cery. I don't know who discovered this, but now clean water is put in the bowl under the bed instead of the wash water from the dead person.

The corpse is laid out on the bed, dressed in clean clothes. It mustn't carry with it to the grave anything that belongs to a living person. The linen used in the coffin to cradle the head, feet, and body must also belong to the dead person. It is said that if any material or object be-longing to a living person finds its way into the coffin, he or she will begin to decompose at the same time as the cadaver. During the wake, and till the coffin is closed, family members take turns watching the body to prevent the appropriation of the dead spirit for use in an *expé-dition*, an evil spell. Someone might slip in a note, some hair, or a personal object belonging to an enemy who would thus be "dis-patched," (*expédié*) with a prepaid ticket to death.

Death is serious business; it's important. What secrets it brings to light! The other day, in the middle of final good-byes before leaving for church, something happened that astonished me: a real scandal. The wife of the dead man began to shriek and ask her husband's forgive-ness: "Paul, Paul! Before you leave for the other side, I must tell you that I've had other men, yes, while we were together. Your daughter Lucinda isn't really yours. . . . "

Leonora: The Buried Story of Guadeloupe

The husband's relatives were embarrassed, but they couldn't shut her up. She had straddled the corpse, a gesture usually indicating that you fear the dead person will come back and torment you.

Here, people believe that the dead have power. While, for some, a dead person is dead and gone for good, for many others, even after they've buried their father or mother, their parent isn't really dead. They'll say to you: Yes, the dead have real power; there are good and bad spirits. The bad ones were evil when they lived and continue to do harm even after their deaths. Good or bad, the dead have power. You might hear: I dreamed of a certain relative, he said this to me, or that, he gave me the recipe for an herbal brew to cure me. Another will have dreamed of a friend: he saw him and heard him speak. He hadn't actually seen the person but recognized him all the same.

Not very long ago, I heard a woman explain to a group of people who had come to rest in the shade in front of her house all the things the dead had done for her. I'm not very interested in these types of stories, but I stopped to listen because it was *Man* Bety who spoke, one of our *grangrèk savann*—as we call our wise men and women. Their learning doesn't come from school but from life and the teachings of the elders.

"Do the dead have power?" wondered *Man* Bety. "That's a thing we can't really verify. Some people say they'll see them again, others that they've disappeared for good; others believe in dreams and still others don't. I have a feeling, however, that there are things I can't dismiss. You dream of someone, of a person you've known, and sometimes this person comes to you with a prediction that turns out to be true. For instance, my godfather appeared to my mother the day after his death to console her for not having received her inheritance. Those who stole it wouldn't profit from it.

'Lusla, to pèd tout biten a to. To pèd tout. Tanto tanto, an toua jou, vista, an toua jou, tanto, tanto . . . '	'Lusla, you've lost everything that was coming to you. You've lost it all. Soon, soon, you'll see, in three days, soon, soon . . . '

"Three days later, the cyclone of 1928 hit and destroyed all his property, leaving the land ravaged. The twenty-one four-room cabins were carried off by the tidal wave. That's why I can't deny that the dead may have power. I can't say either yes or no. I just don't know.

"My sister, who was an excellent seamstress, often repeated to me:

My favorite celebrations, the vigils for the dead

'When I die, I don't want to be buried in just any old dress. Get my cousin Andrée. Don't let anyone but her sew my dress.'

"The day she gave birth, I was running errands in Pointe-à-Pitre, buying vegetables for the special soup given to women who have just delivered. A neighbor came to find me: 'Bety, your sister is ill.' 'Ill? My sister? Impossible! I left her in labor. Oh, my God! She's dead!'

"I passed out. I almost died myself. Then I walked, wild-eyed, around Pointe-à-Pitre with a single idea in mind: to reach Cousin Andrée's house. She wasn't there. I borrowed money from one of my friends who owned a jewelry shop, bought material for the dress and the slip, bought everything necessary. When I got home, adults as well as children were out front, crying and crying. My sister was already laid out, dressed in an outfit Madame Siméis had made for her.

"'That dress can go under her head, as a pillow,' I said, sobbing, 'Cousin Andrée will make her dress.'

"That evening, at the wake, I dozed off. In a dream, my sister came to speak to me:

'Ban, di-ou on biten. Wòb la Man Siméis fè ban mwen la, i ka fè mwen tèlman byen. Bon, ou pa bizouen chaléré kò a-ou. Men an ka di ou on sèl biten, huit pitit an mwen la, enki pran yo pou ou.'	'Listen carefully. The dress that *Man* Siméis made for me fits perfectly. It's fine. Stop worrying. I ask only one thing of you. Take my eight children.'

"Whenever I think of these words, I shiver.

"'And,' she continued, 'there's one other thing, sister dear. Aunt Helene forgot to deliver the afterbirth. Tell her to remove the placenta, I can't leave as long as it's still with me.'

"I called over Aunt Helene. She swiftly delivered the afterbirth and my sister was set free. She had suffered a massive hemorrhage and died as the placenta was being expelled. I was forced to acknowledge that the dead do have power.

"Well, then I couldn't stand the thought of seeing two coffins carried out of the house, one for her and the other for her stillborn child. So I buried the baby at the foot of the coconut tree, where my mother buried her miscarriages. I buried both the child and the placenta. Several days after my sister's funeral in the town of Lamentin, a good friend of hers, Madame Claude, had a visitation from her.

"'Claudette,' she said, 'everything that's been done for me is perfect and to my liking. But what work you've given me! You should have left my child with me. Every day I must go up to Chartreux to nurse it. It should have been close to me.'

"I think there's something to that. My father had asked to be buried on his family's land at Baie-Mahault, in the cemetery where, every year on the festival of All Saints,[33] the dead are honored in the traditional way. When he died, I said:

'Ay, chè, sa ja pasé dimòd téré moun an bitasyon.'	'Nuts! The dead aren't buried in the country any more. It's no longer in fashion.'

"And I buried him in town. I made the decision, but later regretted it and still do. It bothers me just as with my sister's child. I defied his wishes. He came to reassure me: 'I'm comfortable where I am, Bety. I was always a good man while I lived on earth. I'm with fine company, and everybody prays to God for me. My spirit is quiet, I had a good life. As I said to you when I was alive, actions are what really count, not the business of going to Mass. I never ran after the priest, who is only a man like me. I'm a little bored in town, that's all.'

"Some sort of power exists that weaves together the living and the dead. I really don't know. Only recently have people ceased fearing the dead and the things they do. Everyone's getting used to it.

"Previously, we didn't know the names of illnesses. We simply said: he died. Sometimes, if a person suffered at length before dying, nasty tongues would start wagging. The flesh of a person with cancer, for instance, would start to dry up. It might be said of him: 'Look how he suffers. That's a person who has done evil. The poor thing drags along half dead without managing to die.'

"Death is something human that we can't begin to control. What I find extraordinary is that some people know in advance when they're going to die. They'll tell you that they're going to die on a certain day, and they do. I can swear it happened that way to my godmother and my father.

"My godmother didn't get along well with her man and often came to my mother for support. She was a talented seamstress and a fine embroiderer. To help raise her children, she also took in washing and ironing. Her children were always impeccable, spick-and-span. One day she sent one of her sons to ask his father for some money for the evening meal. The child didn't return promptly. Somewhat uneasy, Godmother put down her iron and exclaimed: 'With this wretch of a husband, one never knows what can happen. I'm going to go see.'

"She had ironed; she had sweated. On the way, she fell down all sweaty into the gully. When she arrived at my mother's house, Mamma made her swallow an infusion made from coffee-bean husks, and applied an herbal poultice of *guéri-tout.*

"'Don't trouble yourself so much, cousin, I'm going to die.'

"'What a thing to say!' my mother answered.

"'I tell you, I'm going to die. The thing that bothers me most is leaving you with all the mess of burying me.'

"'Sister, don't speak such nonsense!'

"'Vonette, the beautiful embroidered lace altar cloth that I've been working on for the Baie-Mahault chapel isn't finished. The Good Lord didn't want me to give him what I've made with such love and faith. The tablecloth I embroidered for Elise—wash it well, bleach it, and use it for my burial dress.'

"'Now stop . . .'

"'Listen, sister, make sure people don't speak ill of you. I don't have enough strength left to deal with this tablecloth. I beg you, wash and bleach it.'

"She continued on in a voice laden with sadness: 'And to think I'm going to die without seeing my child again. God, I don't want to die yet and leave my children like this. Go and fetch my sister Amélise so she can wash my hair. I don't want to die with all this filth on me.'

"'What's all this about dying? Wash your hair when you're chilled? That would really make you sick.'

"'Please send for her.'

"When Amélise arrived, my godmother said to her: 'Comb my hair well. Clean my scalp, don't leave any dandruff, scrub hard. Clean out my ears. Vonette, your child must be crying. A twenty-six day old baby is delicate.'

"'No, Godmother. I nursed him just before coming.'

"'Go and see to him, my child.'

"My godmother knew she would die at any moment. Vonette was nursing, and the shock could dry up her milk. Godmother sensed this and refused to die in her presence. She insisted: 'Vonette. Go see to your child. Don't tell me you'll go in a minute. Go, now, and on your way, ask *Man* Ragondier to lend me her rocking chair. I want to see my children. I'll wait for them in the rocking chair. I don't want to die yet. My brute of a husband hasn't sent back the children. Go fetch them for me. Death is in my eyes. I want to see them before I go.'

"After Vonette left, she said: 'She won't have time to get there, but don't call her. Bring all the neighbors. I'm dying.'

"And she died, just like that.

"My father also knew he was going to die. Ill, he suffered from a pain in his knee. One Saturday he got up and said: 'Monday, I'm going to the hospital.'

"He hadn't yet told us he was going to die. In the evening he asked me to gather some oranges for him.

"'Sick as you are, Papa, you want to eat cold oranges? That's too greedy.'

"'Are you the one who's going to eat them?'

"I didn't want to give them to him. Mamma—had she seen a sign in his eyes?—brought two big oranges to please him. He wasn't so sick as all that. He asked for his friends, neighbors, his sister, to whom he said: 'Josephine, today make me some of those sweets you do so well. Today, because tomorrow I won't be here anymore.'

"My aunt made him coconut *doucelettes,* and he ate them. With his friends and my aunt, he stayed there chatting, telling jokes, talking of the municipal elections that were scheduled for Sunday. At a certain moment he called me: 'Bety, how about going for the relatives who live up the road? I want to ask them to make an exchange with you. You'll give them a little more land in the back in exchange for a smaller piece along the road. On this parcel, you'll set up a small store to earn your living. I don't want you to live with your brother-in-law, he'll make too much trouble for you. It's not a joke when I tell you that tomorrow I won't be here anymore. Bety, go and bring all your sister's children to me as well as Cousin Mano.'

"Tenderly he kissed all the children, passing his hand through their hair. 'Kiss Papa Mine, children. Tomorrow he's going to the hospital; he'll be leaving you. And you, Cousin Mano, keep a close eye on my second daughter. Meet with her fiancé and set a date for the wedding. If that *misyé,* that young gentleman, can't decide, kick him out of here.'

"My sister was pregnant, her sixth child due soon. My father drew her near, embraced her belly with his arms, shook it gently, kissed her, and said: 'I'm going to the hospital. I won't get to see this little girl.'

"Two weeks later my sister gave birth to a daughter. A child who would grow up to be a forceful, energetic woman with strength of character. That was normal, people said, since a dying man had shaken her.

"Sunday, at about three in the morning, my father woke me and asked me to make him some coffee. At three in the morning! It was still dark and the kitchen was outside.

"'Get up at this hour of the night to make coffee? Go outside? Do you want the zombis[34] to carry me off, Papa?'

'Oh! So you're content to let me die without even making me a little coffee? That's all I ask from my daughter before I die.'

"'Your wife can wait on you.'

"'Not your mother, you. Make me a little coffee, my girl.'

"I didn't move and remained silent.

My favorite celebrations, the vigils for the dead

"'Will you let me die without my coffee?'

"I didn't understand any of these words about dying. When the sky began to brighten, I made up my mind: 'Papa. I'll go make you coffee.'

"'It's too late. I wouldn't have time to drink it. Fetch your sister, and also Odilia and Andrea. They called me an evil man. Tell them to come see how a man dies a quiet death on his bed. Have them also bring their guardian angel to pray for me at my death.'

"I left, fear eating away at my insides. I had trouble waking my sister, with her pregnant woman's heavy body. And, in her delicate state, how was I to tell her about my father's death without risking her own? She finally woke up and came with me. As for the two young ladies, Odilia and Andrea, I usually didn't speak to them. We hadn't been getting along for quite a while.

"'What's gotten into you, waking me up at this time of night?'

"'My father sent me. He asked me to tell you: Come and see how a man can die, a man who's said to be evil. Come also and read the prayers of the dying for him.'

"'Oh, so your father's up to more of his tricks, is he?'

"'No, *Manzèl,* he asked you to come and bring Andrea.'

"They made the trip. My father greeted them with a broad grin. 'Odilia, I'm going to die a quiet death on my bed. You'll see if I was an evil man.' Having said these words, he suddenly died.

"'*Anmoué, anmoué!* Help, help! Run, my father's dead!'

"My cousin and I wept bitterly, hugging one another. We cried and shrieked. My mother remained unmoved. You see, it hadn't yet sunk in.

"For at least two months I couldn't bring myself to drink coffee. Each time I made some, I'd throw it out or it would spill. I could still hear my father saying: 'Go make me some coffee; before I die, I want to drink coffee made by my daughter's hands.' And I hadn't given him that pleasure. The elders have taught us that before drinking or eating, we should give the dead their share. If we do not honor this command-ment, the food will fall from our hands. I had dismissed the warning . . . "

Man Bety told her story so engagingly that I lost track of time. How-ever, at the end I interjected: "I used to believe in all that, but no longer. The dead don't have any power. I can't agree with you anymore."

It's true. So many stories circulate about the dead, so many accounts of their power: helping people find work, releasing a child from evil spells, setting a fallen woman onto the straight and narrow path. . . . Personally, I can't say the dead do anything at all for me. I just can't say they do. I've already lost my father, my mother, many relatives. If they appear in my dreams, it wouldn't enter my mind to think: that's them, they have powers. Of course I think of them, dream about them giving me things, but maybe it's not actually them.

I've never been afraid of the dead. I don't know why, but the sight of a corpse doesn't make much of an impression on me. I know people who are so afraid of the dead that after paying a funeral visit, they can't sleep even if they cover themselves from head to toe. My neighbor, for example, I wonder what she'll do when someone close to her dies. She can't attend a wake because, afterward, she imagines seeing the person all night long and is terribly afraid.

As for me, I ask how the dead can harm me, frighten me. I say: "It's someone I got along well with, a relative I liked, and if that person is dead, its her body that died." According to my beliefs, the person is dead, I'll die someday too, and we'll meet again. The Gospel gave me this faith. We were created, and we'll die. That's the path we'll all follow. So you suffer, you miss the person, but you have to resign yourself to it. Man wasn't created to live on this earth eternally.

I'm always ready to console people in need, especially those overwhelmed by death, to help them find the courage to go on. They shouldn't be kept from crying, I cry with them, but I don't have that sensitivity toward the dead. I can mourn for someone killed accidentally, someone I've just seen alive and suddenly find dead. But an older person, sick, suffering, I can cry for him but I'm not grieved. That's the way it was with my mother. I lived here, one of my sisters in Pointe-à-Pitre, another in the town of Capesterre. The last one had remained at Carangaise; she had to earn her living and also care for my sick mother. When mother died, her death saddened me but I didn't grieve, because her life had been unhappy. She had plenty to eat and drink, but she suffered terribly, and my brother and sister, who cared for her, didn't know where to turn. God blessed her by calling her to him. I have my faith, and it's always with me. It inspires me when I console family members after a funeral and reflect with them on how well everything went at the cemetery, when I observe how they adjust to the death.

When I don't know the family well, I have the car that brought us from the cemetery drop me off before it arrives at the front door of the dead person's house. I say: "I'll get off here because I'm not going to lay down the dead."

"*Man* Joseph, the dead will stay with you."

Since people know I'm a jokester, that I love to kid around, they don't take it seriously. But after the funeral, almost everyone returns to be with the family in the home of the dead person's master and "lay down the dead." How can one "lay down the dead" since the body was already "laid down" in the cemetery? Are the dead upon us? Perhaps they are, because some people, if they have a sick person at home, refuse to welcome visitors who have just come back from the cemetery. Also, pregnant women shouldn't pay their respects to the dead, the child might be born with its eyes turned inward.

The corpse is left at the cemetery; the spirit of the dead person is brought home, to his house. There it will remain, some say, for the nine days of prayer, and it will leave on the night of veneration when a second wake is held. Others think the spirit cannot leave till after the Mass said in its honor on the fortieth day. If the living have done their best for him, respectfully following the traditions, the dead person will not return to bother them, pull their toes while they sleep, frighten them when they go outside at night.

I don't believe that the dead are on me when I leave the cemetery. Neither do I believe that you can "send a dead person" onto someone. If a sick person doesn't recover, people say: "So-and-so was spiteful, cruel to such-and-such, used sorcery against him and sent a dead person to him. He invoked a spirit at the cemetery and sent it onto that person."

It's strange. In telling this I realize that our ancestors left us all these customs without any explanation. For example, why, after the funeral, do those who came only for the carrying out of the body, also strip the beds, air the sheets, and discard the bath water as soon as the cadaver is gone? I've always seen these things done but never been able to ask why.

Of all the thousands of different things done by our ancestors, we understand only a few. Yet it would be useful to know the reasons for them all. Why do so many Guadeloupeans fear the silk-cotton tree, the "Congolese masks" at Mardi Gras, and all the things left from the time when we were slaves?

As a child, I used to hide under the bed when the Congolese masks passed by at Mardi Gras. Those huge naked devils, bodies all shiny black, always terrorized me. I didn't understand their importance or what they represented. On the radio one day, an old woman spoke about all the things Guadeloupe had lost: Congolese masks, death masks, horned masks, *mokozonbi*.[35] The journalist asked her if she knew the meaning of the masks. She answered no, but that they used to be around. The guy explained that those men painted themselves black to represent the Africans. I laughed, oh how I laughed! So that was it: at Mardi Gras we dressed up as "blacks"! We walked around completely naked, without clothes, only hiding our genitals. And, to become real Africans, real Congolese, we smeared ourselves with black. Black people, already darkskinned, who painted themselves black. How bizarre!

When I think about all these traditions, I realize that they used to have special meanings. Some people know what they are, but most of us repeat the gestures without having a clue. The ancestors went about their business without saying a word. They kept their secrets by keeping silent. And children didn't have the right to ask adults questions. But you, as a child, you're there, watching everything with both eyes open. If you know how to remember things, you'll be able to tell about them afterward: "I saw that." Me too, I watched, I saw things, I did things, but without really knowing. I didn't have true understanding. That's why there are still many things I wonder about today.

For instance, why do certain Guadeloupeans consider it so important to own a family tomb? They say they don't want the earth to fall on their stomachs! But I think there's something else. Personally, I don't give a damn about a tomb. In any case, they'll have to dig the earth to receive my body. There was a time when tombs didn't exist; someone had to set the example. Not just anyone, he would have needed the means. Another person wanted to imitate him, then another. The tombs became bigger and bigger, more imposing, real buildings. Being laid to rest in a tomb signifies that you're someone "of substance." In thinking about it, I've decided that the importance common folk attach to the tomb must come from the time of slavery. The masters lived in beautiful, large houses, and the slaves in small shacks. In death, don't we try to obtain what we couldn't have in life? Each one wants to get even, to be up on top, to become really important. If you don't have a tomb, you're less than nothing.

Even though dying, leaving friends and family, is a very difficult thing, we live with the idea and prepare for it well in advance so as not to mess it up. The first thing people say is: "My *Mare-Gaillard* is paid up."[36] That puts their minds at ease. The money for the coffin, the service, and the rented cars that ferry people around, is all arranged. The family members won't have to hold their heads in despair or call for help. Proud people want what they call a "proper death." They'd like a beautiful house to impress their friends, one large enough to accommodate all the relatives who'll come from far away and stay for the nine days of prayer. Some want a whole train of cars following them, others choose flowers and music. . . . Still others, who must have suffered greatly during their lives, say: "At my death, no flowers no wreaths, nothing, nothing at all."

When my mother built her tomb with the money from her cousin's land, it certainly wasn't out of pride. She never had visions of grandeur. She built it as others of her generation for whom the land had great value might have done.

I've heard another explanation for this obsession with tombs. People don't want to "lose their bones." They fear being dug up. And I must admit that there's no respect in the city cemeteries. Bodies are dug up without care; bones are lost. The gravediggers throw everything away. Nothing is left of the person, not a single bone. The gravediggers earn monthly salaries. A bone from here falls here or there. Once it's fallen, it's fallen. How can you tell where it belongs? The tomb serves as a repository for your bones; they stay with the other family remains.

In your own cemetery, one on your own property, when a skeleton is dug up, all the bones are carefully put back in place. Besides, whoever might dig among the bones would have family ties or ties of friendship with the dead person. They would be there picnicking and speaking respectfully of the dead they had known.

"Look! So-and-so's the most recent. His bones are the freshest."

"And such-and-such. Her hair has grown so long!"

"See how white his teeth have stayed!"

I know bones have a real value because once, in a history book about France, I read about a museum where bones are displayed with labels, "bones of this one," "bones of that one." I can understand people not wanting the remains of their bodies treated disrespectfully.

I wonder about another custom passed on from our ancestors: Why do we mourn a mother for three years—two in deep mourning wearing all black, plus one in partial mourning—and a father for two years, one in deep mourning and one in partial mourning? Of course, a father's not the same as a mother, but I wonder why we give women the best place in mourning, since we don't give them the same place in life. It's worth some thought. How come the woman has a right to the greatest honor, three years of mourning, and the man only gets two, yet she never takes priority over him in life? Why is she only first in the question of mourning? Of course, a mother counts more than a father, but in society, mothers don't have the best place. Yet mothers give birth to the children, carry them in their arms from birth, get up at night. Nowadays I do see some fathers who carry their children and give them the bottle, but I really can't say much about it, since it never happened at my house. Men fear babies for the first five or six months. After that, a few—we should give them credit—do contribute to the children's upbringing and care for them, for instance, when the mother has too much work and throws them out. If we look carefully, we'll find that everything of real value centers around the mother. The man does nothing but put the kid in your womb, then you carry it for nine months. Also, often before the child is even four weeks old, you must return to work, make sure everything is prepared before leaving, and if there's no older child at home to watch the baby, take it to someone else, then later run back for it. While the mother works, she thinks all the time about the baby who's not with her.

What trouble a mother has raising a child! The father is like an appendage to the family. We've all been brought up to mistrust men. Mamma's side of the family is more important. For example, I have a daughter from my first union. The other children call Lucie their sister "on Mamma's side" because they don't have the same father. But if I were Lucie's mother, Joseph her father, and another woman the mother of the other children, they'd say: we're not from the same branch of the family because we're not from the same womb. You can count on a sister "from Mamma's side" whereas you never can be sure of a sister "from Papa's side."

I endured a lot to bring up my children, but I don't want them killing themselves after my death by wearing deep mourning in this sun for two years. Wearing black means nothing to me; it's what's in the heart that matters. The other day I explained this to a woman I met at a *coup de main*.[37] She wore a black dress, her head wrapped in a black scarf. She told me she'd recently lost her mother and had no choice. I answered: "The black dress is unimportant; what goes on in your heart is all that counts. If you worked in an office with cool air blowing on your back, I could understand. But you're a farm laborer and the sun cooks you alive. Take care of your health, put on a light dress—blue or violet—when you're in the cane fields, and wear the black dress when you go out to church or to town. You respect your mourning by avoiding dances and the movies. Don't mistreat your body. After such a catastrophe, a loss as terrible as the death of a mother, you must preserve your strength to go on living.

It seems to me that children are aware of all the trouble their mothers have taken with them since birth. They're the ones who, at her death, put her first.

Nothing is certain with a father. But you're at ease with a mother. She gives you strength. She's always there, through rain, storms, and sunny days.

What is it that we mothers sing to our children, to rock them to sleep?

Pitit dodo, papa pa la, sésé pa la.	Sleep little one, papa's gone, sister's gone.
Sé manman tousèl ki dan lamizè.	Mamma stays, all alone in her misery.
Sé manman tousèl ki dan lanbara.	Mamma stays, all alone with her troubles.

My favorite celebrations, the vigils for the dead

This is the song that my grandmother sang, my mother lulled me to sleep with, and I, too, always sing.

I'm not really sure, but somehow I feel that the words and deeds of the elders and their understanding of the world are rooted in all of us, good as well as bad. And that's what has made us, we Guadeloupeans.

4

Tè, tè a manman, tè a granfanmi,

sé on moso a kò a-ou. Sa pa ka vann

Maternal land, land of the ancestors,

a piece of oneself that cannot be sold

You can take the child out of the country, but you can't take
the country out of the child.

James Baldwin

You cannot, you must not, sell the land of your ancestors. As fingers
are joined together by the palm of the hand, family members are joined
together by the land. First the thumb, then the other fingers, and finally
the pinkie. Together they form a whole. To sell the land of the ancestors would be to tear apart the family because what holds it together
would no longer exist. To sell the land left to you by your father or
mother would be like selling your father or mother, denying that they
gave you life. It would be like the master who sold a slave, taking from
him all he cherished.

If, by misfortune, you sold it, you'd reflect afterward and cry out:
"What have I done?" But what's done is done and cannot be undone.
Yet sometimes, because of the hypocritical blood that flows through
the veins of today's children, selling is the only solution. It apportions
things, brings peace. If one selfish person wants to keep it all without
giving anything to the others, it's better to sell. Each one takes his
money and goes his own way: one traveling, another buying land elsewhere and building a house. You must know how to buy and in what
way. Also, if you build a little house, you should acknowledge in some
small way, with a sign or mark, what made it possible.

For some people, being forced to sell the land of their parents is a
source of shame. For me, its just painful, something that severs family
ties. When I go to Carangaise I say: I'm going to my mother's land, to
my father's land. If I sold it, I couldn't say that anymore. It would become "so-and-so's land." Of course, I'm speaking of the maternal land
or the paternal land you inherit from your parents, the memory of your

ancestors. If a cousin leaves you land, you can sell it. My mother was the sole heir of a cousin's parcel of land. It was her own. She'd been given it and could sell it. And that's what she did. She used the money to build her tomb. She didn't make the decision by herself. We children urged her to sell because one of my brothers wanted it for himself. We said: when our mother dies, a fight will break out. That brother had already behaved badly toward our mother. The court had already intervened. My mother sold the land to one of her godsons. My brother was still going to take her to court. So we decided: something must be done with the money. We thought of a tomb. My mother couldn't be accused of throwing away the money. Thanks to the land left by her cousin, she was able to build herself a tomb.

The ancestral land is sacred, but what discord it creates within families and among neighbors! The hatchet, the shotgun, and the knife can sometimes become involved. Out of fear, many people don't want to hear anything about inheritance problems. Their names must not be brought up before the law. They have respect for themselves. They say: "The land eats away at people; take it for yourself." I agree with them. Some will hand over their shares without an argument; others will fight for what belongs to them, often unsuccessfully. If the court decides, it's like a chair that's been sawed in two, one part for each person. It will never stand up.

Say the court awards you a bit of land. Even if you can't work it yourself, you put someone on it to show that it's yours. But your neighbor, who wants it all for himself, doesn't see the renter, he only sees you, who are on "his" land. Even if you rent it (or sell it, as some do) because you're afraid of him, the problem doesn't go away. He's out to get you. You'll always be at odds with him.

Some people, while they're alive, choose to give a gift to one of their children but others give nothing away, leaving the inheritance to be worked out afterward. Then, even those children who cared for their old father and stayed close with him, could end up arguing. They might have let one of the siblings, perhaps the worst off, cultivate the land himself so he could earn a living. Then, little by little, he tries to take it all. That brings dissension, and the problems begin. If you act according to your rights, you find yourself embroiled in the business of justice and the law. You know in your heart that you're in a situation you don't want. You didn't buy the land; your parents left it to you without your having had to work for it. You don't feel you can keep others from earning a living.

When my mother died, she left us some land. With several children inheriting, no single person has the right to sell. And why sell, anyway? Each heir could take a small piece, or a single person could work the whole parcel. But if that one then decides to sell, the other heirs intervene: "We don't want to sell but agree to rent it out. If you're tired, rent to someone who knows how to work it. Or another one of us could take your place."

My brothers and sisters already owned land. Only one, the youngest brother, didn't have any of his own. He had stayed with mother till her death, working the land. We let him have it. Now he controls it and does what he chooses. One of my sisters who lives in Capesterre has a garden, but if she needs oranges, lemons, or coconuts, she goes to my brother's place to get some. According to her, the creep doesn't even want her to set foot on "his" land. It's true that if he finds one of us there without his permission, he throws a fit and grumbles behind our backs, not daring to say to us face-to-face: "Don't come onto my land."

If my sister and I were nasty we could say to him: "It's our mother's land. Either we divide it up, or you get off it!"

"Divide up this land! After all the work I've put into it, you want to kick me off now?" he'd answer.

Since we all went our own ways and he alone stayed in Capesterre with Mamma, we let it be. We don't want to fight with him over a question of land.

Another source of problems: you might be an heir but not carry the family name or have marriage ties to prove your rights. For you to get a share, a court would have to decide that so-and-so was your mother. How demeaning to be forced to climb the courthouse steps!

When it's a question of land, beware! If one of the heirs says: "I'm most qualified to look into the technical and legal aspects of this property," that means: "I'm the biggest thief of the bunch."

Once he's involved with the business and up-to-date on everything, he'll take over the shares of those who don't bother to get involved. They didn't have their land resurveyed? He'll nibble away a few hundred square meters here from this one, a few hundred square meters there from that one.

Long ago, people were craftier. They took a more serious, honest view of things. Their understanding was based on proof. A xeranthemum plant might mark the boundary of their land. Whenever they planted a xeranthemum, they'd bury a bit of coal and some rusted iron under the roots. If the xeranthemum disappeared, uprooted by a person or a cyclone, only the one who'd been instructed by the elders could hold his own against someone better educated. He knew he could say: "That's the boundary of my land; dig there and you'll find a lump of coal and a bit of rusted iron." Our ancestors didn't covet others' land, but hands off anything that belonged to them!

Maternal land, land of the ancestors, a piece of oneself that cannot be sold

Now we lay down concrete posts to stake out the borders of a property. It's done more or less correctly. And the *lakandas* (cadaster) gets mixed up in it! If one of the surveyors comes and says: "These are the borders of your land," you must accept it without discussion. I've seen these gentlemen at work. One morning, I was with a friend way at the back of her garden, gathering peas. Two men in city clothes and fancy shoes arrived and addressed her: "Here's a paper that describes your land. Please sign for the record."

My friend isn't a person to sign anything without reading it. She examined the papers. "But, sir, you're stealing three *ares* from me."

"No, ma'am. We're not stealing anything. It's all clearly delineated and surveyed."

"I don't know who it was, but someone gave you the boundaries of my land. All I can sign is, 'Yes, it's my land.' I won't sign for the size."

"Then you must arrange to have it surveyed."

"Me? I have my title. If you want to survey, you two are surveyors, go ahead and survey. But for free. I don't need to check my land. You're the ones who want to know. Go ahead and survey, then. You can tell me where the three *ares* have gone."

Many people are hoodwinked in this way. They don't know how to read, and even if they do, they must at least know a little about the metric system. Know how large an *are* is, how many square meters. An *are* is ten meters by ten meters, three *ares* are three hundred square meters; my friend knew that, they didn't just disappear. She wasn't taken in. They tried to say: "It's the canal that absorbed them."

"The canal never took land from my side. I've always known where it went."

"Then it's the ravine."

"Gentlemen, the ravine is the Lamentin River. If it took anything away, it would be from my neighbor's land. He changed its course across his land, and it comes back out on mine."

Those gentlemen from the administration are really awful. They come up with a pile of petty annoyances to force you to resurvey your land or re-mark the borders when you don't have any need to and know your own business well enough.

"What information an old property title contains!" my friend explained to me. "The type of land, its size, where it's located and, especially, information about yourself: who you are, what race you belong to, the professions of your family—so-and-so was a merchant, another a carpenter. . . . That's what the old land titles were like."

The cemeteries also record who owned which parcels of land. Our ancestors rarely established cemeteries in the towns. From generation to generation, they were buried where they lived. All generations— married and unmarried people, legitimate and illegitimate children— all were buried in the same place, together. "Died and was buried on said property," read the death certificates, proof that the people had bought the land. And for those who had been born on the same parcel, it would read: "Born in the maternal or paternal house" and "Died in the maternal or paternal house, in the hamlet of . . . " "Neighbor- hoods" didn't exist the way they do today. One would speak of the hamlet of La Rose Blanche, or the hamlet of Plaisir, and the name of the hamlet provided enough information to research a parcel of land, a dead person, or a birth, so you could find out whether the land came from the mother's lineage or the father's. That way, descendants could learn where they came from and decide how to arrange their affairs.

Our ancestors had another custom. They'd plant a coconut palm to mark a birth and a mango tree to indicate where the first member of the family was buried on a plot of land. Why a mango tree? A mango tree lives a long time. Next to my place, there's one that must be 200 years old because, I believe, it was planted in the 1700s. It's noted on the deed to the land. The tree served as a reference point, indicated a place of respect. Sometimes, instead of a mango tree or a breadfruit tree, flowers, purple bushes, or dracaenas would mark the cemetery. As soon as you saw these sorts of plants, you knew that people were buried there. Now, people grow these flowers all around their houses.

The same friend who had a bone to pick with the *lakandas,* owns many parcels of family land. On each, there's a cemetery that serves as a landmark. One day she went to look for one of these cemeteries in a place she didn't know well and found herself in a field of sugarcane that had been planted by a cousin. Thanks to the mango tree, she could locate the graves. Today, people have no respect for the dead. They even plant and let their animals feed on top of the graves. Our ances- tors planted that tree as a sign of respect for the family, to leave some- thing in remembrance. People should have preserved that custom and maintained the cemeteries. If you don't clean them up, of course weeds grow. No care, no respect.

This woman never neglected her dead. The graves on her land are even neater than those in the public cemeteries in town. One year at the festival of All Saints, on the Day of the Dead, I accompanied her on her rounds. We went everywhere: one day to pull out the weeds, another to *propter,* to clean up. The evening of the illumination, we set out candles both at Chabert and at Bergnoles, where a wake contin- ued all night long with food and drink, games, songs, and a drum, just like the customary wake for the dead. The neighbors all came together.

Maternal land, land of the ancestors, a piece of oneself that cannot be sold

These celebrations occurred up till quite recently. Today, the wake at the festival of All Saint's has practically disappeared.

Till recently, too, on Saturdays or Sundays, the whole family came, either from Pointe-à-Pitre or from another direction—one passing by to pick up the next—to visit "their dead." All that's finished. Everyone for himself. Each looks out for his own best interest without thinking of the ancestor who sacrificed, who chose not to sell, because, as he said, he didn't know what the future would hold for his children.

Some descendants—even if the land has fallen into other hands, even if the new owners have put up fences—continue to maintain the graves. The mango tree, the old graves remain.

For forty, forty-two years, *yo* (they)[38] have opposed burials on private land. I'm talking about the graves of the landowners, not of the sharecroppers or the agricultural workers on the plantations, who are buried in a common grave. Today, when the present owner allows it, the descendants can come on the festival of All Saint's and rebuild the graves of their ancestors.[39]

When you have a cemetery on your land, on your property, the dead are there with you, you're with them, you're together. You can't be selfish and only care about what you can take from the earth without respecting the cemetery. You'd sever the cord. If you keep the graves neat and plant flowers, then the bond remains unbroken. Even if we call a dead person "the departed," his memory remains. Are we really able to understand the meaning of "departed?"

Let's consider a tree, for instance. Our ancestors planted some of them, and we still find the same species. Where did the breadfruit tree come from? It was just there; we always knew there was a breadfruit tree. The fruit of the *denndés* and the coconut palms fall down and the trees grow up. The cacao tree too. . . . We can see the link between nut and tree. You can think: I don't know which ancestor planted it, but the tree is there.

It's easy to confuse the fruits of the breadfruit and the chestnut trees. Both are green and round like a ball, but when they ripen and split open on the ground, they're not at all alike. The breadfruit rots, the fruit of the chestnut tree opens and chestnuts pop out by the dozens. According to the proverb, *Fanm sé chateny, nonm sé fouyapen.* (Woman is like a chestnut that produces other chestnuts, man like a breadfruit that dies once it falls.)

People look at what's most obvious, for on closer inspection, the breadfruit tree reproduces via its roots. Even if the tree appears dead, the roots still live and spread, producing new shoots. The roots of the chestnut tree don't reproduce. If the trunk dies, no more chestnuts. You'd need new nuts to give rise to another tree.

Breadfruit trees, silk-cotton trees, mango trees, red gum trees, huge pear trees,[40] filaos, custard-apple trees—all these trees, all these fruits: no one knows where they came from, but we communicate with them and they're important to us. At your birth, you're detached from your mother and tied to the earth when your umbilical cord is planted along with a coconut palm. The site of the coconut palm is the earth on which you were born. Your memory will live as long as the palm tree. Only a strong cyclone can uproot a coconut palm. My sister's broke during the cyclone of 1966. Mine still lives and bears fruit.

When you die, of course your body returns to the earth and, again, the water used to bathe the corpse is discarded at the foot of a tree, far from the well-traveled paths. From birth to death, we're tied to the earth. The earth gives us life. The earth binds all of us together, the living and the dead. In nature and in the lives of men, life and death are intertwined and cannot be separated.

5

Kouzin Amelya ka aprann mwen

pa détlé douvan lavi

Cousin Amelya teaches me

not to bow down to life

We hadn't stirred, Grandmother and I, and her voice grew
strange. . . . "However tall trouble is, man must make himself
taller still, even if it means making stilts. . . . My little ember,"
she'd whisper, "if you ever get on a horse, keep good hold of the
reins so that it's not the horse that rides you. . . . Behind one
pain there is another. Sorrow is a wave without end. But the
horse mustn't ride you, you must ride it."

Simone Schwarz-Bart,
The Bridge of Beyond

I always say to my children: "You're living in an easy and pleasant time
for children."

As soon I quit school—which I was lucky to have attended—I left
my parents' home to go to work. It wasn't as bad as it might have been;
much of what I learned about life was thanks to this departure for
the city.

I had recently turned fourteen and just barely missed earning my
certificate of studies. The teacher wanted my mother to pay for another
year of school, but she couldn't afford it and I didn't want to go either.

My mother sold manioc flour in Pointe-à-Pitre. One of her clients
owned a shop there. Mamma said to her: "I have a daughter, a very
intelligent girl, who went to school and took the exam for her certificate. She just quit. Do you need someone to work for you?"

At that time, employers took advantage of children, but parents
didn't much care. What counted were the wages the children brought
home. I only became aware of this much later and, even then, not all
at once.

My mother sent me to work in that woman's shop and arranged for
me to live with cousins in Bébian, a suburb of Pointe-à-Pitre. Four sis-

ters shared a house. I don't know how or why, but cousin Amelya was the one who adopted me. "You're my child," she said to me. And she taught me everything.

I'd attended all my classes, but something was missing in that school. How could I have gotten as far as taking the exam for my certificate and not learned to introduce myself, to meet someone, to receive a visitor? I was truly gauche! And I can't blame my parents, it wasn't part of their lives. People stayed in their villages then, where they were born. They didn't welcome many strangers. They didn't look afar for their children's godmothers and godfathers. Everything occurred within the group. We all knew each other, there weren't many occasions to meet people and say: "May I introduce so-and-so." If one of your children has been away a long time and returns home, for example, you don't introduce people to him, because they'd already know his name. You'd just say: "Maximus, come say hello to your uncle."

That's not the same as meeting a stranger who comes to my house, and saying to him: "May I introduce *Manzèl* Dani."

If you don't know how to act, it's because neither your parents nor the school ever taught you. You weren't given the key. To have reached this level of instruction—missing out on the certificate by only two points—and to find yourself tongue-tied in a house with many visitors whenever you're introduced: "This is my niece . . . my cousin . . . a young relative."

You're only fourteen, and small, but you're no longer a child, and you stand there not knowing what to do or say: it's embarrassing.

Cousin Amelya introduced me to everyone who visited. Gradually, I began to answer: "My name is Leonora. I'm from Capesterre, I . . . "

I learned to "make someone's acquaintance." I'd heard the term, heard someone say: "He's made her acquaintance," but I didn't know how to act, how to start the introduction. And I understood that to make someone's acquaintance means knowing how to introduce yourself to that person, saying hello, telling your name, where you live, your home region, perhaps your profession, everything about you. It's very important. I'll never forget this gap in my education.

There were many others. Of course, with five, six, seven children like Mamma had, its not the same as dedicating yourself to only one. Cousin Amelya could give me attention, she only had me to care for. She'd take the clothes I was washing from my hands: "That's not the way, it's not done like that. . . . "

She also showed me how to dress: "When you get home from work, you must change your clothes. You shouldn't wear this housedress

Cousin Amelya teaches me not to bow down to life

when you go outside. If you have an old *robe-case* on, you can't say: 'I'm going to Mass, I'm going to the festival.'"

When I wanted to do things differently, wear my best dress to work, cousin Amelya took me to task: "No, child. That's not the way it's done."

I wasn't angry at her remarks, but I did feel upset and cried. I couldn't stand having to do it her way all the time. I felt she was being hard on me, and my tears fell.

Amelya helped me pick out everything I needed. She showed me different bolts of fabric, hats, but she made the decisions. One day she said to me: "From now on you must select your own things. It's time you learned how." That young woman was quite something, teaching a fourteen-year-old to buy her own things. She had no formal education, but she knew how to let you assume responsibility.

When my mother sent me off to work, she took my pay and bought me what she chose. I still remember the dress she gave me at the end of my first month. It buttoned all the way down the back. Amelya watched everything out of the corner of her eye. One day she spoke to my mother: "Auntie, please listen. The child works now, she lives in the city, we go out, she accompanies us, she needs some money for buying her own things."

Amelya realized I was growing up, becoming a young lady. When I went out, I had to dress like a young lady, clean and neat. No need for the finest fabric, the most expensive, but a dress that buttoned up the back was only suited for the country and even there, only for children.

My mother was very upset. She didn't want to let me keep my wages. Finally she gave in, but continued to help herself to some, even though it wasn't a fat salary.

Thinking back, I reflect: "My girl, you never had much luck with your work." This bad luck began the day my mother found me work with that woman. I worked like a zombi, never got to keep more than a small part of my meager wages, and, in addition, was expected to spy on the others!

I arrived at Bas-de-la-Source at seven in the morning to open the shop. It was a large shop, a real grocery store chock-full of merchandise from floor to ceiling. And what activity! We sold a great deal on credit. I was in charge of keeping the accounts and preparing the bills. Every two weeks, the customers brought in their account books. So much to add up! You had to be good at arithmetic. I didn't make mistakes, and the owner was satisfied. In a sense, I was a bookkeeper, but I also took my turn behind the counter. I liked to wait on customers. That was the only chance to relax and laugh, because many young men came in to buy a Job cigarette, mint candies, soda, but especially to dish out compliments: "Look at that beauty! Where'd you find that lovely skin, soft as a plum? What region are you from? The sun doesn't beat down too cruelly there. That's where I should go, to look for a fiancée. . . . "

It might have led to something, but in that shop, nothing went very far. And no question of meeting after work. At seven P.M., after twelve hours of work, I was dead tired, flat out like a papaya trunk under a wagon wheel. Selling, counting can't be done while talking. You don't have time to make friends. But you're not a cow, you're not stupid, and the clients—young men, women, single men who do their own marketing—all say a friendly word, make a joke. Sometimes you might meet a client in town and she'd come over to say hello and chat a moment: "Oh, my child! *Man* Bibis's is the last place in the world to work. I've seen so many employees pass through there. They appear and then disappear faster than water in a crab's hole."

But you had to be careful and not become too friendly with the clients, not speak with them too long: if you chat on with any of them, the owner will be convinced the person is an accomplice to whom you're passing merchandise.

Adelaide, another girl who worked there with me, stole and stole big. A well-polished thief. She stole whatever was in the store. Occasionally, she'd take the goods herself; other times she'd arrange for an accomplice to buy things at the counter. In the blink of an eye, a pot of lard, a liter of oil, a kilo of rice, a jug of rum would be grabbed, handed over, spirited away. In the evening they'd meet to divvy it up.

The owner saw her goods disappear without catching anyone. Yet she watched, eagle-eyed. Watching was her real work, her only occupation. One eye on you, the other on the wares and on the money that came in. Her favorite place: the cash register. Every few minutes, she'd remove the big bills and exchange coins for them. To better spy on us, she had cut a hole in the floor of her apartment above the shop. She suspected Adelaide and asked me to catch her at it. I was supposed to tell her who wasn't stealing, who was, and how.

I told cousin Amelya everything. "My girl," she said, "be careful! You've never been involved in anything like this before. You're still too young. Don't get mixed up in this sort of business."

When *Man* Bibis realized I wasn't going to denounce anyone, she sent for my mother: "Business isn't going well, I need fewer workers now, I can't keep your daughter on any longer."

Cousin Amelya tried hard to find me work. Finally she located an opening in another store. The woman in charge wasn't really the owner; she was a manager, who hired and fired the workers. There

Cousin Amelya teaches me not to bow down to life

again, no luck! I don't know if I was too good or too soft or what. I was young, but those people didn't care if you were a child, a working child. They treated you like a beast of burden. No sympathy for the employees. Once again, I found myself out the door, without really knowing why.

On the other hand, I remember my third job well: a large shop with two or three employees. My work? Washing wine and rum bottles. I spent almost the entire day in a sort of warehouse, rinsing bottles in a large basin. A girl who worked in the shop, an employee like me, really ran things, acting as if the place belonged to her. I did my work, obeyed, and everyone was pleased. Had I finally found a good job? Dum-da-dum! A new hurdle in my path!

One day, as I was quietly washing the bottles, the other employees invaded my domain. They were laughing because they'd stolen a box of cookies from the shop. They finished them off and left the box and papers behind. The owner found the remains. I was the only one in the room. Who else could have eaten the cookies? I tried to defend myself: "I certainly wasn't the one who ate the cookies."

Nothing doing. I'd stolen the cookies and had to pay for the box. I thought: "Cousin Amelya will tell the woman that I'm not a thief. I'll bring her with me tomorrow."

"This child doesn't touch anybody else's belongings. She's never taken a single thing that isn't hers. If she ate any of the cookies, she'll pay for them, but then everyone must pay."

"Okay. Everyone will pay. I'll take it out of their salaries."

But finally, she only took money from me. Enough to pay for the whole box. Cousin Amelya was furious: "You won't stay with that woman one more minute. Come with me."

She caused a scene at the shop. "This is not a child who steals. You've wronged her, and she won't work for you anymore."

Let me tell you, you can get angry or play a dirty trick on someone for the fun of it, but if you're underhanded and treacherous—watch out! At Baie-Mahault, I saw the girl who had wrongly accused me of stealing. She's gone crazy. I'm not absolutely sure it's her, but every time I run into that girl I think to myself: "That must be Julie, the girl who worked with me." I see a person who looks like her, and yet I wonder: "Good God, this crazy person can't be her."

I left the shop with my head held high, but leave I did. Out of work. I fell ill. I wasn't like most girls here who get their period at nine or ten years old. I was seventeen and still no period. My mother hadn't been able to give me a reason. I swelled up, became very fat. Cousin Amelya sent for Doctor Chartol. When he saw me, he thought I was pregnant. "But doctor, she hasn't yet gotten her period," Amelya told him.

Doctor Chartol gave me good treatment and brought me through that life-threatening situation.

In Pointe-à-Pitre, we all lived in the same room, Amelya, her sisters, and I. One day, Cousin Theresa, seeing my stained underpants, exclaimed: "Ai-ai-ai! Your panties are stained with blood. You've gotten your period, my girl. Leonora, listen well, you're no longer a little girl. Don't let the boys play with you anymore, touch you. You can get pregnant if you speak with them. Once you've gotten your period, it's serious."

That's how I learned about life. It was mostly Cousin Amelya who taught me what was good or bad, and what to do so no one would take advantage of me. I can't say that my mother taught me any of those things. Not even how to wash and iron. Since I'd gone to the river with Mamma, I knew how to wash. But true understanding I owe to that cousin of mine. Of the three sisters, I liked her best. Wherever she went, I followed behind. I was called her little puppy.

At the house, in addition to Amelya and me, lived Suzanne (nicknamed Foufouyi), Victoria, Theresa (called Térézine), a brother named Cholo, and one of their nephews.

My cousins were self-made. Their mother, a Marie-Galantaise,[41] had come to Guadeloupe to live with an old fellow at Goyave. The girls decided to move to Pointe-à-Pitre. Led by the oldest sister, they rented a small cabin. When I went to live with them, my life became intertwined with theirs.

Their father hadn't sent them to school, so they didn't know how to read or write. They decided to train and educate themselves. They managed to pay for classes in a small private school. I helped them write their names, recognize numbers. . . . They weren't educated but figured out how to handle each of life's surprises. They hadn't come to Pointe-à-Pitre to let themselves go and give in to the pleasures of the city. They didn't find any men worthy of them. Yet they finally did marry, even the youngest, a seamstress who was called *zingzing* (dragonfly) because of the graceful way her hips swung. Of the four, only one remained single—the eldest, Amelya, my favorite. No man suited her. She stayed there a long time, wilting like an eggplant in a merchant's stall, drying up, withering. Late in life, a man made her an offer. She went to live with him and remained there for the rest of her life, but she'd married off her two sisters.

We all slept together in the small wooden house, at the end of a courtyard, surrounded by many other similar cabins. Slightly further on, the suburbs gave way to trees, streams, hills, and railroad tracks that carried the sugarcane.

Boulevard Hanne separated the city from the suburbs. Across the

Cousin Amelya teaches me not to bow down to life

canal, you were in the suburbs, and a suburb that looked so much like the country! You should have seen it in the rain. The canal overflowed. To reach Bébian Street, you had to make your way carefully across a wooden plank. In the rainy season, the waters running down from Abymes Hill overflowed and mixed with the ocean near Dino,[42] transforming the suburb into a sea. Mattresses, beds, barrels floated about. From every side, people called for help:

"An moué, an ka néyé!"　　　　"Help, help, I'm drowning!"
"Vin sové nou!"　　　　　　　"Save us!"

No question of going to work, you had to retrieve your belongings.

The smallest storm carried away the planks. To cross, you had to know the place well. Without landmarks, you might easily disappear into the canal. For a small sum, men would lift you up, carry you across the canal, take you out of the area, and deposit you on the sidewalk in front of Monsieur Fostin's store. He was a large, dark, black man who allowed everyone who climbed out of the water soaking wet, to come dry their feet, put on their shoes, roll down their pants legs, and wring out their petticoats.

This Monsieur Fostin was the most important merchant in the neighborhood. His shop, a combination grocery-general store-cafe located right at the entrance to the city, sold everything. It seemed like a large store to me, but it was no more than a *lolo* compared to today's supermarkets. Except for an occasional item bought at Fostin's or in the city, we did our marketing in the small *lolos* of the suburb. You couldn't buy everything in town, you had to do business at a place that would sell on credit. The accounts were paid off every two weeks. I don't remember all the shops of the suburb, but I can still clearly visualize those of *Manman* Atoua and Monsieur Fostin. They ignored the packages you were already carrying when you entered the shop, and they never refused to serve you. In the country it's not like that. If you go into a shop to buy salt or matches with your shopping bag full of rice and codfish, you're told off: "You already have all your groceries, all your food, but since you can't cook it, you come here, to my place, so you can light a fire. . . . Go back and buy your matches where you bought the rest, *manmzèl!*"

The shopkeepers shouldn't do that. They have shops so they can sell things. If I'm a client of *Man* Calixte and she doesn't have what I need, shouldn't I have the right to go to *Man* Bruno's store for it? Should I be forced to do without? No! None of this sick "everything for oneself" attitude. In the city, people don't act that way. Of course, there are many shops right next door to one another. Each one manages to earn a living.

Also we bought from the market women with "dust on their feet,"[43] the itinerants, who didn't wait for clients to come to them but walked about with baskets on their heads. Each one came at a particular time of day and sang a special song. When I'd hear in the morning:

"Mi mabi an mwen . . . frèch frèch, frèch!"	"Buy my mabi . . . cool, refreshing!"

I knew it was almost six o'clock. The peddler women who sold milk, coconut sherbet, "bouquets" of soup vegetables, came by in the afternoon. In the evening: grilled peanuts, warm blood sausage, fresh-ground *kilibibi*, snowballs . . . [44]

On the days when we received our pay, we'd buy cakes, *marinades*, and blood sausages on our way home from work. Sick people and children were entitled to milk. Sometimes on Sunday, we treated ourselves to this delicacy. The vendor would cry out: "Buy my boiled milk, buy my hot milk!"

That day, lunch was also special: rice with red beans, or red beans with manioc flour, and meat sautéed with carrots. In the evening, soup made from veal feet, beef, a drink of *chodo* or, even more frequently, a big bowl of chocolate milk flavored with vanilla and cinnamon, eaten with bread.

Never fresh meat during the week: salted meat, pig's tail or pig's head, salt cod, or fresh fish. Snapper, threadfin, or *grandes-gueules* for the soup stock, *balarous* or sea pike for frying, little *pissiettes* for deep frying . . . with root vegetables: yams, *malangas, madères,* sweet potatoes, green bananas often brought in from my mother's garden.

I never heard of "an entrée" as some people prepare nowadays. I really don't know when this custom came to Guadeloupe.

To cook all this, no kerosene burner and certainly not a butane stove; but charcoal. At *Man* Reyo's, on the market square, we bought it by *ka* or half-*ka* (lard-tin full). When we were flush and had money *an agouba* (to spare) we went to the charcoal market, at the end of the boulevard. There, under the large *salbiyé* tree, the merchants of Anse-Bertrand came by oxcart to sell their high-quality *campêche* wood. We'd buy a whole sackful.

We shared expenses, each one contributing what she could. Together we decided what was needed, one would get the rice, another the fish. I didn't have to chip in money, my mother provided the vegetables. When I worked at the soda factory, I ate both lunch and dinner with them. Then it was a different story, and of course, I paid my share. You

Cousin Amelya teaches me not to bow down to life

find freeloaders who don't want to pay everywhere, but never at home. The cooperative family life really impressed me.

In the evenings, the cabins expanded like accordions with their partitions and walls. Six of us slept in one room, sometimes even eight or nine when my mother or another relative came to Pointe-à-Pitre. We worked it all out, each one finding a corner. We weren't unhappy squeezed together, we got along beautifully. Most often, the four girls slept in the big bed, the young nephew on a narrow wooden couch alongside, and Amelya's brother on a folding cot in the kitchen. No chance of having a "private room" like nowadays. Even in my parent's house. Their house was large; my mother and father had their own room. But it wasn't what you'd call a private room today. If a relative arrived, a straw pad or mattress would be put in the room, and it was no longer private. No matter how big or small the house, each child had his or her own mattress and sleeping corner. Girls and boys weren't separated. You chose the person you wanted to sleep near and then simply lay down next to him or her.

All four of us girls who lived at Amelya's house had jobs. The last one up made the bed, arranged the table and chairs. Amelya and Térézine worked at the same soft drink plant. They started at 8 A.M. Amelya, very clean and slightly obsessive, awoke early to have enough time to do a number of things. Sometimes she washed a few articles of clothing for me. Foufouyi and Victoria worked for a tailor, as seamstresses. They'd offered my mother to take me on as an apprentice. But, even if I was a city girl, I still had to obey my mother's orders. She'd found me work in that store, and so there I had to go. Besides, at the time I didn't much care for sewing. Afterward I was sorry, I should have learned.

The brother, called Cholo, liked his rum. He hung around the docks trying to scrape together a little money by carrying packages or passengers' bags when a boat landed. There was a whole crew of guys: those with wheelbarrows pushed their loads, while the others had to carry on their backs. I don't recall what the nephew did for work. But he was certainly spoiled!

We all got along well together. Of course, we had an occasional disagreement, as happens everywhere, but basically we shared a real feeling of family unity. They took care of one another, helped each other, even though money was scarce. You lived on what you earned, always keeping a little aside in case someone arrived unexpectedly. Possibly even the poorest of the poor, Jesus, might appear in disguise, clothed in torn rags, and ask for a place at your table to test your brotherly love. If your heart remained hard and your hand closed, misfortune might await you.

In today's world, the more money people have, the less they help one another. Also, the bigwig bureaucrats who return to the country full of contempt don't help matters. In Amelya's family, no bureaucrats. My cousins were impressed by my having reached the certificate level. They introduced me to everyone: "This child attended school, she has her certificate. . . . " They were proud and happy.

In the evening, after dinner, we all collapsed from exhaustion. More often than not, straight to bed. Sometimes a short pause outside, in front of the house, for a breath of air. We'd chat together, the adults about their own lives or the lives of their neighbors. I didn't pay much attention to those conversations. Too young to take part, I just stayed, enjoying the cool air for as long as I was permitted.

Sometimes Térézine's fiancé came courting. He sat talking to her in front of everybody, and when it came time to leave, he got up and kissed her on the forehead. No question of fondling or caressing. And yet they must have been doing it somewhere. Normally it happens.

Other evenings, we'd take a little walk, up and down our street. But I think my cousins feared being out after dark. In any case, the streets were empty after eight o'clock. Going into the city for an evening movie was a big event. Only something special, such as the showing of the film *La Passion de Jésus* at the Renaissance Theater would tempt us. And even then, we'd have to find other people to accompany us back, which wasn't easy since the neighborhood people usually went to the movies on Sunday afternoons. We hardly ever went then, because our Sundays were so busy.

The first thing to do upon awakening—get ready for Mass. We'd prepared the meal the night before. The brother, Cholo, slept in his corner of the kitchen, and we didn't wake him. We wouldn't have missed Sunday Mass at Massabielle or at Grande-Eglise for anything in the world. And yet, on every one of God's mornings, Amelya took me to say *Bondié, bonjou!* Up at 4 A.M. to allow enough time for fetching water at the fountain and rinsing out a few things, I washed myself, dressed, downed my mug of coffee, and then—off to church. Amelya insisted on stopping at the church on her way to work. She liked that, was very involved with religion. She might ask a saint for a blessing, beg the Virgin Mary for mercy. . . . I walked behind. I didn't understand much of what Amelya did. I saw her pray to God, visit each saint, speak to them as if they were people: "Holy Virgin Mary, gracefully cast your eyes on this, your child. . . . " "Most Holy Peter, Most Holy Paul, you who have the power to bind and to loose, open the doors that are closed before me, preserve me from falling into entrapment. . . . "

I never asked for anything, never did anything. But I wasn't surprised; everyone visited the saints, it was the custom, the tradition.

Cousin Amelya teaches me not to bow down to life

Later on, when I had known pain and suffering, when I lost my job, I followed the road I'd been shown. I'd seen all the plaques of thanksgiving in the grotto of the Immaculate Conception, under the church of Massabielle. I went to invoke the saints myself, choosing from the Collection of Forty-Four Prayers for Life's Necessities those prayers designated for finding work: "Most Holy Simon Peter, as our Lord Jesus Christ entered your boat, let work enter into my life. In the same way our Lord Jesus Christ filled your boat with fish by the miraculous catch, let my house be filled with work and money. . . . "[45]

Sunday, after Mass, laundry time. First we organized a bucket brigade to the fountain to fill our big iron casks. Bébian lacked running water. And how we needed water for the wash! Luckily, we found a great many iron or wooden barrels. A wooden one, cut in half and kept out of the sun—the sun would crack it—served as a bathtub and a laundry basin. Drinking water was kept in a large jug with a tin pitcher hanging on the side. For the table, we had water in pottery jars.

While the laundry dried on the lines hung across the courtyard, we walked to the ocean. Bas-du-Fort was the closest point, just where their "Marina with its feet in the water" had been built.

"Listen to all this racket," people exclaimed, "look what's happened to this place where the poor used to go and bathe. Impossible now for them even to get near the water!"

We brought with us sardines, soda, and leaves specially chosen to rub ourselves with in the water, to relax our limbs during our "energizing bath." We needed to remove all the impurities that had entered our bodies. The herbal bath was supposed to clean out whatever could be eliminated. What it couldn't remove, couldn't be removed at all. Nowadays, I no longer talk about an "energizing bath." I don't believe in them anymore. But I took lots of them, although I never carried a codfish tail or cloves into the water, nor did I go in for the "special cleansing bath" at midnight on New Year's Eve. The new year should find you clean, healthy, and dressed in new clothes, from head to toe. Nothing better, it was thought, than the ocean waves to wash away the impurities acquired during the year and leave you in fine shape.

All these superstitions meant a great deal to people. In the marketplace, Amelya and her sisters purchased various herbs for bathing in the sea or at home, but I never heard of them consulting a *gadèdzafè*.[46] They never missed a pilgrimage or a walk along the stations of the cross to Abymes. Whatever the distance, even if we might lose our way, off we'd go! Although going to a *gadèdzafè* isn't something you proclaim from the rooftops, I was sure Amelya never did it.

And yet one day, at the time of my great illness and problems with my husband, Joseph, Amelya came to see me: "Leonora, don't fall asleep on your knees, people don't live that way. Try to loosen your limbs, get the machinery moving, go and see a *manti kakouè* for your problems with Joseph, a *séancier* for your illness."

I hardly recognized my Amelya. Life had changed her, altered her outlook on things. Or maybe she'd been influenced by others. . . . She—who'd taken control of life instead of letting it control her, who'd taught me never to give up—had herself bowed down! Because of age or worry?

When I lived with her, life flowed joyfully on, gentle and pleasant. Many people appreciated her; she and her sisters were well respected. We were often invited to engagements, baptisms, and marriages. On Sundays, we entertained at home or went to visit friends. On those days, we'd set off after the worst heat of the day had passed. In the hot afternoons, we'd lie down, outside on a bench or inside on a blanket placed on the floor in the breeze between the two doors. Only rarely on the bed. Here in Guadeloupe, people aren't in the habit of stretching out on a bed that has already been made. The other day, a neighbor told me that she had never lain on a bed during the day.

"My dear," I answered her, "even if the bed is made, when I need to rest, I stretch out on it. I fold back the top sheet and I'm all set."

People say they feel more comfortable taking their siesta on the ground. *Manti a mantè!* Lies of liars! They don't want to mess up their nice, smooth beds. It's not that I don't want to sleep on the ground, I sleep wherever I happen to be, but if I have a nice bed, why not use it? The reason I don't want the children on my bed is because the mattress, made of native cotton, weakens at the edges when you sit on it.

When we weren't visiting, we'd take a walk around Victory Square. More than one mother dressed her children up for the occasion. Kids from rich families strutted about on the arms of their nurses, who wore their best *cancan* skirts[47] and gold bead necklaces. That was the place to show yourself off, walking under the enormous mango trees, between the rows of multicolored flowers. There and nowhere else. We didn't stay long. Night falls before seven, and we had to return to the outskirts, to Bébian, the country where we stayed all week, only venturing into the city on Sundays.

The festivals also attracted us. The feast at Le Moule falls on Saint John's, at midsummer: great fires were lit, the "fire of Saint John." We'd start out in the morning, all scrubbed and dressed up: to the celebration at Goyave, where one of Amelya's sisters lived; to the celebration at Capesterre, of course, with my parents. . . . We made the rounds of all the towns. Pointe-à-Pitre too. I had just arrived in the city when cousin Amelya said to me: "Dress up, Leonora, child. It's the Tercentenary celebration. You'll see wonderful things at Victory Square."

"Tercentenary"?[48] What did it mean? I didn't know, and perhaps

Cousin Amelya teaches me not to bow down to life

Cousin Amelya didn't either. She knew what the priest at Pointe-à-Pitre had told her: "Put on your best *matador* dress, wrap your hair in your most beautiful Madras scarf, honor the visitors to your country."

A boat, the *Colombie*, had arrived from France carrying all sorts of important people. A Mass had been celebrated on La Soufrière. At noon, bells rang out all over Guadeloupe. I don't remember the "Tercentenary Hymn"[49] except the last words of the refrain: "To always remain Christian and French."

In the afternoon, Victory Square was packed, people everywhere, even in the trees, to watch the soldiers parading by in old-time costumes. And then there were games, fireworks . . . For me, newly arrived from the country, it was dazzling.

At Mardi Gras, we lined up along the street. People cried out: "Here come the masks!" I was very frightened, especially by the *mokozonbi*, those enormous giants. They danced about on stilts, and when they leaned over in my direction to gather up the money thrown at them, I ran away, terrorized. When the "death masks" passed by, I refused to leave the house. Wrapped in a white sheet from head to toe, they tried to grab you and prick you with needles. I heard one of them had grabbed a woman and pricked her so hard she bled. It had even gone to court.

Amelya, her sisters, and I were always together; we didn't go out alone. Normally you make friends at work. But here you are, in the city, in Pointe-à-Pitre, a city with a certain reputation. Also, you're a family girl, you can't hang around with just anyone. Amelya gave me tips on how I should treat each of the neighbors: "No need to be rude to *Man* X or Monsieur Y, you can say hello but don't get involved in their affairs."

She was right. One woman who lived in our courtyard drank heavily. She didn't have to be angry with you to "crack open a coconut," create a scene, drive the entire courtyard crazy with her shrieks. My cousin avoided disgraceful people like that. She managed to keep herself apart and explained to me how I should act, handle things, run my life in Pointe-à-Pitre. She took the time to talk to me, inform me, tell me all about life. She helped you discover where you were in it all and if, the following day, you fell into a trap, you couldn't claim: "I didn't know."

I had begun to meet people who introduced me to others, women who were already involved in all aspects of life. Cousin Amelya knew about this type of person and warned me: "Be careful of these people who live so freely, my girl. They live together without being married. I'm not telling you to avoid speaking with them, but don't throw yourself into their arms."

I was approaching my fifteenth birthday. Walking around such a big city alone wasn't always easy. One day, a boy tried to catch my attention: "Psit! Psit!" He whispered behind my back. I didn't turn around, either to look at or to insult him. Much later, when I worked in a cane field at Capesterre, a man came over to me:

"Ou ka sonjé lé ou té Lapouent kon ou té ka ganmé, kon ou té ka fè dyèz. An té ka kriyé ou 'Psit! Psit!' Ou pa té ka menm pran grad an mwen."

"Do you remember how, at Pointe-à-Pitre, you acted so stuck up, walked about putting on airs. I called to you: 'Psit! Psit!' but you didn't even look at me."

Then I did remember him. He was seeing a woman who lived a little way down the road. I can still visualize him wearing his white Panama hat, his hands in his pockets, walking like a cock dressed for combat. And to think that I married this man's brother! Life is strange!

I was wary because I thought girls began having affairs without their mothers' knowledge much earlier in Pointe-à-Pitre than in the country. I knew a girl who let her man into the house as soon as her mother had left for work. How could the mother learn about it unless someone told her? The only way: when the girl comes home with a big belly. Then there's no hiding it. And the mother has no choice but to go out and earn a living. Perhaps it wasn't so in the city itself, but in our suburb, all the mothers worked. The children go to school, but sometimes they prefer to *marronner*[50]—to play hooky—and hang out along the railroad tracks. City men have many opportunities for meeting young girls and more than one trick for attracting them: "Come over to the railroad tracks, let's meet behind the factory. . . . "

Pointe-à-Pitre contains so many hidden corners and isolated, dangerous places. For example, at the end of Bébian Street, past the last cabins, not far from where people empty their toilet buckets, is a little-frequented vacant lot. I don't really know much about it and never went there myself, but a girl I used to meet on the way to work told me about it and how she fooled her mother: "Mamma works late into the evening. I take care of my brothers and sisters. I didn't stay at school very long, but I know how to get along. They aren't unhappy."

We were speaking openly, but she didn't tell me everything. People never tell you everything except when they have a problem and are asking for your help: "A boy spoke to me and asked me this and wanted me to do that. . . . " I never got to that point with her. I liked to see her, tell her why I left Carangaise, how my mother had gotten me work . . . I never saw her again after that.

I also visited other friends my age. I still occasionally bump into one

Cousin Amelya teaches me not to bow down to life

or another of them without always recognizing who they are. We were young then and it must be twenty, thirty, forty years since we've seen each other. Even when I do recognize them, I don't always say hello. One in particular, who had problems with her family because of a Jehovah's Witness[51] who lived across the street.

This girl's mother had been an Adventist since *l'année canelle,* since time began. The Jehovah's Witness converted Suzelle. Then she wanted her mother to join the Jehovah's while the mother wanted the girl to enter her religion. Each one preached to the other: constant conflict. It's not because she was a Jehovah's Witness that I didn't go up and speak to her. We'd lived near each other, and she'd been my friend. Not long ago I marched in Pointe-à-Pitre. The demonstration passed behind the Dubouchage school. I recognized this girl and went to greet her.

To tell you the truth, I didn't make that many friends in Pointe-à-Pitre. I didn't have much time. Up early, a stop at church to ask God's protection, then work till evening. In the shop, no chatting, we even ate lunch in shifts so as not to leave the counter unattended. When I left that exhausting job, I had no regrets.

Amelya got me a position where she worked, at Vacher's, a large soft-drink factory. I don't think she intended to keep an eye on me, but I'd had so many misfortunes in my previous positions, she must have felt reassured having me close to her.

I washed bottles the whole blessed day. We were two or three around the barrels filled to the brim with bottles. Some washed, others rinsed, and still others carried water. An old woman, the overseer of the bottle washing, kept us moving rapidly to her rhythm: "Blokoto, blokoto . . . voukoum, voukoum . . . " Wash, rinse, hang the bottle on an iron spike to dry. Our hands flew. But as soon as the old woman left for a moment, no more music. Rest. We *cocagnions* (goofed off) for a moment.

The soda factory opened its doors at seven in the morning and stayed open till noon. Started up again at 2 P.M., freedom at 5 P.M. It was hard work, hands in the water all day long, with no break, but the job was good. And then Vacher started to lay people off! He complained: "Soda doesn't sell anymore, it will bankrupt me, my expenses are too high. . . . " The owner wanted to make a profit, but that didn't mean anything to us employees.

It's only nowadays we hear the word *profit.* At that time, workers were simply fired. No question of giving notice or paying severance. . . . The owner made his decision: Soda doesn't sell anymore? We'll lay workers off. He changed to making ice cream. Once again, I was out on the street.

Leonora: The Buried Story of Guadeloupe

With Amelya and Térézine I went by Doktové's place. His soda factory had just opened, and he was hiring. Five or six people: the women for the bottles and the men to produce and transport it. The owner of the factory worked too. He needed to, since he was starting up the business and didn't have a lot of money. Just a poor little guy. In a small wagon with one wheel, a wheelbarrow, he himself delivered crates in the city. Later on, he managed to buy a small truck and began selling in the streets.

Doktové's factory had only one machine. Sugar[52] was melted in an enormous aluminum vat. The addition of a piece of charcoal made the syrup clearer. Once cooled, it was poured into containers, each with a different flavor: the soda took on its color. Pink, grenadine flavor; white, anise or apple; green, mint; red, currant flavor or orange. . . . The white-colored apple flavor was our favorite. It tasted just slightly of banana and was pure white. What gave it the taste? A mystery. Perhaps the flavoring came from France or from the pharmacy.

A man took care of the bottling, mixing the syrup with the carbonated water under pressure. As soon as he had filled twenty-four bottles, they were grabbed and packed up. Bottle racks didn't exist. We put the twenty-four bottles into cases, padded with sugarcane straw. With nothing but his wheelbarrow, Doktové couldn't deliver to the countryside. The merchants who were unable to fetch their orders relied on the bus drivers: "Leave this case of empty bottles at Doktové's for me and don't forget to bring back full ones when you return."

My work, for a change: washing bottles. The pace was fast. As soon as you took a minute's rest, the owner would holler that you were loafing. And everything had to be spick-and-span! Not a tear drop left on the dry bottles! If it's not perfect, wipe it with a piece of paper! I don't want to see those bottles cry!

The moment he was out of sight, laughter and the clacking of tongues started up. Each person had some gossip to share, news of the previous evening to tell. I was the youngest, the kid, so I just listened and listened, all ears. It was very interesting: "What a ruckus at Manuel's last night! He shouted at his wench: 'Slap me if you want, but if you dare tell your friends, I'll kill you!'" "I've completely lost my voice this morning. My neighbor died. I served as mourner all night long:

"Pléré, pléré, timoun, pléré, man- "Cry, my child, cry. Mamma is
 man ou mò, pléré, konnyé tèt, dead, cry, beat your head, let
 lagé kò pitit, moun pé ni dé yourself go. People may have
 papa, men yo ni on sèl man- two papas but only one
 man. mamma.

Cousin Amelya teaches me not to bow down to life

"And the women answered in chorus:

"'C'est bien vrai, si yo ba pitit manjé manman yo, yo ka manjé-i si yo ba manman manjé pitit, i ka mò'."	"'Yes, it's true, if children were given their mother to feed on, they'd eat her, but if a mother were given her children to feed on, she'd die'."

"Saturday I saw the wedding at Grande-Eglise. Jesus Mary Joseph Saint Anne! What beautiful clothes! And no *sousounklérant* (imitation-silk lining material) either."

"Young X, all dressed in white for her wedding, with veil and crown, everything . . . and pregnant up to the chin!"

Radio Bois-Patate[53] broadcast full strength, but our hands didn't stop. Watch out so as not to get hurt! There were so many bottles in the barrel. They rattled against one another with an infernal noise and could easily break, cutting your hands.

Sometimes one person would take up the story from another: "Don't say that! I know *Man* Y, a fine woman. Not a person to cause such trouble."

"Tout, jé sé jé, mé fouré boua an fès a makak pa jé."	"Playing around is one thing, but shoving a stick up a monkey's ass isn't playing."

Saturdays, we got a bonus: a bottle of soda. Not a small, wine-bottle size either, but a large, hearty one. Sometimes we managed to get one out after work on a weekday. In any case, while working, we filled our stomachs with soda. Vacher never gave us any, not even a small bottle. He must have thought to himself: "They drink enough behind my back."

Soda has always sold well. I think it's the first drink people bought to serve to guests. Especially to women and young girls. There was a choice: currant, mint, anise, all sorts of flavors. Now only pink, white, and Coca-Cola are made.

At Amelya's, I saw soda, rum, and wine. From time to time, my cousins also bought a small bottle of liquor, Quinquina, or La Meuse beer, the first popular beer in Guadeloupe. To offer guests. But never rum for young girls. Rum was for men. Is a man's flesh different from a woman's? I don't see why it would make a difference for a drink. Some men don't drink at all, while some women like rum. Others will never touch it. They might take a small glass of coconut-rum punch, punch made from genip, juice, or a small drink. Now some people only go for champagne, as I saw when my daughter Emilienne, who works in France, was here on vacation: "If you go visiting," she said to me, "and you don't bring a bottle of champagne, you're no one." How can it be that here, in Guadeloupe, more champagne is consumed than in France?[54]

Oh yes, but where does black folks' taste for champagne come from? I really can't say, but I who'd never even heard of it am now caught up in it too. For my grandson's first birthday I thought: one year old, one bottle of champagne. And yet I'm not crazy about it, I prefer sparkling wine such as Paul Bréan. People say champagne is better for your health, makes you less drunk, and fortifies you. A true medicine for after a birth or an operation, for exhaustion. No party is complete without champagne. Even in the Christian congregation, when we organize a "supper dance," we must have champagne. Such an expensive thing! And we all pursue it like fools!

I really wasn't lucky with my jobs. All those places where I worked and all those unpleasant people who caused me grief! Happily, amidst all this misfortune, one piece of good luck: my friends in the country.

From time to time, I'd meet someone who had come to the city. Occasionally they even came especially to see me: "Leonora, we're planning a dance, come join us. . . . "

"Leonora, it's Mardi Gras, come back with us. . . . "

"I'm living in the city, working, I can't. . . . "

"Just for once, it's a special celebration, everyone up there's waiting for you, come."

One day, I went back with cousin Amelya and all her sisters. I hardly knew how to dance—for Papa there had never been a proper time for us to go dancing—but I had such fun! So I returned more and more often, and these getaways to the country, my rediscovered childhood friends, created a strong desire in me: to leave Pointe-à-Pitre where I'd encountered only unhappiness and misfortune, and return to the country.

It is said that the place of your birth—where you grew up, went to school, made your first communion—is forever marked in the smallest recesses of your body. . . . For me it's true. No matter where I am, no matter which region of Grande- or Basse-Terre I live in, only in Carangaise do I feel at home. As soon as I set foot there, I see things differently, my life changes, even my body changes. You must live wherever you happen to be. You must work, earn money, and, in town, you manage to do all that, but something is missing. At Amelya's, I lived with family, with people I loved. Unfortunately, at her house as well as

Cousin Amelya teaches me not to bow down to life

at work, everyone around me was older. Amelya was like a mother, and a mother is never too old in her child's eyes, yet I didn't feel I was in a place for young people. At work, seated or standing one beside the other, it was just wash, wash bottles, kachouk, kachouk. . . . If you became tired, no one helped you. And even if someone treats you nicely, it isn't the same as in the country. My friends urged me: "You could do this, or that, you could work in the sugarcane fields like us."

I felt they wanted me with them. One day, I didn't return to the city. I got myself hired to tie up sheaves of sugarcane. I rediscovered comradeship, the ambiance of work in the fields, jokes to alleviate the fatigue and the sun that drills into your head.

"Ka ou fè Entèl? Lavi ka menné-ou? Ou ka menné-i?"

"How are you, so-and-so? Is life leading you? Or are you leading it?"

"Ka ou fè yé osoua? Ou si telman avanni."

"What did you do last night to be so tired?"

"Gadé mamnzèl la. Ou konprann sé mwen ké vin rédé-ou jòdla. Maré jouné kann a-ou. Ou las konnyéla. Tandé!"

"Look at this young lady! You think I'll help you today. Tie up, tie up your canes. Now you're tired! Listen to that!"

Ah, yes! Only when I returned to Carangaise did I regain my love of life.

6

Afòs tounéviré pou Kannaval,

an déviré an bitasyon

Mardi Gras lures me back to the country

I figure the year of my return to the village according to the age of my oldest child: René was born in 1941, and I didn't have him right away. Therefore, I left the city in 1940.

At Mardi Gras that year, each girl found her beau: me, Graziella, and Bertille. Some of the girls in our group married, others didn't.

I began seeing Alexander. And there I was, binding up sugarcane. With the city left behind, I plunged into life in the country. Thanks to the festivals, to Mardi Gras, I rediscovered my hometown. Home, with my family, my friends, my boyfriend, I was happy.

Yes, I'd had enough of the city. The shuttling back and forth between Pointe-à-Pitre and Capesterre was happening more and more often. Any reason sufficed: village festival, Mardi Gras, Christmas. . . . One of my friends invited me to her dance. Not just any old dance, but that of the Mardi Gras king and queen. Only certain people were invited. You had to be a young girl. Once you gave birth to a child, even if you weren't married, that dance was off-limits. You could go to the "dance for the fallen tits," for the women, the mothers. The rule was strictly enforced. If, by chance, a "woman with fallen tits" slipped into the young girls' dance, the mothers would yank their daughters from the room, without even waiting for the bouquet ceremony.

During the evening, the guests selected a queen and king for the following Saturday. In this way, from one Saturday to the next all through the Mardi Gras season, the bouquet was passed along.

It happened at midnight: the lady gave her bouquet to her dance partner, the one she chose to be king. Then, it was their turn to organize the next dance, invite the guests. The partner chosen as king gave the queen money for drinks, alcohol. To the queen fell the responsibility for preparing *chodo,* cakes, soup, coffee. The queen was expected to dance with all the guests. If she refused, she could be turned out. The king and queen covered the costs. The guests paid nothing. Only the men, I think, contributed something for the musicians.

I was twenty years old and considered myself an adult. Yet I wasn't grown up: I still had no experience with men. During my visit at Mardi

Gras, I met a young man. He spoke to me. As soon as a guy approached a girl, if he was serious, he'd ask to meet her family. First, he'd present a letter to which the father would answer: "I'll receive you with your family." At the meeting, the parents asked each other questions. "What does your son do? Does he have a good occupation?"

The engagement would be finalized. No ring business in those days. From then on, the boy could come and visit. But not to make love, you understand. You'd be seated here, and the guy there. One chair for the girl, one chair for a family member, one chair for the boy.

If a young man met the family and then went off without marrying the girl—a tragedy! What a fuss! What noise! What dishonor for the entire family! The girl suffered already from the blow, and the scorn of the neighborhood only increased her pain. Yet, if the marriage fell through, there was bound to be a reason. The couple knew why. But people only said: "He didn't marry her."

In her shame, the girl's mother would keep silent. Sometimes, everything had already been purchased for the wedding and, zap! just like that, the boy backed out. Of course he asked for certain guarantees. You could jerk him around and say, for instance: "I'm a virgin, pure, untouched by any man." But, on reflection, it was better to tell the truth. Marrying a virgin was so important to them that they might cause a major scandal if they discovered they'd been deceived. What pride to be able to announce: "My wife was pure!"

It didn't happen that way with me. My father no longer supported me. I lived in the city, earned my own living, was more than twenty years old, so my parents couldn't very well interfere in my love life. Out of respect for their home, I presented the boy I'd met at Mardi Gras. My father accepted him according to custom, but he drank a lot, and when drunk, he harassed my fiancé, disrespected him. When the young man arrived, my father would leave. When he left, my father would come back in. One day Alexander sat with his legs crossed.

"Who gave you permission to cross your legs in my house?" And there was my father, pulling at the boy's legs. I told him not to pay any attention. Seated next to one another, without touching, we spoke about ourselves, our ideas. We worked together in the cane fields, he cutting cane and I binding it into sheaves. We loved each other, shared everything. Yet he never said: "I want to marry you."

We met at a dance. That day, a girlfriend had accompanied me, and he was with a big, dark black man he passed off as his brother. Each guy paired up with a girl. When you first meet, you start talking, and from one word to the next, love progresses. You dance close together and things start happening. Afterward, no need for words. At these dances, each young man had his date, and the girls didn't have to pay. In principle, any boy could invite any girl to dance, but as soon as the music started, each guy took his date in his arms before anyone else could invite her. Between dances, the young ladies sat on a bench, and the boys stood in front of them. We chatted. The girls who weren't yet paired up came with their mothers and left early. They might have had boyfriends in the room, but their mothers were keeping a lookout! A knowing wink, a *zyé dou,* nothing else could happen before the letter was presented. How could you be sure, prior to bringing this all-important letter, that the girl loved you? I've seen marriages arranged without love playing a role. The boy writes his letter, the parents come to an agreement, and the girl is obliged to accept the situation. Sometimes the mothers have their own ideas: this young man is my comrade's son, he's a diligent worker, I'll marry my daughter to him.

That doesn't work out, not at all. Do people marry more often for love today? I see hardly any difference. I love you, you love me, we get married. Fine. What will the family life be like? Yesterday, today, marriage has most often been a *bari boutèy krazé,* a barrel full of broken glass. Maybe it used to last a little longer because the wife was more submissive, the problems less publicly exposed, but that didn't mean love was involved. Even if the woman married a lazy bones—and God knows there are enough of them in Guadeloupe!—she'd hang in there. She had married, and it was forever.

I still see families that force their daughters into marriage with a guy she doesn't love. What can she do? Gather her courage, shoulder her ideas, and leave home? Another woman might build her house on the family land, near her mother, expecting the marriage to fail. At the least little problem, she'd call for help, and the mother would take advantage of the situation to stick her nose into the couple's private business.

Nowadays, whether a couple marries or lives together, everything is already set for the breakup. You keep track of who owns what: the boy brought the living room furniture, the girl the bedroom. If the girl doesn't work, her mother gives her a present of the bed and dresser. When I left my parents' home to set up my own, Alexander and I put everything together. Besides, the words *bedroom* and *living room* didn't even exist. A cabin had two parts: one room for sleeping, the other for everything else—living, eating. A bed, a mattress, a table, four chairs, then six. In time, the number increased as the family grew.

On their wedding day, the married couple would depart at midnight. They weren't ushered out the front door, the way it's done today. They'd just disappear. But they weren't spared being the butt of jokes:

Mardi Gras lures me back to the country

"The champagne cork will pop tonight!" "If the bottle is still corked. . . . "

A girl's virginity was of supreme importance, the honor of her mother depended upon it. The following morning, the mother visited the newlyweds. If the wife's virginity was confirmed, the man congratulated the mother.

I became pregnant. And my marriage didn't happen because of my father. Normally, when an accident occurs, the girl's father calls the man in: "Sir, my daughter is expecting a baby. You've been introduced into my family. What are you going to do about it? What are your intentions?"

He couldn't say: "My daughter has brought me a full belly, but I don't know who filled it."

My father had a letter from Alexander and had given him permission to come courting.

Without saying anything, my father watched for the small bag I hung on a nail every month to hold my cloth sanitary napkins when they needed washing. One month, he didn't see the bag. Without a word, without any explanation, he set upon me. Blow after blow. Finally he totally lost control, broke a broom over my back, threw all my belongings out the door, and accused my mother of complicity. I couldn't remain at home after that. I didn't want to leave Mamma in that situation.

Papa had been driving us crazy for a long time with his stories of poison gas during World War I. What's more, he was often drunk. My mother decided to leave him. One of my aunts had recently died, and her house stood empty. We moved out and left my father "his" house. He stayed there all alone. Mother, the children, and I—we all fled. I was expecting a baby, there was no other choice.

Papa didn't see it the same way and came around creating scenes, cursing us, breaking down the door of the house. . . . As for the fiancé, he squirmed this way and that. Pregnant girl, good-bye marriage!

My father managed to die before the child was born. We returned to our home. That's where I gave birth. The child who had caused all the trouble lived only six days.

Alexander and I set up housekeeping in l'Ilet-Pérou and moved our few things into a small rented cabin. We both worked in the cane fields. We stayed together for a while, long enough to have four children. The first died immediately, the second at six months. Two are still living, a girl and a boy.

Alexander wasn't a very good choice. It didn't last. Because of another woman. I wouldn't have believed that such a handsome boy could have been so badly brought up. That rat hadn't shown it earlier, but now his vulgarity surfaced. His cursing of my family made me ill. My mother had to come and nurse me. One evening, he went off to spend the night at the other woman's house. I made up my mind: I'd weigh anchor. I dropped my things off with a sister, took my children, and went to my mother's.

That man ran after me: "Leonora, if we're going to separate, we must split up the things we bought together when we set up house. What I bought afterward is mine, I'm keeping it."

And if you take this, give me that, and that too. . . . I didn't give a damn about the things. I just wanted to go home to my mother. And that's what I did.

Then he came and raised such a ruckus that I finally let him take the boy with him. He wanted the boy because he was afraid, one day, a stepfather might order his son around. I didn't have the slightest intention of getting together with another man. I stayed at my mother's, with my older sister and my young daughter; I had enough to eat, to drink, I worked, and I lived my life.

Cousin Amelya often came to share our cabin. At Vacher's, her soft-drink employer, business wasn't great. Occasionally she'd come to earn some extra money working in the cane fields. On Sunday, she'd return to Pointe-à-Pitre. Amelya was a city person.

For seven years, I too had been a city person. When I returned home, I wasn't treated as a stranger, primarily because of my attitude. People judge if the city has changed you by the way you treat them and speak to them. Have you become a "snob"? Do you, who sell in a shop, look down on those who work the land? They watch you closely: Is she going to greet so-and-so? Visit such-and-such, who used to be her friend but hasn't done well? . . . Eyes follow you around and tongues wag.

Yes, I'd lived in the city, but as soon as I arrived back home, I was in the cane fields, binding up sheaves of cane like my friends. My mother was sick about it: "Listen, Mamma. I've just left the city, I'm no longer working there. I haven't returned to the country to sit on my rump and gaze at the clouds, or twiddle my thumbs. . . . I've got to earn a living."

I joined one of my sisters, working on the plantations as a farm laborer. A cane binder must pile up seventeen stacks per day. The thin variety of sugarcane, B. H. When it wasn't harvest season, we were sent out to manure the fields, plant seedlings, remove the straw. . . . You worked like a dog, but at two or three o'clock, the day is over, you're free. At home, if you don't find your meal already cooked by your family you fix your *cambuse* yourself, you eat, then you can do whatever you want: visit relatives, join friends to dig for clams on the beach, trap crabs or, when it's the season, run after *touloulous*. Revived by a good bath, each carrying a large bundle of dead wood balanced on our heads, we walked back up the hill to our houses.

Sometimes we'd go as a group and wash our clothes in the river. Each of us chose her own place among the big, black rocks in the current: the rounded rocks for beating clothes, the flat ones for rubbing them. Our hands slapped, and our tongues clacked still faster: we spoke about everything, our childhood, our mothers, our neighbors. We laughed so much that I almost choked. The hot sun reflected off the stones, and we often wanted to jump into the water to cool off. I wasn't a very strong swimmer but, to be like everyone else, I too jumped into the flowing current. If a woman hadn't been there, I would have drowned, really drowned. She held out one hand to me, then the other, and managed to haul me out of the water onto a rock. I coughed, spit, had water in my nose, my mouth, my throat, my eyes, my ears. It took me a long time to catch my breath. No one had seen a thing, and yet we were all in the water together!

My fright didn't spoil the pleasure of washing at the river's edge. Unfortunately, it's finished now. Some people still go there, but the water isn't clean anymore. What has happened to the water in our rivers? Too much runoff, too much of all sorts of things are released into it. They have ruined our water. So we'd be forced into buying washing machines? When I arrived at Grosse-Montagne, I washed my children in the river. Now, nope, not possible any more, they'd get sick.

On Sunday, the big outing: all who believed in God walked to Mass. We'd leave the countryside and go to church in town. The early morning was chaotic. The first one awake nudged her neighbor: "Get up! Mass will begin without you!"

We went down together, shoes in hand—they weren't put on till we arrived at the church—laughing, joking, making fun of the latecomers who ran behind, trying to catch up with the group: "Rosélise, don't count on my tongue to beg the Holy Virgin for you." "Run, Philemon, run, but don't forget to tuck your shirt into your pants when you get to town!"

On the way home, we were more serious. Perhaps the aftereffect of the sermon? We'd often stop at one house or another to get the news.

"Aunt Rosalie wasn't at Mass this morning, let's go make sure she isn't sick."

All Sunday morning was taken up in this way.

Almost every week, I was invited to a party. An engagement, a baptism, a wedding, the family mustn't leave anyone out. Anyone of their class, of course. We knew that the factory owner or his foreman wouldn't invite us to his daughter's wedding, but if your neighbor, who works in the cane fields with you, baptizes her child and doesn't invite you to the party, it will be the talk of the village. Everyone will try to figure out the reason: "Why wasn't so-and-so at the party?" "In her place, I wouldn't stand for such an insult!" "Could it be because her husband . . . "

The rumors spread. Twenty years later, you might still find some people holding a grudge. They'll never forgive the indignity of not having been invited.

These parties were important gatherings, as were the *coups de main,* the convoys: you've harvested your manioc—you invite friends to *grager* it with you, make it into flour, *cassaves.* . . . You want to settle down and build a cabin, clear a plot of land—you ask your neighbors to lend a hand, on condition, of course, that you return the favor one day.

The men don't need any invitation. Almost every evening they gather at the bar for a game of dominos and a mug of rum. Alexander joined them. And, above all, he ran after other women. I loved him, he loved me, we loved each other. And yet our love didn't last. We split up. Luckily, we weren't married. Marriage wouldn't have been useful for us. Times were tough; it was during Sorin's regime.[55]

An tan Soren: that's the way we refer to the period when Germany invaded France. I was still young and didn't know much about this Governor Sorin. One day I heard: "Sorin came by, he found some *sèl a sosyé,* sorcerer's salt, at a crossroads (it had been put there to ward off spirits) and declared: 'If salt can be wasted by sprinkling it around in crossroads, there must be an overabundance. I'm going to hide the salt, put it into storage, and lock up all the *gadèdzafè.*'"

He restricted the sale of salt. We had to use our ingenuity, "make salt" by evaporating seawater. People started speaking out, raising their voices: "This Governor has come to break our backs with his sailors from the *Jeanne d'Arc* and their rifles!"

And then, suddenly, a rumor: "There's no more salt, no more kerosene, no more soap, no more oil, no more of this, no more of that. . . . "

Sorin made us eat "spaghetti à la broad leaf" as it says in a song about green bananas.

Gouvènè kondanné nou manjé	The Governor made us eat,
éspagéti a gran fèy, pandan nou	spaghetti à la broad leaf.

Mardi Gras lures me back to the country

ka mégri gouvènè la ka ri.   While we thinned,
                                              the governor grinned.

Black marketeers arrived in the countryside. But careful! For the smallest little thing: jail. Even *Manzèl* Eleonore, the curé's sacristan, got a taste of it. Everyone who knew her found it loathsome. Putting a woman in prison! She ran a small shop that sold rosaries, holy pictures, all sorts of religious objects. No one knew why she was arrested. Were her prices too high? When they released her, she no longer knew either blacks or whites, didn't trust anyone.

We all ran around looking for food. You'd head off to Sainte-Marie for fish: when you arrived, it had all been sold to some bigwigs. If you killed a pig, you could only keep half. We knew a butcher. He was a good fellow, a friend. I learned of his plan to kill a steer. I stopped him on the road: "Tomorrow, Saturday, I'll be at your place to get some fresh meat on the sly."

I awoke at four in the morning and set out for Cambrefort. It was quite a distance, a good ten kilometers. Upon arriving, I signaled him that I was there. "I'll be with you in a moment."

I waited. I was hungry. I hadn't eaten anything before leaving, hadn't even had coffee, not a thing. All the meat tempted me, and I yearned for some. I waited and waited. Finally, I couldn't stand it any longer. Then I realized that the chopping block was cleaned off, empty, everything gone. I said to the man: "So, you wouldn't even give me a pound of soup meat!"

Money in hand, I cried for that meat. If I'd asked for credit, I might have understood, but to have the money right there and to see all the meat without managing to buy the smallest bit. . . . All I could do was swallow my tears. I vowed never to return to that man's shop, even if it meant giving up meat altogether.

We were living at *Man* Toloman's; I had just given birth. When she returned from work, she'd cook up two small green bananas for me to eat. My man, who worked on the plantations, brought me some too. I ate nothing but bananas, bananas with bananas, plain bananas without oil, without anything, true *ti bandi, ti Soren,* as we called them then. And me just newly risen from childbed! No milk for the baby. We pounded sugarcane to make juice. We gathered and cooked all sorts of wild plants, caught crabs, dug clams. Some people had provisions stored away, and you could always find a pinch of salt, a small jar of coconut oil, or coconut butter to trade for your *cassaves,* manioc flour, vinegar made from *cabosses* (cacao pods). Still, young children and the elderly died quickly.

In our village, there was one man who could predict a person's death. A *vyékò*, always seated in front of his door, staff in hand. When he stood up, all eyes followed him warily. He'd walk slowly by the cabins: "That one won't see his fourth day. He'll die Thursday. This man will be gone by evening."

He indicated my neighbor, who died later that afternoon. I heard shrieks: "Run, quickly, Papa's dead!"

The small cabins, close together, were all dark. In a flash, the house of the dead man was illuminated, glowed. All the neighbors had converged there, bringing their bits of glowing rubber.

Burning rubber, placed on a sheet of metal, gave us light. We found bits and pieces of it on the beach, washed up by the tide, and used them as lamps, since we were too poor to buy kerosene on the black market.

One morning, to the sound of the drum, rationing was announced. This made things easier. It was fairer. So many people in a family equals so many kilos of meat, so many bottles of oil, so much salt. . . . Families that were short of money and couldn't use all their tickets sold them. In this way, you managed to live. Well, not really, because you weren't free, you couldn't simply go into a shop and buy things. You had to fight for your rations, to wait endlessly in line. Sorin had levied a tax on all merchandise and kept a close eye on the black market. Even cloth was rationed. What trouble preparing for a wedding! You'd get a coupon for one sheet. Nothing without a coupon. The people hated Sorin. He inflicted so much cruelty on the Guadeloupeans. When he left, people sang in the streets:

Viv Dégōl viv Lézalyé	Long live de Gaulle, long live the Allies
Soren tonbé pou létèrnité	Sorin has fallen, never to rise
Péyi an nou la dou	Our land so pleasant, our land
Gouvènè ké régrété-i	so fine
Soren mó é antéré	For it the governor will always
Konplis a-i ka pléré	pine
Yo ka régrété	Sorin is dead and in the ground
Milyon la i pa séparé.	His accomplices raise a hue and cry
	Regretting
	The millions they were denied.

What a time it was during Sorin's regime! The war, men leaving to join the resistance.[56] They took small fishing boats to meet up with de Gaulle in Dominica. I don't know how they made out over there. They claimed to be against Sorin's leader, Marshal Pétain, who was in

France, and were going off to defend their country. But I don't think we were French yet, even though we belonged to France. Everyone spoke of de Gaulle. In Carangaise, no one owned a radio; *Radio Bois-Patate* broadcast the news: "De Gaulle issues a call to all men. We must join him in London to defend our country."

After the war, we found ourselves "assimilated." As the song went: "Before we were *asi boukèt* (seated on an ass), now we are *asi milé*[57] (seated on a mule).

We didn't know what assimilated meant, nor département[58] and even now, who really knows?

Afterward, a good long time afterward, we realized the importance of "Sorin's regime." A time of suffering but also of work and creativity. We had nothing, yet had to go on living; so we were forced to learn how to get along and, anyway, *débouya pa péché* (resourcefulness isn't a sin), especially at that time.

We learned to make use of everything: coconut meat for oil and soap, coconut *parche* for straw pallets and brooms, coconut shells for spoons, forks, and bowls. . . . The utensils of the poor regained status. Coffeepots, mugs, plates, *chaspann* to dip water from the large jugs were made of clay or crafted from milk containers or empty food tins. The tinsmiths created vessels—mugs, pitchers, *roquilles*—with a flick of the wrist. They repaired your basin or chamber pot, soldering with lead retrieved from old batteries or pipes. . . . Flour from dried bread-fruit; hats, bags, and mats woven from sugarcane straw. . . . Some people still say today that they make grass mats and bags thanks to Sorin's regime.

Everyone contributed something handmade to a wedding. We fashioned a beautiful satin headpiece for my sister, and her consort wore a straw hat woven of cane leaves sewn together with thread teased out of flour sacks or *karata* lanyards. What you couldn't make yourself, if you spent all your time in the cane fields, you'd buy from someone else, who could then earn a little money.

The other day at a gathering, young people of the M.R.J.C.[59] talked of Sorin's regime as a time when potatoes were grown at Matouba and garlic at Trois-Rivières, a time when cars ran on gas mixed with rum. I hadn't known about that, the country people walked. For us—who occasionally walked as far as Basse-Terre or Pointe-à-Pitre wearing *ko-vadis,* sandals with soles of wood or old tires—Sorin had trees planted along the main roads. They provided shade. Now, we have lovely lines of filaos and flame trees in our town. I'm not talking about the alley of palms at the entrance to town, up which General de Gaulle rode on a white horse when he came to Guadeloupe. I think those were planted earlier. The youngsters of the M.R.J.C. insist that the Guadeloupean people learned to be self-sufficient. I don't think they learned anything at all, because they didn't continue. Circumstances forced them to do something, so they did it. Maybe too they've been taught how to be dependent again. After all, department stores like Prisunic must do business! I learned one important thing from that time of dried breadfruit: not to fear any earthly misfortune. I can eat anything; I'm ready for any situation. I don't throw things away because I never know what might happen. I use butane gas, but I keep my charcoal and kerosene stoves, just in case. I have the bottle of butane, but I don't worry when the truck doesn't make its regular delivery to the shop. In my housing development, I'm the one the neighbors come to for kerosene when the electricity fails. I share with them, but I secretly feel they should be better prepared, that perhaps they haven't lived through the hard times I have.

Certain old people, who have forgotten all the bad times, speak of Sorin as a fair man: he applied the same rules, the same law to everyone. Those who had a right to three kilos wouldn't get five. You have ten children, ten tickets. You're alone, one ticket.

Of course, many things were kept hidden from us, and those who had a connection and money received more food. But black marketeers, black men as well as white, he dumped in jail. So, the old ones say, we need a strong man like Sorin to keep the country running. We blacks don't move unless we're whipped. The blacks are bad. You want independence? So blacks will lead blacks? If black people don't feel the whip on their skins, they won't work.

Only words, all that. Yet we hear them repeated often here. Words against ourselves. The least snag and it's the black man's fault. Blacks scorn blacks. I don't agree with these disdainful words, this scornful judgment of blacks, of your brothers. Those people act as if we're still slaves. Yes, it's true, the whites made the blacks jump by whipping them. It's part of our history. The whites too have their history, but it seems different from ours. What we must search for is agreement among ourselves. Then we could live well, live normally. Under Sorin, nothing was normal.

Sorin's boss was Pétain. Every morning in the schools, our children were made to sing to the flag: "See us here, Marshal, the savior of France." While under their breath they sang: "Our only hope: General de Gaulle, He'll come and save our land."

Tan an nou sété bon tan	Our time was the good time,
tan dé plézi, tan dé bonnè	was the pleasure time, time of joy,

Mardi Gras lures me back to the country

Touarivyè pa té ni dola	Trois-Rivières didn't know the dollar,
on ti sou té ka sifi	A little penny would always do.
Aprézan la lavi touné	Now life's not like that at all
toutbiten chalviré	Everything's upside down.
sèl èspoua nou tini	Our only hope: General de Gaulle,
Jénéral Dègōl ké sové nou.	He'll come and save our land.

After Sorin's regime, I came of age, I could vote, I took part in the elections.

My first vote: to elect Paul Lacavé mayor. That election wasn't a small-time affair. Paul Lacavé represented the Communist party and, at the time, the Communist party dominated Capesterre, was held in respect. I believe Lacavé's opponent was an Indian named Moutou, said to be a puppet of the Marquisat factory owners.

Each candidate campaigned, traveled throughout the region. When Lacavé came to Carangaise, "Viva Paulo!" resounded everywhere. But not all the people supported him. Even within families, people came to blows, remained estranged for the rest of their lives.

Neither party gave the other an easy time. Paulo won. His followers immediately organized a parade: the parade of the *boua-boua*. The puppet they created to represent Doctor Moutou was the most successful: the spitting image of him. With a long white robe and small satchel, it turned its head from right to left, causing its long Indian hair to flow out behind. The procession halted in front of the houses of party supporters and opponents. People shouted, sang, beat on tin jugs, pots. . . . Each one took advantage of the situation to settle personal grudges. Cousin X opposes Lacavé, let's go announce our victory to her with music. After such an insult, she'd be angry with you for the rest of her life.

First election, first victory. Around the mayor, the company grew. Lacavé held office till his death, winning resoundingly in each election. I remained his loyal supporter, working to prevent his defeat. But he was tough. Of course, some deserted him the way a crab sheds its claws or a lizard its tail. One, for instance, didn't get the position he wanted in the mayor's office; another, the house he'd requested; a third, a job for his wife or a nephew. . . . They decided not to vote for the mayor again, but they pretended they would. On election day, they'd sign in, get their card stamped, and then deposit a blank envelope. That way they'd take revenge on the mayor but not lose their influence. I'm not sure how but these things were always known, and the gossiping started up again at each election.

The election of representatives was even more heated. The people of Capesterre wanted to send Paulo to France as their representative. He registered as a candidate. I don't recall the name of his opponent; on the other hand, I do remember very well that, to make fun of him, a pig was locked in the prison the night of the election. The following morning, Lacavé was declared the winner. The pig was then released and ran wildly through the streets of the town. Everyone was outside, armed with pots, pans, tin or aluminum jugs, anything and everything that could make a noise. Even the drums were pulled out for the occasion.

"A pig has escaped from prison! After it! Catch it!"

You should have seen the fuss and heard the noise! One big swarming mass. Capesterre was alive!

"Hooray for Paulo! Long live Lacavé!"

The defeated candidate and his supporters, cold as ice, dug themselves into their holes, retreated into their shells.

Paul Lacavé continued as mayor of Capesterre for almost forty years. He took charge of the township at a crucial time, in 1945 I believe, when a major strike erupted among the sugarcane workers. I don't know if another mayor would have dared do what Lacavé did that day. Everything was at a standstill. No cutting or binding up of cane. The owners went off to hire foreigners, people from Sainte-Rose, to take our places in the fields. For us, a "foreigner" is anyone whose umbilical cord isn't buried in Capesterre. I've lived in Lamentin for more than thirty years, yet I'm still a "foreigner" here. We had all gathered, ready to beat up the foreigners if they dared go onto the fields. People came from everywhere, from all the plantations: "We won't let them do it, we won't let them break the strike!"

Who did we find in front of us? The security police. We sent for the mayor. He appeared with his sash of office around his waist. He approached the troops.

"We have enough workers at Capesterre. We don't need anyone else to cut cane. My people are demanding a decent salary, a fair price for their day's work. As long as their demands aren't met, not a cane of sugar will be cut, not by anyone."

The line of security police advanced on Lacavé. He removed his red, white, and blue sash and held it out to block their passage. We all shouted: "*Woulo* (bravo)! Hooray for Paulo!"

It began to get nasty. I don't know what would have happened had rocks started to fly. At that time, the workers couldn't control themselves very well, not the way they did later at Grosse-Montagne. Brawls, rocks, fistfights—that's what we knew.

Lacavé called to them:

Mardi Gras lures me back to the country

"Pa touché pèp an mwen!   "Don't lay a hand on my people!
Tchouyé mwen!"   Kill me!"

He stood there, facing the security forces, unmoving, fearless. Victory.

From that day on, Capesterre became known as *Capesterre-la-Vaillante* (Capesterre the courageous). Now it's called *Capesterre-Belle-Eau* (Capesterre of the clear water) and things have changed greatly.

It is said that life changes; man's status rises and falls, and that's evolution. I think, rather, that people change and then change everything around them. Life continues, always the same.

"People can't stand each other any more," a man explained to me, "and it's all because of money." He continued: "Till recently, money wasn't deposited in banks, in all those accounts. If you managed to accumulate a small reserve—one you kept well hidden—it would be for an emergency. Now everyone runs after the millions. Every man for himself. The life of sharing, of solidarity is gone."

Money was scare for my family at Carangaise, but we weren't unhappy. We never had to buy pork, for instance. Almost every Saturday, you'd be awakened by the cries of a pig being led to slaughter. You knew that a brother, a cousin, or a friend would send over a piece, expecting some in exchange when your pig's Saturday arrived. The same for manioc. On the day to *grager,* everyone who helped earned a share of the flour, of the *cassaves*. . . . Each person had a turn: one day at *Man* Tata's, another at the Nadirs'. Every family worked a small plot of manioc, of *dictame*. The children wanted to go to all the *coups de main* because, in addition to getting a nice coconut *cassave,* they could gather the *kakapannyòl*—the *cassave* remains—on the cooking platter. We loved these manioc-flour pastries. The ones made at home in the *canaris*—*bosokos* as we called them—were very thick and filling. A bit of *bosoko* in the morning with fresh water or weak coffee kept your belly filled till noon. You became strong in body and mind. A reaper, with a whole *bosoko* in his stomach, kept going all day long. Today, the *donbré* has replaced the *bosoko*. It isn't as nourishing, since it's made of white flour from France.

We made many things ourselves, prepared charcoal, planted yams that we could then barter for fish or meat. No question of buying dishwashing soap: the plates would gleam when rubbed with sunflower leaves or wood ashes. When someone returned with a basketful of crabs or a pile of crayfish, the neighbors always received a share. Not anymore. Crayfish sell for one hundred and fifty francs a kilo even if they've fed on bilharzia, the worm that pollutes our rivers and causes a terrible illness. No possibility of eating *kanklo* any longer. Apparently the worm that causes bilharziasis or schistosomiasis grows in these snails. Now if you want to collect crayfish or to bathe in the rivers, you have to go up into the mountains or over to Bois fermé, way behind Lamoisse, to the deep marsh. You can safely eat everything that comes from there—crayfish, fish. The nature killers haven't yet passed through there.

I loved that life of solidarity, of helping one another. My sisters and I helped everyone. We weren't rich or well educated or civil servants or office workers, yet we were held up as examples: "Those three girls are everywhere, always around when they're needed, where they can help most."

Grager the manioc, wash clothes of the sick, clean houses of the dead—nothing intimidated us. That's just the way we were, trying to help others, offering to do things, and I've remained that way. I like to take action, sometimes a little abruptly. But I don't do it for a reward or to hear people say: "Look how kind Leonora is, how much good she does. . . . "

Love pushes me toward others. My sisters and I were judged by what we did, not by what we owned. Now, only money counts. The more you have, the higher your standing. It forces people apart, encourages indifference to one's brothers and sisters. Gone is the solidarity between neighbors, the understanding within families. Life can't proceed decently. Everything can be—and is—purchased, and the more you buy, the more you're esteemed. You don't even need real live money anymore, you sign papers, pay with checks. So you replace your furniture: sofa, table, chairs, and why not the bed and dresser too? What people own counts for so much: "I have a mattress, a real cotton mattress. So-and-so only sleeps on a straw mat; I know, I've seen her."

When young people set up housekeeping, many didn't have the money for a cotton mattress. They used rags and made a lovely pad, so beautiful you'd have thought it was a thick mattress on the bed. Unfortunately, there were usually well-intentioned individuals who felt they had to go and give it a poke, just to make sure it was a real mattress and not simply straw.

Nowadays, from early childhood, you learn to measure a man by his possessions. You work in the cane fields, you're nothing, a zero; in an office, you're already of a different quality; civil servant, teacher, now you're something! That's why all parents struggle so hard to produce teachers. And if you succeed, others are jealous. With money or without it, discord and jealousy will always exist.

Mardi Gras lures me back to the country

Not far from our house in Carangaise, lived a woman who was generous with her possessions. When you visited her, she gave you everything she owned. Then, at a certain point, she'd say some very hurtful words to you. No one wanted to visit her, and gradually she was abandoned by her family and her neighbors. Opposite, lived a woman as gossipy as she, who loved to cause scenes and to argue with people. Her husband, a well-loved and respected man, had recently died. She had only to cry out: "Ai-ai-ai! Aristophanes is dead!" and her home was crowded with people. Some fetched water, others carried chairs, tables, and benches outdoors, still others ran about with brooms and dustrags. The wife of the dead man didn't have to do anything, the house was in our hands. She had sunk down into a rocking chair, unmoving, as if she too had suddenly died in the night. That's how Paul Lacavé, mayor of the town and a relative of hers, found her.

"Sylviane," he said to her, "look at all the people around who have come to help. You're lucky they're here."

I think he wanted to teach her a lesson, she who was so argumentative and relished maligning others, he wanted to show her that we all need one another. Meanwhile, the good lady from across the road was infuriated by all the comings and goings. She hollered out of her window: "Well, look at that now! Isn't that something? All the fussing around that old cat! If it were me, not a fly would come buzzing around my head."

At the time, I thought she was jealous, jealous of the help given to the dead man. Today, I wonder if she didn't have another reason. The dead man had been a fisherman, but his son attended a fancy school, one of his daughters was a teacher, the other worked in a hospital, and, most importantly, he was related by marriage to the Lacavé family, one of the finest in the region. Paul Lacavé was mayor of Capesterre. Did all those who threw themselves into the task want to be seen in a favorable light so as to obtain a favor at some future time?

I didn't think of it then. Many things happened that you didn't suspect. People knew how to keep a secret. They didn't repeat everywhere and anywhere, to all in sight, what they had just learned about this person or that one. A father, returning home, could have said: "I met a friend. Do you know, he told me . . . " But no. He'd wait till he was in bed with his wife at night and, if he decided it was important, he'd tell her about it. No one else. The children wouldn't hear a thing. As the elders said:

Pawòl lendi pa pawòl dimanch.	Monday's words aren't Sunday's
Vométan dépafoua bouch rèté	words. Sometimes it's better

fèmé. An bouch fèmé mouch pa ka rantré.	to keep your mouth shut. Flies don't enter a closed mouth.

If the walls and the savannas could talk, they'd be able to share many secrets and complaints. Complaints of women who'd been battered, humiliated, forced to endure the worst kind of suffering.

I'd had my fair share. I wasn't the least interested in another domestic relationship. A second man came to speak with me, Monsieur Joseph, the watchman on the plantation where I worked tying up sheaves of sugarcane. I didn't want to be in the power of another man, find myself again embroiled in these affairs of husband and wife. What had so disgusted me? I started off badly with my first man. After getting out from under Alexander's grasp, I felt myself alive, alive and free. I lived with my mother, I worked, I could feed and care for my children. No more problems with a husband, a man who wants to control everything in the house, who insists you wait up for him no matter what hour he chooses to return. . . . I had managed to claw myself out of a crippling situation, I wasn't going to lock myself into another.

But then I thought long and hard about it. I'm a young woman. A woman of twenty-six can't stay with her mother for the rest of her life. Nor do I want to live alone and have all the other women accusing me of stealing their husbands. Especially since I was lively, liked to laugh and joke around. You should have seen me at that time, in the small hamlet where I was born. All the young men sought me out. They'd compete to see who could invite me for a drink, for some sweets. . . . I wasn't in love with any of them. Maybe because I knew them too well, had grown used to them, and remembered all our childhood arguments, I couldn't see myself living with this Peter or that Paul. Having fun, laughing, enjoying life together: okay. They all kissed me, called me *Abo,* but I didn't feel romantically involved with any of them. I couldn't leave my mother's house to set up on my own. If I did, a man's simply talking to me would have started rumors: "Look, Leonora is stealing husbands."

| Sé on fanm a kokot chatou. | She's a woman with an octopus between her legs. |
| Fanm a kokot chatou pi fò pas Bondyé, pi fò pasé Dyab. | Women like that are stronger than God, stronger than the Devil. |

I wanted to be respected. I refused that kind of life.

Joseph pursued me for a long time, continued to pressure me. He was very much in love with me and said he waited for me the way

Mardi Gras lures me back to the country

parched earth waits for rain. His manner pleased me, and I finally accepted, so as not to stay at Mamma's any longer. We set up house together.

I must have remained in Carangaise for four years, long enough to have one child with Joseph, then twins. After that, we moved and, for a second time, I left my birthplace. Joseph had just been hired as steward on a plantation in the township of Lamentin. I was to become "Madame Steward."

7

Man lékonòm ka mété pannyé asi tèt

Madame Steward takes a basket on her head

and goes on her way

The settlers extract as much work from their blacks as possible. . . . But what makes their work so difficult and annoying, I believe, is its futility. For they know that all their sweat profits only the masters, who, even if they gathered mountains of gold, wouldn't share any of it; the blacks wouldn't get to see even one ounce of gain for all their suffering.

Père Dutertre,
Histoire générale des
Antilles habitées par les Français, 1654

Even before leaving Carangaise, Joseph had given me a lecture: I wasn't any longer a little sugarcane worker in the white man's fields, free at the end of the workday to run around with friends and plunge into the ocean. Nor could I work in the factory. Of course, I could help him cultivate his own land, but on the plantation, I had a position to maintain, I had became a lady, Madame Steward.

1952. For the second time, I left my family and my birthplace. I retain vivid memories of my life from that moment on. I see it very clearly, with no haze clouding the mirror. Years of suffering and battling to hold my family together, come what may. An ongoing struggle with life to raise my thirteen children in honor and respect.

When I arrived at Lamentin, no one knew my name, they all called me *Man* Joseph. If you're *Madame,* then you're married. Yet I wasn't. When I made friends with a few people, I gave them my own name. Why hide it? I don't consider marriage an honor. It's the church that brought the custom here. Before that, we blacks formed couples and started families without the priest's blessing.

Then they invented all sorts of nuisances to humiliate, annoy, and frustrate those who didn't get married. Exclusion from taking communion unless you renewed your conversion[60] and renounced the pleasures of the flesh. A separate day for baptizing children of unmarried

Madame Steward takes a basket on her head and goes on her way

parents. Lowest category of burial: the body simply blessed at the church door. . . . And yet it was clear that the women who took communion weren't more faithful because they were married; they just carried on with wedding rings on their fingers.

For me, what difference did it make if I was married or not? I had more serious problems; Joseph turned my hair gray. In the beginning, at Capesterre, things went well. Joseph wanted me very badly, and I felt a kind of love for him. Then problems arose, the same ones I'd known in my first relationship, with Alexander.

I can't claim that Joseph didn't bring his pay home—he gave me enough to raise my children—but he always ran after other women, and I couldn't stand that. I also missed a family life: father, mother, children, all together. Already with my first man I hadn't found it, and I again ended up in a situation I didn't want. Makes you believe that when something is going to happen, it happens no matter what. Besides, you shouldn't dream in the noonday sun or bank on the promises a man makes before he ensnares you.

Even worse than his passion for women, Joseph took to drinking once we arrived in Lamentin. How many times did I say to myself: "Leonora, get out before it's too late. Leave this man." But how could I do it with six children to care for already? I had to think of them first—their education, their future.

Mothers carry their children for nine months, give birth to them, and generally mothers are the ones who help them reach adulthood. If mine have succeeded, managed to do so well—I have an elementary-school teacher, a high-school science teacher, and perhaps another teacher, since my last girl, who's in high school, is doing very well— it's no thanks to their father. He gave me all his pay, but it was up to me to slice, chop, multiply, and divide it so that it would last for two weeks. Up to me to sew, iron, cook, and do all the housework without grumbling. Up to me to care for the children, make sure they were clean for school, learned their lessons, led proper lives.

My husband never helped, never lifted a finger to do the least little thing around the house. As soon as he was awake, I had to make his coffee, sweeten it, pour it, serve it to him. Then fill a *koui* with water so he could wash his face, and give him his clothes, prepare his snack. . . . When he came home from work at two or three in the afternoon, the table was set, the meal steaming hot. In the evening, even if he returned at midnight—or at one, two in the morning—I had to get up and serve him something to eat. I treated him the way I'd seen my mother treat my father. I helped him develop this bad habit, and then, when I wanted to get myself out of it, it wasn't easy. One day I made him understand that a woman can't get up like that, at midnight, to feed a man. "If you arrive while the children are still doing homework, then it's the most normal thing in the world for me to serve you. But it's just plain inconsiderate to insist that a wretched woman of my age—one who has given birth to thirteen children, who has worked so hard—get up at night to wait on you. If you keep this up, it will become really serious, the children will get involved."

I consider this custom truly awful. Some men will take care of themselves if they return home late and their wives are asleep. It's a question of disposition. Most consider the woman their slave, their servant, always at their beck and call. A "house slave" who toils all day long without tiring.

That's the way our mothers raised us: it was less a question of love than of obedience. The man gives the orders in the family, goes off to work, and the woman obeys. It's how things are done. The men want to interpret the Bible literally. When Adam and Eve got in trouble, God chased them out of Paradise saying: "Adam, by the sweat of your brow you shall work and you will bring in money. Eve, you will stay at home."

If there's a place where you sweat out all your body's water, it's in a field of sugarcane. Sweat water and blood, with a head that is split in two by the sun, slave away, that's work in the cane fields.

As the morning's first *pipirit* birds[61] chirped out their name, Joseph was already up, greeting the workers who came from afar to work by the day, assembling them with those who lived on the plantation, assigning a job to each, a place, a section of the field. Depending on the number of reapers and their ability, he'd group them by twos or threes, accompanied by binders.

At that time, a day's work was measured in sheaves of cane. The reaper cut. First the plant at the base of its stalk, then its top—the leaves, the *zanma*—which were used to tie up the sheaves, then the stalk in two or three parts of approximately one meter each. Behind the reaper, a woman bound twelve pieces together using two *zanma* and formed stacks of twenty-five sheaves each.

The number of completed stacks in a day's work varied according to the age of the sugarcane. For cane planted in the current year, tender and easy to cut: fourteen stacks. For the second shoots of the previous year's cane: nine stacks. Third-year shoots: eight stacks. Fourth-year shoots: seven stacks. With this system, the most skilled reapers managed to cut one and a half or two days worth of cane. The owners quickly caught on to what was happening. They increased a day's quota to sixteen stacks. The less skilled could no longer manage to earn a full day's wages. No one exceeded the norm.

The fastest reapers completed their day by 10 A.M., the others by

Madame Steward takes a basket on her head and goes on her way

eleven or noon. No special hours for rest or meals. Each person arranged his time as he chose. Some workers purchased their *didiko* from the peddlers who sold food along the edge of the fields, others brought leftovers from home and only paid for a soda or beer. They didn't have the twenty-five cents for a *donkit* or even the five cents for a *marinade*. Still others chose not to eat while working and waited till they'd finished their quota before stopping for refreshment.

Even after the cane was cut, tied into sheaves, and stacked up, you still couldn't leave. You had to wait for the steward to check your work. Did each sheaf have its proper number of stalks? Were the stacks fluffed up to look as if they contained extra sheaves? How many stacks? That was Joseph's job. All by himself, he had to check on ninety reapers. Starting at ten o'clock, an unruly swarm:

"Mister Joseph, I'm done, come count mine."

"No, over here Mr. Joseph, I finished before he did!"

"No, it's my turn!"

"No, it's mine!"

After verification, the names of the reaper and binder were marked in the book, together with the job accomplished; then Joseph supervised loading the sheaves of cane onto the oxcarts that entered the fields. The carts ferried the cane to the trucks waiting alongside the roads. Bundles flew from hand to hand, stuffing those huge Titans.[62] The work became harder and harder as they filled up. One man stood in the middle of a ladder erected alongside the truck, leaning back against the cane. The guy in the cart threw him a bundle and he sent it off, over his head, to a third man on top of the pile who untied the *zanma* and packed in the cane as well as he could. The worst placed was the fellow on the ladder. In addition to his arms and legs tiring, he received a shower of ants on his head and neck, all the red ants that released their grasp, interrupted in the middle of their meals. Angry and frightened, they bit viciously.

When the workers felt Joseph delayed unnecessarily in checking their work, they criticized him: "Look at this steward, he wants to do everything himself. He makes us wait till noon even though we finished at ten o'clock! He doesn't want to take on a helper. He keeps all the work for himself!"

They couldn't see that the owner was the one saving money on Joseph's back by killing him with work.

Mechanization came later. It started on Grande-Terre, where they gathered the cane with a *kanodè*, a crane-type machine that grabbed the cane with big iron claws and dumped it directly into the trucks. That's cane cut "by surface area." Each worker was assigned four rows of cane to reap, each one eighty or ninety meters long.

Of course it seems easier. No tying sheaves, no building stacks, no awaiting verification. You cut your allotment, and your day's work is done. Ah, yes! But you had to be able to do it: ninety meters of sugarcane, four rows wide, is equivalent to ten or twelve tons! Not everyone managed, far from it. If you wanted to earn your day's wages, you had to cut, cut, cut, thinking of nothing else and taking care not to hurt yourself with your finely sharpened machete. The ants bite, ignore them! The rain drenches you, ignore it! The sun scorches you, ignore it! Cut . . . cut . . . cut . . .

The weakest, the women—for they too had taken up the machete, since they weren't needed anymore to tie up the sheaves—might only have cut twenty or thirty meters by noon. They were paid accordingly. The women also made a extra little money as *kanodèz,* by going through the fields after the machine had passed, gathering up the canes that had been missed and piling them up so that the *kanodè* could grab hold of them. Joseph's workload lightened a bit. No need to check the work or to count piles anymore. He measured the distance cut with his large wooden compass, and that was it.

He was first on the field, in order to organize the work, and last to leave. Then he met with the overseer to give him an accounting of the day's work. The children had long since gone back to school when he returned home. They never ate together.

By this time, they all attended school, and it became an increasing financial burden on the household. To try to keep it all afloat, Joseph took on a little more than two hectares (five acres) of land as a sharecropper, one parcel in Chouchou, the other in Castrade. At first, it helped a great deal. Even after paying the workers for harvesting and the factory for its services, the sugarcane brought in a nice sum.

When the factory started paying for cane according to its sugar content rather than per ton, our return dropped to less than nothing. An evil, yes, but one that at least yielded some good, because it showed the peasants their true situation and forced them into action. Having the price of cane set according to its sweetness upset everything, brought about total chaos, opened the eyes of many people, including me.

No one favored the change, not even the government officials, who voted against it. It happened anyway and no big surprise, since the factory owners and their group make all the decisions. When the cane arrives at the factory, they analyze a sample for its sugar content. The factory owner himself does the calculation and can pay whatever he chooses for the cane. If the cane waits outside the factory too long, it dries out, and the sugar content falls. The owner first takes his own

Madame Steward takes a basket on her head and goes on her way

cane, the harvest from the plantations, while the small grower waits in line. When he can finally deliver it, he's told his cane is worthless.

Did they intend to take revenge on Monsieur Steward? The cart drivers arranged to come for Joseph's cane last of all. It dried out in the fields and didn't measure more than a five or seven in sugar, while that of the factory was always assessed at ten, twelve. Joseph found himself trapped, along with many other small growers.

The first year, the factory purchased the cane half according to sugar content and half by weight. And they gave generous sugar-content readings to all. The growers were caught in the trap. But they learned quickly. Last year, some were paid for a sugar content of two, when normally it ranges between nine and twelve. That's downright thievery! They found that, with this system, after having paid for fertilizer, herbicides, transportation, and loans from the Agricultural Credit Bank, instead of receiving money from the factory, they were in debt to it. And how could they project their earnings if they didn't know whether they'd get any money and, if so, how much?

Previously, if they cut X tons, X tons would be paid for, even if the factory stole several hundredweight. They could estimate and request the correct amount of credit. Now, when they bring the sugarcane to the factory, they're giving the owner a gift. If they've employed workers for the harvest, often they must sell a steer to pay them. . . .

Things began to boil, to seethe in the sugarcane business. Work in the cane fields isn't for the lazy. Plowing, furrowing, planting, hoeing, weeding, fertilizing, reaping, binding, carrying—with cane paid according to its sweetness—it was like farming the ocean! Total gain: zero! And no one around to defend the peasants. There was, of course, the C.G.T.[63] which went to speak with the owners, but without transmitting the complaints of the workers or even asking the peasants their opinions. The representatives returned, announcing a five-cent increase for a day's work, or five cents per ton cut. . . . One year, a strike broke out spontaneously, just like that, but it didn't last. Someone always took charge—never a small farmer or a worker—and went to speak with the owner, then came back saying: "We've won! They've agreed to a raise of this much or that much. Now we can go back to work."

What a joke! Nothing changed and the peasants slipped deeper and deeper into poverty.

The workers began to realize that their representatives, the government, and certain Guadeloupeans were demagogues and all in it together. Several growers, like Chicaté, and two or three "intellectuals" began to make the rounds of the farmers and workers. They asked: "Are you satisfied? How much do you earn for a day's work? Can you live on that? You work out in the hot sun, in the rain, yet you earn less than the factory workers who, sheltered from the elements, keep the machines running. Is that fair?"

They helped the cane growers calculate how much it cost to produce a ton of sugarcane. "All merchandise is priced according to how much it costs to make. Why not sugarcane too?"

At the same time, they organized mutual aid societies, encouraged people to return to their time-honored traditions: *coups de main*, convoys, communal efforts to cut, bind, and transport the cane. That's how, after many discussions and meetings in all parts of Lamentin and Sainte-Rose, the Agricultural Workers Union (U.T.A.) was created.[64]

The *coups de main* had always existed. Neighbors and friends would work together to build a house, to clear land. The cane harvest was predominantly a family affair. Parents would assemble their six, eight, ten, twelve children. They were assured of cutting their cane. They didn't look further than that. Like my parents, they didn't count the cost of their labor or their children's. Nor did they calculate what they paid for fertilizer and herbicides. They only thought about the money they received at the end of the harvest. Selling cane by its sugar content forced them to open their eyes.

The U.T.A. came and said to them: "There's a meeting this evening, together we'll try to figure out how to solve this problem, we'll join forces."

Previously, the workers would have answered: "We don't have time to waste on that." Now, they listened carefully. Chicaté explained: "The harvest used to last six months, six months of work in the fields and in the factory. Now, with mechanization, we're offered only three months. Can a man feed his family by working only three months a year? And what work! The cane is burned so the machines can work faster, all the charcoal dust enters our bodies. The white man has begun the harvest without stating how much he'll pay per day or what price he'll pay for the cane. I don't see why we shouldn't stay home tomorrow. What would we be doing in the fields, anyway? Tomorrow morning, all on strike, let's not go to work."

And old man Chicaté came onto the plantation, stopped by each cabin with information, told the agricultural laborers not to work without a fixed wage, urged them to support the small growers by refusing to cut on the white man's cane plantation till the price per ton was announced. "Tomorrow morning, no one in the fields," he said.

The following day, almost all the workers were in the cane fields. The beginning was very, very hard. This union didn't speak at all like the others; people were worried. The owners sent out their saboteurs to create mistrust between cane growers and farm laborers. They understood the strength of the iron the U.T.A. was forging and didn't want it to cool down, to take shape.

When the U.T.A. called for a strike in 1971, many ears had already heard their words and the scales had fallen from many eyes. The workers stood up to be counted. With each one pulling hard on the chain, it tightened and tightened. Work came to a halt on all of Monsieur S's properties, then throughout Guadeloupe. Not a stalk of cane was cut, not a factory belched smoke. Chicaté and the other leaders never slept. Like *klendendeng* (fireflies), they were everywhere at once, blocking a road here, keeping an eye on the strikebreakers there, evading the *képis rouges*,[65] who swarmed like bees.

The strike continued. The owners refused to negotiate with the U.T.A. They said: "This union isn't representative, it's nothing but a small group of irresponsible people."

The U.T.A. had only recently been created, and its coffers were empty. The strikers tried to collect some small things to help those most in need: food staples, rice. Father Chérubin Céleste, a Guadeloupean priest who took an interest in the sugarcane workers—he was chaplain of the M.R.J.C.—also lent his support. He collected money and food from those who could spare it. The following year, he was appointed priest of the Lamentin parish.

Some people didn't hold out—they had to pay their bills at the company store—and returned to work. Others totally disagreed with the strike. "*Man* Joseph," one of them said to me, "what a farce to strike! If anyone prevents me from working, I'll punch him in the face."

And he did.

"That crew at U.T.A. can do whatever it wants," a friend confided to me, "I'll go to work, and whatever the others get by striking, I'll get too."

"What do you mean, sister? You don't want to join those who fight, and yet you expect to take advantage of their gains? Shame on you!" I was furious. My problems were beginning with people on the plantation. Each day I made a point of finding out what would be happening, the places of work stoppage. I helped in whatever way I could. I gave each person a little something from my husband's pay. Today, fifty cents to help one family pay for school lunches, tomorrow, fifty cents to help another. At least that way, I figured, the children can eat at noon. I shared as I could, in secret, because people licked their tongues in delight when they could gossip about Madame Steward, and besides, I didn't want my husband to learn about it.

Joseph didn't take part in the strike, nor did he oppose it. He had to be at work, so he went and twiddled his thumbs. One of the guys who worked with him denounced him to the overseer: "Monsieur Joseph does nothing, he doesn't try to pressure the workers into returning to their jobs."

Monsieur S had Joseph watched closely. He had managed to recruit several reapers and stuck Joseph out in the field with them. A striker, Monsieur Lotelier, set off together with others to stop the harvesting. He saw Joseph there, but didn't take any notice of him. He entered the plantation, and all the others followed. The work was brought to a standstill. When the owner learned that they had entered onto "his" plantation, prevented "his" workers from harvesting cane, he started to sweat, became as red as a cooked crayfish. He appeared in person at our door: "What's going on? You let Lotelier onto my plantation!"

"Monsieur S, there were so many people! How could I, alone, have stopped them?" Joseph responded very dryly. Trouble was brewing. He had already earned a reprimand for allowing the strikers to enter. And he never tried to recruit workers to break the strike the way the other stewards did. Monsieur S was furious twice over.

"Be careful, Joseph! Figure out a way to get me workers for next week. Go to Petit-Bourg, Goyave, anywhere you want, but bring me back people."

What could Joseph do? He left, pretending to scour the countryside. All along the road, he found only security troops and strikers. He came back empty-handed.

He didn't support either Monsieur S or the strikers, and Monsieur S realized that he couldn't count on Joseph. He sent him to Bellevue Hill to station a car across the road, prevent the strikers from passing, and let in only those who wanted to work. The overseer accompanied him and didn't leave his side for an instant. Joseph succeeded in his mission and got everyone to work. Strange work: cutting, not by surface area nor by stacks, but *an pangal* (every which way) and quickly, for a fixed time, just to break the strike, and for this you'd receive a full day's wages. The overseer congratulated Joseph: "You see, Joseph, when I'm looking over your shoulder, you manage to get things done."

Some of the workers didn't dare stop on their own but rejoiced when the strike interrupted them! A real party! I watched from a distance, because I couldn't risk getting caught on that cane field. As soon as the strikers appeared, all the workers, in unison, dropped their machetes. What a beautiful sight! I questioned everyone who passed my door: "What's going on? What news? Where are you coming from?"

"The union came up behind us. We're on strike."

Sometimes the overseers went to find workers on Grande-Terre, as far as Grands-Fonds-du-Moule: "Come with us. We need reapers."

They never described the situation to the men. When the U.T.A.

blocked the road and explained that the union was demanding an equitable salary, not for itself but for them, and that prices in the stores kept rising although a day's wages didn't, they turned back.

Some were afraid. They'd heard so much about this new union, how it attacked those who wouldn't join. At Cadoux, several workers were out in the fields cutting, protected by the security forces. A large group of strikers arrived. When the scabs saw they were outnumbered even with the *képis rouges,* they leapt into the swamps and took off into the woods.

I realized that many things were changing on the plantation. The strike had thrown everything into confusion. Previously—just as my father had done and I, too, for ten years at Capesterre—the workers would arrive, earn their meager wages in the sugarcane fields of the white man, and leave without questioning things, complaining, or discussing, simply accepting all the decisions of the owner: You'll be paid per stack; they worked per stack. You'll be paid by surface area; they worked by surface area. We'll burn the cane; they inhaled the smoke. Well, things started hopping! Gatherings, meetings, discussions in every corner; mutual help; solidarity. The U.T.A. managed to unite small cane growers and farm laborers. Now, when I see how the reapers all stop working if the small growers are suffering and not getting a fair price for their sugarcane, I cheer the U.T.A. and men like Chicaté who put this union on its feet.

Even though life became increasingly difficult and I was placed in a delicate position on the plantation, I followed it all with a sense of satisfaction. Not so Joseph. After the formation of the U.T.A., Monsieur S felt obliged to keep an eye him. He couldn't do what he wanted anymore. For Joseph and his boss, life was less rosy, sparks started flying.

To pay for the children's schooling now that they were in the upper grades, Joseph had borrowed money from the agricultural bank. His boss had guaranteed the loan. I knew nothing about the conditions of the loan. He simply gave me money. In fact, he'd borrowed more than he'd told me. He needed cash for all his women. And that kind of woman doesn't come cheap! Always after the man, asking for more. Finally, he wasn't able to meet his payments. He didn't have a cent left. How could he afford to pay people to cut and harvest his sugarcane? It dried out while still unharvested and lost all its sugar. Yet how could he give up working for the white man just to take care of his own land? The owner didn't hesitate a moment. He gave Joseph's account to a bailiff and appropriated his fields.

I could sense Joseph's worry, knew about his troubles, but he wasn't the sort of man to confide in his wife, sit down with her and speak seriously, try to resolve life's problems with her.

Through the years, Joseph and I had grown apart.

Apa ti masko Jozèf té ka ban mwen. Daprè-i, i té vlé fè mwen pwan dlo mannyok pou lèt. Kòd a yanm maré yanm, é Jozèf touvé-i pri.	Joseph brought me in a boat. He wanted me to drink manioc juice (poison) instead of milk. The yam is attached by its runners, and Joseph was caught in his own trap.

But I'd be lying if I said he only gave me money on the end of a whip, that I had to beg each and every one of God's mornings to be able to light the fire.

Religiously, every two weeks, the money was on the table. I paid for the rice, oil, salt cod, salted meat, French flour, and dried beans bought on credit at the shop; paid for the bread; and gave each child what he or she needed for daily transportation to school. For the two weeks between paydays, I struggled to meet the everyday expenses. Counting, recounting, calculating, dividing, what a headache! I tried hard to economize, to save some money, but before the two weeks were up, my kitty would be empty.

When a child fell ill, I'd have to go to Joseph: "Lucie isn't well, she has a fever. I want to call in the doctor but I don't have any money."

"What do you mean, no money? I gave you all my pay!"

He only thought about his biweekly pay! With so many children at school and things in the stores so costly, how could we live on that meager pay? Dress the children, buy food, pay the doctor ... I breathed a little easier when distribution of the government family allowance fell on payday. The drum announced to the workers' families that it was time to go to the mayor's office with their cards. Later on, we picked up our allowance at the revenue office.

As long as the children attended primary school at La Rosière or classes at the C. E. or C.M.,[66] they needed only small, inexpensive notebooks. With the meager pay Joseph brought home, plus my small family allowance, I could meet their needs. Then, one by one, they changed schools. The boy in middle school moved on to the next grade, at the school in town. Another finished C. E. and entered high school in Pointe-à-Pitre. I had to pay for noontime meals, for big and expensive books. . . . Biweekly pay and family allowance no longer sufficed. So, you sell a head of cattle, borrow against the year's harvest, dig yourself into a hole.

Madame Steward takes a basket on her head and goes on her way

How the start of the school year turns our hair gray, us mothers! Some, the *manfouben,* don't bother about their children. You go to school, fine. You don't want to go to school, okay, don't go. That's how they were brought up, that's how they bring up their children. Most mothers want a good future for their children. They kill themselves working to produce a schoolteacher, a civil servant with a steady income. As the opening of school approaches, it's not the time to *kalanjé* (drag your feet). They run around everywhere getting together what's needed.

I've always considered school matters important. Well in advance of October, I began preparing for the start of the term. As soon as I'd save a few cents, I'd buy a small bag for one child, a slate for another, colored pencils, fabric to make their clothes, shoes. . . . It's not enough to send kids off to school just any old way. Each one gets a new outfit for the opening of school. After that, they must stay clean and properly dressed. That means washing hurriedly in the evening so things will be dry by morning, ironing, sewing, running around to assure that your children get a perfect score when they're examined from head to toe on the way to school. Here in Guadeloupe, people are quick to criticize: "Have you seen? *Man* so-and-so doesn't look after her daughter, she's wearing the same sweaty dress as yesterday."

Sometimes the teachers would call in the parents because a child wasn't dressed carefully enough. "That's not proper dress for school."

No need for new clothes, it's true, but don't let your child wear torn, dirty, or wrinkled clothes, that's disrespectful. Mothers who are proud, work themselves to the bone to maintain their reputations, even if they have ten or twelve children.

Everything rests on their shoulders. They conceive the children, give birth to them, and help them grow up. I know very few men who help their wives resolve the problems associated with the start of school. At this difficult time of the year, I would have liked Joseph to sit down with me and say: "Leonora, school opens soon, how are we going to handle everything for all our kids?"

I would have answered: "Well, first we have to set aside money for the one who's going to Pointe-à-Pitre, then for the boy who'll be in town, and finally for those in school near the plantation."

I thought about it this way: the money went first for the one who traveled farthest. I explained why to the children: "Mark will be going to high school in Pointe-à-Pitre, he must have everything he needs—in the end, I never managed to get him everything anyway—he comes first. He'll be entering tenth grade and needs good shoes, clothes, many books, money for his daily transportation. Emilienne, you'll be at school in La Rosière, just next door. You can come to me and say: 'Mamma, the teacher asked me to bring in something, I need this or that,' and we'll come up with a solution together."

I couldn't afford to pay for room and board. At first, my oldest daughter commuted from Grosse-Montagne to Pointe-à-Pitre. Then she stayed with an acquaintance of mine. It wasn't exactly boarding: she ate and slept at this friend's house, and every week I sent a bagful of root vegetables,[67] yams, *malangas,* breadfruit, a chicken, pork when we killed a pig. When I could, I added a little money.

When my son's turn came, demipension existed, he could take his noonday meal in the city and return home every evening. It was all expensive, the cost of living increased, but not the household income.

On the plantation I'd gotten to know a very interesting woman, a peddler. She stood in front of the factory and sold *akras, donkit,* sandwiches of spicy flaked cod, all sorts of good things. We talked together, woman to woman.

"I don't know if the pay is too short or the two weeks too long, but there are always three or four lean days. With all these kids at school, I can't seem to make ends meet anymore. I must find a way to bring in a little extra money. My husband's the steward, I can't work in the cane fields, he forbids me. . . . "

"Why don't you do what I'm doing? You know how to cook. Food always sells."

I thought about it. The steward's house, my house, was located at a crossroads. Whether they went up to Jouala or down to Lamoisse, the workers had to pass by my door. I opened a small, informal shop at home. I sold soda, beer, *marinades,* fried fish, and also our favorite drink—but in secret, because I didn't have a license to sell rum. My sales flourished, especially by selling on credit. Every two weeks, on payday, I went up to the plantation with my account book to collect.

As long as sugarcane was cut nearby, customers came regularly. When the harvest moved to more distant fields, on the other side of the river, my clientele disappeared. I wasn't the only vendor. They'd buy their *didiko* on the spot. So I took my basket on my head and went on my way.

A young boy I'd helped returned the favor by carrying the bottles of beer and soda in his wagon. I hadn't told my husband. I couldn't simply say to a man as proud as Joseph: "I'm going off to sell in the fields." He wouldn't have allowed it, and yet I had to free myself because I was squeezed and couldn't manage. One day a friend came to warn me: "Leonora, Joseph recognized you in one of the cane fields. He did a double take. . . . He muttered: 'It's not possible. That can't be Leonora. . . .'"

Madame Steward takes a basket on her head and goes on her way

But it certainly was I, Madame Steward, who defied my husband. Not to prove I was the stronger one, but to give luck a helping hand. Joseph threw a fit and wanted me to stop. His fit didn't bother me. The children and their schooling—that's what was sacred, and I would have done anything at all. So there, Joseph! And I continued my business.

As soon as the workers spied me, it was, *Man* Joseph over here, *Man* Joseph over there, only one *Man* Joseph. They were always happy to see me. I had a smile for each of them, a friendly word, a joke. They came by the house for a drink of water, I knew them all. They'd say: "That's a special woman, not another one like her. For a steward's wife, she's not snobbish."

The *marinade,* fried cod, *donkits*—everything, gone in the blink of an eye. I'd return with an empty basket.

How much I managed to do at that time! The Good Lord must surely have been with me. I arose before dawn to be ready for my earliest customers. First, of course, I had to prepare that man's coffee then, a frying pan over here and a *canari* heating over there, I bustled about.

I had fried the cod the night before and prepared the dough for the *donkits:* some French flour, a little water, a tad of yeast, all well beaten together. Finally, a couple of drops of vinegar and the dough was set to rise overnight. In the morning, I cut it into small, five-centimeter-square pieces. Dropped into boiling oil, each one became a large crisp dumpling. The *canari* could hold three of them. The *donkits* brought in a good profit. If I had sardines or mackerel, I'd mix some of the fish with hot pepper and make sandwiches.

When the customers paid me, I'd simply put the money on the kitchen shelf. That way, when the children left for school in the morning, they could take their daily coins. They still tell how the money from my small business aided them, allowed them to stay in school, and how they occasionally helped themselves to some behind my back.

After my last customer left, around 6 A.M. or 6:30, I'd make the rounds of the fields, not returning till about ten o'clock. I had to rush around like a mad woman to make sure everything was impeccable at home, since that man wasn't pleased about my working. I swept, cooked, and—hop!—off to the river to wash clothes.

From all the going up and down, moving between hot and cold, I got sick. I kept on but, one day, wasn't well enough to go out and sell. Only a few people came by, and I was left with some food. Instead of throwing it out, I gave it to my neighbors, had some brought to my sister in Pointe-à-Pitre. The children wanted to help me: "Mamma, since we're on vacation, we'll go sell for you."

Leonora: The Buried Story of Guadeloupe

I think they realized that everything I did was for them. Emilienne woke up Ernest, the little *chabin:* "Get up, we're going out to sell!"

Ernest had always been somewhat lazy. Off they went with what I'd made, not too much.

Back on my feet, I took over again. But a moment arrived when I got discouraged: people had begun to play hide-and-seek with me, to no longer pay me what they owed. I tried to corner them on payday. When I heard their name called, I ran over to them. They had sent someone else to pick up their wages!

I loved those Saturday paydays, the whole plantation celebrated. All the workers gathered in front of an *ajoupa.* As they waited for the paymaster to arrive from the factory in a chauffeur-driven car, tightly clutching a bag of money, the workers shared jokes and broke into laughter at the smallest thing. All of them were excited, they were going to get their money. Downright little money, but theirs nonetheless, sugarcane money, money for all those days spent suffering in the rain or under the sweltering sun. Each new arrival took his turn at being the butt of a joke.

"Mésyézédanm, gadé vant a Jo, i égal pyèt égal modan èvè poch a ré?"

"Ladies and gentlemen, take a look at Joe's belly, doesn't it resemble a ray's pouch?"

"Vizé tou a né a konpè an mwen, ou té jen di sé la makak ka joué grenndé?"

"And my friend's nostrils, isn't that where the monkeys play dice?"

Laughter was better than worry over whether the meager wages would even cover the debt at the company store. The men also joked among themselves about the women, who had dressed up for the occasion. No question of wearing old work clothes on that day. But clean and ironed dresses, heads wrapped in knotted Madras-cotton scarves, earrings . . . as if they were going out. When their names were called, they'd slowly sidle up, swaying their hips, seeking admiration, laughing at the compliments. Sometimes they'd answer back sharply if a man got too fresh, and then he became the target of his friends' comments.

Drawn by the smell of money, peddlers of all sorts would arrive by the cartful. Men selling vegetables, chives, spices, beef, fish: red snapper, blue and yellow catfish, threadfins, long-nosed sea pike. . . . Women selling sweets: *tourments d'amour,* cream-filled pastries, *sik* (candies), *pipilits, douslèt, kilibibi.* . . . Vendors arriving in cars with dishes, *canaris,* pans, red clay pottery jars; fabrics (twill for men's pants, Madras cotton for the women); hats (Panamas, funeral hats with veils). . . . A real open-air department store!

When the paymaster arrived, he set up at a table with the overseer. The steward remained standing, notebook in hand. The roll call began. One after another, the workers went forward to receive their pay. Often someone would receive less than he thought he'd earned. A day's wages were missing. Joseph would step in, he was in charge of that:

"You say you're missing some money?"

"Yes, Monsieur Joseph, I worked nine days."

"Let's see, you worked which days? Monday, Tuesday?"

"Yes."

"Wednesday?"

"Yes."

"And which other day?"

"Friday, I cut at Jaula, the next Monday at Merlande."

If my husband saw that the man was correct, either he paid him right away or, if he didn't much like him, carried the money over to the next payday, two weeks later. If they couldn't agree, the tension would start to rise, and others got involved, causing a scene. It could even lead to a fistfight. The man was furious: he'd sweated an entire day and the steward had forgotten to mark down his name! You can't fool around like that with a man's living! How well I know that every cent counts. And whereas I had a husband who brought his entire pay home, that wasn't the case with everyone.

Plenty of men gambled and came home totally cleaned out. Sometimes even the woman's pay went the same way. I remember Fernand, a worker on the plantation. Unfortunately, his wife asked him: "Pick up my pay." She waited on the doorstep, surrounded by her children. He came back empty-handed, with nothing to eat or drink. No tempting aroma of sautéed meat filled his cabin that evening. The fool had gambled it all away. Playing dice? Lotto? Or that beloved game of *bingbiling* that's played with steel balls recuperated from car bearings or distillery machines? Young and old alike were addicted to it. A triangle was traced on the ground and each player put in a coin, most often one of those large five-cent pieces that don't exist anymore. Each player sent his ball rolling. When it touched a coin, "biling!" he'd pocket it. A good shot could win several coins in a single roll. Some men put down one-franc pieces. At that rate, the pay quickly evaporated.

Another game, that's no longer played even around the cockfight pits,[68] is *lika.* On payday, it turned up in front of the houses. A wooden plank with a row of small doors was placed on the ground. A narrow corridor led to each door. The player, standing at a good distance, rolled a ball and tried to get it into one of the doors. If it went in, you won! The men made their own balls, from cement. They polished and repolished them till they were perfectly round and smooth. Each player had his own *lika* box. And how money changed hands on paydays!

Those were the Saturdays of the wildest *léwoz*. *Radio Bois-Patate* worked overtime: news traveled by word of mouth. "This evening they'll be a *léwoz* at so-and-so's place, in such-and-such a shop on the plantation. . . . " In any case, those who hadn't heard the news in the morning ran as soon as the drum began to sound at sunset.

Certain snobbish Guadeloupeans might say that they don't like the drums, that the *léwoz* are dances of *vyé Nèg*, but as soon as they hear the "boum! boudoum!" of the *gwoka*, they're drawn to it like a hummingbird to hibiscus flowers.

The *léwoz* took place in front of a house. The owner supplied food and drink. Each person brought either a bottle of rum or a string of blood sausages. Before the music started, while the *boulayè* and *makè* tuned their drum skins by gently tapping on the circles that tightened them, we exchanged the latest news of the plantation.

When the *tanbouyè* made more compelling noises, people drew near and formed a circle. Suddenly the singer's voice rang out:

Mwen kontré Lolo	I met Lolo
Lolo ka balansé an lari la. . . .	Lolo who danced in the street. . . .

or

Kenbé rèd, frè	Hold on, brother,
Kenbé rèd, sitou pa moli	Hold on, don't give in,
Pa moli douvan misyé la	Don't give in to the master,
Misyè la ka kenbé fouèt la.	The master who holds the whip.

Once the rhythm was established, the drums joined the dance. First the two base drums, the *boula,* which would maintain the rhythm throughout the piece, then the *makè,* with its clear sound. The *répondè* answered the singer, everyone began clapping, loosening their shoulders, legs, backsides. The boldest decided to enter the circle: the dance had begun. It was a contest between the *makè,* with his drum, and the dancer, with his whole body, to see who was more agile. The dancer tried to embarrass the *makè* by doing increasingly complicated steps. The drum was obliged to follow, but the dancer couldn't lose the rhythm. Another dancer soon replaced the first, whom he took by the hand, twirled around, and sent out of the ring. His turn now to prove he wasn't flat-footed. And so it continued till morning. . . .

What stories circulated about the *léwoz!* At the full moon the she-devil came and danced. The she-devil! A beautiful, fair-skinned woman, her lovely face set off by a large scarf, golden rings in her ears, a long dress drawn up on one side revealing her fancy, embroidered petticoat, but also, if you looked closely, a cloven hoof that replaced one of her feet.

She danced and sang. Some man always tried his luck with her. The she-devil went off with him, even slept with him. In the morning, the poor man found only a pile of bones in his arms.

The men became more careful, kept a watchful eye on the *léwoz* and braided whips of *mahault* lianas. When an unknown woman arrived, beautiful as the Holy Virgin, they watched closely as she danced, and if they glimpsed a cloven hoof instead of a foot, they chased her away with their whips. She couldn't tolerate cigarette smoke. If you walked home alone at night, you'd be well advised to smoke so as not to get abducted.

But the she-devil took her revenge. She couldn't come and dance anymore? She'd make you run around in circles. One Saturday evening you heard the drum beating, people singing, and a hot, hot rhythm. . . . Not far away, like from Prise-d'Eau to Baimbridge. You thought to yourself, lets go to this *léwoz*. You started out, the moon lighting up the way. When you arrived at Baimbridge, the *léwoz* seemed to be at La Rosière. At La Rosière, no one. The drum called you to Chartreux, and so on all night long. The she-devil made you run after a phantom *léwoz*.

Nowadays *léwoz* happen only rarely. The militant separatists have organized a few in the region. They used to occur every Saturday. The young people lack experience, they don't know how to dance the way the old ones did, and it's a shame.

After my arrival at Lamentin, I hardly attended any *léwoz*. Monsieur Steward didn't like me being too friendly with the people from the plantation or socializing with the farm laborers from nearby. According to him, we weren't any longer in the same class as the reapers and binders: "You have your house, it's your own place, you don't work, yet you want to socialize with people who cut cane, who break their backs working in the fields. I don't understand you."

He spoke to me like this in private, not in front of other people, and it caused me pain because I didn't agree with him. My neighbors, my friends, everyone I met daily worked on the plantation. They were like me, I was, and would always be, like them. Besides, how can one person consider herself better or worse than another? We're all made from the same flesh. We all lived together on the same plantation, I couldn't hold myself apart, even though I was Madame Steward. One of the women was my child's godmother; one of my children, the godfather of a boy; and I, myself, the godmother of several of them. . . . I went from one house to another with advice on how to treat a child, suggestions on keeping the cabin in order . . . and Joseph wanted to forbid me from talking with them all, visiting them, welcoming them in my home!

Really, Madame Steward didn't stay in her own class! I socialized with everyone, worked my garden instead of paying a gardener, and, worst of all, could be found hanging around the cane fields with a basket on my head. I had to give luck a hand and squeeze money out of somewhere. The children were growing and our expenses with them, but not the pay. Joseph should have realized. It gnawed at him, made his blood boil, yet he had no choice but to allow me to do something, take my own affairs in hand. He never attacked me directly, but complained to my friends: "Leonora didn't say a word to me, off she went, just like that, to sell her things, turning up in the cane fields among the workers I supervise. She, my wife! It embarrasses me!"

I didn't worry about him. He would probably have preferred that I socialize with the overseer's wife, but the overseer kept his distance. He was Joseph's boss, and Joseph had to call him mister. He made his rounds on horseback, checking to see that his steward was at work keeping after the *latilyé*[69] as the workers reaped, hoed, spread fertilizer or manure.

Since his wife had troubles, I did occasionally speak with her. She'd been a teacher, but since her marriage, that husband of hers had forbidden her to work. She was, therefore, totally dependent on him. Her new job: having children. That's how I found her when I arrived on the plantation. She suffered terribly because her husband was a great womanizer, could have all the women he wanted, and didn't restrain himself. He treated her horribly. Sometimes when that man of hers left her alone, she'd wait for him under my balcony. I don't know what occurred when she returned home. She came under my balcony, but I never entered her house.

If my husband was sick, the overseer would come by to see him. He also came to the house when I lost one of my children and told Joseph that he was at his service, ready to help him. But he wasn't a man who socialized with Joseph; it was always work, work, period, that's all. Joseph had his pride and kept to his own class. Like many others, he could have chosen his boss as a godfather for one of his children. But Joseph was a stickler for custom. You have your class, I have mine. They were in the upper class and we were one class lower down.

8

Maladi an mwen vin a chouval, i pati a pyé

My illness galloped in and

crawled off

I was pregnant and dying.

In 1953, when that terrible illness crashed down on me, my life became truly unbearable. My neighbors, friends, family, everyone advised me: "*Man* Joseph, go for a consultation, have a *séance* with a healer. If you can't get there, send someone in your place. A good *gadèdzafè* will find out who had a spell put on you and be able to release you."

How this faith in *kenbwa*, in *machann kakoué* (beliefmongers) is rooted in us! Father Céleste is right, it won't be easy to free us from it. It clings to us like a shirt to our bodies, and no one in Guadeloupe can honestly claim to have a mind completely free of those things.

Joseph didn't believe in *gadèdzafè*. Neither did his relatives. I wonder, how did they manage to be spared? One day, when I had suffered a particularly strong attack, a neighbor spoke to Joseph: "Didn't anyone tell you? There's a spirit in this house. It's attacking your wife. Is on her. You can't simply let her die. She must be protected. I know a good *gadèdzafè*, come with me for his advice."

A friend from the village came by to see me and offered the same advice. Each person who visited pushed Joseph in the same direction: I was set upon by a spirit, evil had entered my body, only a gifted sorcerer could counteract my enemy's curse.

Finally Joseph gave in. My good friend accompanied him to a well-known *kenbwazè,* who threw them right out the door. Why? By chance, they had stumbled onto the sorcerer who was working against me! A comrade of mine had left his wife. Furious, she claimed I was to blame and paid to have a spirit sent to destroy my body, suffocate me. She talked about it everywhere, I knew, but since I already suffered from asthma and often experienced bad attacks, I didn't pay attention to her threats. Yet everyone remarked on how my attacks had worsened, that only an evil spirit could bring about such seizures. I had to "take precautions."

Another friend came to my aid: one of his neighbors' daughters had the gift and an excellent reputation. Joseph went to see her but had to wait for her to pick a good day. Not every one of the Good Lord's days would do. Joseph never was given an appointment.

My older brother came to see me. Frightened by the state of my health, he called in a doctor, who prescribed various treatments. Nothing worked. I saw another and still another, took medicine in drops, pills, capsules, and injections. I continued to suffocate day and night, with the child in my body moving about restlessly, rising up to my throat.

Joseph learned about a *gadèdzafè* at Vieux-Habitants, on the other side of the mountains: "Oh, sir," he said, "your wife is pregnant, I can't do anything for her before her delivery. Give her juice of the custard apple and tamarind, make sure she eats lots of tamarind.[70]

He hadn't done a *séance* or even spoken of the spirit that invaded me, but simply prescribed fruit juices. I followed his advice—not bad, really. I felt less oppressed, and the child in my belly rested more quietly.

That year was terrible. Attack after attack. Joseph didn't know where to turn next. He didn't even want to go to work because, each time I had a seizure, someone would go for him. And each time his heart would leap in his chest. He expected to hear: "Your wife is dead." He tried very hard during my illness! That's why I forgive him much of the misery he made me suffer afterward. Not knowing what else to do, he asked one of my sisters if I could spend a few days with her, perhaps till the baby was born. I stayed there three months, three months of suffering, choking, discomfort. My mother often came to see me, we got along very well.

When I felt an attack coming on, I'd lie down on a chaise longue. I couldn't see, hear, or think about anything, not even my children. I just suffered. In the quiet moments between attacks, I worried: "I'm with my sister, we get along, she takes care of me as well as the hospital would, but she has ten children of her own, and even if Joseph brings us food, I can't impose on her forever. And my home is split up! I had brought my two youngest children with me. The three others stayed with their older sister at Lamentin. It all cost money, I wasn't able to save anything. And Joseph who loved carousing . . .

One night, I thought I was dying. I couldn't breathe. Never had an attack been so strong. I was taken to see a doctor. I was lucky, I happened on Doctor Nyambi, a very skilled physician who treated me for many years afterward. He bled me and managed to control the attack.

My whole family had been very worried. My sister, who worked for a white woman, shivered at the thought of my dying and not having a Christian burial. She was embarrassed to admit to her employer that her sister lived with a man she wasn't married to. At that time, the church refused to conduct funeral services for unmarried women who died while pregnant or in childbirth. Had I died, people wouldn't have seen my corpse carried through the church. Little I cared about that: "If I die, bury me, with or without a service, it won't matter. *Bèl antèrman pa paradi* (a fancy funeral doesn't guarantee entry to paradise)."

Every person has things that touch his pride, but that wasn't one for me. So-and-so died, she wasn't married, we won't go to church, but will meet at the cemetery instead. Isn't that where we're all buried anyway?

In any case, my family united in pressuring Joseph, the father of my children, into marrying me. He didn't want to marry a woman who was on her deathbed. He wanted to have me well and standing at his side. I didn't die and gave birth to my sixth child. The day of the baptism, I married Joseph.

The child who caused me so much suffering only lived five months. It had ingested all sorts of medicines in my womb. All those remedies I swallowed killed it.

I felt better. The air of my childhood home, the care of the good doctor Nyambi brought me great relief. I went back to Lamentin. During my long absence, tongues had started wagging like *raras* during Holy Week.[71] "Ah hah! She went to "protect" herself against his mistress, who has been returning her blow for blow. . . . " "After having cast an illness spell, she sent her off to Capesterre, to get her out of the way. . . . "

Saint Dispatcher didn't do her work well, because I returned married.

Ah yes! I was married, but it didn't matter to me one way or the other. I wasn't too interested in marriage nor was Joseph. Our family and friends pushed us into it. As recently as the other day, one of my old friends, Madame Alphonsine, proper as can be, was priding herself on her role in the affair. "I said to him: 'Joseph, Leonora may die, you must do something for her so at least she could have a proper funeral. After all the time you two have been living together, you could at least put a ring on her finger.' And he listened to me."

"Okay, *Man* Alphonsine, we got married. But it's not a ceremony—a beautiful wedding with fancy clothes, good food, champagne—that makes a couple strong and keeps them together. The church benefits most from marriage. If people married only before men and not before God, the church wouldn't occupy its present place in society. People wouldn't bother about it so much."

I also reminded her how Joseph, drunk as a pig, couldn't make it to the prenuptial medical visit. He had sent a friend to take the X-ray in his place. "It wasn't exactly him I married, *an mayè èvè lonbraj a-i* (I married his shadow). Perhaps that's why we couldn't get along or live out our lives together."

It's true, each time he visited me at my sister's, Joseph arrived full of rum. I refused to see him. "Me, marry a man who can't even stand up straight? Impolite when he visits my family? Never!"

My parents wouldn't hear of such a thing. Their daughter was asked for in marriage, such an honor. I embarrassed them by refusing. When Joseph told them of the child's birth and promised to marry me in my own village on the day of its baptism, they exclaimed: "*Woulo!* Bravo!" Not I. And had I offered up to God even the smallest sprig of flowers in order to receive a blessing on the marriage, I would have regretted it.

Ka ou vlé fè, sa ki la pou ou, dlo pa ka chayé-i. E mwen, pou chayé an chayé. Jou mayé la sa sé té kouri dèyè bonnè akoudpyé pou ranmasé malè a dé men.	What do you want? What is destined for you isn't carried along by the water. And how I carried things on my back! The day of the wedding, I kicked out happiness and, with my two hands, gathered up sorrow.

Upon my return to Lamentin, oppression settled on me even more heavily than before. The evil spirit of the house was again upon me. I reminded Joseph of his promise to the *gadèdzafè* at Vieux-Habitants; that he'd go consult with him after I gave birth. I suffered terribly. Joseph refused to go: "He didn't cure you when you were pregnant, what could he do for you now?"

So my illness dragged on and on for eighteen years. What sort of illness? One that ran in my family. My father had talked about his grandfather's attacks. One of my aunts died of them. My sister's children also have asthma. I first caught it at age twenty-two. Just after giving birth, I suffered that attack, but I recovered quickly.

When I moved from Capesterre to Lamentin, I had a young baby. My friends warned me: "If you go to Lamentin, protect yourself. Those people have a reputation for being powerful sorcerers. They don't fool around."

Our house, the one reserved for the plantation steward, was close to the canal. In the morning, after having cleaned the house, I would ask my neighbors to keep an eye on the baby while I went up to the canal to wash clothes. When it was time to prepare the meal, I returned home. I went back to continue the washing and then left to meet the children when they came from school. After the noontime meal, I went back to the canal. All these comings and goings caused a serious "imprudence."[72] I was newly up from childbed, and moving from the warmth of a charcoal stove to the cold of the river brought on a relapse of my illness.

I was knocked flat. It was as if I had received a "transfer," something that had melted over me and pinned me down, preventing me from ever climbing back up on my mount. Perhaps that's what it was and perhaps not. In any case, it was the first time I had seen anyone suffer so much and fight back so hard with all her will from the bottom of the sea.

My mother prayed: "God, Jesus Christ, deliver my child, save my child."

She also implored Saint Anthony of Padua, reading from the Collection of Forty-Four Prayers for Life's Necessities: "Evil, whatever you may be, wherever your home, whatever your nature or source, in the name of Jesus Christ, he who is obeyed in Heaven, on earth, and down into the fires of Hell, I order you to depart from Leonora, God's creature who is present here. I order you out in the name of the Father, the Son, and the Holy Ghost."

She tried her best to help me. Every time I gave birth, she came and spent several days with me, doing whatever she could around the house. She even wanted to go to the river and do my washing. Although she was old and her work wasn't perfect, she was there with me, for me. She too saw something unnatural in my illness.

Today, I admit that Joseph was right in refusing to visit the *gadèdzafè* at Vieux-Habitants a second time. As the proverb says:

Tousa ou pa konnèt pi gran pasé ou . . .	What you don't understand is bigger than you, goes beyond you . . .

but sometimes it's better not to know.

When a *gadèdzafè* sets out to find the answer for you, he always discovers something new. You must visit him often and spend lots of money. He takes on your problems, your husband's, your children's. . . . He might have seen, for example, that a spell would make my daughter fail her exam. And then maybe Lucie would have come back in the same condition as that poor girl who, sent by her mother for a consultation, found herself pregnant after the *séance*. A lovely time indeed the fellow had with her!

The *gadèdzafè* would surely have directed my thoughts toward my friend's wife. We'd had an argument, and she'd already threatened to get me. She convinced herself I had destroyed her home.

Leonora: The Buried Story of Guadeloupe

We were neighbors on the plantation. Her husband was the watchman; he guarded the sugarcane. He walked about the plantation, his badge visibly displayed, eyes darting everywhere to protect the white man's cane from being eaten up. That was his job, to watch over the sugarcane and the cattle that found their way onto the fields. We lived in the same type of wooden cabin with two rooms and a balcony, but she acted the fine lady with me. She showed off her living room furniture, her deluxe tableware with porcelain plates, her wine glasses. My household consisted of nothing at all: gourd *kouis,* iron cups, and lots of children, children who attended school. I didn't covet *bèl bèbèl,* beautiful frivolities, but only school, the one door worth knocking on to help your children escape the cane fields and a life of poverty.

But we spoke together as neighbors and called each other friend, sister. She and her husband had been having trouble for a long time. She wanted to bend him to her wishes, and he chose to do whatever he liked. They had already separated four times. With lots of racket, involving the law and the courts. The fifth time was for good. The household split up, and she blamed it on me. She predicted I'd have the worst misfortunes. A few simple words from the *gadèdzafè* would have convinced me that this woman was working on me, was the cause of all my problems. He would have persuaded me to defend myself, and I might still be in his grip, pouring all my money into his hands.

One night as I slept, a close friend who had recently died appeared to me. I had a vision of the two of us together, she caring for me, bathing me, rubbing my body. She reminded me: "Don't forget the ingredients of the bath, Leonora—Val Fleuri cologne, chicken droppings, Indian tamarind."

She disappeared, and my whole body, normally so cold, so freezing, became warm, burning, like the *wòchgalèt* (cobblestones) at high noon.

The following morning I prepared the remedy. It was the same brand of cologne that I used for the baby. I asked for fresh chicken droppings. They were cold, but I bathed in them anyway. Why? I don't really know. A dream had told me to. For the second bath, my sister wrapped the chicken droppings in a cloth. I suffered so much pain that I was ready to follow any advice. I even bathed in hot pepper! I tried everything that might bring me some relief.

And so I managed to resist from one day to the next, to see a slight improvement. All by sheer will power, without even sleeping in a red cotton night dress that is said to frighten away the spirits. When you struggle so persistently against evil, it ends up turning against the one who sent it. You can hear the person moaning with his own malice.

Eighteen years of my life, eighteen years spent fighting the illness

My illness galloped in and crawled off

and suffering. I didn't want to stay in bed. My body had to be upright. The more time you spend lying down, the deeper you sink into your malady. Whether the attack struck during the day or at night, by the next day, I was up. Trembling, I'd climb out of bed, pull on a sweater to warm my chilled body, take some of this liquid, some of those pills, following the advice of the doctors as well as our herbal cures. Stuffed with medicines, I more or less managed. As soon as my stock was depleted, a new crisis and again a visit to the doctor.

Everyone cried, "Hosanna!" and threw up their hands, understanding nothing at all about my illness.

One woman, claiming she came to comfort me, pressed on a sea-urchin thorn sticking into my skin: "Leonora, my poor dear, Monsieur Joseph must be disgusted. His money certainly doesn't have time to burn a hole in his pocket. It all goes for the doctors and medicines."

I have many reasons for reproaching Joseph, but that's not one of them. I forgive him a lot because he never grumbled about my care or about spending money for whatever might bring me some relief. He cared for me like a precious doll and didn't spare himself. His infidelity certainly aggravated my condition but it didn't cause the illness the way those nasty tongues wagging in the public square wanted everyone to believe. "Look at Leonora, she's choking on the feathers of her pillow. She has been crying into it for so long."

It was just at the time of my worst attacks that national health care, *Sécurité sociale,* was brought to Guadeloupe. I had recently gotten married and was entitled to it. No offices in the rural townships then. If you wanted your money, you had to get yourself to Pointe-à-Pitre by 4 A.M. The doors opened at 8 A.M. and closed at 4 P.M. During the long wait, you got to meet other people. We spoke to one another, especially about our health problems and what we'd found for cures. . . .

"I woke up one day," began one woman, "with the sole of my foot riddled with holes, as if it had been eaten. It frightened me. I consulted a friend. He told me: 'Rub it with ground glass.' That night I had a dream. Someone I didn't know, had never seen before, came to me. A pale, little woman, very short but white as can be. She leaned over me and said: 'Kiss me.'

"Since I wasn't too eager to do it, she continued: 'Then I'll kiss you.'

"And she gave me several kisses. Then she spoke again: 'You have a problem with your foot.'

"'Yes.'

"'Go to the port in Pointe-à-Pitre, to the docks. Buy blue soap. Carefully wash your foot with it and you'll be cured. Don't you recognize me?'

"'No'

"'I'm your father's grandmother. I've given you a cure, try it.'

"No sooner said than done. Never have I seen so many holes in one foot. Holes and holes and holes! If I believed in sorcery, I'd have said: 'A spell was put on me!' I still don't know what it was. My skin, *on vré nich a poulboua*, a real termite's nest. Had I stepped on something? I really don't know one way or the other. So I bought a piece of blue soap with a white stripe in the middle, the kind used for bar soap. I washed and soaped my foot. The holes disappeared."

"And," continued another woman, "I'll tell you how I was able to extricate my daughter from the claws of a *kenbouazè* who had ensnared her. He had made her drink some sort of concoction. My daughter obeyed that villain, did whatever he ordered her to, day as well as night. I went for a consultation, no sorcerer wanted to work for me, the other man was too strong. Someone suggested Malyenmé. I hesitated, I didn't have much money. . . . "

"You were right, my good woman. Malyenmé! Ai-ai-ai!"

"Malyenmé! You must be careful of the Indian goddess. She has great powers, especially to help you have a child when you're *branany* or to cure afflictions. But watch out, friends! If you don't keep your promises, Malyenmé's anger is terrible and unforgiving."

The poor woman couldn't get in another word. Everyone wanted to tell something about Malyenmé's vengeance. Recently an eighteen year-old girl had received a favor. She had broken her promise to the goddess. A truck hit her as she was leaving Chanji's temple. . . .

Finally the woman continued: "So much the worse for those who don't keep their promises. I sold a pair of oxen to buy all the things necessary for the ceremony: roosters and goats for the sacrifice, food and drink for the guests who were transported from Anse-Bertrand to Chanji at Capesterre in a rented bus. I spent a lot, but my daughter has been freed."

"All that frightens me. I had a *séance* done to learn the cause of my sickness. Now I take *razyé* medicines, herbal cures given me by the sorcerer and also those things prescribed by the doctor."

What words tumbled out of those mouths! I tried not to miss a single one. I too spoke of my illness. Someone told me about recipes and remedies to help me out. I listened and tried one thing after another. Slowly, I fought off the malady, regaining control of my body.

One woman I met that day advised me to buy a hand pump at the pharmacy. A little aspirator that could be filled with liquid. Whenever I gasped for breath, I opened my mouth wide, pumped away, and was able to breathe.

People were appalled to see me do this.

My illness galloped in and crawled off

"Watch out Leonora, that pump looks dangerous to me."

"If it were, it wouldn't be sold in pharmacies."

That pump brought me great relief and also saved many visits to the doctor.

I really wanted to pull through the illness. It couldn't last forever. I was tired of hanging around and not being able to do much at home. Fortunately, my oldest daughter had taken charge of the household. She went to school and also ran the house, washing clothes in the river with her brothers and sisters. Bless that child, she helped me so much. Also her brother, Dominick, my little Didi, how I love that child! Among your children, you always have a favorite. People think Mark is my pet because, being a teacher, he gives me money, supports me, and helps with his brothers and sisters. But I've always had a weak spot for Didi, who lives in France now. He could pull a dirty trick on me and, at the same time, with a word, a smile, lift my spirits up.

One day I went to the river with the children. I decided to be careful. I'd caught the illness at the river. I didn't go into the water but washed in a large basin, letting the children rinse the clothes which I then spread out on large, smooth rocks. Joseph was waiting for us when we returned: "Great! You're off doing the wash. Do you think it's funny if you get sick again? I give up on you!"

"But Joseph, I can't let the children do everything. They have school to worry about. And the women you send to help with the washing, well, some of them aren't clean, they don't do a good job. I have to use the ones you find, but they're not to my liking."

In fact, all those women must have been subjected to Joseph's whims. He had as many women as he had canes of sugar, Joseph did.

I began to regain control of my body. Doctor Nyambi treated me, and I asked him question after question. Could I stay out in the sun? Bathe in the ocean? In the river? What must I avoid?

"Madame," he answered, "asthma is a very annoying illness. Dust inhaled, a moment of inattention, and the attacks could begin anew. You can bathe, but not like healthy people who dive and swim and stay in the water a long time."

He was right. Not long ago, I went to see my sister. I met one of my nieces, and we went down to the ocean to bathe. I was happy, and forgetting the advice of the doctor, I lolled about in the water, unconcerned. I don't know if the water, the sun, or the wind that blew the sand about was the cause, but I suffered an attack. My niece took me by car to the doctor on call. Luckily, it was the good doctor Nyambi. After all the years he had been treating me, he knew what to do: he bled me and gave me a shot. With the excess blood removed, I felt better.

"Doctor Nyambi!" People from Capesterre pronounced his name like that of a god. *Sé Bondyé Sènyè a yo*, this Indian from London who took up residence in Guadeloupe. He married a young woman from Capesterre, she too a doctor, but she got in trouble and they divorced.

I know I must be careful for the rest of my life. When I breathe in dust or smoke, I feel a weight that travels up to my throat, but, thank God, the attacks have subsided.

Having galloped in, my illness crawled off.

9

Apatoudi menné koulèv lékòl

sé fè-i sizé asi ban ki mèt

Leading the cobra to school is not enough; to

be its master you must make it lie down

> "Life is a thread that doesn't break, that is never lost, and do
> you know why? Because every man ties a knot in it during his
> lifetime with the work he has done. That's what keeps life going
> through the centuries—man's work on this earth."

Jacques Roumain,
Masters of the Dew

In school, the teachers don't teach diligence or admiration for those
who work with their hands, sweat under the hot sun, wear themselves
out plowing the earth.

The ideal: to become a person who uses a pen, who will never work
with sugarcane or bananas. If you don't learn well, the worst threats
rain down on your head: "You'll end up guarding the oxen, digging in
the earth, cutting cane!"

I don't know how teachers threaten lazy students these days. Even
with a high-school degree, you can't guard the oxen or dig in the earth,
there are few oxen left and little earth to cultivate. The only solution:
head off to France to work, for example, in a hotel. First you serve in
the dining room and then in the bedrooms . . . that's the way they get
our young people involved with drugs or prostitution. They should
find a job when they leave school, but that's not what school is for. It's
just to teach you how to speak French, that's all.

School is also the cause of many problems and much envy within
families. Several of your children succeed, advance. Several become
teachers. None of your sister's children do. She gets envious, hate grows
in her heart. Whenever she has a problem, she feels it's only normal
for you to take care of her. Your children have succeeded, you're better
than she is, you've left her behind. She doesn't want to accept that the
diplomas aren't yours, or the paychecks. Of course your children give

you a little money to live on, but the paychecks belong to them. You can't support your sister's needs, so she gets angry with you.

School also causes quarrels between siblings. It's important to them. If one does well, gets good marks, the others accuse you of loving him best because of his grades. That's the way they see it, and maybe they're right: unconsciously, you're proud of him, try to push him so he'll succeed. . . . The others are jealous.

My oldest daughter flew along in school. On prize day, she carried off all the awards. First prize in French, Lucie. First prize in math, Lucie. First prize in this, first prize in that, her name rang out each time. You should have seen her walk down the platform steps, hidden behind an enormous pile of books—so small and thin that she was nicknamed *Zègèlèt*. Her grandmother swooned with joy.

"Luckily you didn't leave her with me at Carangaise," she said to me. "By being first in everything, she'd have made many people jealous. Her path would have been blocked by some *kenbwa!* You must have been inspired by God when you took her back from me."

My mother's belief in all this sorcery was as strong as nails, and she worried about her little darling. It's true, I was right to take Lucie from her. And about time too, she spoiled her rotten. She adored the kid and never required her to do any chores around the house. If, even once, she'd ask for help in sweeping the doorstep, all the child had to do was whimper and say she was tired for my mother to get up and do the work herself. Insisting would have made a martyr of her granddaughter. What a lousy upbringing! My mother wasn't like that with any of her other grandchildren; Lucie occupied a special place in her heart. Nothing was too beautiful or too expensive for her little girl: hats, floral fabric, printed dresses. . . .

I had a devil of a time undoing it. The little lady had become so accustomed to doing whatever she wanted—that is, nothing at all—that as soon as you asked for a little help, she'd just about collapse. My sister laughed and made fun of me: "My goodness, that child's so small and thin, brought up with kid gloves, she'll be carried off by the smallest breeze!"

And let's not mention the quarreling between neighbors! Your children do well at school. Your neighbor's don't. That's not normal, people say; witchcraft must be involved somehow. You've had a spell put on them.

For a long time I was thought to be "gifted," to have "the touch." My powers were exhausted after the success of three of my children. My second daughter failed three times to receive her certificate of elementary studies. So, were my powers gone, or was a stronger force than mine at work? What incredible things people said! I got a good laugh from it all.

Leading the cobra to school is not enough

In fact, I really do have a gift, but it's the simple understanding that each person has his or her own intelligence and willpower: success also depends on what one wants from life.

We give birth to children but don't create their temperaments. Each child is born with its own mind and follows its own path. I treated all my children alike. One of my sons, Ernest, who didn't do much with his life, said it himself: "If I haven't succeeded, it's not from lack of care. I could never claim that my mother didn't do enough for me."

After middle school, I sent him on to Pointe-à-Pitre for two years, then for an apprenticeship to learn to be a house painter. He couldn't stand it. He dropped it all and took a job in the rum factory.

Mark is a teacher. From his elementary school years right up through high school and university, he never experienced what you'd call a failure. And of all my children, he was the one who most loved to play. Every little field beckoned to him, and off he'd go, to play and laugh with his friends. Even by himself, he invented all sorts of games . . . and now he's a teacher. What counts is what you really and truly desire.

My daughter Emilienne also wanted to succeed, but she's too much of a busybody. At school, she already stuck her nose into everyone else's business. This one did well at school; that one wasn't very good. . . . In sixth grade, she was in a class with a friend's daughter. I heard all about their family life: Isabelle got a thirteen out of twenty in math, a fourteen in geography. Never a word about Emilienne's own grades. She was always looking over someone else's shoulder. She worked toward a secretarial proficiency diploma. She failed. I'd paid for three years of private school. I decided not to spend any more money on schooling for those who'd be sent packing. My son Mark urged me: "Mamma, you can't keep Emilienne at home. Pay for one more year."

I let myself be convinced, and she failed again. That's when people began to whisper that I'd lost my "gift." Why? Because I wasn't producing any more teachers. As if everyone had to be an elementary or high-school teacher! For me, the question is simply one of working, of each child having an occupation. Here, success is measured by a high-school diploma. They talk as if every Guadeloupean must earn one.

Emilienne could have succeeded at school, but her mind was too preoccupied. Even while washing dishes, she'd squirm around all the time: a plate washed, a glass and—hop!—she'd be out in the street. Restless as a latch on a new door, she'd jump up at the slightest noise. I tried to calm her down: "Emilienne, stay still, you're doing dishes, don't get so excited!"

Today she lives in France. She finally managed to get her hands on a certificate of professional aptitude and works as a secretary in the armed forces. She's still the same: the gossip she tells me on the phone cracks me up with laughter just the way her stories about school used to do.

For Justin too, people said that somebody "had it in for me," that I could do nothing against the power that crashed down on me and my children. He earned his certificate of elementary studies and was ready to enter middle school. When I went to enroll him, I was told that there weren't any more places, that he'd have to go back a year, into his younger brother's grade. He refused to go to school, possibly out of a sense of wounded pride. I found him an apprenticeship with a lathe worker at Fouillole. Two years later, he was employed in the Darboussier factory.

At the end of his military service, no more job. Walking the streets, watching the clouds roll by, running after the girls—these became his new occupation. The Bumidom[73] sent him papers so he could leave for France. At that time, I wasn't as well informed as I am now, otherwise my son wouldn't have gone off. Yet perhaps, with his mania for running after women, it was for the best. And France wasn't yet such a hellhole then.

My husband, Joseph, didn't approve of Justin's departure. But since he too was a ladies man, I feared he'd be a bad influence and, instead of getting the boy back on track, would teach him how to run around. He said: "No, Justin won't leave. I'll buy him a bus. He'll stay here, period."

He wasn't worried about his son getting lost in France, he wanted to keep control over him.

Guadeloupeans didn't travel then the way they do now. I wasn't nervous about France. It hadn't started to heat up, get really tough . . . so I urged him to go. After several training courses, he earned a certificate of professional aptitude. He works in a factory, married a white woman, and has never returned home.

Dominick joined him there. After his military service, he stayed in France, at Roubaix. A tough place where there are only whites and no jobs. I wrote and suggested he return, but he didn't want to hear a single word about it.

"I'm not dependent on Justin, I'm 'unemployed.' I get money, etc."

Then he went up to Paris. He works in a hospital, feeding the patients, I believe. I hope he'll come home during vacation and tell me about his life.

As for Viviane, the little black one, the youngest of my daughters, if she gets her diploma, she'll have to decide what she wants to do. When she gets that far it will be time for her to make up her mind. One

Leading the cobra to school is not enough

day she wants to become a stewardess, the next day to go to Martinique, to study English, Spanish. . . . I hardly listen to everything she tells me; she's always changing her mind. But she's well on her way to getting a high school degree.

Are there so many failures on this list? Of course, there is José, the youngest, who causes me so much trouble, keeps me awake at night, makes my blood boil, occupies my mind day and night. Such a hard-headed kid, so stubborn, so uncooperative, so disrespectful to me and to his older brothers.

"That one really had an evil spell put on him. *Man* Joseph, you must find a sorcerer who is stronger than the one working for your enemy."

Evil, Evil, everything that happens is blamed on Evil! A person loses his job, Evil's at work. A merchant sees her business slack off, the *menné-vini* lotion that attracted clients isn't working any more. She goes bankrupt and closes the shop, its because an envious competitor engaged a sorcerer to put out a trap. Newly married, pregnant Marie doesn't watch where she's walking, slips, falls down, and loses her baby. Her husband's mistress had a spell put on her to kill the baby, to get rid of it. One of your children doesn't do well at school, strays off the right path like my Ti-Jo.[74] Someone jealous of your success is behind it all. . . . Envy is really the sister of sorcery. Not everything should be laid on the back of Evil. The child's lack of interest and his abilities have a lot to do with it.

So, what to do with Ti-Jo? Follow what's in vogue and send him to France because he doesn't work at school and he misbehaves? I heard one woman say: "I don't have enough money. But if I could afford the price of a ticket, I'd send my daughter to France. I can't stand seeing her misbehave. If she's in France, at least my eyes won't have to witness my shame."

She saw France as a place to hide the unacceptable behavior of her daughter. A cloak for failures. She's over there, on the other side of the ocean.

Sa zyé pa vouè, kè pa'a fè mal.   The heart does not suffer from
                                    what the eyes cannot see.

In addition to the youngest, who causes me all this grief, I have another son who drinks heavily. His sister repeats all day long: "In France, only in France, will he be able to straighten himself out."

And a neighbor: "*Man* Joseph, you can say all you want about France, but if this young man can find work there, shouldn't you send him? He's a nuisance to you here."

I answered yes, but it wasn't a true answer from my heart. I haven't made up my mind, because I know the sorts of things that happen to blacks in France. I don't want to see him go there. And, anyway, it would be giving in to life's problems, letting them carry you along.

You have ten fingers. If one of your fingers smells rotten, can you say okay, I'm going to get rid of it? Can you? No. If one of your children isn't good, you don't have the right to reject him or her.

Of course, we'd like all of them to follow the good path, but it's not too surprising if at least one gives you trouble. A difficult challenge when it happens, as I know well. My José is truly disobedient. I accept it because I believe in the Gospel and know you can't have the resurrection without Good Friday. Yet his unkindness can sometimes cause an intolerable pain to spread through my body. When he was twelve I was told: "Be patient, he's changing, it's a difficult age."

Now he's turning fifteen: no improvement. I wonder if he could have a real problem. From the time he was a little boy, I let up on the reins and gave him his head. His father wasn't at home much; the child ran about freely, from one house to the next. Now I want to keep him on a tighter lead. Does he feel it and rebel? I don't know how to handle it. Yet I'm sure I shouldn't act like those mothers who keep their child at home, close to them, and treat him differently from the others, as if he weren't theirs. He'd become even worse.

From time to time, I notice a slight improvement in Ti-Jo. Yesterday morning I asked him to clean his room, put his things in order, and wipe the floor with a wet rag. He began to howl: "Dammit! I'm busy. I've had enough, you talk too much, my head is splitting."

And off he went. In the living room I'd arranged a dry branch in a vase to look like a tree. On its ends, I'd hung hibiscus flowers. It looks very pretty but wilts quickly. I found my little tree all hung with fresh flowers.

"Ti-Jo, was it you who arranged the tree so beautifully?"

"Yes."

"I didn't ask you to, but you decorated it so nicely. Thank you, Ti-Jo."

I was very happy. For the first time, he'd done something for me without my having asked. He'd gathered the hibiscus flowers just after his noisy departure from his room.

Occasionally, he'll do something thoughtful, but most of the time he's unbearable. I fight with him over school and so does his brother, the teacher. Ti-Jo doesn't put in any effort or pay attention.

Today the Guadeloupean unions[75] proclaim:

| Lékol a yo pa bon pou nou, fò nou changé-i! | The French schools aren't good for us, we must change them! |

Leading the cobra to school is not enough

In the meantime, school is there, it doesn't go anywhere. Only a few teachers try something new, speak an occasional word of Creole. Yet we must send our children somewhere.

Ti-Jo attends but doesn't study. At fifteen, in seventh grade, he's way behind. Only one thing interests him: drawing. He draws incredibly well. He wants to become an architect. But when I look at the architects here, I see they've had a good deal of schooling. They crammed many things into their heads before they succeeded. Perhaps Ti-Jo heard the word *architect* without knowing what it meant, but he, at least, has an idea of what he wants to do.

It's difficult these days to predict one's children's future. Before, even if parents weren't educated and didn't expect much from school, they could choose for their children: this one will become this, that one will go there. Now the teachers say no. It's up to the child to know what he wants to do, up to us teachers to decide his future occupation. The teachers side with the children, say they'll help them. They can also lead them into all sorts of stupid blunders. All a child has to do is stand up to a teacher, be insolent, for the teacher to block his way and prevent him from continuing his studies. The child might be capable, but the teacher doesn't like him, and so trips him up. Those people who work in the schools are paid to do their jobs; they don't have the right to control everything in the family, present and future.

Many teachers don't agree either. They understand that things can't stay the way they are, students and teachers in a school that doesn't function well. They'd like the parents, students, and teachers to work together. Are they looking for a way to change what isn't right with the schools? Whenever there's need for a demonstration, they call on the parents. I've often taken part: for better food in the cafeteria, for scholarships. . . . In that latter case, I didn't totally agree. When it concerns a request for money, we must be very *véyatifs* (vigilant) and think carefully before getting involved.

At the C.E.T.[76] in Lamentin, the third term was already well underway but the scholarships for the first term hadn't yet been paid. The students themselves decided to go and demand their money. They asked their parents to support them. I went along. Afterward I decided: I won't go again. The scholarships help parents pay for the children's transportation, buy a few books—just barely though, because they aren't large. So if you have to fight for the small sum of money the government owes you, they might as well keep it. If they award a scholarship, they should pay it out on time. They can't pretend to be generous and then hold me tightly around the neck and force me to come crying to get what's owed me. Maybe I react badly, with too much pride. If the youngsters want to fight for their scholarships, to go on strike, let them. But I won't go running after the government's money again.

Another time, the parents were called together by the C.E.T. We wondered why they needed us. Several teachers waited at the gate. They escorted us across the courtyard. As we advanced, a horrible smell grew increasingly stronger. We neared the toilets. That's what they wanted to show us: the water had been shut off ages before. The children lived in unsanitary conditions, couldn't even use the toilets anymore. We formed a group and marched in the streets yelling: "Turn on the water! Turn on the water at the C.E.T.!"

We went down to Pointe-à-Pitre, to the office of the vice-rector.

The parents were called on soon again for another problem. One of the professors was sick. He had assembled his students in the courtyard around a drum and made them play the *gwoka*. I'm partial to the *gwoka*, and maybe he invented a new activity for his students. But he was known to be somewhat sick in the head. It frightened everyone. In addition, he'd disappear for three months at a stretch and then terrorize colleagues and students when he reappeared. The vice-rector didn't care. At a meeting, we discussed his case. Everyone present signed a petition. It wasn't a question of asking that the teacher be thrown out, but rather that he be given a pension or a position in an office without students to teach. We were all supposed to bring the petition to the vice-rector. Only a few parents turned up in Pointe-à-Pitre. Even though the problem didn't directly concern my children, I was there for support. Three parents were received. They left empty-handed: no way to do this, no way to do that. I lost interest in the affair and don't know how it ended.

One thing is certain. If we want to win, we must band together. Teachers alone, parents alone can't do anything. Teachers, parents, students all united can exert pressure on the vice-rector. Unfortunately, many parents don't want to get involved, don't even like it when the others take action. Especially if the local of the S.G.E.G. union leads the way. "Look at them, listen to them, I don't like that kind of person. Teachers speaking in Creole! What do they take us for? Animals? I don't even talk Creole to my goats!"

At the parents' meetings, Creole disturbs people. Even if you say something worthwhile, as long as you express yourself in Creole someone will grumble and others will dismiss your ideas. Words must flow well in French to be considered important.

Nowadays, people dare to criticize the teachers openly. They aren't the all-powerful lords they once were. To be sure, there are more of them, and they aren't from the same stock. Sons and daughters of farmworkers, of fishermen have become teachers. They act refined, think they're someone important, but for their village neighbors, they still haven't become "sir" or "madame." We knew them as children, saw them grow up in poverty. They remain *"pitit à Man Bayadin"* (*Man Bayadin's* little one) or *"Man* Grégwa's." If, when newly promoted, they put on airs, act superior, they're in for it.

"Look at little Myriam, now that she's a teacher, she won't give us the time of day. She has forgotten where she came from, forgotten that she had to run to the end of the garden when she wanted to go to the toilet. She doesn't have time to talk to anyone, not even to say hello. Little snob!"

All mothers take pride in seeing their children clean, well behaved, taking the right path, succeeding. From early on, you can discern good stock. A child who starts off well begins to take an interest in his body and comes on his own to ask for help in washing and dressing. Later, when he's old enough to go to school, he's involved in learning. He begins to read, to learn proper behavior. He greets people in the street. That's a child a mother won't have to hold in a vice, dictate to: "Go get washed, take your book, get ready, it's time for school. . . . " "Look at *Man* so-and-so's daughter. She's already up and about, has put out the plates, is washing the dishes and hurrying off to school."

This kind of discussion doesn't happen anymore.

What I hear at home is rather: "I'm not the girl next door, Mamma, I'm Emilienne."

It would have been unheard of for me to answer my mother: "I'm not the girl next door," when she gave me a similar example. Mouth clamped shut and off to work. How many children were scolded because they didn't get up early enough to wash the dishes, sweep the house, or hang up the washing before leaving for school! They weren't any less lazy than children nowadays, parents simply didn't discuss things. Now parents ask themselves questions about their children: What's in his heart? Why is he listless? Is he comfortable with himself? Parents didn't used to bother about their children's indisposition.

Besides, children weren't often sick—under-the-weather occasionally, but not sick. On condition, of course, that you followed the advice of your mother, avoided going directly from hot to cold, didn't eat genip or custard apples when you were overheated from running, didn't lean against a cold wall when you were sweaty, etc. From your earliest years, you were taught these precautions, knew you mustn't treat your body stupidly and should avoid *blesses*.[77] Plant extracts helped maintain health: *sémèncontra* tea, purslane for worms, citronella to aid digestion, custard apple to help you sleep, country brew for the liver, couch grass to revive you before a purge. . . . Flu? Fever? A good hot drink made from *paroka* and *fleurs de sonnettes* and your cough would be gone.

These herbal cures worked for us. I've kept up the custom: each eve-

Leonora: The Buried Story of Guadeloupe

ning at home I prepare an herbal tea. My granddaughter, who came from Paris to spend her vacation with me, mentioned it to her mother: "Why don't you make tea in the evening the way Granny Joseph does? It helps me sleep."

People change, customs evolve, but for all Guadeloupeans, from the richest to the poorest, taking care of their bodies remains important.

For me, reason number one is that cleanliness protects children against sickness. A clean skin won't let infections in. In the housing project where I live, each house has a shower. I have an ongoing battle royal with Ti-Jo to get him to wash. A child can't go to school, play, run, then come home all sweaty and go to bed without washing. Even a boy. Ti-Jo goes into the shower, turns on the faucet, and comes back out with his feet totally dry. He hasn't washed. How can he have so many faults? The boys don't always wash their *kòk* or their behinds, but not even to wash their feet before going to bed? Pigs!

Neither of the two plantations on which I lived before coming here had showers, washcloths, or facilities for keeping yourself clean. My mother advised me: "Rub hibiscus flowers under your arms, squeeze them well to press out the juice, and rub your private parts."

Teeth gleamed when rubbed with *agoman* leaves. Those without a tub—a tub like the large, wooden half barrel we bathed in—crushed leaves in a large *koui* (half gourd). You'd stand on a rock or board, rub yourself, then pour water over your body. In the evening, before going to bed, you'd sprinkle your legs and feet. We went to the river when we wanted a good bath. In any case, children who fetched water at the spring came back thoroughly soaked after playing around in the water.

To keep away bad sweats, illness, your skin must always be spick-and-span and so must all your body's orifices. Each mother kept her children clean. In the morning, when they awoke, she'd wash their faces and hands by scooping up water from a barrel in front of the house with an empty condensed-milk can. If she had to leave for work too early, the oldest sister would wash the little ones before going off to school, remove the peepee-soaked diapers from the babies' beds. By the age of three, children had to know how to wash themselves and their underpants. It was up to you, the mother, to undertake the serious evening cleaning, check that all their orifices were clean—nose, ears, private parts, behind. When the little boys began to feel more grown up, some of them didn't want to be checked by their mothers. They took advantage and stopped washing altogether.

I don't understand why we expect girls to keep themselves cleaner than boys. Is it because our sexual organs open into our bodies, whereas the boys don't have any problems if they don't wash?

Leading the cobra to school is not enough

When my grandchildren visit me, I keep a close eye on their washing habits, boys as well as girls. "Have you washed your feet?" is heard every evening in all the houses. And in the morning, you wash your face, comb your hair, change the panties you slept in.

As a child, I didn't wear panties at night, but a few years ago I adopted the custom. I wonder if children in France sleep with underpants on. My son who lives in France married a white woman. When his children come here on vacation, they sleep with me in my bed. I asked the girl: "Why don't you wear panties when you sleep?"

"Mamma told me not to."

"Here, little girls don't sleep without panties," my daughter Viviane told her.

When she returned to France, the first thing she said was: "Mamma, Grandma and Auntie told me to sleep with panties on."

My daughter-in-law must have her hands full with her now. I don't know where this custom came from nor why I adopted it, but now I'm hooked. I'm more comfortable, don't feel naked. And yet women have problems when they sleep with panties on. It's a fight with the gentleman who wants to rip them off. I'm not in favor of nightly battles, but no question of giving up my panties.

Our mothers didn't wear any underpants at all. They had long, full dresses, and I remember seeing my mother lift up one side of her dress, wrap it around her and crouch down to pee behind the kitchen. Later on, as things changed, they must have started wearing underpants. But who knows when. Or why.

Apparently, wearing underpants keeps children from playing with themselves at night. As if that made any difference! With or without underpants, they do what they want. I see some mothers smack their children for doing that! You should love, care for, and discover your own body. My mother never said to me: "Don't touch your private parts." We were brought up together, girls and boys. We used to go to the river together, without thinking much about this sex business.

Some children touch their weewee, others suck their thumbs, still others do both at once. A kid who sucks one thumb and holds his weewee tightly in the other hand gets a good feeling from it. There's nothing wrong with that. But once he starts school, he can't continue, it mustn't become a habit that he can't break.

Ti-Jo sucked his tongue and his finger. I managed to get him to give up the finger, but I regret it. He continues more than ever with his tongue. You should see the scene at night in his bed! A tongue—long as this—outside his mouth, his hand twisting a cloth. Because he needs a cloth. For others it's a pillow, a corner of a blanket to rub against their noses. . . . Take it away from them, and they can't fall asleep.

I did my best with my children, tried to get them to abandon these kinds of habits without hitting them. You can't hit a baby, it might be left *tèbè*, handicapped for life. With little children, you must restrain your arm and slap your mouth twice before speaking. In a film on TV, a father kept repeating to his son: "Don't go near women, don't go near them, don't talk to them." When the son grew up and met women, nothing happened, zero. Finally he murdered that father who prevented him from learning how to love, who condemned him to a living hell.

Today, you hear everywhere that if things don't work properly in a child's mind, if he gets into trouble, it's the parents' fault, its society's fault. Society, society, that word is on everyone's tongue, but it means something different from what it used to.

"Behave properly in society," my mother would tell me, "you can't wear that dress when you're going into society."

For us, society was a gathering for a wedding, a baptism, a party for a group of coworkers. We went into society to meet people, have fun. Nowadays, society, like Evil, has a broad back upon which we heap many things. A nasty business, a sordid affair? It's society's fault; society has made people act like that. Is everything that happens society's fault? Does it control your mind, guide your hand when you act? A young man convicted of theft explained that the porno books caused him to steal! But just because porno books are now sold in Guadeloupe doesn't mean you should steal, should do whatever you want!

For me society means people. All sorts of societies exist. The most important, the strongest, is the one that wants to clothe you in a suit it has tailored for itself. That's the one that organizes everything, with its mayors, representatives, police, school. We must try to understand how that one works. Ever since the "dissidence," the time when Guadeloupeans went to join General de Gaulle, we've heard about that society.

People say we have new problems in life, problems unknown to our ancestors. But atrocities, violent acts, especially toward children, have always existed.

Today, when I take my kids home to my family in Carangaise, for a "change of scene," they want to be treated like little princes and princesses. "Look at that, won't you! They don't even want to fetch a bucket of water, the hills frighten them!"

"But they aren't used to it, they don't know how."

In fact they do want to run about the hills, but aren't capable of carrying water back. And, also, times have changed, my children will never work as hard as I did. Yet some are still forced to slave away all the time. It depends on the family's attitude. I can't stand seeing children treated so badly! Children tire too! Just because they should help their parents, learn to work, doesn't mean parents should take advantage of them. On your right side you hear: "That child is already a woman, she must work," and on your left: "She hangs around too much in the streets, spends all her time with her friends, she must be kept home, working."

One of my neighbors treats her children that way; they must work, work, work all the time. I said to her: "Let them take a break, the stricter you are with them, the tougher they'll become, and their hearts will harden against you."

Mark also remarked to me: "She exploits her children."

I don't totally agree with that word: *exploit*. Capitalists exploit, not parents. It's too strong a word for me, a word currently in fashion. Even if it means "profit from," like our Creole word *profitasyon*, it doesn't apply within a family. I'd say rather: "That's not the way to treat a child." But "exploit?" No! Mothers will always tell you that a child must learn to do things, help around the house. If he's lazy, she'll fight against it, pull the cord tighter, but that's still not exploitation.

A mother's authority is part of normal life. The relationship between a mother and her child is not that of "capitalist exploitation." Some children never see by themselves what has to be done; they must be told everything. Others do their chores naturally, following the example of their young friends. Still others can only work in a group. You may even find children who willingly wash dishes for a neighbor, run errands for her, go up and down all the blessed day for her. But the moment they walk in the door at home, they pull a long face if their mother asks for help. On top of all that, you'll be criticized: you brought them up badly, it's your fault, you're handling it the wrong way. . . . Perhaps. But I think that when a child doesn't want to do anything, never wants to help at home, resistance is already part of his nature. It's a question of outlook.

Generally, things go well with the first one, who doesn't grumble if asked to help out. When it's the last one's turn, he refuses to pitch in. Yet everything is well organized: before leaving each morning, I know what I have to accomplish and I do it. It's the same for a child: he knows that before going to school he must wash the dishes. He gets up, washes the dishes, no problem. Oh yes! But with José, the youngest, it's a devil of a job. He knows, but still doesn't do it. What a cross to bear when you have a child like that! I'm not the only one in this situation. Yesterday as I left a meeting, I complained: "You wouldn't find it funny, ladies and gentlemen, if you saw what my sons' rooms look like: as if hit by a cyclone. I've been battling with them ever since I moved to this housing project. Zero, I'm talking to a blank wall!"

"At least, Leonora, yours are boys and are still young. You should see the room of my three big girls! The bed never made, dirty clothes dumped on the floor, issues of *O.K.* and *Girl*[78] all around. And if you think they give me any help, think again!"

This woman isn't strict with her children, doesn't "exploit" them. She's not the type to sit in a chair and order everyone about, ruling with an iron hand: "You! Get me a glass of water, I'm thirsty. You! Gather me some mangos, I have a craving for mangos."

My little José doesn't want to understand any language. When I get tired of seeing his room all topsy-turvy, I straighten it up a bit. But on leaving the room, I get an asthma attack. I prefer to close his door and not look at the mess. Even his bed: from afar you think it's been made, the bedspread pulled flat. But lift up a corner and you find the sheets all wrinkled, not even shaken out.

As for my other son's room, "the grand gentleman," you can't even find a place to put down your foot. Books, newspapers scattered everywhere. And don't you dare touch a thing!

The children are always out somewhere or other. I have a television: José never watches with us. It's as if he's all alone when he's with the family, with his brothers and sisters, who are, it's true, much older than he is. He prefers to meet his friends and watch TV with the other kids. Every evening he goes out, and I've had to give him a curfew for returning. But it's discouraging to own a TV and still need to wait up for your son till 11 P.M. because he's out watching a movie at someone else's house. That's late for a young boy. I would never have let my daughter do that when she was his age. Oh no! But perhaps I wouldn't have been able to prevent her. When my TV was broken, Viviane would say: "Mamma, I'm going over to *Man* Bigaro's."

My husband, Joseph, forbade her to go, but I allowed it. Up to a certain age you can forbid things, but when a girl reaches nineteen, you can't stop her from going to watch TV two houses away. That wouldn't work; it means you don't trust her. I'm not like that. I was raised in openness and truthfulness. I will not become suspicious of my daughter! With José it's different. He simply informs me: "I'm going over to Remi's house."

Remi is his school friend so I shouldn't have a problem with it. But it's his tone of voice. He's always so harsh with me. He seems to be constantly in a fighting mood. I try speaking with him, but he only tosses his head as if to say "keep on talking," implying I've already said too much. I find it very hard to take. I tell myself, and let him know too, that of all my children, he's the only one who's so rebellious. He stiffens up and doesn't want to listen.

Mark divvied up the household chores between Viviane and José. José has dishwashing detail on certain days. He does it, but never a thing more. If I ask him for help with any other small job: "I have the dishes today, that's my job, you assigned it to me, nothing else." So when I really need him for another chore, I end up with the dishes! He's tough, that kid, really tough.

When Viviane's schedule changed, we had to reassign dishwashing duties. Tuesday is Ti-Jo's day. I go and iron at my daughter Lucie's house. If I return before José, I don't think about the schedule, I do the dishes. To tell the truth, I prefer it that way, they're cleaner. Since he must contribute to the chores at home, he has his turn with the dishes, but I'm rather ashamed of my plates and *canaris*. He washes, but don't count on him to scour or polish them. Zip! A little wipe with the detergent, but when you've cooked red beans, they stick and the pan must be scrubbed. . . . And you should be able to see yourself reflected in the shining bottoms of my *canaris!* From time to time, Viviane can't do the dishes on her day and makes a trade with José. But he doesn't always stick to the arrangement, and the dishes end up falling to me.

What problems in a household! You must know how to paddle your boat on the waters of life.

10

Mayé? On ralé mizè, on bari boutèy krazé

Marriage? A truckful of

misfortune, a barrel full of broken glass

It's not when a man comes courting you at mamma-papa's nor once you're a woman and he's running after you, trying to seduce you, that you can tell who he is, what kind of person you're dealing with. He only reveals his true self when you live together.

After Joseph and I had lived together for several years, he wasn't the same man. *Sa té ka siri,* it turned sour. That's why, when he married me after our sixth child, I wasn't particularly keen on the idea. Your love changes according to what you find in front of you. No one will ever convince me that love doesn't fade. Anyone who suggests the opposite is perfect, like the Good Lord. Occasionally, after having dimmed, love may shine brightly again. For that to happen, loathing can't have taken its place, the way it did with me. My husband so misused, so totally disgusted me, that love between us is no longer possible.

Marriage! What a hopeless mess! A barrel full of broken glass in which the wife is trapped and injures herself at every turn, a masked ball that sometimes ends in tragedy.

There you are, the wife, accepting everything, submitting, and nothing improves. One day you feel you're living in a house with a man, and there's nothing more between you. You have children, you're there to take care of them, cook, clean, and let yourself be mounted when he, the man, gets the urge. That has nothing to do with love. To love is to desire, to accept one another, to talk together, to discuss problems naturally when they arise, without fear. Who can show me where it's written that a man can have several wives? The law gives him only one. In Guadeloupe, since there are more women than men, a man doesn't hold back from having up to five women! It suits him. In any case, married or living together, a man should respect the woman who keeps his home. But, on the contrary, the more women he has outside, the more he harasses you.

All this leads to trouble in the family. Some people say that it's different with white people, that things don't happen the way they do in the households of blacks. That's stupid. They don't think, they say whatever comes into their heads. At Prise-d'Eau I saw a white man beat his

Marriage? A truckful of misfortune, a barrel full of broken glass

white wife. So why always say that the whites are like this, the blacks like that? Always the blacks, the blacks, the blacks . . . the blacks aren't the worst. If you look carefully, all groups of men argue and fight. It's not a question of race. White or black, a man is a man, and each man has his own particular way of behaving. Not really behaving, rather a way of living. Some have a way of living freely, others eat themselves up inside. I've known women who have been killed at home. They accept everything, never share their pain. After a beating in the evening, they show you their bruises the following morning and say: "I fell down." Why all the secrecy?

I wouldn't act that way! I don't shout everything in the market-place—some things must be kept to oneself, they could come back to you later—but in general, when there were problems at home, the following morning I opened my mouth wide and told it loud and clear.

Yes, it's true, I do like talking. Why would I hide my husband's abominations if I'd be the first to let everyone know when he gave me an armoire?

One day I said to him: "If I were treating you badly, I could say we made each other equally miserable, that it's only fair. But I'm here to love you, and what do you give me in return? You wrong me, try to humiliate me. Oh yes! When we're in company, when your friends are around or your family, it's my wife this and my wife that, no man has a better wife than you. Well, I don't want you to praise me in front of other people only to tear me apart as soon as they leave."

I can't stand hypocrites. I say what I mean. I'm a free woman who cherishes her freedom, and no one will keep me from being free. For me it's a question of honor.

In our arguments, I resisted. Joseph fumed. Must a wife endure everything, accept it all without fighting back? That's how men "devour" women. They consume your will, your pride, turn you into a baby. Then they're happy, they're the masters.

Of course, not all men bring disorder into their marriages, and they shouldn't shoulder all the blame without some resting on us women. Yet more often than not, the source of trouble is the man who has another woman. Every wife loves her husband. If he takes another woman, she can't accept it. When, unfortunately, she's not able to control herself and, in her shame, can't open up to anyone, her pain is even greater. And all the words flying about that she must listen to!

"I saw your husband yesterday evening with Armandia. . . . "

"Oh, poor dear! As I was on my way to work early this morning, before sunrise, your husband was coming out of Suzelle's house. . . . "

"Near the mango tree, in the bottomland, Joseph was on top of Fernande, they weren't bored. . . . "

You love your husband, your heart aches. The worm has entered the hog plum and will continue enlarging its hole.

Before reacting, you must make sure not to create a scandal as soon as a so-called friend comes to tell you your husband has a mistress. You suffer already, the money the man brings home is meager, you have trouble running the house on it, so it's in your best interest to keep your mouth shut and not look for trouble. And no question of talking it over. So, when you can't bear it any longer, when he comes back from a game of dice or dominos or from the woman, you greet him with those words that all wives say:

La ou sòti la, sé voyé yo voyé ou ban mwen.	"Where you've come from they don't want you anymore so they've sent you back knocking on my door.

Men can't stand this little jingle. The "Where you've come from" suffices to bring on the storm, to start the rod ringing and the tin roof singing.

Some women return blow for blow: you take a woman, I'll take a man. And the more men she has on the side, the more she spoils the one at home, with caresses, special dishes, and this, and that. But at a certain moment, the husband opens his eyes. Some men, when they discover that their wives have made a cuckold of them, take steps to get out of this *manjé-kochòn*. Others call their wives dirty bitch, *bòbò*, and yet don't hate her and simply go along with the situation. There are all sorts of men.

I don't agree with these women. I'd be stifled, feel tied up by this kind of life. If a man has a mistress he doesn't want to give up, then let the couple separate. Once apart, if my heart desired, I could seek out a companion. But while he's leading this filthy life, do the same thing? No. And how about the respect due my children? Even if I managed to hide from them, they'd learn about it one day. In a village, tongues clack away, and ears stand as wide open as trumpets, listening. Even today, my husband speaks of me with respect: "I'm sure my wife didn't have other men, that no one climbed on top of her after me."

There, you see, a man can have fifty women, steal them from other men, and never allow his wife to do likewise. He'd feel degraded, dishonored. He's the one who breaks up the marriage, sleeps around, and he's also the one who gets annoyed if his wife has another man. Even when he lives elsewhere and after many years of separation, he can't stand hearing: "*X*'s wife is living with *Y*." When he marries you, he believes he has purchased you, *mofouazé* (metamorphosed) you into part of himself. You're no longer yourself. In fact, it's not him you've dishonored but his name.

"My name is dragged through the streets and the back roads. Madame so-and-so is with Monsieur what's-his-name. I, Monsieur so-and-so am here. What will people say about the so-and-so family?"

And they continue reeling off the entire family tree. The honor of one's name leads married men to divorce their wives for the smallest trespass, to remove their name from the woman, particularly to prevent any male child from carrying it.

Personally, I agree with those women who register under their maiden name a child they've had with a man other than their husband. One of my nieces by marriage had a falling out with her husband. They split up. She wasn't yet divorced when she had a child. She gave it her own name. At the mayor's office she was asked the reason: "I'm afraid of the man," she answered, "that's why I don't give the child his name."

Yes, there are also women who can't see a pair of trousers without wanting to jump into them. They often justify their actions by complaining of their husband's inadequacy. True? Not true? I can't say. I know one, it's not her husband who can't do it, he's more than able, but she doesn't want him and goes elsewhere. Is her blood too hot? Does she desire one and not another? These affairs are complicated and full of nooks and crannies. I haven't been through it, can't really speak from experience. Especially since those involved don't usually go into any great detail. Only one thing is clear: that woman is hot, hot as a little rabbit. . . .

On the other hand, there are women who swear: "Once I'm married, I'm married."

Me, for example. I always said to Joseph: "I respect myself, I respect my children. It's not because of you that I don't go running around. I could have done whatever I liked with my body. I'm not less of a woman than another, but I love my body."

I don't know much, but somehow feel that a woman should love herself, respect herself; it's a question of honor. She shouldn't sell her body to obtain beautiful objects or money. As we say here, "sell her flesh." A real market of bodies. Those women sell their flesh because their husbands can't give them everything they desire. They sell themselves to buy cars, furniture, clothes, idiocies. . . . In this society, you must be strong to avoid giving in to envy. What temptation when you go to Pointe-à-Pitre and see so many things you need. A new refrigerator, for example, to replace your old one that's always breaking down.

Leonora: The Buried Story of Guadeloupe

One of my friends told me a sad story about her daughter. For a long time, a guy had been running after her, promising mountains and marvels, heaven and earth. She didn't love the man, nor did she wish to sleep with him. She fell on hard times and ended up in dire straits. This fellow, who'd secretly continued to follow her, again made his proposition. She relented to get out of her predicament, thinking: "After all the time he has pursued me, he'll certainly give me 'a nice little something.'" What a nasty surprise when, after having had his way, the guy didn't give her a cent. He said: "We've had our pleasure, my beauty, isn't that what we both needed?"

The poor girl, how she cried! And regretted having given in to him.

Men can't be trusted very far, especially if it concerns money. And when, in addition, the relationship between you and the fellow starts sinking as fast as an old barge with a pierced bottom, things are kept hidden, secret, unfinished. You don't know everything, and even if you did, you couldn't interfere or say anything. Had Joseph been more open with me, he would have said: "Let's see, Leonora, how are we going to make ends meet? I earn this much, let's put that much of it aside for hard times, for a death. . . . "

But, when a man has other women on the side, frankness can't exist because, of course, he must sneak around, organize a whole mafia to work it out.

"I bring you all my pay, but you'll never know what I do to earn extra money so I can support my mistresses."

Living well is having a husband who comes home regularly. He's not obliged to make love to you every night, but the world can see that he sleeps at your place. He can go out on Saturday, to the pit to watch a cockfight, to a dance or a *léwoz,* for a game of dominos, it doesn't matter. One night he might even forget to return home, as long as he tells you about it, explains: "Leonora, I didn't make it home last night, I was with friends in Boucan. We didn't realize how late it was, we found ourselves caught. . . . "

Caught up barhopping, perhaps. Men have the right to a good time. But trust is what's important.

Kat zyé kontré, manti fini.   Lies have no place to hide when
                                        eyes meet.

The man works, brings home his pay, hands over the government family allowance and, when a problem arises, you talk it over and decide together. For instance, the start of the school year is approaching,

Marriage? A truckful of misfortune, a barrel full of broken glass

you sit down to calculate: How can we manage to send all the children to school?

If the wife is ill, the man takes her to the doctor, cares for her as if she were a baby. If it's the man, the entire household is turned on end, with the continuous comings and goings, upstairs and down. Wife, children, all are on call. The husband is the one who brings home the bread, he must be gotten back on his feet so he can return to work. In my family, the women were always around to care for their men, but Joseph was a difficult patient. My sister Lélina's husband—now that's a man you could nurse back to health. He knew how to care for his body, didn't drink things that disagreed with him, and swallowed without a fuss the remedies his wife prepared.

When your husband comes home from work, you're waiting to welcome him. You've prepared his herbal bath, left a basin of water warming all day in the sun. You've crushed into it hibiscus, custard-apple leaves, sandalwood that smells so fragrant. You might add salt, several drops of alkali. I never put any "come-hither," "love water," or "mistress of men" lotion in Joseph's baths. Some people call herbal baths "witches' baths." I consider them simply relaxing baths. Preparing them for your husband is a way of showing your love for him.

Another demonstration of love is your considerate treatment of his family when they come to visit. And he does the same with yours.

Those are the kinds of things that to me represent a family life with love. As long as a husband and wife talk, the household can run, even if the man cultivates another flower elsewhere.

I lived years of harmony, pleasure, and happiness. But one day my eyes and Joseph's no longer met. Not only did he have other women, but also friends who watched our marriage grow and urged him to destroy it. They'd never known this life of love and understanding. They were envious. Those with shaky relationships, *é ni on latilyé,* are numerous, they outnumber those who tow the line, and they're only content when they succeed in breaking up, smashing to bits, the marriages of others. They begin by saying to the husband: "Your wife is a strong woman, she knows how to run her household . . . and her husband. It's clear who gives orders, who holds the reins."

They try to make fun of him: "We're going out this evening. Ask your wife for permission to join us. If you're afraid, I'll go in your place."

That's what Joseph's "good friends" did to him. Result? With his pride sharply stung, he threatened me: "My friends say you rule over me, watch out!"

From then on, all he did was enter and leave the house. No more discussions, no more chats. More serious still, he began going out on weekday evenings, not returning home till the following morning.

Spending his nights elsewhere! I don't know how other women handle it, but I wasn't prepared for such a thing. Even my father, a hard and authoritarian man, never insulted my mother that way: spending the night under another roof, away from his family.

Joseph always had other women, his affairs were like a knife cutting through water, passing unnoticed. We had a home together, slept together. From time to time, he'd slip away, telling me he was going to a wake or a wedding. He might not return till morning, perhaps having slept with a woman, but he didn't really spend his nights away from home.

When I was so sick, Joseph hired a woman to stay with me, do the washing, ironing, and take care of the whole house. Rumor had it she was sleeping with Joseph. I didn't believe it. That young woman was married. Then her husband died. Her house became empty, and Joseph jumped at the chance to go and spend his nights there. I was forced to open my eyes to the truth.

"You brought someone into our house, saying it was to help me, to handle the household chores, and I find you're together with that person!"

"If you wish, she won't come anymore." That's all he found to answer me.

In our neighborhood, tongues had been wagging for a long time: we two women were *konbòch*,[79] we shared Joseph, and people chanted:

Artémiz é misyé Jozèf, zafè a yo   Between Artémise and Joseph
    ka maché rèd, rèd.   things are tight, tight, tight.

I was perhaps the only person who hadn't gotten it into my head. I kept telling myself: "Those nasty minds, those gossips see that I get along well with Artémise, that Joseph took her out of the cane fields and pays her for helping me, they're jealous."

Then Joseph left me alone at night. I was really *dékalé*, thrown off-balance, I lost what was supporting me in my suffering. How hard-hearted men are! Luckily, they seem to die younger than women do. They give us a taste and then go off, leaving us behind in fine form. The way Joseph was heading led only to separation from him or death. To be young and feel one's body dying, what terrible pain!

He'd return in the early morning, often drunk. I found him repulsive and, just at those times, he wanted to make love. My whole body revolted, closed up. Should an unfortunate woman like me, who had already borne so many children, have to accept a man in that state, live

Marriage? A truckful of misfortune, a barrel full of broken glass

in such a situation? No and no again. From time to time, I was obliged to go through with it. I didn't derive any pleasure from the act. There was no love between us any longer; worse yet, it was like a murderous parody of love.

I tried to distract him, offering a thousand little excuses: "Joseph, I must be up before dawn tomorrow. . . . I'm tired. . . . " And I don't know what else. No sooner had I opened my mouth, than I found myself on the floor, kicked out of bed. When I refused him like that, Joseph would sometimes go off again, dead drunk, to that young woman's house.

I tried to stay calm with her, not look for any trouble. I threw out several snide remarks, innuendoes, for her to wear if the shoe fit.

"Oh these women, like double-edged swords, who cajole you on the one hand and then stab you in the back by taking your husband. . . . "

She never answered me back or did anything to anger or vex me. Joseph was the one I was angry with.

I'm hot-blooded. When worked up, I'm capable of hurling baskets full of stunning curses. I don't hold myself back. I couldn't greet Joseph with a rod, so I beat him with my words. To no avail. Joseph is a calm man, not like me at all. He refused to discuss the matter, didn't admit his guilt, made no effort at reconciliation . . . and went off the next evening to spend the night with that wretched woman of his. The more he slept away from home, the greater my anger, the louder my shrieks. One of my friends advised me: "No, Leonora, try to keep calm. When he comes home, don't say a word to him, don't concern yourself with him. Serve him his coffee, have his clean clothes ready."

I couldn't do it, I really couldn't, even to try to get him back. I was also advised: "It's because of a tea Artémise gave him to drink. Surely she's wearing come-hither lotion. You must go for a consultation if you want your man back."

I don't believe in these *yo yo di,* nor in the song *Anmann* sang: "You've stolen my husband; you'll give him back thanks to ten cents worth of precipitate . . .

"Adalisya ban mari an mwen	"Adalisya, give back my husband
An ké pwan pannyé kobèy an mwen	I'll take my basket
Adalisya	Adalisya
An ké désann Bémaho	I'll go to Baie-Mahault
Adalisya	Adalisya
An ké alé aka an gadèdzafè	I'll visit a *gadèdzafè*
Adalisya	Adalisya
An ké alé aka an man Rovélas	I'll go see *Man* Rovélas

Leonora: The Buried Story of Guadeloupe

Adalisya	Adalisya
An ka di-ou, ou ké ban mari an mwen	I'm telling you, you'll give back my husband
Adalisya	Adalisya
Man Rovélas gadé pou mwen	*Man* Rovélas looked into my problem
Adalisya	Adalisya
Mwen sòti aka man Rovélas	I left *Man* Rovélas
Adalisya	Adalisya
Mwen pwan chimen Dèstélan	I took the road to Destréllan
Adalisya	Adalisya
Mwen désann an vil Pouentapit	I went down to Pointe-à-Pitre
Adalisya	Adalisya
Mwen antré adan on kenkalri	I entered a hardware store
Adalisya	Adalisya
Mwen achté on kannari	I bought a *canari*
Adalisya	Adalisya
Mwen alé adan on boutik grési	I went into a grocery store
Adalisya	Adalisya
Mwen gannyé toua chandèl pou dé sou	I bought three candles for ten cents
Adalisya	Adalisya
Mwen mété tousa an kannari la	I put them all in my *canari*
Adalisya	Adalisya
Mwen alé adan yo fòrmasi	I went into a pharmacy
Adalisya	Adalisya
An gannyé kat sou présipité	I bought ten cents worth of precipitate
Adalisya	Adalisya
Mwen gannyé kat sou menné-vini	I bought twenty cents worth of *menné-vini* lotion
Adalisya	Adalisya
An mété tous an kannari la	I put it all in my *canari*
Adalisya	Adalisya
Mwen alé anba plas maché	I went to the market square
Adalisya	Adalisya
Mwen achté on baton lélé	I bought a *lélé* stick[80]
Adalisya	Adalisya
Mwen désann akaz an mwen	I went back home
Adalisya	Adalisya
An pwan baton lélé an mwen	I took my *lélé* stick
Adalisya	Adalisya

Marriage? A truckful of misfortune, a barrel full of broken glass

Mwen mété mwen a lélé kannari la	I stirred the mixture in the *canari*
Adalisya	Adalisya
Mwen ka antann 'bim, bim, bim!'	I heard 'Boum, boum, boum!'
Adalisya	Adalisya
Mari an ka pilé Adalisya	My husband was beating Adalisya
Adalisya	Adalisya
An ka tann 'anmwé! Alasasen!'	I heard 'Help! Murder!'
Adalisya	Adalisya
An ka di-ou, ou ké ban mari an mwen	I'm telling you, you'll give back my husband
Adalisya	Adalisya
Obou toua jou mari an mwen vini	Three days later my husband returned
Adalisya"	Adalisya"

As soon as a man starts neglecting his own family to spend time regularly with another woman, sorcery gets the blame: "He can't free himself. That woman has bound him, *magoté* in a big cucumber."

Of course there are women who know how to catch a man and hold on to him in their own way. They make love with him as you'd never do. Your guy finds himself caught by her. The feelings of these man-thieves for your husband are totally different from yours. She sleeps with him in all sorts of positions, at any hour of the day, even at noon! Always ready. You have your children, you're always busy with housework. Only in the evening, despite your weariness, are you available, but then he simply takes you on the fly when the desire seizes him.

He spends his nights elsewhere, while you're there, at home, crying into your pillow at night, then listening to his grumblings in the morning when his coffee isn't hot and waiting for him. After days and years of this, love dies and disgust takes its place.

At a certain point, at my wits' end, I thought about packing my bags, leaving, finding a place where I could live. But where? With a relative? Even if she receives you cordially, does all she can to put you at ease and make you feel at home, a day comes when you say to yourself: "I must leave."

Abandoned, adrift, you could take refuge at your sister's house. You go and speak with her, confide in her, stay three, four days eating, drinking, sleeping, but move into her home permanently, no.

Before walking out, you must think carefully about it. You don't have a house or work, only a wagon-full of children. How could you pay rent on a cabin? With what would you buy bread, oil, rice? Take another man? After having endured so much, I didn't really have that in mind, not one little bit. Already, after my first experience, I didn't want to put myself under the authority of another man. Yet I did accept Joseph. If I freed myself from him, I wasn't going to take a third chance.

Today when I take a bitter look back over my life, I find I did the right thing by not giving in to that desire to leave. A departure must be well organized, something Joseph didn't know how to do when he left me. Because he was the one who finally left. Now I sense that he'd like to start again, but once disgust has taken love's place, no reconciliation is possible.

11

Pawòl a Jézikri vin fè kò èvè vi an mwen

The Gospel enters my life

As public prosecutor of the aforementioned island, I will demonstrate how it came to my knowledge, via public rumor, that
last Sunday, at about ten in the morning, in the Church of Saint-
Louis in the city of Basseterre, in the slaves' parish, during the
celebration of Mass, Father Marée, a Jesuit, took the pulpit and
preached. That having delivered his sermon on the Holy Cross,
he pronounced these words: "Let men revolt against God; let the
blacks revolt against the whites and thus avenge God; and let the
time be not far off." What I fear is that these ideas, enunciated
from the pulpit of truth by a religious leader in whom the slaves
have total confidence, and based on the holiest and most sacred
of religious passages, will inspire in these same slaves feelings of
revolt and treason against their masters.

Letter from the public prosecutor of
Guadeloupe to the judge of the island,
8 May 1733

In the past and, in fact, not so very long ago, when we went to Mass,
the priest was the only one to speak. Each of us came for his or her
own personal reasons: to ask Jesus of Nazareth to untie feet bound by
the power of an enemy, to give thanks for a blessing bestowed, or even
to invoke the aid of a particular saint in bringing misfortune to a
neighbor.

Things have been different since Father Céleste's arrival. Monsignor
Ually, the first black bishop of Guadeloupe, had reorganized the
country into districts. Why? Because of the shortage of priests. Baie-
Mahault had its priest, Lamentin too, but he left; and the one in Cadet
was sent to Sainte-Rose, a large township. When Father Céleste arrived, our district included Lamentin, the center, and also Baie-Mahault, Cadet, and the chapels at Grosse-Montagne and Castel.

Other districts had been planned all across Guadeloupe, but a district involves work. A map was laid out, and each district was asked
to prepare a report. The bishop dreamed of a kind of federation, but
it didn't work out. Only our district functioned. And how we were

maligned! From inside, as well as from without. The other priests didn't like us, not at all, and the only thing we ever got from His Eminence was an unspoken pledge not to criticize our work. Yet it was a source of strength for us.

So there was a shortage of priests. And soon it will be even worse: they age, retire, and no young people enter the church to replace them.

Céleste was the chaplain of a youth movement, the M.R.J.C. We'd already seen him at meetings in Lamentin and Grosse-Montagne. Father Céleste immediately chose to say Mass in the little chapel near the Grosse-Montagne factory. Perhaps because there are many young people in that area and perhaps also because a family particularly active in the church lived there.

Father Céleste astonished us right away: his way of saying Mass, of preaching—in French because, at that time, Creole hadn't yet entered the Church—was unlike anything we'd ever heard. On the way back, we talked it over: "We've been sent a prophet!"

We knew the words of the prophets and found these same words on his lips. People thought they were hearing Jesus Christ. He preached against malice, against revenge. His preaching wasn't theoretical like the other priests who reminded you: "Paul said this, Paul said that, wake up, it's an order, you must love God. . . . "

Agreed: you must love God, if that's your belief, I can't prevent you from believing. But how can you get me to love God if you command me to do so and don't provide any explanation? Céleste helped us relate to these questions of belief in a totally different way and you understood better. He taught us to share everything.

One Sunday at Mass, he told us how, at Anse-Bertrand, in a little remote corner of the country, he'd seen people who had nothing to eat. He asked if we could bring in green bananas, sweet potatoes, yams, anything at all that he could give to this family on Grande-Terre. Silence. When he saw that no one said a word, he began to cry. Seeing him cry like that made a strange impression on us. We'd never seen a priest speak so simply, cry in front of us. He was a man like us! Everything spun in our heads. We asked ourselves all sorts of questions. People really are willing to give, but they were surprised and hesitated, perhaps calculating: What will my husband say? Will I have to buy things? Father Céleste must have thought: not a single person in this whole crowd to offer even a few bananas! It hurt him deeply and he cried. That was how he started, pushing us into small acts, small acts of sharing.

Not long after his arrival in the parish, he asked if we were going to continue like that, with him coming, saying Mass, giving his sermon, and leaving. Do you find that good? Can't we do something else together? Those who would like to go further could gather by neighborhoods and study the Bible. If we didn't know the Bible, he said, we couldn't live with dignity.

We answered yes, but not everyone, only those who wanted to work, the most progressive. The group from Grosse-Montagne agreed first. But where could they meet? Not all could or would offer their homes. What problems!

One felt her home wasn't yet "decorated," not attractive enough and she couldn't bear to hear: "We met at so-and-so's house; there weren't even enough chairs. . . . "

Another made fun of that. Even if people called her house *tòl sanblé*, a pile of sheet metal, the important thing was to bring blessings on her household. So, she invited the group to her home three times, then had enough and disappeared.

"Come to my place," proposed another. But maybe she's angry with her neighbors and can't invite them. Yet a neighborhood meeting means a gathering of all the people who live near you, in the area. If we're always the same group, we don't progress. Occasionally, because of an old falling-out, someone didn't dare include a neighbor even though the person expected an invitation. And afterward she'd announce: "I wasn't invited." Instead of moving toward a reconciliation, they became even angrier with one another.

At our first meeting, we didn't have many problems. The Alexis family, "good people" from nearby who followed Father Céleste right from the start, immediately offered their home for anything and everything related to the church. Quite naturally, we met at their place.

Thirty of us, more or less. Céleste distributed pages of a text from the Gospel and questions. We had to understand the text in order to answer the questions. It was difficult, we had to work at it, and we weren't accustomed to using our brain cells that way. At first, two or three of us spoke out, the most fearless who, like me, had tongues that didn't trip too badly over the French. Especially Adele, daughter of the Alexis family: being a teacher, she was used to it.

Almost everything related to the Bible. Everyday things didn't come out then, as they do today. Each person brought her sheet of paper, each brought her Bible. We had to open the Bible, look through the Bible, search in the Bible, and many were content with that. They remained tied to their Bibles, immersed in them, and didn't want to move away from them. They said there was no need to worry, the answers to all questions were in the Good Book.

We soon found it difficult not to stray from the text if we wanted to study the reality of our country, to answer questions regarding our lives in Guadeloupe. Some passages in the Gospel don't touch on real life, but others lead you very far along. When someone shares problems about her children, another about herself, her husband, or her sister and we try to resolve them through Jesus Christ, the Gospel no longer remains simply a book, it takes on life, becomes part of life, part of our lives. We came for help, for support, and life gushed out of us, we made life spring forth.

Things weren't so clear for everyone when we started. We floundered about. Afterward, some people were trained as group leaders. The leader selected a text with questions, handed out the sheets. At the meeting, the leader had the text read and then asked the questions. Each one contributed her thoughts, said something whether she spoke clearly or not. Everyone had to participate. When it became too confused, the leader added her two-cents worth, but so did the others. The role of the group leader is to draw out ideas—green or ripe—and get the whole group involved. Occasionally, people came to watch, to listen, without really being part of the group. That's already the first step. After everyone had spoken and we'd made the rounds of the questions, we closed up shop and ended with songs or prayers that sprang from our souls.

Sometimes we had so much to discuss that we'd still be at it past midnight. And the meetings started at six o'clock!

Pawòl a Nèg pa ni bout.	Words of black people, words without end.

That's the truth!

At Sunday Mass, the spokesperson for each group summarized its work. Then everyone could speak. Some people went too far: they wouldn't come to the meetings but took advantage of the discussions, of all the issues raised in the neighborhood groups, to insult the group leaders or bring up, right in church itself, their own personal stories.

One day at church I intervened to stop a fight. A woman, known always to be quarreling with Peter or with Paul, with one person or another, had a falling-out with her brother over a parcel of land. Since her sister-in-law was mamma-catechist and group leader, she interrupted Mass at Grosse-Montagne to insult her: "See this woman, she leads religious instruction, goes to Bible meetings, well she's her brother's accomplice, she wants to steal my land. . . . "

I said no: "Those words don't belong in church. Come and argue about your problem at the neighborhood meetings, don't cause scenes in church. The church at Grosse-Montagne is already called the gossip church, the church of the Creoles; if you come here with your land problems, the rumors will never end."

Must we accept these people who only come to church when they have a problem to expose, who use the Gospel as cover? You can't, for instance, go to church in Lamentin or Capesterre and, without ever having participated in the meetings, speak out when the priest reads from the Gospel: "Jesus Christ says 'You gave me no drink . . .'" and you ask someone: "Did you help your sister the way Christ asks you to?"

And another, who resents a neighbor because she refused to lend a franc or a bit of food: "Father, yesterday evening I asked my neighbor for a small bowl of rice, she gave me nothing. And yet Jesus Christ told us to love one another. . . . "

Besides, what meaning do those words have? None. Those people have no ties with us, don't know about our lives, don't help us. Quite the contrary; they only speak ill of us, call our church the gossip church when it is they who themselves come and create the disturbances.

Simply because we speak out in church, in Creole, try to share our everyday problems and seek solutions, people speak of "gossip."

One Sunday at Mass, a new land problem surfaced. The two parties were present and each told her side of the story. We couldn't decide who was right.

"They sold me some land and now they want to take it back! They're dismantling my house before my very eyes! Every day they come and take away some sheet metal, a plank, what will become of me?"

"It's not true, I never sold that land, that woman is occupying it illegally!"

A real hullabaloo inside the church: those who knew about the situation added their two-cents worth, those who didn't opened their eyes and ears wide. . . . The celebration of Mass that day went on and on.

At the neighborhood meetings, everyone can speak out, all can bring their sufferings, their difficulties, and receive consolation, help. Studying a passage from the Gospel means figuring out, first and foremost, what the passage tells us, then what Jesus Christ did, and finally, what we have to do today, because it's today that we're living. After the reading aloud, each person bears witness, relates her problems to the group. Often the solution is difficult to find because we still aren't candid enough, many things remain hidden, we don't open ourselves up completely.

The affairs involving sorcery are the most difficult to resolve. One woman accused a neighbor, who had argued with her husband, of driving him crazy. Apparently she'd grabbed a broom, turned it on end, placed a hat on the end of the broomstick, and taken advantage of the man's illness to do her witchcraft and provoke fits of madness.

"Listen, listen to the evil of this woman. Instead of helping her sick neighbor, look what she did to him!"

The relatives got involved, each wanting to support one side or the other. Happily, the accused woman, who was present, didn't answer back. Afterward, she was able to make up with her neighbor.

Sometimes, Céleste attended our neighborhood meetings but never to lead them. One day we said to him: "Since you're here, lead the discussion."

He answered: "Deal with your problems yourselves, I can only help enlighten you."

I agreed with him. In Guadeloupe, we have a failing: if we're doing something and an important person arrives, someone better educated, we immediately want him to take charge of the situation.

At one of the group-leader meetings, the issue of the woman I'd interrupted at Mass was brought up. I explained how and why I made her hush up, that I didn't agree at all—not one bit—with people who came to church to cause disruptions. I told that woman not to come back, to stay at home, to deal with her problems somewhere other than in church.

For me, church means not the walls, but the assembly of people, it's the church of Jesus Christ and must be respected. There are plenty of other places too, places of respect, where you can't simply say whatever you like. I believe in Jesus Christ, so I respect his church.

Father Pélage explained to us that, the next time, no matter who came to tell her story, we must allow the person to speak without interruption. Interrupting is what creates a disturbance. Some take one side, some the other, and tempers flare. . . . Let the person speak and, at the end, find some of Christ's words in answer. He gave us the example of Mary Magdalen: when Mary Magdalen was brought before Jesus Christ so he could stone her, he bent down and began to write in the sand. No, before bending down he said: "Let him who is without sin among you cast the first stone."

Then he bent his head. No one dared moved. He said: "Let no one condemn her. Go and sin no more."

That's how, gradually, we learned to lead a meeting, not to talk all at once, but to share. I was like that too; I didn't know how to discuss, to allow a person to speak, and then to ask for a turn before speaking out myself.

It's not a question of simply replying to people: "What you just said isn't right," because that leads to an argument. When, after reading the text, the group leader asks what it's telling us, I offer my opinion. It means something else to the next person. The text reminds her of a problem at home, and she describes it for us. It might be a disagreement between neighbors or in the community. A thing normally difficult to speak of, that you choke on.

One evening, a woman confided to us how hard she had fought against going to a *machann kakoué,* a healer. Things were very bad for her, she was obsessed.

"I must go for a consultation. But at the same time, what I hear here, at these meetings, tells me, no, don't go. I'm tortured by the idea, and the battle between 'Don't go! Go!' rages in my mind. It's making me sick. One day, I take my Bible. I make the sign of the cross along the edge, close my eyes, and let my finger pick a page. With the Bible open, I read the words that are meant for me. When I close the book, I'm almost cured."

That woman's mind was torn apart. She believed that all her domestic problems, whether with her husband or with one of her children, were caused by witchcraft. Someone had put an evil spell on her, to create disorder, to pursue her. She might even die of it. She discovered that, in our neighborhood meetings, we dealt with problems that are usually kept hidden, not spoken of. And yet nothing serious happened to us. On the contrary, it gave us strength to resist. A strength made up of small bits of strength put together, of the attention we all gave to the problems of each one, and, especially, of the Gospel that we studied together. If she had stayed at home, she'd still have the problems on her mind.

Some people use the Bible for all sorts of intrigues. A few even attend our meetings hoping to acquire an understanding, a knowledge they could then use in their own way. They quickly learn that they won't find it with us.

Perhaps it was to prevent these practices that people in former times used to be prohibited from owning a Bible. You went to Mass, not with the Bible, but with a missal. The priest read an epistle, those who had their missals followed along, but many just listened. Even with a thick missal, you couldn't understand everything, and I'm not even speaking of the Mass in Latin, but in French, because if we'd been obliged to continue in Latin, we'd all have died *tèbè* (idiots).

On Sundays, it was the epistle, the Gospel, the priests reading as they had to and you following along as best you could. First we were read to from the Old Testament, then we were shown what God had asked of the Apostles and how they split up into several groups. . . . But what real understanding did we have?

Of course the church never urged us to do evil, you won't find that in the Gospel, but did it help us to become more perfect, even if that's what we wanted? We were part of the church, and we accepted it without questioning.

Since I went to Mass, so did all my children. I had problems with my husband so I visited all the saints. I knew that I shouldn't ask them all for help, only Christ who is at the entrance to the church. And yet I prayed to them as did everyone else. "Most Holy Anthony, grant me this, Virgin Mary, enlighten me, send me light. . . . "

I didn't beg them to do evil, but I had so many troubles, and I believed the Virgin would solve my problems. Later, it was explained to us that everything happened through Jesus Christ and that He alone is all-powerful. If you asked the Holy Virgin for something, she'd pass the request on to her son. During the wedding at Cana, when the Virgin saw there was no more wine, she said to her son: "There is no more wine." Had she been in charge, she'd have changed the water into wine herself.

In Lamentin, when Father Céleste removed the statues from the village church, the people were furious:

"Labé la ay krazé Bondyé!"	"The priest has destroyed God!"
"Ni moun ki di: 'ban yonn.'"	"Someone said: 'Give me one.'"
"Labé la fou! Sa pa ka fèt."	"That priest is crazy! He can't do that."

I was afraid for Father Céleste, even worried he might be harmed. Some people are still angry with him.

Chérubin Céleste never said: "The saints aren't what's important." But when he saw that the Easter candle was stolen, that the flowers placed on the altar disappeared as soon as Mass ended, or that threatening letters imploring Satan rather than God appeared at the feet of the statues, he wanted to show that we shouldn't adore the images.

We group leaders asked why he provoked the anger of the people of Lamentin in this way. He answered that, one day, when entering the church, he came upon a small boy looking at the large statue of Saint Michael killing the dragon. The boy was crying. "Why," he asked, "is even God cruel to the blacks?" That shocked Father Céleste and he began by removing the statue of Saint Michael.

Before that time, Mass never helped me much. Yes, the priests spoke about faith, about the church, but they preached for themselves, their sermons ran over us like water over a *malanga* leaf, without stopping or penetrating. We didn't find anything in church to help us advance, to live our faith. Now our faith is enriched. In our district, the priests no longer conduct their little Mass the way they used to. They explain things to us, and the more we develop our knowledge, the more we grow, the more we understand.

Instead of confession, for instance, we have a "service of repentance." A text is selected about sin, about reconciliation, which someone reads and comments on. Finally, each person renounces his sins, and we sing the song of forgiveness or publicly ask God's mercy.

But it didn't work for everyone. People would say all sorts of nonsense: "God, forgive me, I hit my children . . . I argued . . . "

Or they would speak of their neighbor, while fearing to speak of themselves. I admit, it's difficult to confess this way, in public, but if you go to confession, it concerns you, what you yourself have done, you can't go and confess for your neighbor! It was a real hodgepodge. Some were sincere and spoke the truth, but very few.

Those who didn't want to confess in public could meet with the priest. But I think they repeated the same *bwi-bwi* (trifles) behind the little window that they confessed to in front of everyone. Would they confide in the priest and ask for guidance if they got angry with their neighbor, cursed her? Would they dare acknowledge: "I woke up at four in the morning, me, a Christian, to go kill a black hen in a crossroads?" Would they say: "At noon, outside, I recited the prayer to Saint Bouleverse (Confusion): "O Most Holy Bouleverse, you who have the power to throw the world into confusion, you are a saint and I a sinner, I implore you and take you for my only defender, go, go, I send you to X's house, mess up her head, mess up her mind, mess up her heart, overcome her, make her spin round, break all her bones, bring on the thunder and let loose the storm, sow discord at X's house. . . . Amen."

The service of repentance helps me much more than the old way of confessing did. When I experienced all my domestic troubles, I said to myself, let's go and see the priest, he can talk with me, help me see things more clearly.

"Father," I said to him (in French, of course, since he didn't speak Creole), "I've come because my husband spends the night with another woman."

"Does he feed your children?"

"Yes, Father."

"Well then, there's no problem. Go in peace, my daughter, do your act of contrition, recite a second rosary for your repentance."

So, as long as a man feeds his children, he can sleep where he wants. The priest didn't exactly say that, but he took the man's side. I had to accept it, not cause a scene.

Not all the priests in Guadeloupe conduct services of repentance, and they don't all agree with what we call a "service of faith." We gather together, and one of us, a brother or sister, leads the service, delivers the word, and conducts the communion. The priest isn't indispensable, it's not his presence that provides comfort, rather it's a question of faith. A brother can speak to you as well as a priest, except the priest has different training and he alone has the right to consecrate. He always leaves consecrated hosts in the tabernacle for the service of faith and we put them out on the table.

This type of service caused many people to leave, particularly those who felt we weren't passing out real, consecrated hosts. They, therefore, couldn't use them for witchcraft. They also said we shared bread and not the host, that our service wasn't valid.

They hadn't understood a thing. Nor had I. I'd believed that the actual substance of the host was something sacred, that it wasn't made from flour, a product of human hands. Father Céleste explained to us: normal bread has nothing holy about it, but when the priest places it on the altar and blesses it, the bread becomes consecrated like the host. When Jesus met with his disciples, just as he was going to sacrifice his body, he picked up some bread and said: "This is my body, take and eat; this is my blood, take and drink." He didn't say: "This is the host."

For me, it could be a piece of yam, some rice. During Jesus' time, the country produced wheat, so they used bread. Later on, since bread gets stale, they used French flour to make the host, but it's similar to bread.

We cut a quarter loaf of a bread into small pieces, they're consecrated. Those who want bread, take bread, those who want the host, take the host. At Grosse-Montagne, to follow the words of Jesus, "Take and eat," we don't hand out the host. If I give, you're not taking. If you feel worthy, take some and eat it. And if you take it yourself while being unworthy, you condemn yourself.

In general, people aren't very eager to take the bread, especially if it has been brought in by a member of the congregation. You don't really know what it contains. A long time ago, at Mass, bread represented something else. You'd tell the priest your troubles. He'd ask you to bring in two or three loaves of bread. He put them on the altar. After communion and before the end of Mass, he handed out pieces of your bread and, in doing so, shared your problems among the whole congregation. Many people refused: "I won't carry someone else's troubles home with me!"

Others helped themselves to two or three pieces: "I'll bring home some bread for my children."

At other times it was cake. People handed out basketfuls during Mass. Soon it was apparent to all that bread, cake, and even the pilgrimages only served the needs of a single person.

"Madame so-and-so has problems, she hands out bread, cake, takes us on pilgrimages, she needs to distribute her pain to others. On the pilgrimages, she's the one who leads the prayers all along the route, gets us to bathe, compels us to do all sorts of things. . . . We won't go anymore. If we want to go on a pilgrimage, we'll go alone. And what if we've been pulled into the work of a *gadèdzafè?*"

Yes, it's true, some people only come to church to carry out the orders of a *gadèdzafè.* In Guadeloupe, sorcery isn't anywhere near being ended. I fight against these practices, give advice, but without many illusions. No one can stop magic and witchcraft. The other day, I explained to a lady: "You don't feel well, you believe your mind's full of evil spirits. You go to a *kenbouazè.* Right away, he tells you that someone is sending evil onto you and, he always adds: 'It's from envy.' 'Haven't you bought anything for the new year?' 'Yes, I've redecorated my home.' 'Oh, you see! I told you so, that's the reason.' And he has you trapped. You ask yourself: how did he know, I bought those things in secret? And you do whatever he tells you to."

I'm not sure she understood, but I knew that she'd just redone her house, bought a ton of furniture. People are said to be jealous, but does anyone need to buy a ton of furniture? No, I say. My bed dates from the time of *nanni-nannan,* long, long ago, and the two middle doors of my wardrobe are broken.

At exam time, plenty of children at the Jarry Chapel,[81] many "Hail Marys" recited along the route. Once there, there are prayers, baths, drinks of water, walking in the footsteps of God to obtain what you need. It's not really wicked, no evil in it, but it still is a kind of superstition.

My daughter was to sit for her university degree, I asked her to go and pray to the Virgin of Abymes. Lucie, who was already well trained, answered that it wasn't necessary to go to church to ask God's grace. I got after her and forced her to go to the chapel. She went, against her will, and she flunked the exam. Her aunt blazed: "God punished you because you didn't want to go to church. If you'd gone with a pure heart, he'd have given you your degree."

Imagine that! Looking upon God as a middleman to whom you come, as you did during Sorin's time, bearing coconuts to exchange for soap. If she didn't succeed, it's because she wasn't meant to. She tried unsuccessfully several times, whereas she obtained her high school diploma on the first try. To my youngest daughter I said: no pilgrimage, no prayers, no request of any sort.

Besides, in Lamentin, all that fussing is over. No question now of opening the church at 5 A.M. on New Year's Day so people can fight in front of the door to see who'll be the first to say *Bondyé! bonjou!* and thus receive a special blessing. The *gadèdzafè* are the ones who send you to do those things in church. They want to use God to fool the people. They'll indicate one saint or another you should implore to release you from an evil spell, prevent a neighbor from having a hold over you. . . . He's not the sorcerer, God is, and yet he rakes in the money this way.

In our neighborhood Gospel meetings, we work differently. We work to bring about reconciliation. Someone speaks out, saying: "So-and-so is angry with me, but I don't know why."

Then the floodgates open, and the others explain what they know, what's being said and being done. We discuss the situation, sometimes hotly, but because we're in a group meeting and take Jesus Christ as our model, we make up, and we embrace one another.

It is said that two mountains can never come together and neither can two people whose families have been enemies for generations. Well, our sharing of the Gospel produced such a miracle. The Molière family had been at odds with the Louidor family for as long as anyone could remember. It had gone real far, as far as to the courts. A Louidor had won the case. One of her descendants took the first step toward a reconciliation.

Madame Molière was sickly, getting thinner and thinner. . . . She prayed often at church, hoping to be cured, asking forgiveness from God and from all the people she'd wronged. At the end of one of our meetings, the daughter of the Louidor family went over to her, wished her good evening, and said: "You've already been to many doctors, and none has cured you. It seems to me that your illness is due to great fatigue. Buy three bottles of Quintonine to take every morning, and for eight days drink juice made from raw carrots, papayas, radishes, celery, leeks, oranges, green bananas, and tomatoes, all crushed together."

It was clear *Man* Molière had been waiting for that. She threw herself into the Louidor girl's arms and embraced her.

"Sister, in a dream I was told to reconcile my differences with you."

"Sister, I know you don't hate me because you still have the red bowl my grandmother gave yours."

We all laughed, and they continued their conversation. At Mass two weeks later, old Madame Molière gave thanks to God: "For a long time, I've been running from doctor to doctor without result. I made up with my neighbor, and she prescribed a remedy. I haven't even finished drinking it, and I'm already cured. I obeyed God, accepted the greeting of my enemy, and I'm saved. Thank you, God."

This reconciliation astonished people. The relatives of the two sides couldn't understand how it happened, and some of them were furious.

The Gospel enters my life

Yet sometimes one might want a reconciliation and the other refuses, categorically refuses. One time, the relatives were present, and the refusal came from them: "That will never happen, never, she'll never make up with that girl!"

And it didn't happen. She didn't love her neighbor well enough. Such a beautiful idea, love of one's neighbor, but so difficult to follow.

As soon as you stop wishing a person good day, it's serious, you must have something against her. Being angry with a neighbor who lives close to you, a person you meet every day, isn't funny.

Some people find it completely natural. They don't greet you, don't speak to you anymore, that's their business. You attend the neighborhood Gospel meetings, hope for reconciliation, that's your business. But you may be the one with a greater understanding, you speak out, feel you can't continue to be blocked by the situation, by that person. So you take action. If she rejects you, refuses your outstretched hand, it's not your fault, you've taken the first step. She alone is responsible. You don't have to pursue her constantly, go over to her every time you meet, give her a chance to make up. Your overture already testifies to your good faith. She may never make up with you but, then again, perhaps after three or four days, she'll come over and greet you. Today it might be a simple "hello," tomorrow a hug. You must let things happen in their own good time.

As group leader of the neighborhood, I couldn't allow myself to give advice about reconciliation, to speak out, if I myself remained angry with someone. I'm not yet perfect, I still must progress further. That's how we can judge true faith.

We debated all this in our meetings. Oh! It isn't always easy to speak out. In the beginning, we spent all our time on God, Jesus Christ. Slowly, we began to talk of our own troubles, of our sufferings, but even today, not everything about our lives comes out so easily. If the Gospel passage we're studying closely touches on a personal problem, we speak of it but not thoroughly, only providing select details.

But at a certain moment, and I don't know how, it came to the attention of our husbands. They saw red, didn't understand that if we shared personal secrets, it was to find help, not to start rumors.

"So! You bring my private affairs into your neighborhood meetings. I forbid you to set foot there ever again. I forbid you to open that thing (the Bible) in my house!"

One woman stood up bravely to her husband: "If I were going to dance the *léwoz,* I'd understand and obey you. But at these meetings I'm following Christ."

"So, she's following Jesus Christ! Admit it, you're following Céleste, the husband of all you women."

"I prefer to follow him than to follow your friends. No one can keep me from attending those meetings."

"That priest deserves to have his face bashed in. The Bible is the greatest witchcraft of all. He has trapped you with it. He's up to no good, he's causing trouble in our homes. All those women are gossips. The only thing they want is to know what goes on in their neighbor's house. Go tell your stories at church, my house isn't a church."

The men also complained because the meetings finished late in the evening. I'd formed a group on my block with my neighbors. We met at my house, and things went well. The other groups, however, had problems meeting. So we created one single group that met at different homes in turn. But then my husband said: "No more meetings in my house. I don't want to see anything more of this. As for Father Céleste, he'd better not hang out at my door. So Madame tells the priest how I make love to her, eh!"

All that because I confided in Father Céleste, telling him how, for three days, Joseph hadn't appeared at home. He advised me: "You must separate, it will just get worse." "No, Father, I can manage."

At that time I hadn't thought about a separation. But things weren't getting any better, and one day Father Céleste came by to see Joseph. He knows how to handle things, he didn't breathe a word to Joseph about his habit of sleeping away from home.

"Monsieur Joseph," he said, "when you argue with your wife, you might occasionally hit her. Once the fight is over, you leave. You go to work or out with your friends, you joke, you laugh, you have fun and forget everything. Your wife stays home. The hurt she feels keeps working inside her and her heart hardens."

Yes, my heart was hardening. And when a woman's heart isn't open, her body can't open either. That's it, her body closes. A woman can't have a man unless she has the desire for him. Father Céleste tried to explain this to my husband, and he took it badly. Not in front of him, but with me, afterward.

All the households were seething, but we held firm and, thanks to our meetings, made much progress. Today, I don't find the same enthusiasm, the same excitement. Perhaps people are tired of speaking or of hearing the same things over and over again. A silence pervades our meetings. Is it weariness? Is it the fault of the leader who preaches too much when her role isn't to moralize? I don't know, but I feel that the neighborhood meetings are losing their strength. People are retreating into themselves, into their *kò*.

Some think that the meetings no longer serve much of a purpose. People are being organized elsewhere. I don't agree, they haven't stopped coming because of other meetings, they don't go anywhere else

The Gospel enters my life

instead, they're nowhere. If there has ever been a place where people don't go out, it's in the housing development where I live. No meetings, no demonstrations, no church services, nothing at all. They won't go out for anything in the world, not even for their children who take religious instruction. They stay at home, curled up like cobras, thinking only about buying new furniture or a new car. The more they have, the more they want. They're hopeless.

In reality, people weren't ready for the kind of work we began or for the new kind of Mass. And then too, there's politics! In Guadeloupe, if you try something new, many people will follow you at first and then, very quickly, pull out, give up, most often for political reasons. For instance, at a neighborhood meeting, a word is said against the mayor. One of the participants, who works at the cafeteria, stops coming: "If the mayor learns I go to meetings at which he's criticized, I'll lose my job."

These are all excuses, they put themselves in this situation. It's a way of hiding their "I won't come anymore." Because, when it comes down to it, the mayor won't get involved in all the little details. He might bump into you and say: "Oh, so you go to Father Céleste's meetings!" but he won't fire you for it.

Yes, those people fear for their jobs, but mostly they're not open to the word of God so that it can work on them, get them to do things. They must be thinking: "Why should I stay here listening, listening so I can hear, hearing so I can understand, understanding so I'll want to act, even though I'm not ready? No! I won't do it!"

Others, who joined the U.T.A. or U.P.G. and had continued to work with us, no longer come. They claim to know already everything that's talked about in church and have better things to do.

I also have a great deal to do and could give up. I believe a certain number of people must stay in the church so it can continue, continue as the church we experience at Lamentin, the church of Jesus Christ, the man who appeared on earth to be crucified and who created the apostles to carry on his work. We're believers, our faith is incarnate, we cannot abandon it.

Jesus Christ sees those who have abandoned the church and work for the people. They shouldn't expect us to quit the church too. We can unite and work together. I don't know how the unions currently behave toward those people who remain active in the church. When the U.T.A. was formed, it didn't create any problems.

In our district, we discuss a great deal in church and act upon our discussions. We don't broach the subject of independence in every meeting, it brings out such strong feelings!

Not long ago, one of our priests, Father Berka Pélage, used inflam-

Leonora: The Buried Story of Guadeloupe

matory words in church to discuss the death of Monsignor Romero, bishop of El Salvador: "Why have we heard about it? Because this time, a bishop was assassinated. Think of all the peasants who have been killed, who are killed each and every day, and whose names remain unknown. Think of all those who died during the funeral. Are you really apostles?"

He criticized and criticized, spoke of the prophet Isaiah, who'd been beaten, tortured, suffered his beard to be ripped out, "who never gave in and never questioned his faith.

"If your beards haven't yet been ripped out, your tongues have. If you were true apostles, wouldn't you bring your husbands into the church? Only two or three men come to Mass. You aren't even capable of preaching the Gospel to your own families. . . . "

Angry, annoyed, some people kept silent, but others answered him back: "Bring our husbands! It's already a challenge for us to come."

"Every Sunday, it's a battle."

"Even when we prepare the day's meal in advance, they holler."

"They criticize our way of saying Mass."

"They call our church the gossip church. . . . "

Oh, it heated up, tongues certainly hadn't been ripped out.

"You can get as angry as you want," replied Berka, "but you refuse to hear the truth and you do nothing."

At that point, one of the few men in the congregation rose to his feet. "Generally, I prefer to keep silent, but twice now I've been accused of doing nothing. It's just too much. Being aware is the only thing that counts."

I intervened: "Listen, brother, there's no reason to get yourself so worked up. When words like these echo in our chapel at Grosse-Montagne, they aren't especially addressed to you or to us. All the people in the district are involved, those from Lamentin, Baie-Mahault, Cadet. Don't take it personally."

He threw himself into the discussion even more intensely, getting into the question of independence: "We've all seen what doesn't work. We all have children who can't find jobs, we all see that more and more white people come to Guadeloupe, we're all aware of the gravity of the situation. Yet does that mean we should dive into something without first reflecting, fight for an independence that might well be worse than what we have now? When we observe a massacre, does it mean we too must begin to kill?"

Many people ask themselves these same questions. They aren't members of any union, don't attend any meetings where they might hear arguments in favor of independence. They're part of the church, and that's the only place they go.

The Gospel enters my life

And, besides, people don't take on these kinds of commitments at the drop of a hat. We're not yet like the Christians of El Salvador, not yet too uneasy.

If Chérubin is correct in wanting to bring the faithful along with him in the fight for mankind's liberation, he must understand that not everyone will be able to keep up. They have their families. If I were still with Joseph, could I go about as freely as I do now? Would I be seated here, telling the story of my life? I would have had to obey my husband.

Of course, eyes see and ears hear, and increasing numbers of people realize that Father Céleste is following in the path of Christianity. He has also altered his method slightly: in the beginning, he went outside the church to bring people in, wanted to draw people into the church, to open the doors of the "church of the poor" to everyone. Now, I believe, he's trying to form small groups of active, committed people, here in our area but also at Cadet and Baie-Mahault. So if hard times come to Guadeloupe in the future, we'll be accustomed to speaking out and bearing witness. If the partisans of independence want to chuck out religion, if they come and say: "You don't have the right to speak out, you don't have the right to criticize," those of you who, in your little groups, have grown accustomed to speaking out on anything and everything, giving advice freely, will frustrate them. And even if they silence you, people will realize: "In that group, so-and-so spoke out. What's going on?"

Céleste's sermons had an impact, the neighborhood meetings intrigued people. Politics, people hollered. Of course it's politics, but not just any old kind, not politics that would oust a mayor, not electoral politics, but politics of faith.

If one looks closely at the Bible, it too is political. The priests don't teach you that. Céleste came and opened the Bible for us, opened our eyes, enlightened us. And when you open people's eyes, isn't that a political act?

Céleste is truly an intelligent and sensitive man, who knew how to interact with us. When a new person arrives somewhere, he can't simply enter into a group, there's a way to become accepted. Céleste began by explaining the Gospel to us, then asked if we wanted to take action: the neighborhood meetings were born, and little by little, he managed to awaken in us the word that lives in his innermost being.

We didn't agree to everything he proposed. The discussions were sometimes heated. Chérubin Céleste became increasingly radical. He supported Guadeloupean independence, okay, but I must say that he often wanted to move too quickly, to take on too many things at once. We said to him: "Within the ranks of those who follow Jesus are good folks and bad; watch out, you aren't Jesus, you're a man, your work will kill you."

But he had his own ways. When he couldn't get us to do everything he wanted—all he thought right—there was friction. We wanted to progress, and to progress together with him, but not too fast.

Personally, I've reflected on it and realize that the problem wasn't the speed but the desire to take on too many things at once. Out of the many things we begin, two or three always fail. We start in one direction and then discover a more urgent need. We drop the first, then the second for a third, and so we fail to do anything well. As long as we live, we'll set things in motion, but we can't be in such a rush. Let's proceed with measured steps and careful examination, questioning everything, because, through our action, we can be dragged into evil deeds.

Sometimes Céleste would find himself trapped. Seeing he was a man sensitive to suffering, many people brought him their worries, asked for help. We warned him: "Yes, misfortune is widespread in our country, many are poor, but you must know them before distributing charity, don't be stopped by the tears of all who cry misery. The very same people who come to eat at your table are the ones who give their food money to the capitalists running the stores."

It's true, Father Céleste lived with the poor, but he didn't see everything. Father Pélage seemed tougher, perhaps because he analyzed things well. Their training was different: Berka Pélage entered the seminary as a very young man; Céleste was already grown when he chose the priesthood.

Among the congregation, Céleste is seen as more committed than Berka. It's true, Berka deals more with Mass and baptisms while Chérubin is involved with the life of the district, but they agreed on this arrangement, they worked it out together. If Berka didn't keep the church running, Chérubin wouldn't have time to go around everywhere in the community.

Each has his own way of working, and Father Pélage has already made progress, I like him very much. His method isn't worse just because he speaks French more often. It's slower, and so he helps us discover all sorts of things, from the beginning to the end.

Berka spreads some butter, a bit of lard, a little oil . . . and Chérubin, how direct, how dry he is. Many people no longer follow him. He puts them into a relationship with the church that they've never experienced before. Go to Mass, say the rosary, speak to the Lord about your small problems, light little candles—that's what they practiced. Even if they were mad at someone, they'd take communion; they simply refrained from saying hello to that person when they entered the church, that's all. Now we shake hands and embrace. Previously, the priest would chant: "My God, give us peace." He didn't say: "Brothers and sisters, give one another peace." But simply: "Jesus said, my peace I bring to you, my peace I leave with you."

He didn't insist that we share the peace the way we've been taught: I'm sitting next to you in church; I give you my hand or embrace you.

At the church of Prise-d'Eau, Father Lasserre found he had to descend among the flock to show them how to share the peace. They didn't obey when he charged them, from high up in his pulpit: "Share the peace with one another."

Since they were expected to respond, people avoided sitting next to a person they were at odds with. At Grosse-Montagne, no obligation: "Brothers and sisters, share the peace with one another. Let those who wish to give, give, and reciprocally."

You were never forced to embrace just anyone. That's also why we insist so strongly on reconciliations in our neighborhood meetings.

I myself experienced what they can bring to a person. What had been my habits? I can't say I didn't love my brothers and sisters, but in what way? I just loved them, without knowing how or why. They needed a service, I provided it; an object, I gave it to them. But as soon as they said a word against me, I began to grumble. I didn't yet have this understanding: when you do something good for a person, he may turn against you tomorrow. Now I know that when you give, you mustn't expect to receive something in return.

Of course, I don't always manage to control myself—it must be admitted, I've been taken for a ride—I haven't progressed as far as I possibly can, I'm a poor sinner, I'm not Jesus. . . . Yet since the arrival of Father Céleste, by working through each passage of the Gospel, by putting it into practice, I've acquired a different understanding of faith.

I can say to myself: you've changed, Leonora, but you still have a long way to go. As long as I live, I want to keep growing. I'll never free myself from the word *sinner;* Peter himself fell three times, and he followed Jesus, walked with him, shared with him.

A change has occurred in my life since I met Céleste. I began to understand myself and to see the possibility of another kind of life, yes, another life. If my husband, Joseph, and I had shared a different relationship, maybe we wouldn't be separated today. When one of us said "Chop," the other answered "Cut."

I didn't have the clarity I now have. My marriage turned sour, but perhaps that misfortune is what permitted me to find myself as a witness in the church. People can say what they want, clack their tongues, but I know what I am, I respect what I'm doing.

You must make an effort if you want to act, especially if you're blocked in your marriage. Taking part in the neighborhood meetings already represents a hurdle. If you manage to overcome these obstacles, the ambiance you find there may provide help.

Now, instead of listening quietly, I speak out—in church, at neighborhood meetings, at parent groups, everywhere. The Gospel helps me speak; the Gospel entered into me. Those neighborhood meetings gave all of us—especially us women who were the most numerous—something special. Forever, I believe.

12

Nou tout, ni on koudbòdalo pou nou fè

In each of us, there is room for madness

And the being of man not only cannot be understood without
madness, but it would not be the being of man if it did not carry
madness within it as the limit of its liberty.

Jacques Lacan,
Speech and Language in Psychoanalysis

As soon as you act, live passionately, you're said to be possessed by
one madness or another. In this way, many think Leonora's passion for
the Gospel is an obsession. And it's true, the more the Gospel enters
my life, the more I find to do, the farther I must progress. That can be
called madness of sorts, but not the kind that leads to an asylum. All
the saints were considered mad. Bernadette, for instance, saw the Holy
Virgin in a dream and spoke to her. She told of her vision. People said
she was off her rocker. Still today, if you speak of following the teachings of the Gospel, you're thought to be crazy. Simply put, you have an
ideal, a notion strongly fixed in your mind. The Gospel provides direction, leads you to do this or that, always good things, always along the
righteous path. If I see a child drowning and spring to its aid even
though I can't swim, and I risk my own life, the Gospel is speaking to
me, but if I leave him in the water and turn my back, my fear, not the
Gospel, is leading me.

In each one of us, between what happens in life—in your life—and
what you want or don't want, there's room for madness.

The madness of my oldest son and his group of friends—the fight
for independence—could lead them up the courthouse steps. The farther they advance, the more they speak out, the greater their risk of
being imprisoned. They sow their ideas among the people, there is
good and truth in what they say and do. Yet people exclaim: only madmen could risk so much for ideas. Yes, mad, mad for change.

All these madmen, whether obsessed with the Gospel or politics,
don't march to society's drum. Those who agree with everything, obey
well—who always answer: "Yes, sir, Yes, chief, Yes, boss"—they'll
never go mad. They cry out against anyone who tries to change things
and refuse to hear, refuse to exercise their brain cells. You and I, we're

mad because we reflect on things. People say we're on the road to the insane asylum and wish us a good retirement there, at Saint-Claude.[82]

This earth certainly doesn't lack for varieties of madness! One of the most widespread is lovesickness. I've always heard it's incurable. You become mad without knowing how, but I can recognize the man or woman who has gone mad from love.

Sometimes just seeing a person once is enough to enflame your heart and entrap your mind. All day long, all night, you think about him, you're possessed by him. And maybe he doesn't even see you, turns his back if you try to start a conversation. Meanwhile, since you're totally absorbed with him, your mind simply lets go. That's what we call being lovesick.

A person can also be driven mad by someone playing around. A man can make you believe he loves you. He courts you, charms you, you fall in love . . . and then he leaves. You threw your heart and soul into the love affair simply to find yourself jilted and forsaken. Your mind snaps.

Love isn't the only thing that drives men and women mad. There are plenty of ways to disrupt the pathways in our brains, to turn us upside down!

You don't have a job or any government allowance, but you do have children to care for. If your good will deserts you, you can end up doing almost anything. It's this good will that makes you want to work, to care for your children, to encourage them in life. If an evil will takes its place within you, you no longer have the desire to do anything, you let everything go and drown yourself in drink. Rum becomes your master. It is said that the mind guides the body, but if you let your guiding angel—your good will—escape, the destroying angel—the evil will—can enter your mind and you no longer follow the virtuous path. That's a different kind of madness.

There are others, many others. . . . Some people study too hard and try to reach beyond their capacity. They go mad. They lose everything within them that was good. Their guiding angel goes off and leaves them.

I know a boy who, after receiving his high school diploma, went to France to become a doctor. In his fourth year, he joined the Communist Party. They took advantage of him. He worked and participated in social action at the same time. A brilliant boy, who'd never flunked any exams, he lost his marbles, pushed himself too hard. I don't mean it was the Communist Party's fault—each person chooses his own party—nor that activism is a bad thing—when you participate, you stay alive—but this boy was always thinking about things, always working his mind. And his mind couldn't take all the pressure. Trying to know too much, swallowing too much knowledge, can lead to madness. Studying, thinking, all the time like that, and poof! a screw loosens. It can happen to anyone. You might not necessarily become mad, but you could lose your memory. Like it's starting with me, for instance. Of course old age is partly to blame, but my memory's all a muddle from working so hard, taking part in many activities. I hear about a case, and I take it on, another, I take it on too. . . . I respond like that, always wanting to do more. And the old bones don't keep up. It can even lead to loss of control. Madness isn't far behind. All manner of foolishness becomes possible.

You often hear: "So-and-so went mad, he wanted to push himself beyond his limits, to do more than anyone else, to know everything, to follow a path right along the cliff's edge. . . . " Yet some people give of themselves totally, take on enormous tasks, and never go mad. Father Céleste carries a mountain on his shoulders, he can be worn-out, dead tired, but he doesn't drift into madness. It may be, as people say here, that some of us are born to madness. And if the militant men and women of the independence movement drive themselves mad, can we say they were seeking total knowledge, wanted to take God's place? Remember the story of the invisible man. The apprentice wanted to take his master's place. He followed his every move and, during his absence, made himself invisible. What he needed was a better situation in life. If misfortune befell him, it was certainly his own fault.

Here in Guadeloupe, people always have an explanation: "My dear, evil was done to him. Someone wanted revenge. And sent this . . . " Or else: "His ancestors were evil, and he's paying the price." But those who know the real cause of madness would never speak like that.

I knew a boy who had a gentle sort of madness. In the hamlet where he lived, his neighbors received many letters, but not him, no, never. So he started writing to himself. When the postman handed him his letter, he took it with great ceremony, making sure everyone saw. Apparently one day a neighbor surprised him when he unsealed the envelope. He'd written: "Dear myself." Poor thing, he wanted to become part of society. If you don't receive any letters, you're not part of society. That's how I explain his madness. He had no contact with people, no one stopped to chat with him. People didn't even see he was there. He must have suffered greatly. So he tried everything he could to make people notice him. Those letters he sent to himself made him visible. His madness wasn't harmful, a madness of our times.

Everyone I meet tells me: "I'm so rushed, I don't have time, I can't stop to say hello, to chat for a minute. . . . "

If we no longer have time to do anything, time to visit, to go see our parents, perhaps time itself is escaping us.

Leonora: The Buried Story of Guadeloupe

When I say: "I don't have time," I know why. So I make an about-face and decide: "No. I must find the time. Even if it's brief, time to visit my family, to help my neighbor, to do this thing, and that. . . . " I try to organize my life so as to free up some time. I don't know how it came about, but we don't seem to have as much time as we used to.

Is it a question of laziness? We used to keep some time for living; we took charge of life without letting it take over, the way it does today. Once our day's work was done, we washed up, put dinner on the fire. If we wanted a rest, we lay down for a short siesta, then headed down to the sea. We had time.

Now, everyone complains: we don't have enough time! Nor money, it seems, since, instead of changing and going to visit friends, family, or acquaintances when work is done, people dig right into their gardens.

Our eyes are beggars. It takes plenty of will power not to buy the merchandise displayed in the shopwindows and on the tables of the Syrians in Frébault Street.[83] We all love beautiful things, but this love of *bèlbèbèl* and of cars is dangerous, can lead to the insane asylum.

A friend of my husband's and his wife worked in the white man's cane fields from six in the morning to one in the afternoon. As soon as they returned home, the wife prepared the meal while the man rested in his rocking chair. With the meal gulped down, he hurried his wife along. No question of saying I'm tired, I want to take a rest, it was off to the garden. They wore themselves out that way to save money for a car. And stingy too! The man didn't join in activities with other people but always kept to himself. He never thought of giving away a few yams at harvest time or of offering you a drink for a celebration. Work, eat, work, leave the cane fields of the white man to attack his own garden—that's all he did. And in the evening, closed up in his little cabin with his wife and three children. When he finally managed to save enough money to buy the car, he fell sick. Instead of going to a doctor who would have told him: "My dear sir, you're exhausted, you're killing yourself by overworking, you're crushed like a papaya stalk under a cartwheel, stop, rest," he went to consult the "beliefmongers." The *mantikakwè* persuaded him that, out of envy, his first cousin had an evil spell put on him. After that he had to work to pay the *gadèdzafè*. His savings melted away with each visit. He was constantly buying the necessary objects for new *kenbwa* because, the sorcerer said, the cousin was keeping busy. "See how he's building a beautiful house? He didn't want you to buy a fancy car, so he blocked your way. . . . "

The poor guy began to lose his mind. He saw his cousin everywhere. Spoke only of him: "The only way to get out of this," he said, "is to kill him. He's the one who put this evil spell on me, he's the one who's

In each of us, there is room for madness

causing my money to melt away like sugar in a cup of coffee. I'm going to chop his head off!"

He broke down and was sent to the hospital. The medicines he took caused his mouth to droop, but he regained some of his health. After eating up all the man's money, the *gadèdzafè* worried that his client might slip through his fingers. He advised the wife to take him to a doctor.

When the man left the hospital, he stood dazed, contemplating the large, concrete house his cousin had built opposite his own little wooden cabin. His wits departed for good and he ended up in the asylum.

Everyone talked about his case. Of course, he hadn't put up a poster announcing his desire for a fancy car and had never confided in anyone about consulting a *gadèdzafè,* but there's no such thing as secrecy in this sort of thing. People observe the remedies you take, the herbs you bring home, and know you haven't bought them at the pharmacy, know you're not following the advice of a doctor, although often the two treatments are combined. All agreed that he drove himself crazy by slaving away in order to buy things too fancy for his station in life.

Many years ago, each village took care of its madmen. They were tolerated, loved. Along with everyone else, the madman lived with his family, in the village. No thought of sending him to an asylum. Besides, there weren't any then.[84] Today, it's almost impossible to keep your madman at home. I know, I've lived through it.

A few years ago, one of my brothers went mad. Theodore worked the land of a white man, either as a sharecropper or a tenant, I don't quite remember which. He owed money to the factory, bought his provisions on credit at the company store. You can imagine how the harvest was eagerly awaited! He worked hard, cutting his cane all alone, having it transported to the factory. When it arrived there, it wasn't credited to his account, but to that of the white man. At the end of the harvest, Theodore went to pick up his money. The other man had pocketed it all a long time before. Then what happened? He began to turn around in circles, hands on his head. How would he pay his debts to the factory? And his bill at the company store? He had counted on his harvest. It had been stolen from him. He barely managed to retrieve two cartloads of sugarcane and have them credited to his name before cracking up. His poor little wife had her hands full with him. She brought him home, to us. Mamma pampered him, cared for him, served him meals, drinks, whatever he wanted. He knew he was sick and spoke to my mother about it, but she refused to listen. One day he bought a lottery ticket and won millions. He gave all of us money saying: "Look, it's me, the madman, giving away money!"

To see if he was improving, he left to visit relatives. First he went to the home of a cousin who lived on the maternal family land, a close relative to whom we'd given one plot on which to build her house and another plot to cultivate. Theodore entered her house and began to make a mess of things. He tried to provoke her into a fight. She answered back and jumped on him. We reproached her for her behavior. "You know what's going on," I told her, "you know Theodore is ill. When he arrives all excited like that, you must try to calm him down before reacting."

Another day, he visited one of my sisters who lived in town. He began to insult her, to treat her with scorn. Finally she got worked up and gave him back in kind, letting curses rain down on him. "You're supposedly well brought up," he said to her, "why do you talk to me like that? You must tolerate me. Don't you understand my condition?"

No one in the family wanted to admit that the madness had dug its claws so deeply into him. Finally, my mother was forced to take him to a mental hospital. He destroyed, broke everything he could get his hands on. His guardian angel had deserted him forever, gone somewhere else.

Only one word crossed Theodore's lips: money, money, money. At Saint-Claude, he improved slowly. He was put to work as an ironsmith. The doctor decided to release him and signed his exit papers. He was supposed to leave Thursday. On Wednesday, in his workshop, a nail entered his foot. He didn't mention it to anyone, hid the pain because he wanted to leave the following day. Gangrene set in and he died the same evening. Would his release have caused problems for the family? Is madness really curable, especially madness over money, a mad love for money? With all he'd endured, is it any surprise that he became enraged, crazy enough to be put away? Working all alone with your wife, planting cane, fertilizing it, weeding out the Guinea grass so sharp it slices through your hands, stripping off the straw, cutting the cane, tying it up into sheaves, piling them onto the carts, carrying them to the factory, and then, when you joyously go to receive the fruits of your labor, the money to free you from your debts, you get nothing, not a cent, not even enough to buy a loaf of bread! How can a mind keep from cracking?

It seems that we now have more people than before who, mad like my brother, end up in the insane asylums. Personally, I've never stepped through the doors up there, but with everything that goes on these days, I feel we're all only out on bail. Madmen abound, but not dangerous, angry madmen. From time to time you learn that so-and-so broke up everything in a house, the way my brother did, or that another person took to drink and went off alone into the bottomland to act like

In each of us, there is room for madness

a monkey. Some of them are frightening and people say: "That one's really not well, he's only out on bail." Yet to put someone away in the asylum he must be truly dangerous, have done something serious. People aren't put away for just a simple fit of madness.

Often, problems arise between neighbors. One gets on the other's nerves, ticks him off, unleashes his goats to eat his neighbor's lettuce till finally, totally exasperated, the neighbor grabs a machete and sticks him one. He isn't crazy. An attack of madness seized him. The police might be called, not the doctor.

People can also be driven mad on purpose, so they'll be committed. That happened to one of my acquaintances, a woman with a good head on her shoulders, sharp as Brer Rabbit.

Authoritarian, fierce, and always ready with a retort, she isn't easily taken in, that woman. When it comes to questions of tradition, what's acceptable and what's not, she doesn't compromise. The word *honor* is of the greatest importance to her. The earth is meant for planting *malangas,* Angolan peas, chives, yams, sugarcane, bananas, not for concrete.

She was the principal heir to some family land and refused to sell it even though the other heirs wanted to have it developed. "No concrete forest on our ancestors' land," she said.

And nothing could convince her to sign. So they hatched a plan to drive her crazy. One headed his car at her, threatening to run her over, another released his cattle in her garden where they wreaked havoc. . . . She shrieked, raged, aroused the people, nothing worked, they continued their circus. She fell ill, her blood pressure rose to 200! To add to her misfortune, the water in the neighborhood was shut off that day. She was very hot and went to buy bottles of mineral water so she could wash. Neighborhood scandal! Amélise is crazy, she bathes in mineral water! A niece, one of the heirs, quickly appeared on the scene armed with a doctor's certificate and dragged her off to the mental hospital. Amélise didn't even have time to get ready, comb her hair, put on a proper dress. She was bundled into a car just as she was. That's what really shocked her. To appear in front of the doctors uncombed, in a housedress—and she, such a proud woman—what shame! Immediately the next day, all her nieces and nephews were at her bedside, urging her to sign the infamous paper. She mocked them: "I knew you weren't very smart, but I didn't think your heads were this empty. You say I'm crazy and yet you want me to sign the paper. A document signed by a mad woman isn't valid. You should have thought up another plan, used force. . . . "

After that shock, Amélise went to a rest home to regain her health. Her first vacation in at least fifty years. When she returned home after a month, she was in fine form, looking younger than ever. There they all were, awaiting her, the thieves, sitting around as if at a wake. They made her feel she was living through her own death. Enough is enough. She really cracked. To keep her from having to return to the insane asylum, a friend, who'd been following the circus from the start, welcomed her into her home to recover. Now she's better, but they were close to the point of driving her mad for the rest of her life.

Those who suffer from madness of a gentle sort aren't dangerous, don't threaten anyone. You can tell that their minds are disconnected by their gestures, their way of smiling, of looking at you. I know a young woman like that. People say she's lovesick. I think, rather, she's crazy over men. When the urge seizes her, she must have one. She dresses up, all clean and well groomed, and takes up a position alongside the road. But she doesn't stop just any old car or any man. She chooses the cars driven by white men and climbs in. She has a gentle madness yet knows exactly what she's doing. All her children are cared for by public assistance. Her family tells how a spell was put on her, that a *gwonèg nouè* she once snubbed sent a spirit to work on her. . . . But I believe that to drive someone crazy, you must plant something in her mind, something that eats away at her.

At church, a man told us that, if he believed in the ability of one person to put an evil spell on another, he'd have gone to consult a *gadèdzafè* every time he bumped his car. After thinking about it, he observed himself at the wheel. He found that if he paid better attention, he managed to avoid the small accidents. Examples such as these help us see, at church, what's really behind the stories of Evil. Yes, Evil exists, and if you're afraid of something, you meet exactly what you're expecting. If the *gadèdzafè* predicts an accident, as soon as you take the wheel, your mind begins working, you think about it, lose control of your body, and crash. Of course, you say the evil spirit X sent to work on me is to blame. If X has had a falling out with you, he'll gloat: "I knew he'd smash himself up in a car accident!"

Manti a mantè, lies of liars! Evil always gets the blame. Just the other day, a fisherman drowned while he was diving to empty someone else's traps. The legitimate owner went around announcing that his nets were "protected" and the guardian spirit reserved the same fate for anyone else who dared approach them. No one interfered with his fishing again. And yet they all knew that one day that old walking barrel of rum would end up at the bottom of the sea.

No need of evil spirits to drive mothers crazy, their children do well enough. These days, no one can pride herself on having well-mannered children. Life itself makes children rebellious. A mother who gives birth to ten children adds ten different sensibilities to society. All from

In each of us, there is room for madness

the same womb, yet all different. A mother must realize this so she can do her best for each one. If she doesn't accept that the second is different from the first, the third from the second, etc., she's done for, overwhelmed, and will quickly have enough of them.

At home, my oldest son is everything: father, foster mother, the household runs thanks to him. And if I wanted Lucie, Ernest, and Joseph to be like him? Then I'd work hard to make them resemble him. I'd drive myself crazy, and even then, I wouldn't succeed, because each child is born under a different star and faces its own destiny. In my parents' home we were four sisters and five brothers. Each one of us was different. If my mother had wanted to make us all alike, she wouldn't have lived to age eighty-three, at least not outside an insane asylum. People live to be very old in there! A friend's father was put away fifty years ago. His relatives collect his pension. When the volcano, La Soufrière, came to life, his son went to get him. He couldn't keep him at home for long. The old man screamed, bawled, thundered throughout the housing development. Yet another one on whom "they" put an Evil spell.

Good, Evil, it's all a question of faith. I bring my religious conviction to everything. God is the father of all, Father Pélage often says, of believers as well as nonbelievers. We, his children, have never seen God, but we speak of Him. We try to understand: how did one thing come about and not another, why does one being exist. . . . Even if you aren't a believer, you can't say that Good was created for me, Evil for others. God created Good. If you follow another path, you meet the Devil, because God is Good and the Devil is Evil. God loves all his children, all those who listen to Him. It's up to you to avoid the path of Evil.

Jesus Christ had such deep love for us that he gave his life. That's also a kind of madness. Perhaps that's why we speak of the folly of the Cross. The Cross isn't simply that bit of wood on which he was crucified, it's everything he suffered for others. They nailed him there to give him the message: that's your place, you who thought yourself so strong. We're stronger than you.

Jesus Christ set an example. In following him, some people want to forget who they are, go beyond themselves, push back the limits of human existence. Of those who begin, many stop and a few crack, ending up in an asylum. The farther we advance, the more of them there are. I wonder if Guadeloupe itself is sick like that and if it's even possible for us to leave this society behind, to change it, before all of our minds are turned inside out.

13

Enmé palé fwansé,

on maladi ka rann moun brak

The love of French,

a malady that drives people mad

Chaj an mwen sé mwen, sé lang an mwen, sé-y ki ka di ki-moun ki ka palé dèyè mwen. An pa ni dwa mété-y anba plat a pyé an-mwen. An pa ni dwa lésé-yo toufé-y pas toufé on lang sé déboujonné Limanité.

My language is my burden, it makes a spokesman of me. I don't have the right to trample it underfoot, don't have the right to see it stifled, because stifling a language removes a bud of Humanity.

Hector Poulet

Some Guadeloupeans feel that a well-brought-up child is a child who always speaks French.

What does the French language have to do with a good upbringing? A properly raised child is one who listens to adults, says hello, and grows up the way his parents endeavor to raise him, with respect and a sense of honor.

An té vlé konprann pouki Gwad-loupéyen enmé palé fwansé konsa.

Pouki Nèg ka méprizé kréyòl, lang yo konnèt palè.

An pé di sa lèd: ou pa konnèt palé fwansé, sé fwansé ou vlé palé.

Fò ou brak menm pou ou rété adan on sitiyasyon konsa.

I'd like to understand why Gua-deloupeans so love to speak French.

Why the blacks scorn Creole, a language they can speak. Oh, how ugly! You don't know how to speak French, yet it's French you want to use.

You must be nuts to stay in such a situation.

The love of French, a malady that drives people mad

Is this malady caught at school? I think so. When I was young, the most important thing was to learn French. That's why you went. And it hasn't changed much. Today, if you don't know French, you're considered an complete person.

We never saw pictures of blacks in our schoolbooks. No black mammas or papas. Only now, when I revive all the memories of my childhood and my life, do I realize that I never noticed: all the people in our books were white. That's a real problem. You know it's a photo, a drawing, you recognize a papa, a mamma, but don't see it's a white lady, a white gentleman! And they didn't say to us: this is a white man. They couldn't tell us. We never saw black people in books, they simply weren't there.

It didn't shock us not to see Guadeloupeans in our books. It wouldn't have entered my mind to ask my mother: "Why is the lady in the book white?"

I absolutely couldn't have asked that question.

They showed you a pa-pa, do-do, ba, be-bi, bo, a bob-bin. Now I see it all clearly, and I am disgusted when, in my granddaughter's book, they call you Valerie. Valerie who goes to school, that's you, with her books and her little brother, a leather bag on her back. We don't have leather schoolbags! We go to school with bags made of canvas, of *véti-ver,* or with a small basket. . . . In remembering this, I realize that we don't think about these things, really not at all.

At school, nothing was explained to us. We simply recited, the Gauls this and the Gauls that, the Caribs rubbed their bodies with *rou-kou* . . . Kept in, dismissed, without understanding a thing.

Now I travel, I discover: hey! what I recited in local geography really exists! We heard about "the Rose River," "the Sarcelle," "the Lézarde," but how were we to know they really flowed in Guadeloupe! "Guiy-ono," "Bayarjan," all these names seemed foreign to me, and I recited them with pleasure. But to situate them in a region! It all remained a mystery to us.

The teacher didn't provide any explanation: keeping you quiet and speaking French was her job. Nonetheless, you did learn something but your mind wasn't engaged in finding out just where you were, who you were.

We didn't know about slavery. I heard something about "white slaves" in the history of France. . . . So many things were kept hidden from us. Why?

Some time ago, I went to a lecture about how the blacks had suffered under slavery. A man stood up, angry enough to eat his mother-in-law: "I don't agree with any of this. What an idea to bring people here in order to rehash all these sufferings of the past. It can only renew hatred against the whites."

Did he, perhaps, live with a white woman? What was he afraid of? If you haven't experienced all those atrocities yourself, you're not forced to hate. But even if I wanted to, I can't obliterate slavery, it really and truly happened. Always hiding, hiding our history!

Even though I didn't know about slavery, I thought I was well informed about the *Nègres marrons*. You'd hear: "A *Nègre marron* escaped! Children, watch out, go straight home from school, don't dawdle on the way!"

The *Nègres marrons*—killers, robbers, bandits, evil people who escaped from prison and who were evoked to frighten us children: "If you're not good, if you don't say your prayers at night, the *Nègre marron* will come and carry you off into the woods."

Only recently did I learn who the real *Nègres marrons* were: rebellious blacks, who stood tall, refused the whip, and fled the plantations. I learned, thanks to all those meetings, lectures, get-togethers, upheavals of the last few years. We were forced to grow rapidly, and if I hadn't paid attention, I'd be worse off than many other Guadeloupeans, blinded. It's true, I'm not lying. When Lucie, my oldest daughter, was at school, I fumed when the boys came to chat with her in Creole. I thought: that's not a person she should see; in her last year of high school and allowing boys who don't even speak French to flirt with her! I didn't say a word to her, but I thought it. On the other hand, I certainly wanted her to speak with other people, perhaps less worthy than those boys, but people I knew, neighbors, for instance. I didn't see things clearly at all. Such thoughts should never have entered my mind. At that time, a young girl preparing for her high school diploma wasn't allowed to speak with just any little black boy. All us mothers shared this attitude.

Stepping back, I realize it was stupid to think that way. Now I've learned that those who are meant to advance, advance and those who are meant to slip back, slip backward.

With this French business, "they" caught us like crabs in a trap. Still today, many people are shocked if a child is addressed in Creole. And when it comes from a teacher, the parents and grandparents react angrily:

"Sé moun ki ja konnèt palé
    fwansé ki ka di lézòt pa
    bizouen-i."

"Those people who already speak French are the ones telling others that they don't need it."

The love of French, a malady that drives people mad

"An ja maléré kon lapyè, an pa tini hak, fo timoun an mwen palé fwansé pou vouè si li ka trapé on sitiyasyon."

"I'm already as unhappy as a stone. I own nothing. My child must speak French to land a good job."

"Pouki ou ka palé gwo kréyòl konsa pou timoun la? Palé fwansé pou-i trapé bon labitid pou-i kapab réponn on gran moun an fwansé, menm si moun la palé kréyòl ba-i."

"Why are you speaking that peasant Creole to this child? Speak to him in French so he'll learn good habits, be able to answer an adult in French even if he's addressed in Creole."

"Gadé, on gason pé palé kréyòl, on fi non. Sa pa bon si li vlé fè on bon mayé.

"A boy can speak Creole, but not a girl. It will interfere with her making a good marriage."

And so on and so forth. . . .

Father Céleste told us about a discussion he'd had with his godmother: "Chérubin," she said to him, "your mother brought you up in the Kalakaz woods, at Dèyè Bwa, in the hills above Trois-Rivières, but she spoke to you in French! She sent you to school, and far away too. And now I hear that you speak Creole in church and encourage others to do the same! What's this business of Creole in the house of God?"

To her, preaching in Creole showed disrespect for the Lord. And she's not the only one to think so. For many, using Creole in school or in court would also be disrespectful.

Those who don't know how to read or write are the most outspoken critics of Creole, especially in church. They're already trapped, tied up, have lost whatever belonged to them. My God, how sad, all those people who can't even say "baked bread" in French want to forbid the use of Creole, prohibit their children from speaking Creole, detest Creole! French was given to them, so it's the language they must use. They're head over heels in love with French!

That's why a priest preaching in Creole or we faithful coming to church, speaking Creole into the microphone about how the Gospel inspires us, didn't happen overnight.

The idea was that everyone, even those unable to read or write or speak French, could take part in commenting on the Gospel. In our neighborhood meetings, we rolled along in French at first. People hardly spoke up, even those who had something to say. In Guadeloupe, we make too much fun of people who speak French poorly. You're careful before you open your mouth, because you know that all your descendants may have to live with your mistakes.

There's a young lady nicknamed "I seen you" because, one day, her grandfather spoke to a beautiful woman in French: "The first time I seen you, my hurt went boom boom."

And a Mister "Gligli": "I love you like a *gligli* perched on a dry *zaboka*." (I love you like a bird perched on a dry avocado branch.)

When I went to hear political speeches, I was particularly interested in the words the speakers used. I poked fun at them, laughed at all their mistakes, and tried hard to tuck them away in my memory, to be shared with those who weren't there.

How I laughed at hearing a candidate rail against the Communists: "We wanted to hold a market to sold this year's good harvest of *bou-kousou* beans. The Comminis Party has *kouyé* (killed) it! We wanted a clanics to treat for sick's booboos. The Comminis party has *rou-kouvé* it!"

And that other one who found himself "constipated" by the state of the mayor's office and the monument to the dead!

Even those who aren't fluent in French love to laugh at the mistakes of others. And how they applaud beautiful French phrases even if they don't understand the meaning.

I find it quite amusing to hear a person ask the time of day like this: "Miss, could you put me in direct contact with the palpitating progress of time?"

Chérubin knew all this, and also that some people who don't speak French well are embarrassed. He chose to employ our language as a better way of spreading the word of Christ.

When we used French to comment on the Gospel, we couldn't say much, couldn't go into it very deeply. The written text was there, we just repeated: Christ said this, Christ said that. In Creole, it was differ-ent. You can express yourself, all your ideas flow freely, you bring the text to life. If you really want to explain how the passage affects you, you can't do it in French. You search for words, don't find them, trip yourself up. You don't manage to say what you feel, and the others don't understand you. Rather than floundering around in a *miganné*[85] French, speak your own Creole!

The group leaders understood this, but for some of them, it required an effort. Adele, for instance, is a teacher, she teaches school in French, her family raised her to use French. She was accustomed to the Mass in French—impossible to ask her to dive into Creole all at once. She did it slowly, at her own pace. When she saw the trouble people were

The love of French, a malady that drives people mad

having at the meetings, she advised them: "Say it in Creole," and then she carried on in Creole. She made the effort.

What problems with this Creole business! I often criticize Chérubin because he gets into arguments with the youngsters over it. For instance, he wants them to compose songs in Creole. But religious songs aren't written off the cuff! It takes talent. Simply finding words in Creole isn't enough, you must know how to arrange them so they flow—and then there's the music. A young woman in charge of the choir expressed it well to Céleste: "I'm not a musician, I never learned music, I can't compose songs. We were taught the songs in the book, we repeat them, we sing them."

Without the emergence of the U.T.A. and U.P.G. unions,[86] Chérubin never would have dared to introduce Creole into the church and no one would be using our language at the meetings today.

We spoke it, but as for making a speech, using Creole in public *tou-longalè* (for an entire discussion)—no way. The people from U.T.A. were the first to say: "We're talking to agricultural workers who can't read or write. If they belong to our union, we shouldn't speak to them in French but in Creole. That way they'll be able to understand us."

They came to the factory gates to explain their business.

At that time, in 1971, I wasn't much involved, but I kept an ear open and tried to find out what was going on. I was at a friend's house, at La Rosière, when someone came by with a report of the meeting: "That band of little niggers! To hell with them! I thought they were coming to say something important, but all they did was speak Creole!"

He hadn't listened, hadn't understood a thing. He didn't know if the union men had talked about the price per ton of sugarcane or a prohibition on cutting cane by surface area, he only remembered one thing: "A band of little niggers speaking Creole came and acted like idiots."

For the first time, the cane workers had been able to express themselves and their demands in their own language. After that, Father Céleste, who lived among the small farmers and agricultural workers and who, as a man, had joined them in many protests, must have said to himself: Why not? Why not use Creole in church, at our Gospel meetings. Creole is the language of the poor.[87]

The idea caught on, but with the speed of a *mòlòkoy* (tortoise): once something has been drilled into your head, it's not so easy to change. For those immersed in French, taking part in a Gospel meeting or a Mass in Creole was a major upheaval.

Some people didn't want to hear a word about it, considered it unacceptable. They'd never seen anything of the kind, not here in Guadeloupe! And yet:

Kréyòl sé zépon natirèl an nou. Dépi an vant a manman nou, nou ka bennyé adan. Sòti ou sòti, sé sa ou ka tann palé a kaz a-ou. Fwahnsé sé on lenj prété. Yo pòté-i ban nou è nau enki varé adan-i kon bèf a tchou fon. E nou touvé nou pri.	Creole is our natural spur. In our mother's bellies we're already bathed in it. We heard it spoken at home from the moment of our birth. French is a borrowed garment. They brought it to us, and we plunged into it like a raw-boned bull. We found ourselves trapped.

As for me, I went to school, I speak French, but still don't know all its nuances, don't know what exists in the depths of that language. I'm told I read well, and, at Carangaise, I was the queen of the prayers for the dead. Through force of habit, I managed to recite the words without faltering. But if I'd been asked their meaning: zero, I didn't understand a thing.

Since Father Céleste began explaining everything in Creole, we know what the words of the Bible mean. As for the Latin chants, we filtered them through Creole:

Ave Maria became *lave larí la* (wash the streets)
laudate, dlo glasé (ice water)
miséricorde, miziré kòd (measure the cord), etc.

As *maman-catéchisme,* catechism mother, I realize that children today aren't any farther along than I was yesterday. They don't understand French. The other day, they were asked to draw a picture representing the words: "Jesus was with his disciples, then he went apart from them."

"*Man* Joseph," one of them said to me, "I can't draw that, it's impossible, how can I draw Jesus cut into parts?"

He understood *apart* as having the Creole meaning: cut in parts, split.

My daughter Lucie has a four-year-old son. She speaks to him in French. She doesn't like to use Creole with such young children. Her brother Mark and I gallop along in Creole all the time, with everyone. I don't feel Creole has a bad influence on us. In my youth, a mother would never have said to her child: "I forbid you to speak Creole!"

That custom hadn't yet made its appearance. The older people knew

The love of French, a malady that drives people mad

Creole, period, that's all. They weren't entangled in this language business as we are today. They didn't question things, felt free.

A cousin from Carangaise had two daughters. He set his mind on
bringing them up using French exclusively. As soon as he opened his
mouth, everyone laughed. He lost his temper: "This not first time you
laugh through your sleeve to me. You think *sé dé ti* shame you me
shame!"

My cousin didn't know French. His desire to bring up his children
in this language seemed bizarre. A strange *migan* came from his children's lips. Even if an adult addressed one of them in Creole, she'd
answer in French, in her own version of French, torturing the language:

"Mamma is down below back, she says like that to send her a
pepper. . . . "

"Rain, go chase, you stop me, don't sit on the ground, come take off
the wet linens onto you."

And so the mania to "speak French" gained ground. I myself began
it with my own children. With the last ones, if I remember correctly,
although I'm not sure exactly when or how.

I'm more or less fluent in French, but I never got involved in school
affairs, correcting homework or their way of speaking. Mothers who
want to direct everything without realizing that they're not up to the
level of their children are real pests. They interfere every which way,
correcting what shouldn't be changed, adding mistakes where there
aren't any.

"Mamma, where's that ya lay down the comb?"

"Ah already say to ya like that, it's them comb."

They forbid Creole in their homes even though they can't speak
French.

I never used that method, and in fact, French quickly disappeared
from my house, to everyone's great indifference. I kept my traditions,
my way of life. I don't speak French at home. When I meet "French
speakers," I address them in French. When I'm with my son Justin and
his wife, I speak French with him. He married a white woman who
doesn't understand our language. She might suspect I was criticizing
her. You must show respect for the person you're with. That's how the
overseer of the plantation treated me. He spoke Creole with Joseph
and addressed me in French.

With friends, in shops, in the street, everywhere, it's Creole. My
daughter who lives in France phoned me the other day, in French. I
answered in Creole. If she'd acted surprised, I'd have said: "My girl,
I haven't changed. Did we ever chat together in French at home?"

I don't see how it would be possible for me to state categorically: I
don't want to hear Creole spoken! These days, parents drum into their

children's heads: "Don't speak Creole, it will interfere with your learning French."

My children can't reproach me for having had ideas like that. Their father caught the French bug. He didn't forbid them to speak Creole, but he always addressed them in French. Not I. I was raised using Creole and my children too, whether they went to school or not, the small school or the big one.

What problems we have today about the use of Creole, it's in vogue. The teachers keep after you. They insist: "Too much Creole harms the children, they can't write their homework in proper French!"

They see the problem their own way, but I'm not a teacher and always say what I think, express my ideas—at parents' meetings, for instance: "I've never spoken French to my children at home, and it didn't interfere with their learning French. I even have one who astonished everyone on the plantation, especially my brother-in-law. A sugarcane worker's child, and he expresses himself so well in French! Extraordinary! All my children did what they felt they had to do. Those who stopped their studies—it was their own fault, the result of their laziness and bad company. They all had the potential to succeed, and I did everything in my power to send them to school."

So I don't have any problem with this business—speaking French, speaking Creole—and when Father Céleste shifted to Creole, I cheered!

The use of Creole greatly changed our way of interacting, changed, for instance, the relationship in the community between a teacher and a farm laborer. The common people have so much to say, but they didn't express themselves before. Now, thanks to Creole, they dare to speak out. I realize that our language, Creole, has a real value, but "they" had killed it.

There are several ways to kill someone: you can physically strike him down, with a mortal blow, and he falls. You can also kill him, and he's there, left standing, but not really there, not aware of himself. He's dead. What is he? Nothing. A zombi. His eyes are wide open but he's blind, his mind can't see.

That's what's called killing a person without him noticing he's being killed. And how could we react? There was no one to help us see what we should have seen, discover what there was to discover. We'd heard of important blacks like Félix Eboué. Now the Guadeloupeans are trying to discover who they themselves are. I still don't know who I am, where I come from. I say: "I'm Guadeloupean." My identity card reads "French nationality." It's as if a woman has acknowledged me the way a stepmother acknowledges her children.

When I'm told: "Without France we couldn't live," I answer: "That's normal. When you assume responsibility for a child, you give it enough to eat and drink. Otherwise, you're letting it down, deserting it."

Not so long ago, I couldn't say I was either Guadeloupean or French. I didn't really know what was meant by a French département or by the word *assimilation*. Since I've taken an interest in the new movements, I've discovered the importance of knowing "who you are," "where we come from." Of course, we all come from our mothers' wombs, that's our only real birthplace, but France controls everything.

As for this money that seeks people out without their having to work and falls into their hands like a ripe mango, it overwhelms heart and mind, sets heads spinning. This money, earned without sweat, destroys your balance, vanquishes your comprehension.

Sometimes I try to explain where all this is leading. I'm told: "*Man Joseph*, you have a son who helps support you, a daughter who's a teacher, another who works in France. . . . "

Oh, yes, they're right, I can't deny it even if I only receive a one-hundred-franc note each month. And yet you shouldn't just stand there, waiting, simply because the government's family allowance is convenient. Yes, France gives now, but will it always?

The first time, we received seventy francs at the start of the school year, the second time, slightly more. Everyone griped: "Oh, lordy! How far will seventy francs stretch for seven children? They can just keep their money."

When the subsidy rose to four hundred and fifty francs, their song changed tune, it was: "Hallelujah! Long live Mother France!"

At the beginning, those who received the special allowance for single women didn't brag about it. Then the rumor spread. Each unmarried woman filled out her request, especially those who didn't work and so weren't eligible for the family allowance, *l'argent braguette*, trouser-fly money.

Lajan bragèt	Family allowance
Timoun a laloua	Children supported by the state
"Pa ni pi bon mari pasé lasékir- ité."	"There's no better husband than *Sécurité sociale*."
"On timoun andikapé, sé konn- yéla on bénédiksyon adan on kaz."	"Today, a handicapped child is a blessing for a home."

Words that hurt, words that dishonor us women. Money, money, the French government's hold on us, it causes trouble in families and among the people. What sort of children will our "single women" raise? Children who aren't told their father's name, who see him ske-daddle out the window when the inspector who checks on "women sleeping alone" comes by. . . . Of course, these women are wrong to act like that, but from there to "ripping apart their charity," destroying their pride at public meetings . . . By ridiculing them, repeatedly telling them that they're "assisted," we'll turn them into "beggars."

Chérubin himself puts too much emphasis on this business of "assisted" and "beggars." Before judging each other, we must understand how we've gotten to where we are, all the destruction that the *poux-de-bois,* the termites, have caused in our minds.

They have changed the way we use our own things. We're in the century of electricity, it's normal to have a refrigerator. Yes, gas rings, kerosene stoves are found in the kitchens, but why not retain your terra-cotta jars that keep water so cool, your charcoal burner that gives grilled fish such a wonderful flavor, your gourds?

Today we want everything all prepared for us. Instead of raising chickens, killing and plucking them ourselves, we buy them ready to be cooked. Instead of planting yams, we add water to an instant mix. We no longer make any effort to get our food. Why not prepare meals the way we used to? We ourselves rush in and accept their customs.

Many people are caught up in it. I'm speaking of those who can afford to buy food and merchandise in the large stores like Monoprix, not of the poor. The bureaucrats are the ones who started this mania of eating like the whites, dressing like them, speaking like them.

All the things displayed in the stores were brought to Guadeloupe for the bureaucrats. And because of them—and their enjoyment of buying armfuls of things—the poor suffer. The bureaucrat's paycheck comes regularly, every month. The administration knows how much he earns, so it knows how much to charge for a pound of meat. The poor must buy at the same price. Little money, big price. Can a binder of cane, who occasionally earns a day's wages on the plantation, give her children milk, meat, the balanced diet of a bureaucrat's son or daughter? Never. And yet you, who aren't part of that group, want to imitate them. If you have a child who's a bureaucrat, he always gives you a bit of money, occasionally brings a couple of pounds of apples from France. If you go to the hospital, you get grapes, pear juice. . . . Once you've tasted all these new things, you dance to their music, no longer to the rhythm of your own drum.

Returning one day from a visit to the doctor, I arrived in my housing development. One of my neighbors nabbed me: "*Man* Joseph, come and see, they're installing a telephone at Cecile's."

"Cecile?"

The love of French, a malady that drives people mad

"Yes, the woman who's squeezed in between two families, who's angry with both. . . . "

"But, my dear, that's not possible, she only recently put in her request. I submitted mine much earlier. I'm not going to ruin my health trying to get one before its my turn, but all the same . . . "

I was simply talking off the top of my head, not thinking about causing any trouble, and wouldn't you know it, the guy who'd come to install the phone overheard me and came over to us. "What's that, ma'am? Did Madame C only submit her request a month ago? I'll check the orders. Some people have been waiting for five years."

Cecile didn't get her telephone that day. Others in the development had priority. I was quite embarrassed. I'm not a person who wants to hurt others. I should have kept my mouth shut. Certain people gloated: "It serves her right. She has delusions of grandeur, wants to act like a civil servant, to run after us and do everything we do, have everything we have. I'm a civil servant, so is my husband, I'm the one who can get a telephone put in!"

The tone of this woman's voice made you feel she really wanted to say: "I don't consider you a human being, you're not like me. Since I'm a civil servant, I'm someone important, I can buy whatever I want. You, *tikyap,* poor little thing, you try to be in my class, asking for a telephone, but to call whom? What gall!"

From what height did she speak, that of her paycheck? Nasty words like those lead to conflict. Not only was Cecile angry with her aristocratic neighbor, she began to hate her. One day, she could hardly contain her glee upon hearing that the bureaucrat-husband had been in a car accident.

That's where this mania of possessions and of keeping up with the neighbors leads us, here in Guadeloupe. People aren't happier because of it, quite the contrary. They've lost the meaning of life. And, besides, how can you hold onto it when you live in a housing development? It's all gossip and the like. Nothing is shared, nothing done together as neighbors. What counts is themselves, their friends, their families, their house, their furniture.

Two cars in almost every family, one for the gentleman, one for the lady. The families of *gwokyap:* teachers, bureaucrats. A fisherman leads the life of a bureaucrat thanks to all the strings he pulls. Everyone lives for the grandstand. How they make me laugh! To appear to be something, they bleed themselves dry.

In one household, the paycheck of the husband, a civil servant, arrives each month. The wife raises pigs, chickens, rabbits, saves leftovers, cuts grass along the side of the road. All this work to redo the living room! To put money into the pockets of the white man in his store!

Her chairs itch her backside, she says. She bought four huge stuffed things, but careful! Children are forbidden to sit on them, relatives prohibited from moving them. Maybe once a year, at New Year's, the family will be invited to try them out. . . . Meanwhile, there they sit, for display, to show off.

Not much in my house. Four small armchairs my daughter gave me when she came for vacation two years ago. My six chairs didn't suit her.

"If you don't like them, add whatever you'd like."

She wanted to furnish a small living room for me: a low table and four wooden armchairs. They're used as horses by all the children who come by. Everyone is allowed to sit on them or to move them around.

How do you expect those people, well entrenched in their positions with all their debts, to lend a hand in changing Guadeloupe? They'll be at your side for a few demonstrations, but they'll say no to independence—without even knowing what it is, they don't want it. And how could they know? They don't go out, don't go to meetings, and the independence parties themselves keep their plans secret. Without knowing *a* or *b* about something, you can't really want to take part.

We must kick these rotten old shoes off our feet. But the majority of Guadeloupeans don't want to hear anything about independence. Agreed, nothing works in the country; agreed, everything is going wrong and our situation isn't great, but still, independence . . . Even those who might consider the idea hang back, timidly, not knowing exactly where to go or what to do. Look at Haiti, they say, how long that country has been independent! Must we endure what the Haitians have? People ask themselves all sorts of questions. They live badly, but they live. They're sure of what they have. They don't know what they'll find at the end of the road to independence.

Es nou ké rétouné	Will we return
èvè twa wòch a difé,	to a wood fire in a triangle of stones,
dèyè chabon,	to charcoal,
chèché sèl òbò lanmè,	to getting salt from the sea,
limyè a chaltouné?	and light from a torch?

They ask questions simply to ask them, but they don't listen to the answers. How can they be moved along if they don't go out, don't even go to meetings when they're about everyday concerns of their lives?

The love of French, a malady that drives people mad

When the company that provides water to Lamentin wasn't doing its job well and our faucets ran dry, when we saw the mayor's office slapping a heavy tax on the bills, we held a public demonstration. Only three people from my housing development joined in. Afterward, everyone was pleased not to pay the local tax, but no one had done anything about it. It's the same with the rural Christian community center. They don't come, they're afraid of the priest who brings politics into the church. On the other hand, they send their children to the summer camps that he organizes. Yes, that's convenient. But to guide them along the road to independence, that's something else entirely. It will be hard, very hard. Some people think voting will be enough. We won't get independence by voting, only its likeness! So we must talk, explain . . . but not indiscriminately. I carefully choose the people I speak with. Discussing with people who don't think, who haven't yet understood and don't want to understand, who take part in nothing and resolutely oppose it all, simply gets their backs up, causes problems.

While you see independence as a hope, they see it as a catastrophe. How can you fail to get worked up and quarrel? And harsh words, angry words, tumble out anywhere and everywhere, in meetings as well as at Mass. Unfounded words, words without any real meaning, ironic, nasty words, and words not everyone can accept. A few months ago, at the La Rosière festival, I met a friend, and, quite naturally, we began to discuss the question of independence. Angelina, another acquaintance, was behind us. She joined our conversation: "If you want independence, why don't you just take it?"

"It doesn't happen like that, my girl, I'm getting ready for it, I take part in all the demonstrations."

"Are you also getting ready to suffer?"

"Suffer? From what? Whether we live under France or under independence we'll always manage. Today, I have a gas burner, so I buy gas. If tomorrow it's charcoal, I have charcoal at home. If I have to light a fire, I'll burn some wood to cook my breadfruit. If it's decided that everyone must work in the cane fields, I'll give a day's work without suffering. Of course, employees, people comfortably off who raise their children in cotton wool, who have lost the taste for work, might feel it in their backs. Even the young people today—who agree with and take part in *coups de main,* who find it amusing to cut cane and bind it into sheaves—I'm not sure they'd hold up if they had to earn their living that way. I don't have a garden now, in the housing development, but I know how to raise chickens, a pig. I'm not comfortably installed anywhere, independence won't bother me."

"You have confidence that the blacks can run the country? Look how they behave as soon as they work in an office. They take leave of their senses. Just ask them for directions if you want to see. And if they were in the government? Blacks will eat blacks, that's for sure."

Olyé nou wantré anba Nèg vo-métan nou rété anba Blan.	It's better to remain under the white man's thumb than to fall at the hand of a black man.

I feel that blacks don't have confidence in themselves, so they can't have confidence in other blacks. They're uneasy, they want to know. They have their lives, their customs. Would they be allowed to keep their belongings? their salaries? their pensions? And how about freedom?

I believe we must identify everything that frightens people, know the fears that keep them from struggling, listen, allow others to speak, to say what they have in the back of their minds: "I don't want independence for this or that reason. . . . "

So many things surface. If the Communists govern Guadeloupe, they'll divide everything up: if you have two radios, they'll take one, four chairs, they'll take two, eight acres, half will be confiscated. . . . I try to explain: "How could your furniture, your household, be targeted?"

I remember at Capesterre, when the Communist Lacavé won so many votes in the election, I was warned: "Leonora, if you vote for the Communists, you'll never be allowed to go to France to visit your children. They'll make you sign papers, you'll never be free, you won't be able to do this, or that. . . . "

Sometimes even my daughter Viviane reproaches me: "Mamma, no matter where you go, you only speak of the Gospel and politics."

But I don't speak about them enough! It's true, as soon as something happens, I give my opinion and urge others to get involved. If I die tomorrow, the younger generation will continue suffering.

Although I'm somewhat informed, I can't figure out what's in the hearts of those who lead the fight for independence. What government would they install to replace the French? How will they go about it? We shouldn't be sentimental, but too much violence isn't good either.

I'm a believer, I have faith. I don't mean I'm better than the U.P.L.G. militants.[88] Even though they don't go to church on Sunday, they carry on a more important work than we do, we Christians of the congregation. Besides, they too are believers. We shouldn't reject their faith. They believe in the liberation of Guadeloupe. That faith keeps them fighting and gives them strength. They're right, life today has turned upside down because *Yo* (They) crush us, beat us. I don't know when or how, but *Yo* have killed us. I'm beginning to see clearly and to understand how they killed us, from bottom to top, gently over a low flame, without touching us. Here, everyone knows that you can kill someone without touching his body. France casts a spell over us, wipes out our customs, our thoughts. And the representatives, the council members, the Guadeloupean senators, are the ones who carry out the orders. They too are *yo*. Who tells us to vote for president of the French Republic? Who delivers the propaganda: "You are French, you must vote"?

In 1978, Guadeloupe sent three R.P.R.[89] representatives over there. "Without France, no rice, no work, no money, no *Sécurité sociale*, no government allowance," they cried. People were frightened. France owns our bodies, and it's France that directs our lives, not us. Even if we manage to tackle a few small things, we're forced to recognize that France is in command here. What belongs to us? France began to capture us through the vote when we were made into a *département*, to steal the history of our people, a history I'm just beginning to discover at over sixty years of age.

As soon as you vote for president of the Republic, as soon as you vote for a representative or a councilor, you're playing by the government's rules, you can't claim you're not French. With this business of the vote, they slowly took possession of our minds. The vote came with the French citizenship cards, and happy as can be, we didn't see the lasso that began to tighten around our necks and to choke us.

By going to meetings, I learned the real truth about our representatives. I thought: "If that's the way it is, I don't see why I should go vote for these gentlemen. Once in France, our small brown coffee beans will be lost in a big pile of white aspirin tablets."

Yet I still don't know whether the priests will retain the right to say Mass when the independence party governs the country. If our bishop, Monsignor Oually, continues to remain neutral, not supporting either those of us who fight for the liberation of our people or our critics, all Christians will suffer when independence comes. You must act while a thing is being organized, not on the day it happens.

Tomorrow, the independence fighters won't be able to do everything they want to in Guadeloupe. The Guadeloupean people know how to say no. It's fine to escape from under the thumb of the colonizers, but not simply to give ourselves over to the next thing that comes along. I'm free. This afternoon, I came to see you. Tomorrow, if I want to go out and someone comes to ask: "Where are you going?" that's not good. Controlling people and things, no way!

What's hidden in the bosom of independence? When the U.P.L.G. appeared, it said: "One people. One path: independence. One organization: the U.P.L.G."

One people, of course. One path, well, we'll all become independent. But this business of one organization, what does that mean? I must ask them.

In the meantime, my brain cells are working: How is it possible? One person will be responsible for everything? But several groups are working for independence! If there's only one organization, there won't be the church. The "one organization" will be in charge: you must say this, you must do that. If it says "eliminate the church," you get rid of the church. What will that mean?

Maybe they'll be forced to see things differently. I don't know whether or not these words provoked suspicion, but you don't hear them much anymore. They must be preparing something else. If they sense resistance, they'll be forced to change tactics, to warn themselves: "Uh, oh! Watch out!"

Father Céleste is always changing his methods. He knows that, although almost all Guadeloupe is part of the church, the church itself doesn't support independence. Only a small segment of the Christian community has started along the road to liberation.

Some think independence will come soon. I don't see how. France realizes great profit from us because it has set up all its businesses here. We don't have much remaining that's really ours. That's why we're now searching for what we've lost. We must become Guadeloupeans again. I too have started to remake myself, and I couldn't speak like this if I weren't involved in social action.

For me, being Guadeloupean means first speaking one's own language, Creole, which is perhaps the most important thing we've retained, aside from the death wakes, even though, nowadays, people rarely hold wakes like they used to. If they do, the wakes are silent, in the style of the white folks. They've lost the enormous Guadeloupean laugh. Their laughs are restrained, small, closed. Nor do they want the *gwoka*.

As for me, my whole body starts shaking as soon as I hear its music. I agree that only the *gwoka* should be played at a wake, but at a wedding? I don't even think that it used to be that way in the old days. At weddings you find accordions, maracas, triangles, people singing Creole songs, all sorts of old songs, and dancing the quadrille.[90]

La coquette fi-la jalou nou . . .

Nowadays, we can't dance the whole night long to the music of the drum, it's too loud for our ears. Today's ears aren't like yesterday's. They're not used to the sound of the drum.

The love of French, a malady that drives people mad

People who were raised without the drum—I mean the younger generation—well, they're the ones who clamor for the *gwoka* and demand the use of Creole.

Kréyòl, gwoka, biten an mwen menm.

Creole, *gwoka,* you are mine.

Kréyòl, gwoka, fout zòt ja pran fè,
fè kon fè trasé.

Creole, *gwoka,* how they've shown you a thing or two, made you bear the impossible.

Lékòl, légliz té èskonminyé zòt,

Excommunicated by school, by church,

men zòt té la an biskankwen toupatou ka véyé jé a zòt.

yet you were there, hidden everywhere, watching.

Zò té la, ti la a zòt ka véyé lanm, zòt té sav zafé a zòt zòt té sav lalin ka chanjé katyé.

You were there, in your corner, watching the waves, certain that the moon would wax and wane.

Jodijou zò ka voyé douvan.
An ka mété pon moun odéfi fé zòt pé.

Today, you forge ahead.
I dare any and all to quiet your voice.

14

Lavi oben lanmò: afòs rèté san manjé,

Pè Sélès mété-i ant yo dé

Father Chérubin Céleste begins a hunger

strike and places himself between life

and death

. . . man is a *yes* . . . *Yes* to life. *Yes* to love. *Yes* to generosity. But man is also a *no*. *No* to scorn of man. *No* to degradation of man. *No* to exploitation of man. *No* to the butchery of what is most human in man: freedom.

Frantz Fanon,
Black Skin, White Masks

The strike in the cane fields had already lasted a month and a half. Negotiations stalled. The union men who led the strike despaired. The factory owners were letting the strike degenerate. In addition, they brought in scabs, Haitian cutters, to launch the harvest, to further weaken the workers, to break the strike.

In March 1975, we were worried: *képis rouges* everywhere, surrounding the cane fields. On the plantations, the Haitians worked under the eyes of the C.R.S.[91] Several of us had received orders from the bailiff to remove our cabins from the lands of Monsieur S, owner of the plantations and the factory at Grosse-Montagne. We all felt things were going badly and thought to ourselves: all these battles, all this suffering, and for nothing!

On Sunday, 1 March, the congregations of Castel and Grosse-Montagne met at Lamentin. They gathered in silence, deeply moved. After the sermon on the passage about Lazarus, many people called out: "But we're the ones rotting away. Up to our necks in this mess. Will we be able to get ourselves out?"

Father Chérubin Céleste begins a hunger strike

"Of course, it must be possible, since Jesus Christ was able to revive a man who had already completely rotted away."

"There's certainly a way to revive these people who are hopelessly mired in poverty."

"With the help of Jesus Christ, we can find a way out, since he was able to raise Lazarus from the grave."

The story of Lazarus, of death transformed into life, gave us a starting point. At the end of the meeting, we felt more cheerful, this passage from the Gospel had put us back on our feet. Before breaking up, we agreed to meet later in the week to figure out what we should do next.

Two days later, I was at Rosita's discussing all this. Father Céleste arrived. He'd already been to my house. He wanted to speak with the group leaders. We went to find Monsieur Alexis, his daughter Adele, and Monsieur Etienne and all met at Louise's.

Father Céleste was worried: we couldn't sit by and let the situation deteriorate further. We must quickly assemble all the members of the congregation.

We all agreed, and Monsieur Alexis called the meeting. Many people came. I was astonished to hear Monsieur Alexis declare: "You won't succeed."

He, the leader at first, already discouraging the others. We were shocked. His daughter Adele said to him: "Papa, even if we're not sure of success, we must try."

I couldn't believe my ears. At thirty-five, Adele was the most obedient daughter I knew, well brought up and everything, respectful, and there she was, daring to speak out against her father! She had finally assumed the responsibility of an adult, had begun to conquer her fear.

We decided to go the mayor's office and let him know that even those people who wanted to work couldn't do so: they were afraid of the security forces that surrounded the cane fields. He'd have to come with us to the plantations and see for himself what was going on.

Simply mentioning the name of the mayor, Dagonia, caused tension. In the church we'd already witnessed confrontations between Dr. Dagonia's followers and those of the former mayor, the teacher Toribio. Politics[92] had already made its entrance into the church, but we didn't want to enter politics. Madame Plaisance called out that Dagonia was a coward and we should send as many people as possible to him.

"Yeah," hurled another, "he might run and hide."

Chicaté, general secretary of the U.P.G., didn't support our idea. "You'll be taking an incompetent man to the cane fields. Dagonia doesn't know anything."

Off we went, people from Cadet, Castel, and Grosse-Montagne. When we arrived at the mayor's house, we went around the back. We knocked, and he appeared at the door. We told him everything that had happened: he must come with us. He telephoned his assistant, asking him to come along since a delegation wanted to take him to the cane fields.

The first problem arose when we arrived at the bridge of Ravine-Chaude. To get to Douillard, one of Monsieur S's plantations, you must cross there. The bridge is narrow, the width of a car, a cart. The guards had gone for Monsieur S, who declared: "No one will enter my plantation. It's *mine,* private property."

"We haven't come to cause trouble, Monsieur S, we simply wanted to verify something. According to the radio, there aren't any troops in the cane fields. We've come to see."

He wouldn't listen. He sent for the commander of the security police. Father Céleste was furious and began to get agitated. Finally, we were told that only two people could enter. Dagonia threatened: "You won't let me enter? Well then, I'll resign."

Dagonia acted like a real man that day, threatening to resign!

"I want to go in!" shouted a man who happened to be there.

"No. You won't," said Father Céleste, "those who came here should go in. We're a delegation."

Crossing the bridge seemed more and more difficult. We had to talk and talk but hold firm. We couldn't accept that only part of the delegation would enter, the rest staying outside. The delegation had come to confirm something, it should go in and accomplish its task.

During all this time, they hid the troops, removed them. When only a small detachment was still visible, Monsieur S agreed: "Okay, come on in, but don't lay a hand on any of my workers."

His workers! The only people we found were Haitians. We started talking with them, writing down their names. All of a sudden, Germaine glimpsed her brother. He was following Monsieur S around like a puppy. The poor woman's heart broke: to belong to the congregation, to come as part of a delegation, only to discover her own brother rounding up people to work, recruiting Haitians!

"You're not your brother," I told her, "don't fret."

When this fool of a brother saw us, he ran to tell the Haitians to hide, to refuse to give their names. The bravest stayed put. Father Céleste gathered a few of them together. One managed to explain: "Some man came to get us. People from Lamentin were supposed to join us. They aren't here. If they come and work, I'll stay and cut cane. If it's only Haitians, I won't work."

Another added that they didn't have any health insurance or government allowance. They didn't even know exactly how much they'd be paid for a day's work. We talked and talked. . . . Monsieur S arrived: "Ladies, it's over; the visit's at an end."

A man who carted cane passed by. At the word *ladies* he spewed out all his bile at us, brought up from his stomach the dirtiest curses he knew, created a disturbance:

Fanm a labé, fanm bouzen, gadé yo! Yo ochan kon rat ki pèd grenn a-i an siklòn 28.	The priest's women, whores, look at them! They're scream- ing like rats whose balls were ripped out by the cyclone of 1928.

Oh yes! Except for Dagonia and Céleste, we were all women. We'd counted on Monsieur Alexis, but he hadn't come. Besides, men are as scarce in the congregation as blue-eyed Negroes. Whenever we undertake social action, the women are on the front lines.

On the way back, we went to Dagonia's house. He called the prefect—Adele held the listening receiver[93]—to have the security police withdrawn. For two or three days they weren't seen on the plantations. Then they reappeared.

The following day we held a meeting. Our action hadn't produced a great change, since the troops had only disappeared temporarily. Father Céleste asked what we'd decided to do. We couldn't see a way to move forward. But he had his own idea.

We called another major meeting at the Grosse-Montagne chapel. Everyone spoke at random. Words here, words there. People were into party politics, into all sorts of things. Adele and I were in the forefront. I described where we'd started, our activities up to that point. People from all over attended the meeting. Father Céleste had called on the youth movements, the U.T.A. and U.P.G., even the bishop showed up, but he had other commitments and didn't stay long. Each person gave his opinion: I'd do this, I'd do that . . . but no serious plan of action developed.

At the end of the meeting, Chérubin announced his decision: after the service of repentance on Saturday, 22 March, he would begin a hunger strike, because he couldn't "spread the word of the Gospel without fighting for justice."

"I'll fast till union negotiations resume (which will signify for me that the workers have been recognized as partners in labor disputes and not as slaves who simply obey their masters' orders) and till Monsieur S ends the unfair and illegal practices that allowed him to begin the harvest thanks to the disinterest or complicity of our political leaders. I'm refusing, in advance, all treatment till the previous conditions have been met."

It was a great day. The assembled group seethed with excitement. Everyone spoke at once. One girl cried out: "It's suicide, Chérubin!"

He responded that, throughout the centuries of colonialism in Guadeloupe, our lives had been taken from us, our lives as a people. He wanted to give his own life so that the poor of Guadeloupe and elsewhere could move along the path to freedom.

Perturbed, each of us interrupted to express an opinion. As for me, if I'd been asked what a hunger strike meant . . . who knew? It's when someone refuses to eat. I had no idea of the organization it required. Céleste himself didn't realize he'd need a doctor to care for him.

Anyway, he'd made his decision. We were obliged to accept it and to respect his wishes. There was no question of changing his mind. The only person who could have convinced him to renounce the fast, he told us, was his mother, and she was already dead.

Things were quickly organized. Adele and I oversaw everything. Yet it was the people from the youth movements and the unions, with their greater experience in these things, who took charge. They assigned teams: for first aid, political action, on-duty volunteers, bodyguards— in sum, they began to get us organized. As for Chérubin, he warned us not to let anyone come and check on his health, because they might give him a fatal injection.

Our first work stoppage[94] took place at Paul, not far from the chapel. Those people who had returned to the cane fields were pointed out to us. We all assembled: people from the congregation, the two unions (U.T.A. and U.R.G.), the J.O.C.,[95] the M.R.J.C. Céleste's act served to bring everyone together.

Several members of the congregation seemed somewhat worried before we left. They weren't agricultural workers, didn't have cards for *Sécurité sociale*. "We can't go into the cane fields. If one of us is wounded and has to be taken to the hospital, he'll be asked what he was doing there."

We'd all agreed: we'd help the workers, go en masse to compel them to join the work stoppage. No sooner had we arrived, than the union leaders wanted everyone to enter the plantation! We were already divided, accused of wasting time. Our agreement was broken. Adele, who'd come despite her parents' opposition, wasn't pleased: "We're not accomplishing anything! What's all this? Wasn't the strike started up again thanks to the Christian community?"

It was true. The workers' and peasants' resolve had weakened, the union wasn't playing a strong role, the owners were breaking the strike.

In addition, Chérubin hadn't consulted with the U.T.A. on his course of action but with us Christians, and we'd advised and supported him.

Yet there we stayed. No troops in evidence that day. When those who were working saw the long procession, the crowd that advanced on them, they took off to the left, to the right, abandoning their work, darting in front of the large wagons[96] and causing them to swerve.

Some were afraid and hid, but we managed to talk with others. We told them that, since the pay for a day's work wasn't set, they shouldn't work. Nor should they have faith in the prefect's "monkey business." The drivers of the large wagons agreed with us. Only one protested: he didn't want to leave the cane fields. So with the large wagons in front, we announced our intention of heading up to Monsieur S's office The people followed behind, brandishing sugarcane *zanma*. That was the start, the real beginning. I was so tired, had run back and forth so many times—up and down, down and up—that I was collapsing from exhaustion.

We arrived at the Grosse-Montagne factory. They entered Monsieur S's office. Adele represented us. They talked a long time. Apparently Monsieur S said: "Yes, I understand, I understand."

Since I wasn't present, I can't say how the discussion proceeded.

It began to dawn on us that we couldn't simply protest against Monsieur S. The affair had grown. The hunger strike had shaken the entire island. Pamphlets appeared, distributed everywhere, in all the churches. Mass was celebrated every evening at Grosse-Montagne. Céleste chose the text from the Gospel. We'd begun organizing to protect Céleste, to proceed with our work stoppages, to sleep in the church. I carried over three mattresses.

How many things, how many people moved in and out of that church! One day, members of the island's ruling council arrived, those high-brows, those fine gentlemen. Céleste had asked them to come. "Here we are," said the president of the regional council, and then he left. In other words, it was as if no one had come at all. So we continued.

Work stoppage, work stoppage, every morning at 6 A.M. we left to go out and stop the work! But the *képis rouges* got organized, too. Beginning at 5 A.M., guards were posted at every entrance to the plantation and they were also the ones who, with their trucks, brought in the scabs. So we got up even earlier, at 3 A.M. The union men hid in the fields scheduled for harvesting. Some of them even slept there. While the *képis rouges* blocked the way, they were already inside. When the workers arrived at their places and raised their machetes, the union men rushed onto the field shouting: "Stop! Join the strike!"

Leonora: The Buried Story of Guadeloupe

And each time they explained why the workers shouldn't be cutting cane, not yet.

When Monsieur S saw that, he threw up his hands: "Hell! There's no way of stopping them!"

The evenings weren't for sleeping but for celebration of Mass, with the church overflowing, people flooding in from all corners of the island. And those who came offered to help and stayed to talk, sing, eat, and drink with us. We needed good organization to handle it all!

How can we ever forget that time of Father Céleste's hunger strike! I know I never will. There were good things and bad. But what joy! When we left for the work stoppage, what banter, jesting, riddles accompanied us the whole way. How we chatted, laughed, had fun . . . till we arrived at the hot spot.

But some envious people set out to wreck our beautiful organization. Before we arrived, Combat Ouvrier[97] would send guys to the cane fields to beat up the people who worked. If you want a man to join the strike, your job is to explain things to him, not to beat him up. We who reject violence said no, no beatings, when we saw the attacks. We were always on the scene, and both the union and the youth movement agreed with us. In 1975, they didn't advocate violence. I don't know what ideas they have these days, but so far they haven't encouraged violence.

Each day after the work stoppage, we organized an on-site meeting. We explained in greater detail why work must be halted: there had been no negotiations on the price per ton of cane, nor on working conditions or day wages. In any case, it would be shameful to work under the eyes of the security forces. Not a single stalk of cane should be cut! Not a factory would belch forth smoke!

We covered all the countryside of Grande-Terre. I knew every corner. We went everywhere, telling the settlers, the small farmers: don't cut your cane, don't feed the factory. Those gentlemen mustn't continue to have complete control over the way they treat us.

The harvest was brought to a halt almost everywhere and we held out at the chapel. All Guadeloupe filed through. And what had the prefect found to do? Send his little soldiers. As if that would frighten us.

On the other hand, Céleste hadn't eaten for eleven days. People began to say: "He must stop. You can't go beyond nine or ten days of a hunger strike."

An attractive woman, a fine lady, defended this opinion. "Father Céleste might die," she said. The following morning, she brought coffee for Father Céleste. The nurse from the M.R.J.C. categorically refused it. We must respect his fast. If Father Céleste dies, people said, it will be the M.R.J.C.'s fault, they'll have killed him to assure their own success, their movement is just for their own personal glory, etc.

Céleste alone had made the decision on his hunger strike. Bringing him food wasn't virtuous, it was working against him. Many people truly feared Céleste would die. They wanted to feed him on the sly, but that would have been very bad. If it were discovered that Father Céleste had food in his stomach, people would have said: he's not on a hunger strike, he's jerking us around.

One day Chérubin called me to him. I asked how he felt—not to lie to me but to tell me honestly if he could hold out. He said that if things weren't going well, he'd decide himself, and in case he collapsed, no one was to treat him. And he never said a word to anyone about wanting food.

So he continued with his fast, and we, together with the unions, pursued our job of explaining the situation throughout Guadeloupe. Adele spoke all over the place, at Pointe-à-Pitre, Basse-Terre, Moule, everywhere. At first, many of us didn't dare speak in public. I spoke in meetings at Duzer-Sainte-Rose, Colette at Baie-Mahault, and Suzette at Petit-Bourg. In Basse-Terre we were even mistaken for Jehovah's Witnesses because we went into the most remote areas, leaving pamphlets in every house. "We're neither Seventh-Day Adventists nor Jehovah's Witnesses," we'd say, "we're bringing a message to help a priest who has undertaken a hunger strike to insure that 'the workers are recognized as partners in labor disputes and not as slaves who simply obey their masters' orders.'"

The people from Basse-Terre helped us enormously. They formed a support committee and organized a huge rally, the likes of which had never before been seen at Basse-Terre. The prefect and many officials live in Basse-Terre, snobs who rarely leave their elegant homes to walk through the streets.

We had supporters everywhere, but we had to be careful. I remember one very intelligent guy who agreed with all the laws but didn't follow them himself. He acts like he's on your side, asks you this and that. If you're a fool, you tell him what's going on. Then he goes and tells "the other side" everything. And so the other side learns all your plans and movements. The U.T.A. knew how to spot that sort of *mako* (mole) better than we did. If we decided one evening, for instance, to go and picket at Morne-à-l'Eau the following morning, Combat Ouvrier would be there before us.

From then on, we worked together. The U.T.A. explained to us: since some people want to sabotage this protest, we must organize ourselves differently. We no longer knew ahead of time the site slated for a work stoppage. Only the driver of the first bus knew, the others followed him. When the first bus stopped, we all got out. Generally the protest went well: neither fights nor arguments. But one day, they beat two guys who were very hesitant. Even for the unions that's bad, it creates disorder in our ranks. We'd come to say "Stop!" to those who worked. Some understood why, others didn't. It's a complicated business and must be untangled. It's not a question of showing weakness, but neither should we be violent. If most people join us, why run after the two or three who want to hide?

Those are the kinds of problems we encountered on the outside. In the church itself, what hassles! One day, we surprised a young man standing by Father Céleste's side, staring at him with a strange expression. His eyes looked wild when he turned to leave. He began to speak: "If I confess now, I could be saved. I saw Father Céleste's face. I can't do it. I was given money, lots of money, to kill him. Me take money to kill a priest? I'd never do such a crazy thing."

Then all who were in on the plot began to denounce one another. We tracked down the man who had promised a large reward for Céleste's head: "If you're willing to give so much money to kill that priest, he must be worth a great deal more. We need men like him in Guadeloupe."

Suspicions flew here and there, rumors circulated. A price had been put on Father Céleste's head, they wanted to blow up the chapel. . . . We organized our defense.

The entrance to the little room near the choir, where Céleste lay, was protected: sheet metal on the outside, benches barricading the door on the inside. At the hour for Mass, the crowd pressed in from all sides, people needing to see Father Céleste. We discussed among ourselves which ones to let in. Sometimes we said no, he's tired, his state has worsened, he can't get up. In any case, those who were let in couldn't have done anything, since, when they left the room, they were still inside the church.

Oh, it was so well organized! As the days passed, new ideas came to us. After having arranged protection for Céleste's small room, we decided to put lights all around the chapel. The men took turns standing guard round-the-clock. We'd been able to find many men willing to sleep there. Some of them were capable of staying up all night long so they wouldn't miss any of the tales, word games, and stories Chicaté told. What a man! A real master of the night. He had his own words to describe our poverty, the poverty of the workers: "As recently as five years ago, could we voice our complaints, say anything? The boss decided: 'Okay, the harvest has begun. The pay for a day's work is posted near the manager's house. I need so many reapers tomorrow morning.' You could ask for nothing, complain about nothing. The salary was fixed and the price per ton of cane too. And just to pay for the hole-in-the-wall where the master housed you, you needed to cut seventeen sheaves of cane each day for free! Poorly paid, poorly housed, ripped off by the company store, how could a worker defend himself? No union, no organization to lead the fight. He had to be sly if he wanted to live, sly like Brer Rabbit."

And Chicaté, with his great laugh, would tell of the thousand-and-one tricks of Brer Rabbit. Then, he'd move on to slavery: "I'm not a person who went to school. I've only probed the problem of slavery since the U.T.A.'s creation. That's how I learned that the priests were the defenders of the landlords. You know that during the time of slavery, the slaves rose up: they burned the cane, poisoned the water, killed the livestock. The priests and the police were the first things brought to Guadeloupe, along with the blacks from Africa. The police to take you to prison and the priests to entice you to reveal your actions so they could denounce you to the police: don't cause trouble, God is a just father, stay in your place, bear up under your suffering. That allowed the landowners, the plantation masters, to exploit, to make a martyr of the slave. The priest was always on hand to keep him on his knees."

When Father Céleste arrived to minister to the congregation in Grosse-Montagne, Monsieur S immediately got after him. He tried to turn the people against him in order to steer them away from the neighborhood meetings. I say that people who do that are accursed, thrice cursed! By assembling people to think about their lives, Chérubin acted charitably. If his enemies would read the Bible, they'd see that Father Céleste followed in Christ's footsteps. I sing Chérubin's praises, acknowledge all he has done. God tells you to help your neighbors, no matter what your situation in life, and when you help your neighbor you're really helping God.

Today, Chérubin is willing to give his life for the cane workers. He knows them well. They've been telling him of their hardships, their lives, for a long time. Through them he came to understand the poverty of the wretched. Not able to give them money, he looked for a way to help them. He chose to act through his hunger strike.

I, too, read the Bible and take from it what I find virtuous. That's why I realize his action is "pitiable" in the eyes of God. I don't know of any other person in Guadeloupe who'd give his life that way. People just talk and talk, that's all. But he placed himself between life and death.

For me, the most beautiful thing was when, early in his hunger strike, Father Céleste could get up and celebrate Mass. But traipsing back and forth, standing on his feet without eating didn't help him much. One evening, despite his frailty, he got up. Seeing so very many people gathered together, he cried out: "Had I seen this before, it would have renewed my strength."

What joy to prepare for Mass by composing songs in Creole, what happiness to share the universal prayer with those thousands of Guadeloupeans. They were present to give voice to the words that flowed from their hearts, their own words. Good words:

Mondyé Mondyé, voyé limyè asi
nou pou nou vouè ola nou yé.

My God, my God, send us light
to help us see where we are.

Evil words too:

Ayisyen ka pwan travay an nou.
Fo nou fouté yo kou.

The Haitians are stealing our
work. We must beat them up.

To those who said that, we replied: "Yes, the Haitians are working in our places, but they've come looking for a way to live too." And we'd start to sing.

Each one of us prepared for Mass in his or her own way, studying the Gospel. At Mass, we began by telling what the Gospel had brought us personally. Then the people who'd come spoke out, Christians and non-Christians alike. In fact, no one made any distinction. I don't know the depths of their hearts, but in those unusual circumstances, it didn't matter. Of course, they weren't aware of how we shared the Gospel together, but we found we were sharing something we hadn't known before: the profound feeling of being one people.

Sété on sèl pèp ki té a Grosmontany. Tout moun té ansanm, tout moun té ka goumé ansanm.

We formed one people at Grosse-Montagne. All of us united, all of us fighting together.

Pa té ni gwan moun, pa té ni ti-moun.

No adults, no children.

Pa té ni moun a misyélimè x moun a misyélimè y.

No followers of Mayor X, no followers of Mayor Y.

Pa té ni, ni gòch ni douat nou té ansanm, é nou té fo.

Neither left nor right; we were united, and we were strong.

I never imagined I'd live through such an event. For the first time in my life, I was caught up in something so exhilarating. I lived my life. I had strength to give to the action, and yet I found myself feeling weak. Weak, not afraid.

Father Chérubin Céleste begins a hunger strike

I sometimes wondered: "Where are we now?" "Will we manage to get out of this?" I was worried. I knew we had to fight on, so the cane workers' strike could continue. On the other hand, the longer it continued, the more Céleste's life was endangered.

My role was to go everywhere. Wherever they took me, I went. But I kept hearing in my mind: Céleste mustn't die. It's true, that's what I was fighting for. I tried to convince people, talked and talked. For instance, I met a guy who worked at the factory. I said to him: "Why aren't you doing anything? People are still cutting cane to keep the factory running. If the factory were to stop, the white man wouldn't have the cane cut and it would stay in the fields. It's up to you to shut down the factory."

He promised me he'd try to do something.

Seeing me so involved, people said: "Look at that woman, the way she drags herself everywhere at once, she'll die before that priest."

Lots of other things were said about us women of the congregation, that we were desperate. . . . The day the C.R.S. bore down on us, we really were desperate!

I remember well Céleste's vision of the previous night. I don't know how many days into the fast he was. That evening, a great hunger seized him. He called the nurse, Laurette, to ask for a little water. He thought: "I'm going to get Laurette to leave because, if she stays, I'll ask for something to eat, I'm so hungry."

He told me how, during the night, he felt himself dying. He saw all sorts of things, *Man* Ibè's beasts who wanted to carry him off. He said to me: "Oh, *Man* Joseph, I saw myself pass away. After the nightmare, I suddenly felt very well. I thought: I'm saved, I'll win the battle."

He got up, climbed over the people who slept in front of the door to his room, and knelt down in front of the Holy Sacrament. The youngsters who were awakened saw him walk by.

"What's the matter?" they asked him.

He made a sign to them: "You wouldn't understand. I've come to thank the Lord."

At four in the morning, he woke us all. "Come and sing, give thanks to the Lord."

He wanted all of us around him. He warned us: "Don't go picketing, don't go outside today."

And, in fact, the C.R.S. arrived that morning.

I must admit, we somewhat expected the move because, three days earlier, during a meeting at the school in La Rosière, the C.R.S. had fallen upon us. New forces, freshly arrived from France, a whole planeful of them that the prefect had requested as reinforcements. They were in blue, with helmets and shields. They surrounded the school.

Leonora: The Buried Story of Guadeloupe

We started feeling uncomfortable inside, but we weren't afraid. One group wanted to stay and continue the meeting, another preferred to leave. Monsieur Alexis began to cry: "They've come for Father Céleste and we're not there to protect him!"

We formed a chain, arm in arm, and calmly left, singing *Solidarity, my brothers!* The C.R.S. troops made way, and we passed through, but we were followed for a kilometer—till we reached the chapel—by a helicopter that hovered over our heads.

It was three days later that Father Céleste had his vision of death and forbade us to leave. When the people saw the C.R.S. surrounding the chapel, they shouted: "Céleste is truly inspired by God. He told us not to go out and look what's come, the C.R.S.!"

We were all deeply united in our faith. I, too, had the same reaction. When someone tells you not to go out, warns that something dangerous will happen that day, and then you see he was right, what else can you think?

Everyone had the same idea: the C.R.S. had come for Father Céleste. I think they also hoped to dislodge us from the chapel, to crush the struggle, to isolate us. Because of Céleste, we were all sleeping in the chapel, and Guadeloupeans from all the towns were gathering here. Even if the C.R.S. had taken him away, would everything have stopped? We'd become so accustomed to assembling, saying Mass, we would have continued.

Still there was a problem. Mayor Dagonia had known since the previous evening that the *képis rouges* would be at Grosse-Montagne. If he knew, why wasn't he outside the chapel?

For a moment, everyone panicked. We could hear murmurs of: "Where are our representatives? Where is the mayor? All he has to do is appear and say: 'I'm the mayor,' and the *képis rouges* would leave."

As it turned out, it's lucky he wasn't there. We would have had a defender, but not a feeling of having accomplished something. As it was, despite all the dreadful things the C.R.S. did to us, we were better off. We defended ourselves, defended ourselves without weapons.

Nou pa té pè ayen	We feared nothing
nou tout té ménasé	all were threatened
vi an nou té an danjé	our lives were in danger
nou pa té pè sé képiwouj la	we didn't fear the *képis rouges*
nou pa té pè zyé sanguinè a yo	with their bloodthirsty eyes
nou pa té pè fizi a yo	and their rifles
nou pa té pè hak.	we feared nothing.

They shoved us out one side, we re-entered from the other. They pushed us from here, we went there. "Break it up! Break it up!"

Father Chérubin Céleste begins a hunger strike

One, two, three—the tear-gas grenades exploded. Inside the chapel, we couldn't breathe. Normally when a tear-gas bomb goes off, you scatter. But inside, they were too tightly packed. Some escaped to the right, others to the left. People fell down, lost their shoes. A young man stumbled. The C.R.S. beat him with the butts of their rifles. Sister Philippe intervened: "I'm white like you, kill me, kill me first!"

What a woman that little sister was! The other nuns also showed their courage, but after that attack, they abandoned us. All except Sister Philippe and Sister Marcelle.

Where was Dagonia? Someone went to get him. His entourage didn't want him to leave the house. He's a brave man, but instead of helping him, they said: "Don't go, don't move, don't go anywhere." Apparently the prefect had ordered: "If the little nigger with the sash shows himself, let him have the tear gas, break his ass."

And, in fact, when Dagonia arrived, what grief they gave him, poor man! People shouted at him: "Where's your sash? Where's your sash?"

Doctor Dagonia took out his sash, the symbol of his position as mayor, as our representative, and said to the C.R.S.: "I've come for my patient."

"You've come for your patient, eh? Well then, take him."

Dagonia entered the chapel, ordered the ambulance backed up, and slipped Céleste in on a stretcher while the C.R.S. were busy guarding the entrance to the chapel.

When they saw Céleste appear, lying on the stretcher, eyes closed, they were thunderstruck. They had only backed away from the front of the church door. Off they went, after the ambulance, but it was already far away. Céleste's supporters didn't waste time; with a hat pulled down over his face, he had been taken away in another car. At the Lamentin presbytery, they changed cars once again. The C.R.S. were completely taken in. They understood nothing at all, not a single thing. The helicopter followed the ambulance all the way to Saint-Claude, but it was empty.

To go back to our mayor, I don't think he did anything extraordinary. His town was threatened, no problem, our "little nigger with the sash" accomplished his job. And even he didn't know where Céleste was taken. Even he knew nothing. Only the nurse and another companion were informed.

When the news spread, it caused an outcry of despair. Heads in hands, the people cried out: "Help! Murder! They've taken Father Céleste!"

Terror, panic, everyone rushed to the chapel, but no chance of getting near, the C.R.S. blocked the roads so no one could pass. And they'd cut the electric and telephone lines. The cleverest arrived through the woods or the cane fields. . . .

When the ambulance left, we remained encircled in front of the chapel. The tear-gas grenades continued to rain down. The C.R.S. must have crossed many plantations to come drop their bombs at Bergnolles! They pursued people into their houses, into all the cabins around the chapel. Monsieur S had guaranteed them: "Go ahead. It's all mine; everything here belongs to me."

"Go on, break it up! Go back home!"

Charles-Gabriel, the mayor of Sainte-Rose, repeated the same words: "Go back home!"

No one moved. We'd never heard such a thing before, telling us to go back home! I shouted out: "We are at home in Grosse-Montagne. You're the ones who aren't at home, gentlemen."

You should have seen us, we who were normally so afraid of the police. That day, we had to restrain several people to keep them from fighting with the *képis rouges*. They angrily threw down the stones they were carrying.

The C.R.S. stayed for quite a while. When they started to shove off, we assembled again. We had sent Rozan Mounien[98] into hiding because a noncommissioned officer, photo in hand, had asked a kid to point out to him a man called Rozan. All the leaders of the U.T.A. had gone into hiding because they were the ones the prefect was after.

The battle had disrupted our group for a while, but it quickly reformed and there were many of us. The union men, the bishop, and Dagonia all spoke. We couldn't say we'd won, but we hadn't lost the fight either. The incidents provoked by the "forces of order" left many wounded but happily none dead. Why? Because we'd kept our heads. If we'd picked on a single C.R.S., I'm sure all of Grosse-Montagne would have been torched and bled.

On the radio and on the TV station FR 3, reports talked of war at Grosse-Montagne, a war started by some sugarcane workers who wanted to force their way into Monsieur S's factory. . . . The prefect had called out the C.R.S. to disperse the demonstrators in front of the factory.

The forces of order had certainly come! But not a single journalist to witness what happened and to inform the people of the truth.

Suddenly we noticed a journalist from FR 3 in the crowd. We let him have it: "So, you arrive when the battle is over! You go shove off, too!"

"I couldn't get here any earlier, the roads were blocked. I took advantage of a break. Tell me what happened."

We agreed, but on one condition: "You must use everything we say, otherwise you'll get nothing."

He wasn't comfortable with this. "You know, in the media, they don't accept things indiscriminately."

Father Chérubin Céleste begins a hunger strike

"That's not our problem. You must interview people live. Give the microphone to those who know what happened, they'll describe what went on."

He was forced to agree, and so all Guadeloupeans immediately learned the truth about Grosse-Montagne. It was the first time an event was described as it really happened here. We didn't have time to say everything. One woman explained how the C.R.S. had turned her place upside down, beaten down the doors, broken her things, her house. Chicaté spoke mostly about the workers' demands, the price per ton of cane, how the salary of an agricultural worker should be the same as a factory worker's. . . . He also explained how, with the system of paying for cane according to its sweetness, the poor peasants couldn't manage to make a living. Another woman also managed to get a word in. But even though it lasted only ten minutes, it was extraordinary, a miracle. The people who'd lived through the events told about it themselves. Never before had such a thing been heard on Guadeloupean radio!

Once Chérubin arrived at his destination, he let us know he was continuing his hunger strike and asked us to stand fast. We continued to meet in the chapel, to celebrate Mass in the afternoon and at six in the evening, but as the days passed, fewer people came.

The prefect issued a statement saying that everyone must accept responsibility. The same afternoon, the union leaders demanded a resumption of negotiations. It was agreed to.

At the news, a dance to the *gwoka* broke out in the church: *"Préfè mako, préfè mantè"* (The prefect's a mole, the prefect lied), they chanted, "yea!"

On the hills, in the interior, the *gwoka* called to people: "Come everyone! Come celebrate the victory!"

A small victory, to be sure, but an important one nonetheless, because Father Céleste had begun his hunger strike so negotiations would resume. The prefect had sent in his C.R.S. and came close to killing people because he didn't want negotiations. Well, negotiations resumed, he was forced to continue them.

Céleste wanted the workers to be treated like men, included in the discussions. He had won. His hunger strike ended, but people kept on speaking of it, of what we had lived through that brought us so much good. Chérubin's name rolled off everyone's lips: "That's a man who was willing to sacrifice himself for the people, so the common folk could live. We need that man as our mayor."

Some thought Céleste might run against Dagonia. They asked me: "Is it true Céleste will run?"

"Céleste, mayor? On no, that's not for him at all!"

His politics aren't the kind that would lead to elected office, not mayor any more than representative or councilor. His politics are to denounce what isn't good and to bring about justice.

After the hunger strike, the problems multiplied. During the strike, everyone was happy, especially the cane workers. Céleste had defended them, had initiated his fast to force the factory owners to negotiate, to prevent them from treating the blacks as dogs. Everyone was involved. But once the strike ended, people returned to their places.

They didn't exactly let everything go, but the Gospel had pushed us into action, had made us more demanding, had penetrated deeply into all the details of our lives. Father Céleste resumed his activities. Meetings at the presbytery and the church of Lamentin became more frequent. People said more forcefully: "It's no longer Mass, it's politics!"

I remember a funeral at which Céleste spoke and spoke, saying how Jesus had taken upon himself all the suffering of his people, how he had acted to help them live, why he'd wound up on the cross, what had been the role of the Pharisees . . . what details he gave! He asked us what we were doing for our people, so that they could live in their own land and not emigrate to France. . . . The members of the congregation weren't shocked, but Monsieur Dagonia, the mayor of Lamentin, went to see him and said: "You're very forceful, you don't mince words when you preach."

"Yes, you're right, but if I speak, I'll speak from the heart, otherwise I'll hold my peace."

Chérubin Céleste isn't your run-of-the-mill person. He took his ministry seriously, took seriously the life of Jesus, which he tries to emulate. He entered into the Gospel, entered it profoundly and deeply. He's a man of faith. He supports the liberation of his country, but not by any and all means. He won't go and get himself killed in a demonstration without a strong chance of success. People criticize him a lot, don't understand him, still don't agree, but those who are fully into the Gospel walk along with him. Chérubin follows the Gospel as it is written in the Good Book, the way it was in ancient times. That's what gives him his sensitivity to the misery of the poor, gives him courage to fight against all the forces of injustice.

I don't know what he has inside him but it is certainly something special, and to fight the way he does, you must have something at your side.

Everything that happened during the strike helped me progress. That's what assuming responsibility as a Christian means to me, fighting against injustice, trying to go as far as possible into the Gospel to change the life "they" have imposed on us.

1975. I'll always remember that year. The Gospel opened my eyes and ears, I understood in what sense we are French.

15

Yo ba Jozèf biyé palapenn

é i kasé èvè mwen

Joseph loses his job and leaves me

Sa i ka konté piplis apa sa ou ka kenbé an plat a men a-ou, men sa ou ka lagé.

The essential in life is not what you retain in the palm of your hand but what you let go of.

Man Fofo,
A Guadeloupean peasant woman

I'll never forget 1975, the year of my greatest joys as well as my greatest sorrows.

In my mind and in my body, I truly felt how the Gospel could help us liberate ourselves from the cords that bind us, help us break them and leave behind our lives of slavery. I understood why, from the beginning, Monsieur S—my husband's boss—was fiercely opposed to our neighborhood meetings, opposed to the kind of Mass that Céleste celebrated in the chapel, only a few feet from his factory, at which we, the poor, spoke out. That's also the reason he stuck his nose into my personal affairs. Monsieur S was enraged to see his steward's wife participating in Father Céleste's demonstrations.

After an earlier strike, in 1973—each year the U.T.A. had to do battle—Father Céleste had convened us, and the congregation had decided to write a petition of sorts, demanding justice for the workers.

My daughter signed it. And I put down my maiden name. As I was signing, a young man from the M.R.J.C. asked me if I was divorced.

"No, I'm not divorced but I prefer to write that name."

Father Céleste explained to everyone that, because of my husband's boss, I could participate but it would be better not to write down my name. Monsieur S had *mako* everywhere who brought him copies of all our pamphlets. Naturally one who'd been at the meeting passed him a copy of the petition. Monsieur S examined the entire list closely. He tried to find out who this Madame Lucie B, teacher, was. He discovered that she was the daughter of his steward Joseph's wife—Joseph, my husband. Can you imagine!

So he set out to destroy him.

"Your stepdaughter signed a petition against me, Joseph; look, here's her name and signature!"

"Monsieur S, I don't know what that has to do with me. My stepdaughter is married, lives in her own house, has two children. I live in Lamoisse, I have nothing to do with my stepdaughter's signature. Her name is Madame B and mine Monsieur Joseph. If she still lived in my home . . . but she's married and has two children!"

Things really went wrong from then on. I continued to take part in social actions, without worrying about either Joseph or Monsieur S. At Sunday Mass, we asked ourselves questions. If they had to do with the rich, we didn't talk at random but openly about rich people we knew.

Once again my husband's boss attacked him. "Your wife is a follower of Father Céleste, she's very active in the neighborhood meetings, she criticizes me in church, you must put an end to it, Joseph, otherwise you'll be in trouble."

Joseph defended himself: "What has my wife done that Madame de Brigotte hasn't?"

"Madame de Brigotte is a saintly woman. She gathers people around her to say the rosary, not to get involved in politics."

Madame de Brigotte, a white woman from Martinique and related by marriage to the factory master, organized small meetings to say the rosary. I, too, had almost been caught up in it.

In truth, Monsieur S had difficulties with Joseph, not with me. He wanted to get rid of him and looked for a way to shift the blame onto my shoulders. Joseph didn't see beyond the obvious and lashed out at me: "Leonora, stop getting involved, running up and down after Father Céleste. I forbid you to attend his meetings. You don't know the problems you're causing me. Do you want me to lose my job?"

"How in God's name could I want something stupid like that? If I had an occupation or money, I might have wanted to take revenge for all your abominations by making you lose your job, but you brought me here, forbade me to earn a single day's wages, I don't have a government allowance or national health care, have nothing saved, you're the one who supports the family. What will we do if you lose your job? Think straight, Joseph!"

It didn't matter what I said, his accursed boss had filled his head with Leonora, Father Céleste. Everything was all their fault, not Joseph's own.

I saw the problem clearly. Joseph had taken to leaving for work in the morning with a good two or three glasses of rum already under his belt. He carried provisions along with him, several pints worth. His friend plied him with more in the field. When the bottles were empty, Joseph went off to drink in the rumshops. His friend substituted for him. Joseph was too drunk to understand the strategy: the friend wanted his job.

One day, the children realized that things couldn't go on this way. They went off to find their father, searched the plantation, looked till dark. They finally found him in the rumshop of his friend's sister, asleep in a chair.

"Papa, Papa, wake up. Monsieur S is looking for you, he's mad."

"Look at these little *doudou* (darlings), they're afraid I'll be kicked out. Go tell your mother to calm down instead."

Rum did Joseph in, rum and women. His friends dragged him around. He no longer gave a thought to his home or his children. He had as many women as there are sugarcanes on the plantation. Each one had to take her turn.

People say men drink because they have problems. I was the one with problems. Joseph? No more than anyone else. Of course, it sometimes heated up at home and sharp words flew about, but at work he was the master who kept the others cutting, chopping, slaving away. With his friends, he was like a child, a top they kept spinning around till he found himself spun out of a job.

In 1975, Joseph received his letter of dismissal. Céleste was on the hunger strike, I was totally involved with the movement. Joseph, his head stuffed with ideas put there by Monsieur S, blamed me and left home.

Oh, Boss Man, you're powerful! You managed to cut this man off twice—first from his work and a second time from his family. And you, Joseph, you accepted his acting like the former masters who separated the slaves from their wives and children. . . . No, we're no longer living under slavery, we can reflect and defend ourselves. If *misyé la,* the man, gets you to turn against your wife, accuses her, you can at least open your mouth, try to defend your family, your home, you can react somehow.

No chance of discussing things with Joseph. He alone had the right to speak. With his friends—well, then he spoke and listened to them bad-mouthing his wife and children, breaking up his home.

He had two friends with him when he went to claim his severance pay. Since the money didn't seem adequate, they told him to refuse it. They had him hire a bailiff, a lawyer. I wasn't aware that any of this was happening. He mustn't tell me anything, because I talked too much. In court, the lawyer—undoubtedly well paid by the boss—dismissed all Joseph's valid arguments. But he did obtain a little more money. Monsieur S appealed and Joseph spent all the extra money he'd received on paying lawyers and bailiffs a second time—and on drinks for his friends.

If he'd listened to my son Mark's advice, Joseph would have contacted Chicaté, the leader of the U.P.G. With the union taking on Monsieur S, the boss would have been forced to shell out the number of bills equal to twenty-five years of work. But Joseph considered Chicaté a little nigger who knew nothing of his affairs. Chicaté, whom Monsieur S feared the way the Devil fears holy water, who'd obtained work for the laborers and a refund for the small farmers. When someone went to Chicaté with a problem, he'd bring it to the manager or the owner in person.

One year Monsieur S had called all the small farmers to the factory, all except Chicaté. They went to warn him. Chicaté turned up. When Monsieur S saw him, he held his head in despair.

"Chicaté, I didn't call you; I don't need you here."

"Monsieur S, if you have something to say to the farmers, you must speak with me. The farmers will never come to see you unless I'm with them. Don't dream, Monsieur S, that you'll ever manage to turn them against the union."

Joseph wanted to fight Monsieur S alone. Finally, he was given fifteen thousand francs. For twenty-five years of work on the plantation, twenty-five years of leaving the cane fields at 5 P.M., of counting, checking, listening to the cries and complaints of the workers.

He invested his severance pay in a butcher shop. Not a real shop, a *loge*, a small shack with a plank of wood for a counter, and in a poor location to boot. Rumors circulated about this *loge* and the ones next to it. No one managed to sell there except for a certain Eusèbe. Only after he'd sold all his merchandise did the others begin to do any business.

Joseph didn't buy the animals himself, he purchased the meat at Pointe-à-Pitre and resold it by the pound. He acquired all the necessary scales, but not an icebox, so the meat spoiled.

Since he no longer gave me any money, I figured: "His children need meat; he can't refuse to give them some." I sent them three or four times. Then Joseph entrusted the shop to one of his friends, rented a car, and ran about trying to sell his meat. It rotted en route and no one wanted it. In addition, Joseph was always drunk. A curse must hang over that man.

He left me in March 1975. He hadn't been living at home since the end of 1974. For fifteen years, he'd been sleeping around, only occasionally coming home at night. We still had a relationship, but not a real one. I protested, didn't want him making love to me.

"You've spent the whole night with your mistress and now you come home to make love to me just to show you're my master; well, nothing doing!"

My body and my blood had grown cold. I had no desire for Joseph or for anyone else. Disgust had chased out love and taken its place. A true disgust for Joseph's body. Still today, ten years after our separation, when I meet him we say hello, kiss, but I'm cold as ice and don't feel any desire.

Joseph suggested the separation first. I agreed. Weren't we already separated? He paid no attention to me, slept around, and I no longer felt anything for him.

He took his things, and I stayed in the house belonging to the factory. In the beginning, he came and went from time to time. He'd arrive very early in the morning, wash his face, come over and press it against mine.

I té vlé vouè ki té an té kay fè ba-i, men an pa jen pwan hotè a-i.	He wanted to see which face I'd show him, but I never let myself sink to his level.

I ignored him. So, he'd go sit down in front of the door for a while, taking it easy.

"How are you, Monsieur Jo? How're you feeling?"

"Hello to you, Aristide! Fine, thanks. I'm okay, holding up. And how's life treating you?"

As soon as he'd exchanged a few words with someone, off he'd go. He had his witness. No one could say whether or not the husband had spent the night at home. I watched his game-playing without saying anything and without getting worked up. If someone came to ask for him, I answered: "Monsieur Joseph no longer lives at Lamoisse."

I also felt he was spying on me: How was I reacting to his departure? Did I cry? He was so proud. After a while, when I didn't beg him to return, he insisted on starting in again: "You're nothing without me, Leonora. You have no money, no work, no house. It all depends on me. You'll lead a dog's life. If you push me out, you'll regret it. Wait and see how much you'll miss me."

"Me miss you? Perhaps I'll live in poverty, lack money, but miss you, never! Your absence sits lightly on me. I'm done with you, once and for all."

Joseph hoped that, without a cent, I'd be forced to give in. Thank God he's still waiting!

Before leaving, he'd put four hundred francs on the bed and written on a scrap of paper "for your livelihood." And with these four hundred little francs I had to eke out an existence for me and my two youngest.

Mark was studying in France; Sylvère, doing his military service. Dominick worked in the factory at Grosse-Montagne and brought home a little money. My only wealth, a garden. I would be able to wait and see. I wasn't accustomed to selling fruits and vegetables, Joseph had forbidden me to do it, but I didn't worry.

When I prepared meals, I made enough for Joseph too, because he hadn't totally left. I also washed his clothes. And how he dirtied them! As if on purpose. One day, I was fed up with washing for that man, tiring myself out. I took the dirty clothes he'd brought and hung them up on a nail in our bedroom so they wouldn't get mildewed. When Joseph arrived to change clothes, nothing clean! He threw a fit, but gathered up his dirty clothes in the blink of an eye and disappeared. The woman to whom he brought his laundry spread a rumor that I hadn't been taking care of my husband, no longer kept his things clean.

My family learned of Joseph's departure. They thought I was responsible for his having been fired, since that's what he was going around saying. They came to see me. I explained everything in detail. I showed them the pile of dirty laundry: "Look at the pile of dirty clothes he brings me to wash. Dirty clothes of a drunkard." One of my brothers handed me one hundred francs. "But it's not for soap to wash other people's clothes. And if this man doesn't give you money, you're not to go on saving food for him every day."

He was right. I told Joseph so in no uncertain terms when, as was his habit, he arrived in the middle of the night to keep an eye on me. "Don't worry, you're wasting your time coming by, I'm not planning to replace you. But as for your laundry and your meals, I've had enough. You can deal with them somewhere else, just as you do the rest."

He gathered up the few things that still hung around our house and went off, once and for all, to his new home. The only thing left for me to do was organize life with my children, without a husband.

When Mark returned from France, during Céleste's hunger strike, he scolded me: "Mamma, why didn't you write and let me know about your problems with Papa?"

"I didn't want to bother you, you were studying for your exams. Now I'm a woman without money, without means, but a free woman."

I didn't view my separation as a personal failure but as a failure of the relationship. A failure of our life as a couple, not of our lives as two individuals. The life Joseph led had never been mine. I was married, enclosed in the marriage with him, obliged to do things through him. Since the separation, I've felt like a different person, do what I want, am content, know how to lead my life properly, in an orderly

Joseph loses his job and leaves me

way. Many people criticize me, I know. But I feel good about myself, in harmony with the life I've chosen.

So when Joseph wanted to get back together five years later, I wasn't interested. And I had new reasons.

I'd changed during that time, gotten involved with lots of activities. Would Joseph have accepted the woman I'd become? I couldn't imagine myself bringing him coffee the way I used to, keeping his place at the table and his meal warm so he could eat whenever he chose to return, if he returned at all! I had shed all that slavish behavior, and Joseph wasn't the sort of man to serve himself from the *canari*. With his departure, the children and I had reorganized our lives: no one waited on anyone else. We all ate at the table together, but sometimes, Thursdays for example, when I went to meetings, I prepared the meal and each one helped himself after school or work.

Can you see Joseph living that way, without anyone serving him? Because my children weren't inclined to do so either.

Get back together? What for? To put on an act for the public? Show that I'd recaptured my husband? I wasn't in favor of that sort of thing, nor was I available. Making up also means making love again, renewing love and caresses. Lovemaking becomes the only occupation. *Mayé nouvo, kochon pa ni bouè* (In the home of the newlyweds, the pigs die of thirst), there isn't time to think of anything besides themselves, their bodies. I'm no longer into that.

I remain on good terms with my husband. We greet each other. When he gets sick, I take care of him; after all, he's the father of my children. He can come to my home, find a place there to sleep, but not in my bed, even if he makes eyes at me and wants me to caress him.

I've closed the door of my body. And I hold firm. People can say I'm a person who likes to talk, laugh, joke around, but no one can accuse me of being a *toupiafouèt,* a spinning top, a woman who will dance to any tune.

I've lived through many misfortunes, suffered much poverty, but I like and respect myself. Joseph met a fine woman. He didn't know how to appreciate her. When you're dealt such a lousy hand, starting over would be like taking *kaka poul pou zé* (chicken shit for eggs), *krizokal pou lò* (glitter for gold), really deceiving myself.

The people of my congregation would be pleased to announce: "*Man* Joseph has reunited with her husband." That's what they want. By going back to live with a man again because you've reached a certain age, you fall in line, rediscover the life of a couple, but it's a life in death, death of yourself. I want to live. At sixty, I feel young and enjoy savoring new things.

And, also, serious things happened between Joseph and me. They killed love. *Bal fini, vyolon an sak* (When the dance is over, the violins are put away).

How can I forget all those words, stinging words that wounded my body and my soul. Not all at once, but gradually, throughout many years, each time we fought. *Blesse,* hurtful words, to reach my innermost being, to crush me. Wounding words.

"You're not a woman, you can't be counted among the ranks of women, you don't even reach to the ankles of real women. Now, Renélise, that's a woman. Renélise. Renélise knows how to make love, Renélise this, Renélise that. . . . "

"But Joseph, we've had eleven children. Wasn't I a woman then?"

"You're not a woman," those words of his destroyed me. He dared compare me with his mistress, a girl who "sells her flesh."

I suffered greatly because of that young woman. Not from her relationship with Joseph—he chased every skirt that passed by and many women who stopped on their way home from work to ask me for a drink of water had to submit to him—but she'd betrayed my confidence.

I'd been warned. I hadn't taken the warning seriously. I couldn't believe that a woman who went to and fro over my floors, in my house, who lived compatibly with everyone, was my husband's official mistress. My children loved her, and so did I. When I was ill, she washed my clothes, ironed. If I couldn't do things at home, she stood in for me. Suddenly I discovered she'd taken my place in bed too! I was shocked. I wasn't yet the woman I've since become. I should have said to her: "Renélise, I know you're together with Joseph. You can leave right now and stay away. I never want you to set foot in my house again."

I simply arranged a way to get angry with her. She understood immediately and disappeared from my home. We stopped saying hello. When someone stops saying hello to you, there's a reason. You have to figure out what it is. Maybe this is a bad custom, since often enough people have a falling out based on a missed "hello" (perhaps one of them was simply distracted) and remain estranged, each trying to figure out why the other is angry, but preferring to die rather than ask for an explanation.

The affair with Renélise pricked me for a long time, like an acacia thorn in a deep wound. Joseph had so many women, and yet it was over that one I flipped. One morning on the way to Mass I saw her in front of me. I pushed her aside with a scornful "out of my way." And yet, yet, with the passage of time, the tribulations, the pain, and the suffering lessened. At a certain point, I let go of that young woman. Gave her up, rid myself of her, pushed her from my mind and my body.

Joseph loses his job and leaves me

One day when I was at *Man* Léontel's, Renélise entered and greeted me: "Hello ma'am!" She didn't address the glass or the cup, she was speaking to me.

I go everywhere spreading the word of Jesus Christ, I can't lock hate up in my heart. If I remained mute, I couldn't continue to bear witness. It was hard, but I answered her.

And finally it left, little by little. You might say she was just waiting for that. Since then, we speak when we meet on the way to church. We've even embraced. My daughter Emilienne can't get over it: "Mamma, it can't be true, you embrace *Man* Renélise!"

Joseph was furious: "I'll never understand you, Leonora, now that I'm not with Renélise anymore, you make up with her. You do it on purpose to bug me, because she's taken another husband."

I haven't become her close friend, but I genuinely get along with her. Get along the way you do with people you'd visit if something happened to them but with whom you don't normally socialize; people you might occasionally spend the day with when you feel like it, whose house you might drop by.

I certainly had my share of pain, chagrin. Her relationship with Joseph consumed me. Yet despite all that, I don't carry her in my heart as an enemy. Perhaps because hateful words never passed between us. We made up silently, the way we fell out. Without insults, without scenes. Each of us withdrew, followed her own path, without looking for ways to hurt the other. The path of women.

. . . chimen fanm plen chouk	. . . a path strewn with traps,
aboua, chadron, tout kalité	sea urchins, stinging nettles,
zòti, poual agraté . . .	itching powder . . .

Since 1976, I've been living in a development of small, single-family homes. It's a change for me, after spending so many years on the plantation. Yet I notice that the women, even with all the conveniences of the development—concrete houses, running water, and, for some, a car and a telephone—aren't any happier for all that. Even those who go out arm in arm with their husbands, aren't free in their movements. The husbands impose too many restrictions: no speaking with other men in the development, no hanging around with the neighbors, no going out alone, no this . . ., no that. . . .

When I look to the past, long ago, I think: "My girl, you didn't have a happy childhood, your two relationships weren't so successful, what's left for you?" What's left is my honor and the pride of having withstood everything to raise my children. And the brand new happiness of having me totally to myself.

Leonora: The Buried Story of Guadeloupe

Is a good life ahead for me now? Difficult to say, because a mother is never done with her children, "if you hit your nose, your eyes water." And yet I feel well, I'm no longer sick. And as an active member of the congregation, I see life differently. Each day I make new discoveries, teach myself; I learn to better understand my country, my fellowmen, myself. I take part in all the outings, all the celebrations. I have fun.

I'm a woman of a certain age but, unlike others, I don't see only the struggle, the struggle, nothing but the struggle. Although you can't spend your life dancing, you must have some fun. Struggle, yes, I agree, but enjoy yourself too, scoop up life by the armfuls.

Postface

Let's recover the speech they tore from us and let's cry out
our differences since that's the reason we're dying.

Jeanne Hyvrard,
Mother Death

The essential, said Jean-Paul Sartre, is not what others do to us but what we do with what they have done to us.

Out of "Africa's crucifixion," out of that enormous crime against humanity that was slavery, the Africans who were transported to the New World had to adapt to this new space in order to survive, had to hang up their gods and their customs. The urgent need to respond to the conditions of a life and death they hadn't chosen, wanted, or de-sired—yet with which they were forced to battle daily—joined with the necessity of knowing the cultural code of the slave society to form a collective consciousness related to the past and the present; to create a language, Creole; to elaborate a special relationship with the body; in brief, to confer, by a desire for cohesion and unity, a sense to this world imposed upon them; to give birth to a culture, the popular cul-ture of Guadeloupe.

Leonora drew her strength to confront life and to raise her thirteen children from this culture. Her dreams, her worries, her hopes, her attempt to reappropriate history, they all unite with those of thousands of unknown and anonymous Guadeloupeans whose will to survive built Guadeloupe.

This buried story, forgotten, never studied, this story that has always thrilled me, is what I rediscovered in the life and words of *Anmann* Leonora.

It is this story too, that, in part, I lived as a child; that marked me deeply and perhaps pushed me into the study of linguistics, ethnology, and sociology; that gave me the taste for observing and for questioning the most common, everyday language, perhaps the richest of all in meaning.

In listening to Leonora, I never felt myself to be an outsider, removed from her inquiry, her doubts, her searching. Much of what she told me sounded an echo in me, resonated in my body, caused forgotten sensations to surface.

My father was the son of an important landowner, my mother a farm worker on my grandfather's plantation. If, by clinging to the pa-ternal branch of the family, I was able to prolong my studies, it was always with the maternal branch that I felt at ease. I maintained real contact only with that side of my family, poor peasants, mostly uneducated.

When Leonora describes the manager of the plantation, I recall the one who forbade us to pass in front of the master's house. We had to make a six-kilometer detour to fetch water from the spring. When I received my high school diploma, all mamma's side of the family, on whom this honor reflected, obtained the right to pass by.

A certain complicity thus developed between Leonora and me that enabled me to help her pursue her thoughts and translate the recitation of her experiences from Creole to French without, I hope, unduly betraying them.

For Leonora was seeking, seeking to understand what had happened to her, why one thing and not another. Why did I do this, why did I think that? And most important, who am I? What does it mean to be Guadeloupean? A black who acquired French citizenship, as the identity card suggests? How can the political future of Guadeloupe and the desire to be Guadeloupean express itself today through the thoughts and speech of the Creole-speaking people?

Mustn't one first exist, be a man, a woman, a person? Reclaim this body stolen by the master, violated by France the assimilator? What can we hold on to, what can we lean on in order to give expression to the deepest part of our beings, the part that slips between our fingers, that doesn't yet exist? How can we vanquish the colonial night and allow the sun to shine for us, Guadeloupeans? We must, of course, drive what is real out into the open, reinvent forgotten gestures, reinvent resistance and combat.

And what if we stopped seeing ourselves through the eyes of the other, the colonizer? If we tried to rediscover our own history? If the term *Nèg mawon* no longer struck terror into the hearts of children and threatened the virginity of young girls, but referred to a heroic resistance fighter, more alive than Joan of Arc, Schoelcher, or de Gaulle. . . .?

We must question everything, everyone. France fashioned our minds, took possession of us from the time we entered school, imposing her language and world on us, severing us from everything that made us who we are and remodeling us in her image. We must be on guard against ourselves. Who is thinking? Who is speaking? Is it really me? No one, no colonized people, can totally escape this alienation, this zombification.

And yet despite all the methods used (school, church, army, etc.), the majority of Guadeloupean peasants and workers think and speak in Creole, eat yams and breadfruit, dance and bury their dead to the sound of the *gwoka.*

There is something strong, deep, and solid in this culture, something fundamental that colonialism hasn't yet found, something that has allowed and continues to allow the men and women of Guadeloupe to resist a violence more than three centuries old and to engage in the battles they are now fighting to liberate Guadeloupe from the colonial yoke.

Perhaps Leonora will help us Antilleans find this something, help us reconcile with that accursed part of ourselves, help us hope in the way Ernst Bloch means when he speaks of an "initiated, proven hope," of a hope that "derives its future existence, its sudden appearance from what is anchored deep inside us and that lays the foundation for our proud advance, head held high."

Leonora may also help others understand that Guadeloupe is not "a bit of France palpitating under the tropical sun," as General de Gaulle declared, but a land of insolent beauty, wounded, oppressed, severed in two.

From the depths of that land, a woman, a peasant, speaks out to proclaim her difference and her contradictions, those of an entire people. A people thirsting after a human future, after justice, independence, and dignity.

Dany Bébel-Gisler

Notes

1. Translation of the French word *nègre* poses particular problems and touches on culturally sensitive issues. The English term *black* or *black folks* is employed most frequently in the translation. *Blacks* is also used to translate *les noirs*. (*Trans.*)

2. Lamentin. The township in which Leonora lives.

3. In the original French edition, the story, along with verses in the text and the chapter headings, was transcribed phonetically from Creole and then translated into French. A French-speaking person phonetically reading the Creole can partially understand its meaning. This linguistic parallel is necessarily and unfortunately lost in the English translation. See the Afterword for a discussion of language issues. (*Trans.*)

4. *Anmann.* Guadeloupean peasant woman who was ninety-eight years old when I [Bébel-Gisler] heard this unpublished narrative about the imaginary return of the slaves to Africa. *Anmann* lived, as did Leonora, in the region of Lamentin. She had married an "African" whose parents were among the last slaves carried off from Africa after the abolition of slavery and imported clandestinely into the West Indies. The narrative transcribed here emphasizes to what extent the imaginary was, and still is, a mechanism of resistance, vital to retaining one's individual being and identity. The return to Africa, so fervently wished for, could be achieved only during the evening gatherings when the spirit, helped along by the sound of the drums and the voice of the storyteller, could take wing and join the ancestors. Another type of voyage was the definitive one of death.

5. Plantation. A landholding consisting of cultivated fields, houses for the owner and the workers, plus workshops. At the beginning of Caribbean colonization, plantations producing coffee and market crops were founded. Due to the enormous profits possible in sugar, however, sugar plantations rapidly replaced all the others and became the dominant feature of the Guadeloupean countryside.

In fact, everything was organized around the production of sugarcane, the driving force of the Caribbean colonial economy, and this brought about the destruction of the human and natural environment. After having eliminated the native people (the Caribs), the colonists imported blacks from Africa and put them to work on the plantations, which they could not leave except by breaking the law and thus becoming *Nègres marrons,* runaway slaves.

Each plantation was like a small, independent state with its own laws, justice, and prison. Covering hundreds of acres, which had to be cleared, the plantation usually contained a house for the owner placed on a hilltop to keep it cool and to provide an excellent view of the property, with the stores selling sugar and rum just behind. Farther away were located the sugar refinery and the cane mill, powered first by wind and later by steam. Finally, on the edge of the fields of cane and downwind because of the odors, were the cabins for the blacks.

The plantation was self-sufficient, producing its own food, building its own shacks, and forging its own tools. At the heart of these rigidly hierarchical microsocieties were knotted the complex social bonds between white masters and black slaves, between mulattos and blacks, and between blacks and Indians. Here, too, was the birthplace of resistance and of popular Guadeloupean culture.

Leonora's story shows us how these relationships have survived today and how life on the plantation retains its colonial structure: the all-powerful master, the horse-riding overseer, the cabins rented by the workers and paid for in cut cane. . . .

With the passage of time, the plantations have been reorganized, the owners replaced by sugar companies. Of the 620 plantations existing in Guadeloupe in 1839, each with its own sugar refinery, 13 remained in 1961 and 3 in 1985. Of these, only one, at Grosse-Montagne (which Leonora describes), is still in private hands.

6. Pointe-à-Pitre. The most important city in Guadeloupe and the commercial capital, located at the junction of the islands of Grande-Terre and Basse-Terre (Basse-Terre is the administrative capital). All goods imported to or exported from Guadeloupe pass through Pointe-à-Pitre.

Founded in 1759 by the English, who then occupied the island, Pointe-à-Pitre flourished under French domination, which began in 1763. The city grew around the harbor, reclaiming land from the sea and from the swamps (which explains the frequent floods). During the last few decades, the city has expanded considerably, with apartment buildings and high-rises dotting the periphery. The old town—with its wooden houses adorned with balconies, its market, its open shops that spill onto the streets—has remained much the same. Many slums surround the city, despite the efforts of the city government to limit them. Unemployed Haitians, Dominicans, and Guadeloupeans live there.

A quiet city that empties out and shuts down at 7 P.M., Pointe-à-Pitre has begun to experience more problems (break-ins, thefts, muggings, etc.) due to rising unemployment.

7. See note 50. (*Trans.*)

8. *Man* Ibè's Beast. Popular culture and Caribbean folktales include an important bestiary. Aside from the traditional animals, like Brer Rabbit and Brer Tiger, one finds imaginary animals, mostly malevolent: the three-legged horse, the monstrous buffalo crab, and *Man* Ibè's Beast, a fearsome animal of indeterminate species and capable of devouring any and all unwise beings. [*Man* in Creole designates an older woman; *Ma* on the island of Trinidad. (*Trans.*)]

In addition, certain humans are reputed to be capable of metamorphosing—*mofwazé*—into a dog, steer, or nocturnal bird (see also note 15, *soukounyan*).

9. "Learning to eat at a table and to speak French are the two most difficult things for Guadeloupean people." (Quote from a sixty-five-year-old peasant woman.)

Sitting together as a family around a table for meals is a custom brought to Guadeloupe only recently. It is observed for special occasions: baptisms, communions, and marriages. Most days, the mother serves each person a share of the meal in a bowl. The father has first choice of the best morsels, then the children. Often the mother eats later, when the rest of the family has left. Each one chooses his or her own favorite corner for eating—outdoors, under the balcony, or, less frequently, indoors.

The meal usually consists of a single dish of rice or root vegetables, garnished with a little salted meat (beef or pork), salted cod, or fish for flavor.

Laborers generally take a cup of coffee with milk before leaving at four or five in the morning. Ten o'clock is the hour for the *didiko*, a solid breakfast. Around three o'clock, upon returning from the fields, they eat their dinner. In the evenings—nothing, or something light.

10. *Kò* in Creole, corresponding to *corps* in French, designates the whole person, the self, the "me."

kò an mwen = *mon corps* = *moi* = me
kò a ou = *ton corps* = *toi* = you

Notes

woté kò a ou = va-t'en = go away, scram.

Man is not made up of a soul and a body. His perceived body—sometimes called *kò* sometimes *kadav*—is inhabited and penetrated by spiritual forces that make a man real and living and more than just a skeleton, a body. A loss of the life forces endangers one's existence, because they are what keeps the body alive. The expression *kenbé kò* means to keep oneself in control, to control one's inner life so that the good and bad spirits that direct it exist in equilibrium; to keep watch that one's "guardian angel," the essential spirit of the mind, remains in place.

To ask about a person's health is similar to asking "How is your *kò?* Do you control your *kò*, or does your *kò* control you?"

The term *kò* also evokes all the bonds that tie an individual to his family, the living as well as the dead, in a symbolic chain that connects sickness, life, death, the ancestors, the spirits, and nature. These were bonds forged during the worst of slavery's violence; they carry this history written in the body and in the Creole language, wherein resides the memory of a world order that was imposed and endured, but was also resisted and subverted by the imaginary and the symbolic.

[The English word *self* is used to translate the French *corps*, as well as the more literal translation, "body." (*Trans.*)]

11. Manioc. Up to a few years ago, manioc served as the main staple of the Guadeloupean diet. A small bush, its roots are grated, dried, and ground into a flour. When raw, it can be mixed with meat, vegetables, or fish. Cooked, it is eaten in patties or *cassaves*, often filled with grated coconut. Few farmers grow manioc any longer or grind it into flour, a long and arduous process. Capesterre is home to the largest cooperative on the island still producing and selling the flour and *cassaves*.

12. The tool used to prepare the manioc, a *graj* or grater, is made out of wood or sheet metal. The same term identifies one of the rhythms of the *gwoka* (or *ka*) and the dance that accompanies the process of grating the manioc.

13. *Boutou.* A type of club, sometimes carved, that served the Carib tribe as a weapon for hunting and for war.

The Creole language contains a certain number of Carib words, like *carbet* and *ajoupa* (which describe types of cabins), *coui* (a bowl made from a gourd), *hamac* (hammock), etc. The Carib, a warrior people who came from the South American continent, slowly supplanted—on Martinique, Dominica, and finally Guadeloupe—the Arawaks, who had been there for a millennium and who, through the art of their pottery, left the remains of an advanced civilization. The Carib exterminated them all, sparing only the women.

Considered ferocious anthropophagi, for more than a century the Carib managed to keep the conquering Spanish off their islands. However, they cordially welcomed the first French, who arrived in 1635, but they revolted when the latter tried to force them into slavery. After thirty years of a long and bitter war, they were decimated. Only a handful of survivors escaped to Dominica and Saint Vincent. A peace treaty was signed. They agreed to remain on those islands, where no European nation would bother them. Their descendants still live there today.

14. *Persil.* French word for "parsley." (*Trans.*)

15. *Soukounyan. Volant* or *soukounyan,* the latter word originating in Africa, designates a human being transformed into a ball of fire.

At night, oral tradition tells us, certain people, most often elderly women, have the power to slip out of their skins, transform themselves into a ball of fire, and suck blood from their victims. To do so, one must know the "secret words" acquired either from one's ancestors or through a pact with the Devil.

Several methods exist for neutralizing a *soukounyan*. Scissors opened in the form of a cross play a large role. The simplest way is to find the discarded skin, always carefully hidden, and sprinkle it with salt and red pepper. If the *soukounyan* cannot reenter its mortal envelope by dawn, it dies.

Almost all Antilleans claim to have seen a *soukounyan* one night above the trees or flying low over a sugarcane field.

16. The story of Persillette was published in Creole by Henri Bernard, with illustrations by the author (Editions Présence Caraïbe, 1981).

17. Hog plum. A tree (*Spondias mombin*) that produces bunches of small, yellow, sweet-smelling plums popular for soaking in rum.

18. Several inconsistencies exist in the original French text. For example, Leonora says she started school at age nine and then, one year later, transferred to a larger school. She then goes on to say she'd soon turn fourteen. At another point in the text, she claims to have stopped school at age fourteen. A second inconsistency regards the number of children Leonora gave birth to and how many of those children were living at any particular point in the story. These inconsistencies may well reflect oversights in Léonora's original oral narrative to Dany Bébel-Gisler. The translator and editors have chosen to retain them in the English translation. (*Trans.*)

19. *Chabine.* As Jack Berthelot wrote in 1981, "to define someone is first and foremost to situate him or her in the color scale of multiple shades between white and black, with its distinct peaks, troughs, and thresholds. . . . Color is lived like a frontier, a gulf."

An entire series of terms classifies individuals by the cross-breeding of their ancestors. *Mulâtre(sse)* or *métis(se)* (mulatto) are the terms most commonly used, but a *chabin(e)* is a mulatto with light skin and fair hair; a *câpre(sse)* the offspring of a mulatto woman and a very dark black man; a *quarteron(ne)* the issue of a mulatto man and a white woman; and a *po chapé* [Creole for *peau-échappée* = escaped skin (*Trans.*)] has light skin (and thus escaped being a slave).

20. *Blanc-pays* or *Blanc-créole.* White person born in the Caribbean, in contradistinction to a white person born in France, who was called a "metropolitan."

21. Indians. The abolition of slavery in the French West Indies in 1848 seriously threatened the plantation economy. The newly freed people were not eager to work for their former masters, even for pay. Help in the cane fields was in short supply. Calls went out to Portugal and Africa, but without much success. The colonists then looked to India's huge reserve of manpower. With the help of the French banks, then thanks to an agreement between England and France, more than forty thousand Indians arrived in Guadeloupe between 1854 and 1889. They came with contracts for specified periods of time, but fewer than 10,000 returned to their home country. They were people from the lowest level in the caste system—the untouchables. On the plantations, as well as in homes and in the fields, they took the place of the slaves. Some of the former slaves continued to work. The two groups intermingled, and a relationship developed. The Indians rapidly learned to speak Creole, and despite a certain contempt for the coolies, the *malabars* [presumably from the Malabar Coast (*Trans.*)], intermarriage occurred, especially in the areas with a limited Indian population. Where their communities were of substantial size (Saint-François, Moule, Capesterre), the Indians retained their own characteristics, customs, religion, and culture. (See also note 24.) Although at first relegated to the bottom of the social ladder, they are more highly regarded today, since educational opportunities have permitted some of them to succeed and become doctors, teachers, and lawyers. They ceased being coolies and became Guadeloupeans.

22. *Doudoumso.* Onomatopoetic work recalling the sound of the drum that the swollen belly resembles.

23. *Lolo.* The *lolo,* a general store that sells all manner of things, is usually housed in a small, one-room shack closed off at the front by a counter. All the necessary provisions can be found in the *lolo:* rice, oil, sugar, salt cod, salted meat, lard, matches, spices, as well as string, nails, and religious objects.

Notes

Although still numerous in the countryside, *lolos* are disappearing in the cities, replaced by supermarkets. They still exist, however, because they continue to play an important role in the economic system: they offer credit. Each family has its account book, and the bill is paid every two weeks, on payday. Sometimes the debts accumulate till the sugar harvest, the only time when new cash flows in.

Generally, *lolos* are run by women, some of them are illiterate and employ an ingenious system of marks to keep track of each client's debt to the cent.

24. Maliémen. [Creole adaptation of the Tamil name Mariaman. In chapter 8, the variant Malyenmé occurs. (*Trans.*)] In South India, Mariaman is the goddess of smallpox. She protects against epidemics and is the most popular and feared deity in Guadeloupe.

Religion is the cultural element that best survived the transplantation of the Indian population, mostly Tamil, to Guadeloupe. Large public festivals, in which many blacks also participate, complement the private family rites. The festivals tend to be offerings for blessings received. Significant gifts are bestowed: jewels, embroidered fabric, natural and artificial flowers; foodstuffs such as huge piles of rice, eggs, milk, oil; and animals to be sacrificed—roosters and male kids.

A procession forms around the temple to the sound of the drum and cymbals. The goddess, a vegetarian, is offered cooked rice, milk, and coconuts. The sacrificial animals are for Maldévilen or Madoura Viran (see also note 25), the warrior deity who guards the temple and the goddess. Should the animal's head not be severed in a single blow, it would be taken as a sign that the god wasn't satisfied with the sacrifice. Finally, the animals are eaten at a great banquet, served on banana leaves.

A night of dance often precedes the ceremonies. The dancers, all men, dress in costumes "of light," brightly colored and often encrusted with bits of mirror or even electric lightbulbs in their headdresses. Many dances recount an ancient legend. A choir of men, drums, and cymbals accompanies the dancers.

While retaining important cultural elements like religion and dance, the Indian population has integrated well into Guadeloupean life and made its mark on the Guadeloupean culture. The Indian gods, in particular Maliémen, are considered to be extremely powerful, and many blacks call on their help. They participate in the ceremonies not just for the sake of curiosity or revelry. Even though most are Catholic, they, nonetheless, ask the aid of whichever god or goddess they believe will be most helpful in resolving their problems. Certain Indian customs have thus been totally integrated, and goat curry, for example, has become a national dish of Guadeloupe.

25. Maldévilen. Also written Madoura Viran (see also note 24). Creole forms of Madourai Veeran, the divinity whose legend is danced and sung in this ceremony. (*Trans.*)

26. *Kristal.* Marbles. The game of *kristal* is very popular in Guadeloupe. Although played today only by young boys, as recently as thirty years ago, adults participated in it too. Several games of marbles are part of the matches (triangle, *larel*, *padkochon*), all regulated by strict rules and an uncompromising honor code.

The marbles can be of terra-cotta, glass (*pèrlouz*), agate, steel (recuperated from ball bearings) or simply little stones polished by the river, or even *kannik* (round nuts). They are thrown in different ways, *roulade, bombe,* or *zingé,* that is released by a flick of the thumb in the angle of the bent index finger. The best players, the *vizè* (precision aimers) were very highly respected and drew a crowd whenever they played a game, everyone trying to mimic their movements and discover their secrets.

27. *Matador* dress. This traditional Creole outfit is now only worn in Guadeloupe by older women or on special occasions such as festivals or ceremonies. It consists of a brightly colored Madras cotton dress, decorated with lace, and lifted up on one side to reveal an embroidered petticoat. A Madras cotton *cancan* skirt and bolero could be worn with an embroidered blouse and petticoat instead of the dress.

Leonora: The Buried Story of Guadeloupe

An important element of the outfit is the headpiece: a bright, plaid Madras scarf knotted in a special and complicated manner. Gold jewelry is an indispensable element: *zanno* (earrings), *collier choux* (necklace made of beads as large as peas), good-luck bracelets, brooches, etc. A woman's best *matador* dress is saved for only the most important occasions.

28. The dead person's "master." A relative of the deceased who is responsible for the wake and for arranging the funeral rites.

29. *Léwoz*. The *léwoz* or *swaré léwoz* (*léwoz* soiree) is a cultural tradition still very much alive in the Guadeloupean countryside.

During the time of slavery, the blacks assembled every Saturday night on the plantation to dance to the sound of voices, drums, and clapping. The *bamboula,* or wild party, lasted throughout the night.

Léwoz is also the name of one of the seven principal rhythms of the *gwoka*, Guadeloupean folk music closely derived from African music. On Saturday nights, especially during the harvest, *léwoz* are still organized in front of a *lolo* (see note 23) or someone's house. The evening proceeds according to a well-ordered ceremonial, in which everyone takes part.

First the two *boulayè* start, straddling their deep-voiced *ka* (drum). Their contribution is to repeat a musical phrase throughout a piece to provide the appropriate rhythm (which could be *graj, woulé, léwoz, padjanbèl, kaladja, menndé,* or *toumblak*). Then comes the *makè* or *chèf tanbouyè* (principal drummer), who sits on a small bench and holds his drum upright, between his legs. Beating with hands, feet, and elbows, he plays the melody by coaxing higher and more varied sounds from his drum than the *boulayè*. Once the musicians have begun, the *chantè* (singer) and the *répondè* (answerers), who surround the *chantè*, begin and carry on a dialogue with the rest of the participants, who clap their hands and sing the refrain.

The other important performers in the *léwoz* are the dancers, who take turns challenging one another in the middle of the circle. The succession of rhythms throughout the *léwoz* soiree follows a well-defined and unchangeable order, each rhythm corresponding to certain dance steps. The singer, the real leader, throws out a key phrase, which is taken up by the *répondè* and the rest of the participants. Beginning with this phrase, he improvises, embellishing on an event, some news, or a person, often playing on words to poke fun.

A new development of this rural folk tradition has added other instruments to the drum and voice—the maracas, flute, guitar, and even saxophone and trumpet. Records are made, and concerts are performed. Other groups continue along more traditional lines. The *gwoka* and the *léwoz*, which at one time seemed relegated to the most isolated corners of the countryside, have regained popularity in the towns. The renewal of interest in these old traditions can be seen as related to the growing interest in Creole and to the search for a cultural identity that marks Guadeloupe today.

30. One part of Guadeloupe, also called Basse-Terre, separated from Grande-Terre by the Salée (salty) River.

31. Simon Laigle. [*Si* = *ti* on the musical scale used in solfeggio; *mon* = the French word *mont* = mountain; *l'aigle* = the eagle. (*Trans.*)]

I [Bébel-Gisler] have located this storyteller whom Leonora describes with such admiration. By attending wakes at which he led the games and by recording his words, I have been able to reconstruct the mythological narratives transformed by this man, who doesn't consider himself a poet but from whom "poetry pours forth, flows from [his] heart like an inexhaustible spring" whenever he speaks.

32. Delgrès. Here Simon Laigle alludes to a tragic event in Guadeloupean history.

Sent by Bonaparte, the first consul, General Richepanse landed in Guadeloupe on 6 May 1802. His mission was to reestablish slavery, which had been abolished by the

Notes

Republic in 1793. The leader of the battalion, Delgrès, a mulatto from Martinique, and Captain Ignace, a former *Nègre marron,* deserted from the French army and assumed leadership of the revolution. After many battles, Delgrès was pushed back to Matouba on the slopes of the volcano La Soufrière. Dug in there with three hundred of his followers, he repulsed several attacks. Realizing the hopelessness of their situation, his men and women chose to perish along with their enemies. At the cry of "Live free or die!" they let Richepanse's troops enter the fort and then blew it up. On 17 July 1802, a decree reestablished slavery, and it wasn't till 1848 that slavery was abolished permanently.

33. All Saints Day. November 1, also called the Day of the Dead; the day after Halloween. (*Trans.*)

34. Zombi. From the word *nzumbi,* "specter," "ghost," used in Angola.

According to tradition, the zombi is a dead person brought back to life by a sorcerer to be his servant. A veritable living-dead, the zombi has lost all its own personality and willpower and obeys its master's orders. It is said that in Haiti, landowners used hordes of zombis so they wouldn't have to pay sugarcane laborers to work the fields. By extension, in Guadeloupe the term *zombi* signifies all spirits.

Today the concept of "zombification" is used by some writers to replace that of cultural alienation so typical of colonized societies.

35. Mokozonbi. A man perched on very tall stilts that are hidden by long pants. This traditional Guadeloupean Mardi Gras costume is worn only by certain specialists. It requires practice to move about, dance, and jump for hours on the stilts, which can be as tall as two meters. The *mokozonbi* are greatly appreciated in the parades, but these giants, with their multicolored costumes, frighten the children.

36. Mare-Gaillard. Cooperative burial-insurance society. Each individual signs a contract that guarantees him or her a burial of a certain quality whenever he or she dies. The person makes monthly payments for the type of burial service desired. This custom is widespread in Guadeloupe, and the society flourishes.

37. Coup de main. Helping hand. The *coup de main* or "convoy," called in Haiti *koumbit,* find its roots in the strong tradition of solidarity associated with slavery. In order to clear land, to plant or cut sugarcane, or to build a cabin, family and neighbors congregate to work together, generally to the sound of drums and songs. The person receiving the help provides food and rum. Of course, reciprocity is expected. This custom was dying out till the nationalist union U.T.A. (Agricultural Workers Union) revived it. Large "convoys" are now organized by the M.U.F.L.N.G. (Unification Movement of Guadeloupean National Liberation Forces) to plant sugarcane on occupied land (1,200 inhabitants in 1985) and to revive an agriculture of resistance, notably by means of a new crop, rice: "plant today for tomorrow's food."

38. Yo. The personal pronoun *yo* (they) carries an important symbolic meaning in Guadeloupean society. It designates the unknown person or persons responsible for all bad things that happen. *Yo* can be the government, France, the administration, local elected officials, everyone who gives you trouble and against whom you have no recourse. The cost of living goes up, *yo*'s at fault; the water is cut off, the electricity fails, *yo*'s fault again; delinquency develops, its up to *yo* to do something about it. . . .

39. The graves are often marked by small mounds of earth that are quickly flattened by the rain and must periodically be built up again.

40. Pear trees. The colonists who landed in Guadeloupe gave names to the local flora. Some of the plants kept their Carib names (manioc, *ananas* [pineapples], *igname* [yams], cacao, etc.). Others, because of a vague resemblance to European plants, received French names: the "pear tree" that never bears fruit, the variety of banana called "fig," currants, strawberries, raspberries, apricots, chestnuts—all of which bear only a very slight resemblance (looks, color, consistency) to their French homonyms.

41. Marie Galantais(e). A person from Marie Galante, a small island (149 km²,

Leonora: The Buried Story of Guadeloupe

16,000 inhabitants) under the control of Guadeloupe, 30 kilometers away in the Atlantic Ocean. Of the same geological structure as Grande-Terre, Marie Galante, an arid island, concentrated very early on the cultivation of sugarcane. Split into small family properties, it was called the island of one hundred mills. At the end of the nineteenth century, the mills were replaced by four factories. Today, only one factory, at Grande-Anse, handles the island's entire production of sugarcane.

The population of Marie Galante is much less racially mixed than that of Guadeloupe. Because of its isolation, it has also better retained its traditions, language, and culture and is a treasure trove for anthropologists; sociologists; and French, Canadian, and American musicologists—all of whom produce scores and scores of articles on this microsociety.

The other islands controlled by Guadeloupe are Les Saintes, a small archipelago ten kilometers from the shore of Basse-Terre; La Désirade, a large rock eleven kilometers long by two kilometers wide situated eight kilometers off the extreme eastern end of Grande-Terre; Saint Barthélemy, an island to the north, inhabited almost exclusively by whites descended from the Normans and now the paradise of millionaires; and Saint Martin, an island that France shares with the Netherlands and that owes its prosperity to its status as a free port.

42. Dino. Working-class suburb of Pointe-à-Pitre built on land reclaimed from the sea and particularly subject to flooding.

43. Dust from the streets.

44. Mabi. A Carib drink made from the wood of the mabi tree and an herb called *ti-branda*.

Bouquet of soup vegetables. A carrot, turnip, cabbage leaf, celery branch, and a slice of pumpkin tied together like a bouquet.

Blood sausage. The spicy Creole blood sausage is a distant relative of the French *boudin*.

Kilibibi. Corn that has been ground, grilled, and mixed with brown sugar. It is sold in cones.

Snowball. Crushed ice sprinkled with a syrup (mint, grenadine, orgeat, etc.) and served in little paper cups.

45. Collection of Forty-Four Prayers for Life's Necessities. A sixty-page booklet containing a collection of prayers—to the Sacred Heart of Jesus, to Our Lady of Lourdes, to Saint Radegunda (guardian of cemeteries), et al.—corresponding to all the difficulties of life. It contains prayers for work, for healing, for finding lost objects, for uniting two hearts, for countering an enemy, and especially for protecting against all the spells that can be cast on oneself.

This booklet, which is sold throughout Guadeloupe in shops and marketplaces, has gone through a great many printings since its publication in 1939. One can also buy prayers "by the piece" for specific circumstances.

46. *Gadèdzafè.* The *gadèdzafè,* literally "the one who looks into things," is a person invested with a magical power who is consulted for many reasons. Either he or she (for many women practice this profession) works with the right hand invoking God to help solve problems concerning health, love, or other matters; to help the client extricate himself from a complicated situation, explain if the problem derives from a spell and, if so, who caused the spell to be put on and wishes him ill; to give advice on self-protection. Or the *gadèdzafè* works with the left hand to invoke the Devil. Depending upon his or her talent and respect, the *gadèdzafè* is either considered a *séancier* (healer), a *machann-kakouè* (a beliefmonger), a *mantimantè* (a vendor of lies), or a *kenbwazè*. While a *kenbwazè* devises *kenbwa*—an assemblage of all sorts of things that must be placed in certain locations to have an effect (in a crossroads, in front of an enemy's house)—

the *gadèdzafè* mostly deals with psychological problems, and his sensitivity and great experience of people often result in sound advice.

47. *Cancan* skirt. An important symbolic part of the traditional Caribbean costume (see also note 27).

48. Tercentenary. On 28 June 1935, the French government decided to celebrate with fanfare the three-hundredth anniversary of the arrival on 28 June 1635 of the French forces who took possession of the island. The event was celebrated both in Paris, with a sumptuous gala at the Opera, and in Guadeloupe, with the arrival of the ocean liner *Colombie,* carrying two hundred important people from the political arena, the arts, and the theater. The population was urged to welcome them warmly. The priest from Pointe-à-Pitre suggested that people dress in their local costumes. The guests visited several towns and moved from one reception and banquet to another. A High Mass was celebrated at the cathedral in Basse-Terre; the sailors from the *Emile-Bertin* and the *Audacieux* paraded through Victory Square, dressed as soldiers of the king. Almost two thousand people took part in the Catholic Congress of the Tercentenary. The Christian aspect of the anniversary was consecrated by the Tercentenary Mass on the summit of La Soufrière, the island's volcano. The population was invited to watch this event of "great Christian and French significance." One thousand people made the climb.

Several works were published on the occasion of the Tercentenary: *Guadeloupe du Tricentenaire* (Guadeloupe at its tercentenary), by Governor Bouge, *Les Etapes de la Guadeloupe religieuse* (The development of religion in Guadeloupe), by Quentin, etc.

R.P.

49. Tercentenary Hymn.
Refrain:
For three hundred years, Christian and French
On La Soufrière, they made their claim
Let us swear by these names, of success and fame
To always remain Christian and French.

I.
On La Soufrière
As we pray toward the sky
Let our prayers
Mount on high.

II.
Let us pray on these rocks
While all around
The sound of our bells
Rings through the towns.

III.
Let us pray for France
Let us pray, seas,
Under the sky immense
Let us pray, mountains and trees.

IV.
To the earth, let us pray
Where they sleep in the ground
Our dead of the war
That in combat were downed.

Leonora: The Buried Story of Guadeloupe

V.
Let us pray for the man
Richelieu, the priest
Who brought to this land
France and the Christ.

VI.
Let us pray for the glory
Of soldiers not seeking fame
Who made history
Yet are unknown by name.

VII.
For the military
The brave sailors
The missionaries
Bearers of the Cross.

VIII.
For those who suffered
Unknown pioneers
For those who were felled
The first ones here.

IX.
Oh, Star let us hail
The queen of the sea
That guided the sails
Of their ships here to be.

X.
May His hand protect
Governor, people, all
May His Grace alleviate
Their labor and toil.

XI.
For the Good Shepherd
Let us pray in the breeze
He is dear to our hearts
As our church he leads.

XII.
From the heights let us pray
Where the clouds confer
For the leader of the way
For our brave highlanders.

XIII.
May the gentle Queen
Christian and French

Notes

Lead us on one day
To the King of Peace!

A.B.
Abymes, 1935

50. *Marronner.* The term *Nègre marron* (*Nègmawon*) gave rise to the verb *marronner* (*mawonnè*): to take off, flee, hide, escape.

At the time of slavery, the term *Nègre marron* (from the Spanish *cimarrón*) designated those blacks who ran away from the plantations to escape the physical, moral, and cultural restraints, and who went into the forest to avoid recapture and to live either alone or in groups. With time, despite the severe reprisals against those who were caught (torture, mutilation, execution), the number of *Nègres marrons* increased. They organized villages and encouraged women and children to escape. Benefiting from accomplices inside the plantations, they organized guerrilla attacks, destroying livestock, harvests, factories, and houses. In certain colonies, such as Jamaica and Surinam, their power grew so strong that an almost warlike condition existed. England and Holland were forced to negotiate with them and to recognize their independence, ceding some territory to them (see *Petit traité sur le gouvernement des esclaves* [Short treatise on the government of the slaves], vol. 2, pp. 166-77]).

On Guadeloupe, several thousand slaves took refuge in the hills, where some of their descendants, having returned to a primitive state, can still be found.

A *Nègre marron* was described by the master as an outlaw, a savage, a dangerous person capable of the worst crimes. This image has persisted over the centuries. Escaped convicts were called *Nègres marrons.* The *Nègre marron* was used as a bogeyman, to frighten children and young girls who wanted to go out in the evenings. Most recently, with the rise of nationalist feeling, the *Nègre marron* has become a symbol of resistance to repression. The Haitian government even erected a statue in their honor. In Guadeloupe, the militant independence fighters of the M.P.G.I. (Popular Movement for an Independent Guadeloupe), sought by the police, have taken to the forests and proclaimed themselves *Nègmawon.* This symbolic action is characteristic of the cultural reappropriation now taking place.

51. Jehovah's Witness. For several years now in Guadeloupe, notably under the influence of Canada and the United States, the number of religious groups has been increasing: Seventh Day Adventists, Pentecostals, Jehovah's Witnesses, Apostles of Infinite Love, etc.

As in all countries where people worry seriously about the future (cost of living, unemployment, deterioration of economic and social life), the sects offer a refuge and ready-made answers to existential questions. They have, however, seen only limited success in Guadeloupe, and the Catholic church retains its clear preponderance on the island. [Since the French edition of this book first appeared in print, the followers of non-Catholic, Christian religions have significantly increased in number, and the evangelical churches referred to by Bébel-Gisler have proliferated. (*Trans.*)]

52. An unrefined, brown cane sugar.

53. *Radio Bois-Patate.* Gossip; metaphorically from the name given to the sweet-potato runner that penetrates everywhere underground, in every direction. [Rumor mill, grapevine. (*Trans.*)]

54. Guadeloupe is the largest per-capita importer of champagne in the world.

55. Sorin's regime. Constant Sorin was governor of Guadeloupe from 1940 to 1943, under the direct authority of Admiral Robert, commander-in-chief of the French forces in the western Atlantic, who lived in Martinique.

Leonora: The Buried Story of Guadeloupe

Defeated France signed an armistice with Germany, and Robert swore allegiance to Marshal Pétain. He then set about protecting the Caribbean islands from a possible British-American occupation. He succeeded, but at the cost of a total blockade. Guadeloupe and Martinique, isolated from the rest of the world, had to rely solely on themselves.

Sorin imposed a police state on Guadeloupe. All the elected officials were removed from office and replaced by appointed mayors and city officers. The Freemasons were persecuted, the youth kept in check, the Veterans Legion created. Vichy ideology prevailed: work, family, country. Pressure was exerted on the Guadeloupeans to get to work. A tax was imposed on fallow land.

If, officially, virtue and civil responsibility were extolled, in fact, protection of one's own interests and the ability to get along, to barter, and to trade illicitly ruled. To get soap, you had to bring coconuts and have oil extracted from them. From this derived the term *bya koko pou savon* (exchange one's coconuts for soap), a play on the word *koko,* which also designates the female sexual organ. It was said that the man who made the soap was a great womanizer.

Although it caused much discontent, Sorin's government found support among the factory and property owners, who continued to hold the real economic power. The church also rallied unconditionally behind the government and even became one of the strongest pillars of a regime that made constant reference to religion.

The time of Sorin's regime was a difficult one for Guadeloupe. However, those who wish to demonstrate the ability of the Guadeloupean people to live without outside help cite it as an example.

56. The resistance. The regime imposed by Sorin was far from being unanimously supported by the Guadeloupean people. Beginning in July 1940, the island's ruling council split into two factions. One wanted to continue the fight. Groups of resisters formed and carried out social actions: notices, marches, attacks on the police and the radio station.... Increasing numbers of men left to join the French freedom forces, responding to the call of General de Gaulle. They became part of the resistance. In fishing boats, they reached Dominica, a British possession. It is estimated that between 2,000 and 5,000 Caribbean men managed to evade the Vichy regime in this way.

57. *Asi milé.* The term *asi milé* means "seated on a mule," but when read phonetically it sounds like *assimilés* = "assimilated." (*Trans.*)

58. Département. A département is the upper-tier unit of local government in France, roughly equivalent to a U. S. state. Each département—including those overseas, such as Guadeloupe—sends senators and representatives to the French parliament. (*Trans.*)

59. M.R.J.C. Rural Christian youth movement.

60. Renew your conversion. A woman who lived with a man to whom she wasn't married or who has borne a child out of wedlock, was required to "renew her conversion" if she again wanted to approach the Holy Altar and take communion; in other words, she had to do penance and vow to give up sexual relations with men for the rest of her life.

61. *Pipirit.* Onomatopoetic word describing the song of the first bird of morning. [By extension, the common name of this bird. (*Trans.*)]

62. Titans. Huge tractor trailers that carry the sugarcane.

63. C.G.T. General Confederation of Labor. One of the large, centralized French labor unions, with a local in Guadeloupe. Other such unions include the C.F.D.T. = French Democratic Confederation of Labor; F. O. = Workforce; F.E.N. = National Teachers' Union. (*Trans.*)

64. U.T.A. Agricultural Workers Union. Founded in 1970, this was the first union of Guadeloupean origin. The others in existence at the time on the island were locals of large, centralized French unions (see note 63). Subsequent to extensive groundwork

among the people, its creation totally upset the existing union setup. It immediately proclaimed: "No real change in the condition of the workers and peasants is possible without a radical transformation of Guadeloupean society as a whole." At first rejected by the owners and the other unions, the U.T.A. gained recognition through its dynamism, the success of the strikes it led, and the importance of the concessions it obtained. Today, it is the only union representing agricultural workers.

65. *Képis rouges.* Red caps. Name given by the Guadeloupean people to the forces of order.

66. C. E. = elementary school. C. M. = middle school (*Trans.*)

67. Root vegetables. Tubers and, by extension, starchy foods such as bananas and breadfruit.

68. Cockfight pits. Round enclosure in which cockfights—a highly esteemed diversion in Guadeloupe—take place and in which bets of considerable size are wagered. [Cockfighting is found throughout the Caribbean. (*Trans.*)]

69. *Latilyé.* A group of workers who carry out a common task, as in French *l'atelier.*

70. Custard apple. A small tree that produces a large, spiky fruit with tender and aromatic pulp. Delicious juice is extracted from it. The leaves of the custard apple tree have curative properties. An herbal brew of the leaves relaxes and induces sleep. [The fruit of the tree is also called bullock's or bull's heart. [*Trans.*)]

Tamarind. The real tamarind, used as a tea for pregnant women, is the fruit of a large tree. Existing as a long pod containing two or three kernels coated with an acidic pulp, it makes an excellent juice. The Indian tamarind is a sweeter fruit, which grows on a bushy shrub and is eaten overripe or soaked in rum to produce a Guadeloupean fruit "punch."

In the Caribbean, there is a successful and well-developed system of traditional herbal cures, which has just recently become a subject for serious medical research.

71. Raras. On Good Friday, in place of bells, the children announced church services to the sound of rattles (*raras*).

72. Imprudence. Name of an illness contracted under circumstances in which one goes from hot to cold.

73. Bumidom (Bureau pour les Migrations Intéressant les Départements d'Outre Mer). Office to encourage immigration from the Overseas Départements. The Bumidom was created in 1963 by the French government to facilitate emigration of young West Indians to France. [The term *Départements d'Outre Mer* (DOM) refers to the four French départements or counties outside Europe and overseas: Guadeloupe, Ile de la Réunion, Martinique, and French Guiana. (*Trans.*)] "To contribute to the solution of demographic problems existing in the DOM . . . reduce the incidence of overpopulation in the West Indies with regard to the employment market and the social structure; help those workers who volunteer to take up residence in France."

At that time, France needed manual laborers, while the Caribbean islands grappled with high unemployment. Transportation was offered (only a one-way ticket). This system functioned up till the last few years, when the employment crisis in France dampened slightly this hemorrhage of young West Indians.

74. Ti-Jo. A nickname that means little José, junior. (*Trans.*)

75. Guadeloupean unions (S.G.E.G. and S.I.P.A.G.) that are not part of a central French union, were created in 1977, and support independence. [S.G.E.G. = Education Workers Union of Guadeloupe. Part of the independence movement, the S.G.E.G. represents all personnel in state education. S.I.P.A.G. = Union of Guadeloupean Teachers, Professors, and Staff. (*Trans.*)]

76. C.E.T. Technical junior high school for those pursuing vocational training. (*Trans.*)

77. *Blesse.* A hit, a fall, a violent movement, an overly strenuous effort, a sensation

Leonora: The Buried Story of Guadeloupe

that something moved in one's body. An internal organ "shifts," the stomach "splits," the uterus "falls," the body is "unsettled." Depending upon the severity of the shock, a *blesse* can be fatal. Pregnant women particularly fear *blesses* that can cause the womb to prolapse, provoke a miscarriage, and cause birth defects in the fetus. A *blesse* is treated by a person called a *blesse masseur*, who has a reputation for being able to identify the affected organ and put it back in its proper place.

78. *O.K.* and *Girl.* Popular teen magazines, sold widely in Guadeloupe.

79. *Konbòch.* Female rivals. Skinny women are described as "thin as Konbòch's cats."

80. *Lélé* stick. Stick or wood from the cacao tree, the forked end of which is used to *lélé,* or stir, liquid.

81. Jarry Chapel. Guadeloupe is rich in places of pilgrimage associated with particular occasions (exams, weddings, work, legal matters, etc.). The pilgrimages are organized either on fixed dates or by the faithful who desire to ask for a blessing or to fulfill a vow. The chapels often contain objects or writings carefully hidden, generally left to hurt other people.

Some of these places have been taken over by one or another of the sects. The Jarry Chapel, for instance, has become one of the pilgrimage spots for the Apostles of Infinite Love.

82. Saint-Claude. The township that houses the first psychiatric hospital in Guadeloupe (see also note 84).

83. Frébault Street. The most important commercial street in Pointe-à-Pitre. The majority of stores are owned by Syrians and Lebanese. Having settled in Guadeloupe, sometimes as long as two generations ago, they specialized in the dry-goods business. Originally peddlers, they have set themselves up in shops over the years. The recent events in the Middle East forced a sizable number of Lebanese to emigrate. Those established in Guadeloupe naturally brought over their families, who have considerably enlarged the local community.

84. Asylum, psychiatric hospital. The psychiatric hospital in Saint-Claude was founded in 1876. In 1890, it consisted of six pavilions, four for the indigent and two for the more fortunate. At first, the few inmates, confined predominantly for their aggressive behavior (assault and battery), were guarded by the military and forced to submit to brutal treatment. This situation was attested to by the maxim: *Vométan ay pléré douvan lapòt simityè ki douvan lazil* (It's better for a mother to cry at the gate of the cemetery than at the gate of the asylum). Till about 1940-46, the asylum mostly housed the mentally ill from the colonies of Martinique and French Guiana. The hospital began to receive Guadeloupeans and to be used to capacity starting in 1954, when the Colson Hospital in Martinique opened.

85. *Miganné.* From *migan,* a dish of mixed root vegetables cooked together.

86. U.P.G. Union of Guadeloupean Farmers.

87. Creole, language of the poor.

"In 1971, during the major strikes that mobilized Guadeloupean sugarcane and construction workers, I had the occasion to watch and take part in meetings where the workers spoke out in Creole. The first meeting I attended, called by the U.T.A., took place at the Grosse-Montagne school, in La Rosière, Lamentin. It was thrilling. A crowd of two thousand, attentive, trembling at one moment, smiling or breaking out in laughter the next. A crowd of workers in complete agreement with these men of their own rank, exposing the situation, denouncing the abuses, demanding rights for the workers.

"I had the impression that, finally, the poor stood up in unanimity, using a common language, proclaiming the value of their lives, rejecting another world that crushed them in the economic, political, and cultural spheres. Arguments were heard at all levels in the discussion.

Notes

"An impression of a profound unity, beyond that of their shared life experiences. Something heretofore buried seemed to rise to the surface. An impression of dignity. I had come to listen, yet felt myself seized by a desire to speak, to express my agreement, which I then did.

"I had no doubt that Creole was the instrument of this profound fellowship. First, it allowed for a clear understanding of the situation. And then, surfacing from the bowels of these men, men like C and M, it expressed, in a most extraordinary manner, their aggressiveness and humor, all the while informing us. Creole was revealed to me as a language perfectly capable of conveying a message, carrying information on economics and politics, areas till then reserved for French. I recognized in Creole the fundamental language of protest for a collective identity, for an individuality, for a refusal to continue in bondage to the economic, political, and cultural world that had always imposed this subservience. The fact itself, is a fundamental argument." (Father Chérubin Céleste, 1972.)

88. U.P.L.G. The People's Union for the Liberation of Guadeloupe appeared in 1978, after the introduction in the 1970s of the independent Guadeloupean unions (Agricultural Workers Union, Union of Small Farmers, Union of Guadeloupean Workers, Education Workers Union of Guadeloupe).

"We have entered a period of unionization and political organization of the Guadeloupean people, with the workers and the peasant at the center." (*Ja Ka Ta*, January 1981). The U.P.L.G. defines itself, not as a political party, but as a union that wants to enable "all Guadeloupean patriots from all social classes to get involved in the fight for national liberation." (Political declaration, 1 December 1978) Since the 1985 conference of the remaining French colonies, the U.P.L.G. has been asserting itself as the leader of the Guadeloupean independence movement.

89. R.P.R. Gaullist political party in France. (*Trans.*)

90. Quadrille. In order to replace in the minds of the slaves the "memory of their infamous dances," so "lascivious" and full of "indecent movements," the masters tried to teach them "the minuet, the coranto, the passepied, and others, so they could dance in groups and jump about as much as they wanted." (Father Labat.) Of all these dances, only the quadrille survived and "quadrille dances," organized by "associations" take place almost every Saturday in one or another of the Guadeloupean townships. These evenings are very popular and attract the older people from the country. Unlike the *léwoz,* with its *gwoka,* this tradition has not caught on with either the youth or the nationalist movements, which consider the quadrille to be a remnant of the French cultural domination of the slave era.

91. C.R.S. National police force noted for its aggressive enforcement of law and order. (*Trans.*)

92. Politics. In the restricted, Guadeloupean meaning of the word: electoral politics.

93. French telephones used to have an additional receiver attached to the telephone by a short wire, which allowed a second person to hear the conversation. (*Trans.*)

94. Work stoppage. An intervention, generally large scale (during a strike), in which the strikers explain the reasons for their action to those who continue to work and urge them to join the strike.

95. J.O.C. Organization of young Catholic workers.

96. The large wagons. Large trailers pulled by a tractor and containing two to five tons of sugarcane.

97. Combat Ouvrier. "The Workers' Struggle," a Trotskyite political organization.

98. Rozan Mounien. One of the founders and leaders of the U.T.A. and secretary-general of the Union of Guadeloupean Workers [at the time *Léonora* was written (Trans.)].

Glossary

Afterword

Glossary

adò: yam.

agoman: plant (*Solanum americanum*) that produces small black seeds. It is used to treat the eyes as well as infestations of intestinal worms.

ajoupa: small shack made of board and sheet metal. The word is of Carib origin. (DBG)

akra: spicy, deep-fried codfish dumpling. (DBG)

anmann: mamma; used as a term of respect for older women.

an tan Soren: in Sorin's time. (See also note 55.)

bakoua: plant whose long leaves are dried and woven into hats, bags, and rugs (DBG); especially the hat itself.

balarous: small fish (*Hemiramphus brasiliensis*) with a long nose.

bèlbèbèl or *bèl bèbèl:* frivolities. (DBG)

blesse: hit, fall, shock (DBG). (See also note 77.)

bòbò: slut. (DBG)

Bondié or *Bondyé bonjou!:* Good morning, God!

bosoko: type of pastry or dumpling made from manioc flour.

boua-boua: marionette; large puppet carried during Mardi Gras.

boulayè: drummer who plays the large *ka* (q.v.) drum. (DBG)

boulèt: crab trap.

boutou: club used by the Carib tribe as a weapon. (DBG)

branany: related to French *bréhaigne*, "sterile". (DBG)

bwa sèk: response of the audience to storyteller's calling out *"tim, tim"* (q.v.)

cambuse or *kanbiz:* meal; kitchen.

campêche: Central American hardwood; named after a town in Mexico.

canari: terra-cotta stewpot. (DBG)

cancan: skirt that forms part of the traditional Antillean dress and that carries symbolic importance (DBG); also rumor, gossip. (See also note 27.)

câpre or *câpresse:* offspring of a mulatto woman and a very dark black man. (DBG) (See also note 19.)

carapate: oil made from ricinus seeds (DBG); castor oil made from *Ricinus communis,* a tall euphorbiaceous plant.

cassaves: patties made from manioc flour, often filled with grated coconut. (DBG)

chabin or *chabine:* light-skinned, light-haired person of color (DBG); *shabine* in D. Walcott's orthography. (See also note 19.)

chaspann: tin pitcher (DBG).

chodo: drink made from milk and beaten egg yolk, flavored with cinnamon and nutmeg.

coui or *koui:* half a gourd used as a bowl. (DBG)

coup de main: helping hand, community activity; same sense as Haitian *koumbit.* (See also note 37.)

denndé: oil palm. (DBG)

dictame: plant, the root of which, once treated, yields a cornmeal-like flour that is used in infant formula. (DBG)

didiko: snack, meal eaten midmorning by workers and peasants (DBG).

donbré: type of dumpling made with water, wheat flour, and salt.

donkit: dumpling.

doucelettes or *douslèt:* sweet made from coconut milk, sugar, and cinnamon.

doudou: small, ornamental shrub with red or yellow flowers; term also used as the equivalent of *sweetheart.*

fleurs de sonnettes: yellow flowers of a shrub that produces a rattlelike pod.

gadèdzafè: clairvoyant, also sorcerer, magician, medicine man. (See also note 46.)

gragé, grager: grated, to grate (DBG); see also *graj.*

graines-l'église: red seeds of a tree used to make necklaces.

graj: tool made out of wood or sheet metal, used to scrape manioc (DBG); also a rhythm of the *gwoka* (q.v.). (See also note 12.)

grandes-gueules: large-mouthed fish.

guéri-tout: heals-all; plant used as an herbal medicine (*Eupatorium odoratum*).

gwoka: traditional drum of Guadeloupe.

gwokréyòl or *gwo nèg:* pure, authentic Creole, spoken by the non-French-speaking blacks (DBG); also by rural Guadeloupeans of East Indian origin.

gwokyap: rich folks. (DBG)

gwonèg nouè: large black man.

ka: measure, lard-tin full; also a drum.

kabanné: fruit ripened after falling to the ground.

kakoué or *kakwè:* see *machann kakoué.*

kanbiz: see *cambuse.*

kanodè: caneloader, cranelike machine used to move cut sugarcane about.

karata: sisal. (DBG)

kenbwa or *kenboua:* assemblage of objects that assume magical powers when placed in specified locations (DBG); also sorcery.

kenbwazè or *kenbouazè:* practitioner of *kenbwa* (q.v.). (DBG)

képis rouges: red caps; name given by the Guadeloupean people to the forces of order. (DBG)

kilibibi: corn that is ground, grilled, mixed with brown sugar, then sold in cones. (DBG)

klendendeng: fireflies.

kò: being, self (DBG). (See also note 10.)

kòk: colloquial term for penis; prick.

koui: see *coui.*

kovadis: sandals made from old tire treads (DBG); presumably derived from *Quo vadis, domine?*

krak: see *yé krak.*

krik: see *yé krik.*

lakandas: cadaster; property plan. (DBG)

lélé: stick or wood from the cacao tree, the forked end of which is used to *lélé,* or stir, liquid. (DBG)

léwoz or *swaré léwoz:* community dance to the rhythm of the *gwoka* (q.v.); also a specific rhythm played on this drum. (See also note 29.)

lolo: small, local general store (DBG). (See also note 23.)

mabonne: woman who accompanies the godmother during the baptism and holds the baby. (DBG)

machann kakoué or *machannkakouè; mantikakwè* or *manti kakouè:* beliefmonger, one who sells beliefs, healer. (DBG)

madère: dasheen (*Colocasia esculenta*).

magoté: layered (horticultural term); a plant is propagated by layers (a twig is induced to root while still attached to the living stock).

mahault: manjack (*Cordia sulcata*); a tree.

makè: principal drummer, the one who keeps the rhythm (DBG); also the drum played. (See also note 29.)

mako: mole, spy, informer.

malanga: cabbage.

man: madam, used with proper names.

manfouben: people who don't care, as in French *Je m'en fous bien* (I don't give a damn).

manjé-kochon: pig feed; garbage; mess.

manman: mamma, mother. (See also *anmann.*)

mantikakwè or *manti kakoué:* see *machann kakoué.*

manti-mantè or *mantimantè:* vendor of lies (DBG); also sorcerer, healer, medicine man.

manzèl or *manmzèl:* mademoiselle, miss.

marinade: salty dumpling.

marronner: to play hooky, run off, run away. (See note 50 for a fuller discussion of the etymology.)

matador (dress): traditional creole outfit. (See also note 27.)

menné-vini: "come-hither" lotion, made from the bitter-almond creeper (*Merremia dissecta*), to which is attributed the power to seduce and attract.

miganné, from *migan:* dish of various root vegetables cooked together (DBG); mixture.

mika: plastic sandals.

mofwazé or *mofouazé:* see *moufwazé.*

mokozonbi or *moko-zonbi:* man perched on tall stilts; traditional part of the Mardi Gras parade (DBG). (See also note 35.)

moltani: soup made from dhal (pigeon pea); mulligatawny soup.

moufwazé or *moufouazé* or *mofwazé* or *mofouazé:* metamorphosed (as in animal to human shape or vice versa).

nanni-nannan: a very long time ago. (DBG)

Nègre marron or *Nègmawon:* runaway slave (DBG). (See also note 50 and *marronner,* above.)

niches à poulboua or *poux-de-bois:* termites' nests. (DBG)

parche: husk.

paroka or *ponm kouli:* Indian apple (*Momordica charantra*).

pè: papa.

pépa: inexpensive sandals made from discarded tires. (See also *kovadis.*)

pipilit: a candy.

pipirit: the first bird to sing at daybreak. (DBG)

pissiettes: small fish used for frying.

poban: small bottle, flask. (DBG)

popotes: flowers of the breadfruit tree; also, playing with dolls.

poto-mitan: mainstay (DBG); also the pole linking this world with the world of spirits in Voudou and related Afro-Caribbean religions.

poulboua or *poux-de-bois:* termites. (DBG)

Radio Bois-Patate: rumor mill; grapevine (DBG). (See also note 53.)

rara: rattle. (DBG)

razyé: herbal medicine. (DBG)

répondè: answerer, as in call and response. (See also note 29.)

rois-sous: large crayfish.

roki: measure of liquid (DBG); also the container used.

roquille: see *roki.*

roukou: annatto (*Bixa orellanca*); a red vegetable dye used by the Caribs, often for body paint.

salbiyé: large tree bearing noncomestible fruit. (DBG)

séance: consultation session with a *séancier.*

séancier: healer. (DBG)

sémèncontra: Chenopodium ambrosloides; santonica; worm bush or Mexican tea.

soukounyan: word originating in Africa that designates a human being transformed into a ball of fire (DBG). (See also note 15.)

swaré léwoz: see *léwoz.*

tanbouyè: drummer.

tèbè: mentally retarded, idiot. (DBG).

ti: small, little, junior, from French *petit.* Used as a prefix with proper names.

tikyap: poor folks. (See also *gwokyap.*)

tim tim: ritual words called out by a storyteller to make contact with the listeners, who respond *bwa sèk!* (q.v.).

touches: veins of a leaf. (DBG)

touloulou: small red crab. (DBG)

tourments d'amour: coconut tarts.

vétiver: graminaceous plant of which the root is used in making perfume and the stalk braided into bags and baskets (DBG); cuscus grass.

vyékō: old man, person. (DBG)

vyé Nèg: old blacks.

woulo: bravo.

yé krak: response of the audience to the storyteller's *yé krik* (q.v.).

yé krik: phrase used by the storyteller to begin a story or to renew audience interest.

yo: they; them (DBG). (See also note 38.)

yo yo di: rumor, gossip.

zanma: leaves of sugarcane.

zègèlèt: very skinny.

zikak: coco plum.

zonbi: alternate Creole spelling of *zombi.*

zyé dou: to make eyes at someone.

Afterword

Convergences

In this book made up of my words, it is my very self that is present. Just as I have told my story, you have written it. But how beautiful the way you have transformed my Creole words into French. And keeping their color, their music, their rhythm. Congratulations for what you have managed to put into it. This is your part of the work.

—Léonora about *Léonora,* quoted by
Dany Bébel-Gisler in "Who is the Other?"

Dany Bébel-Gisler was born in 1919 near Lamentin in the northern part of Basse-Terre, Guadeloupe. After graduating from the Lycée Carnot in Pointe-à-Pitre, Guadeloupe in 1953, she went to France on a scholarship to study modern literature and history at the Ecole Normale Supérieure in Paris. A specialist on slavery and its lingering effects in the French Antilles, Bébel-Gisler holds degrees in sociology, ethnology, and sociolinguistics from the Université de Paris III. Since the early 1970s, she has been active in organizing and promoting social-scientific research projects that focus on the people of the French Antilles and on African and West Indian immigrants in France. Bébel-Gisler's efforts, and the support of Michel Leiris, her mentor and collaborator, resulted in her appointment as a member of C.N.R.S., France's national center for scientific research, in 1974. In 1988, after having conducted several years of fieldwork in Guadeloupe, she was named chair of the sociology department of C.E.R.C., the center for caribbean studies and research at the Université des Antilles et de la Guyane in Pointe-à-Pitre. Her research in Martinique, Trinidad, and especially in Guadeloupe has yielded a number of important publications in the fields of sociology and sociolinguistics, among them *Cultures et pouvoir dans la Caraïbe* (Cultures and power in the Caribbean, 1975), co-authored with the Haitian scholar Laënnec Hurbon; *La langue créole, force jugulée* (The Creole language, a strangled force, 1976); *Kèk prinsip pou ékri kréyol* (Some principles for writing Creole, 1976); *Les enfants de la Guadeloupe* (Guadeloupe's children, 1985); *Le défi culturel guadeloupéen: Devenir ce que nous sommes* (The challenge for Guadeloupean culture: To become what we are, 1989); and the collectively authored study *Le livre d'or de la femme créole* (The golden book of the Creole woman, 1988). All of these books testify to Bébel-Gisler's passionate interest in Creole, both as a language and, more broadly, as a distinctive cultural practice at odds with the educational policies and ideological imperatives that the French metropole imposes on its Caribbean subjects. *Leonora,* Bébel-Gisler's first literary work, is no exception in this regard.

What is *Leonora?* To what genre does it belong? Bébel-Gisler insists on calling it a *roman,* a novel, specifically a *roman-témoignage,* or testimony novel. Guadeloupean and Martinican intellectuals—writers, scholars, and teachers—on the other hand, refuse to regard this book as a work of literature, because it is based on the actual testimony of a living witness to Guadeloupean history.[1] It would appear that to them *Leonora* is primarily a socioethnological case study that documents Guadeloupe's economic, social, and cultural history as it recounts the roughly six decades of Leonora's life encompassed in the book. Read in this way, *Leonora* becomes simply another oral history, one that does little else than faithfully chronicle the daily lives of Guadeloupe's working-class blacks and their Creole culture. As ethnography, *Leonora* also confers cultural authenticity, a valued ideological commodity among those French Caribbean intellectuals who, in the face of their islands' continued economic and political dependence on France, wish to emphasize cultural differences. However, the questions of what constitutes such authenticity and of how it is produced in a written text are both vital and not easily resolved. Does literariness detract from authenticity, or does it enhance it? Whether or not a text like *Leonora,* one that combines literary invention with historical-cultural inventory, is acknowledged as a work of the imagination has a profound bearing on current debates about what Caribbean literature should be or do, about what constitutes a "true" representation of Creoleness (*Créolité*) and of Caribbeanness (*Antillanité*).

A controversial issue in these debates is not only how to use language but what language to use in the first place: French or *kréyòl,* a preferred spelling of Creole. The choices are by no means easy ones as, in addition to involving very practical concerns about audience and marketing, they are also highly politicized. Exactly what is at stake in that uneven blend of colloquial Antillean French and Guadeloupean Creole that characterizes the narrative of Bébel-Gisler's *Leonora* will come into clearer focus once the book is situated, on the one hand, within the context of francophone Caribbean literature and, on the other, in relation to the ongoing controversies about the uses of Creole—in writing, pedagogy, and everyday life—that have attended that literature's emergence. For part of the difficulty in assigning *Leonora* to a particular literary or nonliterary genre stems from the broader problem of defining Antillean literature. Although claims have been made as recently as 1989 that "Caribbean literature does not yet exist. We are still in a state of pre-literature: that of a written production without a home audience, ignorant of the authors / readers interaction which is the primary condition of the development of a literature,"[2] a number of literary histories have attempted to offer maps of francophone Antillean writing from the early seventeenth century to the present. Most notable among them are Jack Corzani's six-volume *La littérature des Antilles-Guyane françaises* (The literature of the French Antilles and Guiana, 1978); Roger Toumson's *La trangression des couleurs: Littérature et langage aux Antilles (XVIIIe, XIXe, XXe siècles)* (The transgression of colors: Literature and language in the Antilles [eighteenth, nineteenth, and twentieth centuries], 1989); and even Patrick Chamoiseau and Rafaël Confiant's *Lettres créoles: Tracées antillaises et continentales de la littérature, 1635-1975* (Creole letters: Antillean and European traces in literature, 1991). While there is little consensus among these critics as to what constitutes Antillean literatures, they nevertheless discuss many of the same authors.[3] Their studies also share a conspicuous privileging of male literary production at the expense of texts written by women.

It is not unreasonable to suggest, then, that gender biases have contributed to the confusion about and marginalization of *Leonora* as a work of literature and to its relegation to the realm of the social sciences. In what follows, we will draw a number of possible links between the questions of genre, language use, and gender that *Leonora* raises. Our hope is to encourage a complex appreciation of *Leonora*'s position and status within the context of Caribbean literature as, among other things, the first testimonial narrative or novel to be written in the French West Indies.

Historically, the vast majority of Antillean authors have opted to write in French, but some have been determined to express themselves in written Creole (see below). Ideologically motivated debates about language choice in written texts have been divisive and virulent. The role that Creole plays in *Leonora* and in other earlier or contemporaneous texts is, of course, inextricably linked to the symbolic, at times fetishistic, value Antillean intellectuals and politicians have attached to the Creole language and, by implication, to orality. A brief commentary on Creole and its literary uses will enable a more complex appreciation of *Leonora* as a text that does not simply exoticize Creole in an attempt to generate linguistic realism and cultural authenticity.

Although, by virtue of their status as Overseas Départements of France, the French Antilles and French Guiana have only one official language, French, the vast majority of their populations, across both race and class lines, is bilingual in French and Creole. Especially for the working classes, Creole is often the predominant language spoken at home, while French is learned later, in school.[4] What, then, is Creole? How did it develop? What is its current role in Antillean society?

Creole is both a proper name and a generic linguistic term. Historically, when two groups from different linguistic communities come into contact, especially in trading situations, they utilize a combination of both languages to enable communication. Called a pidgin, this form of spoken expression is no one's first language and is usually only sophisticated enough to deal with the trade issues at hand. However, if these groups remain in contact, successive generations grow up speaking this pidgin as a first language, which is then subsequently termed a creole. As the creole evolves into a more complex communication system, it is considered a full-fledged language rather than a dialect. In the case of the Antilles, the French colonizers came into contact with the Carib peoples of Guadeloupe and Martinique, and later imported vast numbers of West African slaves. The continuing contact between these different populations, along with linguistic influences from other European colonists (mainly the British and the Spanish), resulted in the emergence of various creoles, now called Guadeloupean and Martinican Creole (or *kréyòl*). The two are slightly different but mutually comprehensible, and share a number of linguistic features with other Caribbean creoles, as well as with Indian Ocean creoles (for instances, Réunion Island Creole or Seychelles Creole). While the majority of the lexicon is French-based, a number of recent studies have shown significant contributions of both vocabulary and grammar from a variety of West African languages, such as Wolof, Ewé, and the Bantu languages of central Africa.[5]

There have been numerous studies on the evolution of language in the Antilles, beginning with those the first French missionaries wrote in the seventeenth century. Attitudes toward Creole and theories about its origins, beginning with a fiercely condescending view treating Creole as a deformation of French, have evolved into a more respectful perspective from which Creole was deemed an interesting language phenomenon of great social and cultural significance. As the colonies became more established and successive generations of both French planters and African slaves were born on the islands, Creole became the predominant form of communication. Keenly aware of the power of language, the French, by means of the 1685 *Code noir,* prohibited African slaves of the same language group from working together on one plantation. This made it extremely difficult for the Africans to maintain their own languages, although some linguists, notably Marie-Josée Cérol, contest the notion that they lost their native languages so readily. The Africans' primary way of communicating with each other and, for that matter, with their French masters, was to speak Creole (since educating slaves was forbidden, they did not learn French). Although the legitimate children of the planters often learned French at home, they spoke Creole with their *da* (slave nanny) and with their slave playmates. Creole became a lingua franca spoken by virtually everyone, regardless of race and economic status.

Still, hierarchies based on linguistic competence developed alongside racial ones: If one could not speak French, one could not be French, and to be French was to be human. Since nonwhite people were considered intellectually inferior to whites, Creole, regarded primarily as the language of the "colored" population, was consequently characterized as limited in potential, as insufficient for expressing abstract or complex thought. Furthermore, the French language carried with it enormous symbolic capital. As Frantz Fanon writes in *Peau noire, masques blancs* (Black skin, white masks, 1952): "The Negro of the Antilles will be proportionately whiter—that is, he will come closer to being a real human being—in direct ratio to his mastery of the French language." Dany Bébel-Gisler explains this correlation and its continuing stigma even today: "A typical feature of our societies is that mastering the master's language, French, has been established as the symbol of the attainment of humanity. An illustration of this can be found in a sentence printed on the cover of school books that are still used in primary schools. 'School of my country, I'm bringing my soul to you. Make this frail soul, which is weaker than the body it inhabits, a French soul, a human soul.'" [6] Clearly, the perception of Creole as a nongrammatical patois is a result of French hegemony in the Antilles. To valorize Creole would have contradicted the systematic denigration of nonwhites. Although it was spoken across racial divides, Creole was originally characterized as the language of blacks and came to be associated with all nonwhite people by virtue of their assumed status as monolingual speakers of Creole.

The issue of language, then, carries great importance for most people in the French Antilles, and *Leonora* is a prime example of this in numerous ways. Most obviously perhaps, Bébel-Gisler frequently foregrounds language issues. For instance, in describing her experience in school, Leonora explains why it was such a difficult experience in the beginning: "The first year I wasn't much interested in what went on in the classroom. The teacher didn't speak my language, Creole, and I couldn't say anything, discuss anything, do anything." In addition, chapter 13, devoted almost exclusively to the relationship of Creole to French, offers countless examples of people's attitudes toward language that still persist today: The title reads "Enmé palé fwansé, on maladi ka rann moun brak" (The love of French, a malady that drives people mad).

Another, no less problematic, view of Creole has been perpetuated by intellectuals and academics, such as Moreau de Saint-Méry, who have studied this Antillean idiom in relation to so-called standard languages since the seventeenth century. Despite their interest in Creole—which some of these philologists and linguists came to regard as a quaint dialect certainly worthy of study—hardly any initiatives were taken to recognize the legitimacy of Creole as a complex and sophisticated language, let alone to institute Creole as the official language of the French Antilles. Even researchers such as Rémy Nainsouta and Léontel Calvert, who defended the study of Creole in the first part of this century, took an assimilationist stance with respect to language. By no means did they advocate that Creole be treated as equal to, or even as a substitute for, French in formal, institutional settings.[7] Perhaps surprisingly, both whites and nonwhites alike have shared the view that Creole has no institutional place. Without necessarily believing that French is inherently superior to Creole, Antilleans tend nevertheless to accept the common notion that each language must serve different purposes, one public, the other private.

A third perspective on Creole has gained wide currency since Guadeloupe and Martinique's becoming départements in 1946. Instead of prosperity and equality, which seemed within closer reach once traditional forms of colonialism had ended, the transition to neocolonial département status brought even greater economic dependence on France and with it a growing loss of cultural autonomy. Nationalism has been one of the responses to this economic and political predicament. In the context of nationalism, Creole became the hallmark of a distinctive cultural identity and practice.[8] The defenders of Antillean culture, whether favoring independence or not, have done much to change prevalent attitudes toward the status and the use of Creole. Churches started offering masses in Creole, and Creole became the primary language of most labor unions and political parties dedicated to political independence. Programs dedicated to the integration of Creole and Antillean culture into school curricula gained significant popularity in the 1970s and early 1980s.

Bébel-Gisler's own abiding interest in the Creole language and culture has reached well beyond the halls of academe. Among other things, it has led to her involvement in public education projects in Guadeloupe, including adult-literacy campaigns. In the mid-1980s, she founded the Centre Bwadoubout, an experiment in alternative pedagogy that is dedicated to helping Guadeloupean youths who, partly because they are speakers of Creole with insufficient performance capability in French, have found it exceedingly difficult to function within a national public-school system dominated by French language and culture. Bébel-Gisler continues to serve as director of the Centre. Its approach to education, based upon the use of Creole as a vehicle for learning, reflects the persistent defense of Creole as a viable linguistic practice that characterizes her scholarly writings.

Bébel-Gisler's approach to Creole would probably appear too pragmatically conceived to some Antillean intellectuals, such as the Martinican novelists Patrick Chamoiseau and Raphaël Confiant, who, together with the linguist Jean Bernabé, authored the now well-known *Eloge de la Créolité* (In praise of Creoleness, 1989). In this manifesto, which was first delivered at the Festival Caraïbe in Seine-St.-Denis, France, in 1988, Chamoiseau, Confiant, and Bernabé view Creole as the "primordial" language to which Caribbean writers return "in order to enrich [their] enunciation, to integrate it, and to go beyond it." Literary Creoleness, then, defined in the *Eloge* as "the *interactional or transactional aggregate* of Caribbean, European, African, Asian, and Levantine cultural elements, united on the same soil by the yoke of history," is the result of transcending the notion of the Creole language as unique cultural source and the kind of regionalism, even exoticism, associated with it in literary circles. Bébel-Gisler would no doubt agree with Chamoiseau and his collaborators that it is necessary to "turn away from the fetishist claim of a universality ruled by Western values in order to begin the minute exploration of ourselves."[9] But her own literary and sociopolitical strategies, intertwined in *Leonora* and in evidence in Bébel-Gisler's continuing social work, are distinct from the overwhelmingly aesthetic preoccupations of the *Eloge*.

The difference between Creole and *Créolité* is clearly one of ideological perspective. For Bébel-Gisler, Creole designates a set of specific linguistic and cultural practices whose rehabilitation may be a vehicle toward Antillean independence. Creole, for her, does not refer to a self-consciously multilingual literary practice and thus to the aesthetic values held by a small cultural elite. It should also be added here that, although the Créolité group acknowledges Glissant as a heroic model of sorts, his transnational and transracial concept of *Antillanité*, a theory that is fundamentally rooted in the realities of the Antillean landscape, must not be confused with the rather restrictive and decidedly elitist ideology of Creoleness that emerges from the pages of the *Eloge*. Bébel-Gisler's work, and her often confrontational politics, serve as reminders that Antillean literature's recent attempts to triumph over diglossia—that is, the domination of one (colonial) language over another[10]—may have little immediate effect on the continuing repressive policies with which Creole speakers in France's Overseas Départements have to contend on an almost daily basis. Maryse Condé's criticisms of the Créolité group follow similar lines: "Although West Indian literature proclaims to be revolutionary and to be able to change the world, on the contrary, writer and reader implicitly agree about respecting a stereotypical portrayal of themselves and their society. In reality, does the writer wish to protect the reader and himself against the ugliness of the past, the hardships of the present, and the uncertainty of the future?"[11] It would seem that Dany Bébel-Gisler is one of relatively few writers who refuse to participate in such consensus rituals.

Given Bébel-Gisler's emphasis on the linguistic value and viability of Creole, it is perhaps ironic that *Leonora* is not completely or even predominantly written in Creole, although there would have been ample precedent for this among French Caribbean poets and novelists. At this point, the list of twentieth-century Creole texts ranges from the *Fab Compè Zicaque* (Fables of Monsieur Zicaque, 1958) by the Martinican Gilbert Gratiant, the poetry and novels of the Haitian Franketienne, and the politically militant verse of Sonny Rupaire (whose "Mwen sé Gwadloupéyen" [I am Guadeloupean] Bébel-Gisler quotes as an epigraph to *Leonora*'s narrative), in addition to Hector Poullet's Guadeloupean poetry and folktales from the 1970s. More recent contributions to this body of work are novels by Martinique's Raphaël Confiant—who, since 1988, has published fiction in French rather than in Creole—and by Monchoachi, as well as plays such as *Misyé Molina* (Monsieur Molina, 1988) by Georges Mauvois and a collection of poems by Thérèz Léotin, entitled *An ti zyédou kozé* (A little starry-eyed chat, 1986).[12] Bébel-Gisler's decision to mix French with Creole places *Leonora* in the company of other texts that also combine both languages in varying degrees. There are examples of this bilingual literary practice dating back as far as 1901, when the Haitian writer Justin Lhérisson incorporated Creole into his novel *La famille des Pitite Caille* (The Pitite Caille family) in direct discourse, in proverbs, and in songs. Other examples include Jacques Roumain's classic novel *Gouverneurs de la rosée* (Masters of the dew, 1946), and, more recently, Daniel Maximin's *L'Isolé soleil* (Lone sun, 1981) and Maryse Condé's *La vie scélérate* (The tree of life, 1987).

The original text of *Leonora* is the result of a transcription of the Creole, in which Léonora and Bébel-Gisler conversed during the actual interviews, followed by a reorganization and translation not into academic French but into colloquial Antillean French. But Bébel-Gisler also decided to retain a significant amount of Creole in the written narrative. Most of these phonetic transcriptions from that "unofficial language associated with Guadeloupe's lower-class population, whose written forms have not been fully standardized,[13] are visually set apart from the narrative, almost as if they were being directly quoted, and appear in the original text side by side with their respective French translations. But the boundaries between the two idioms, suggested from the very start by the two-columned bilingual versions of both Anmann's tale and Sonny Rupaire's lyrics, gradually dissolve as we discover that the body of the narrative itself includes an abundance of Creole words and phrases, some translated and even annotated by the author, others not. Bébel-Gisler's insistence on including Creole at all renders *Leonora* controversial at the more subtle level of textual politics. Is Creole, in *Leonora*, merely a folklorized remnant? Or is it, as for instance in Simone Schwarz-Bart's novel *Ti-Jean l'Horizon* (Between two worlds, 1979), "discourse that comes to terms with French in a dual and contrary movement of convergence and separation"? According to Jean Bernabé, the fact that Schwarz-Bart writes exclusively in French and does not include any Creole at all signals her refusal to succumb to a "facile exoticism."[14] But is it the case, conversely, that any inclusion of Creole in a French text relegates that text to the realm of the exotic? And what if Creole appears in a variety of discursive settings and not just in characters' dialogues, where it can be read as an attempt at realistically representing spoken language? A careful answer to these questions requires a consideration of *Leonora* as an interdisciplinary or intergeneric narrative.

In the same way that *Leonora,* as a translation, positions itself at the boundary between two languages—in its English translation, it is obviously a rather different kind of bilingual text—it also occupies an uncertain and exceedingly unstable border space between sociology / anthropology and literature, a line where systematic inventory subtly shades into imaginative invention, and vice versa. *Leonora* is perhaps best described as a text that resides between generic dimensions and is the product of a practice at once social-scientific and artistic. The point is that *Leonora* purposefully straddles divisions between fictional and nonfictional, between literary, historiographical, autobiographical, and social-scientific discourses. Such in-betweenness is not an unusual phenomenon in Caribbean writing. It has in fact been the hallmark of a number of now-canonical texts from other parts of the Caribbean, most notably George Lamming's *The Pleasures of Exile (1960),* C. L. R. James's *The Black Jacobins* (1963), Fernando Ortiz's *Contrapunteo cubano del tabaco y el azúcar* (Cuban counterpoint: Tobacco and sugar, 1940), and Alejo Carpentier's *El reino de este mundo* (The kingdom of this world, 1949).[15] Like these other hybrid texts, *Leonora* is in many ways rather unscientific, even as some of its formal apparatus gestures toward a set of established ethnographic practices. Clearly,

Afterword

Leonora is something other, something more than a collection of interview transcripts edited and rearranged for publication. It is something other even than an academic textbook, despite the fact that sociologist Bébel-Gisler retains some of the methodological conventions of her chosen discipline by adding often-copious annotations to the narrative. But why, one might ask, would this renowned Guadeloupean scholar write a book that might put at risk her standing as a social scientist?

That *Leonora*'s reception as an oral-history text has not actually left Bébel-Gisler's professional status uncorroborated is quite irrelevant. Much more to the point is that her case is remarkably similar to those of other social scientists who were also, as Frantz Fanon called them, native intellectuals trained abroad, many of them, like Bébel-Gisler herself, in Paris. Two writers who come to mind almost immediately are the Cuban Miguel Barnet and the Peruvian José María Arguedas, both of whom were students of Roger Bastide in Paris. A little farther removed in history, there are the Brazilian historian Gilberto Freyre and the African-American folklorist and novelist Zora Neale Hurston, both of whom studied with Franz Boas at Columbia University in the 1920s. All of these native intellectuals are, much like Fanon himself, former "'objects' of observation" who, as Bébel-Gisler's mentor and collaborator Michel Leiris predicted, "would begin to write back" once they returned to their respective "homes" equipped with what Hurston called "the spyglass of anthropology." [16] The Guadeloupe that once was home for Bébel-Gisler, specifically the peasant culture of her family's maternal side to which she refers in her Postface, is now inevitably reframed as the field of investigation. It becomes a professional space where people like herself, or, at any rate, the self she used to be, now become informants, objects of study, or both. However, *Leonora*, much like Hurston's *Mules and Men* (1935), is evidence that this is not all they need become.

Without oversimplifying matters by suggesting that all "native" social scientists—as well as the conditions under which and to which they return—are alike, it is useful to ponder the kinds of questions Benigno Sánchez-Eppler poses in his essay on Hurston and Freyre.

> If one goes to the field to operate as a participant-observer, what are the consequences of *realizing* that one had been already a participant before restructuring one's subjectivity with discipline-specific observational and narrative strictures? If a discourse like anthropology arises, primarily or historically, from the displacement of a subjectivity into a field that is not home, what happens when a

subject travels away from home to acquire a disciplinary
discourse and returns to enact and inscribe its gaze at
home?[17]

What happens, with some frequency it seems, is that methodological
strictures are loosened and even bypassed as anthropological narrative
begins to assume the guise of literature. This is clearly the case in
Freyre's *O escravo nos anúncios de jornais brasileiros do século XIX*
(The slave in the Brazilian newspaper advertisements of the nineteenth
century, 1963), much more so than in his better-known studies of race
and culture in Brazil, *Casa-grande e senzala* (The masters and the
slaves, 1933) and *Sobrados e mucambos* (The mansions and the shant-
ies, 1936). Similar situations obtain in Hurston's *Mules and Men*
(1935), Arguedas's *Los ríos profundos* (Deep rivers, 1958), and Barnet's *Biografía de un cimarrón* (curiously translated into English as
Autobiography of a Runaway Slave, 1966). Granted, the narrative
strategies these texts employ vary considerably—it is worth noting that
Hurston is the only one who both exercises the subject position of the
"native" in her former Florida hometown and "fictionalizes the activity of the field-worker to the point that she becomes a storyteller."[18]
But however different from one another, what all these texts hold in
common is a willful noncompliance with the methodological require-
ments of their authors' professional culture in situations where academic practices meet, and clash with, postcolonial identity politics.
More often than not, such clashes yield texts that demand that readers,
whoever they may be, take a more skeptical look at the professional
production of cultural authenticity. *Leonora* is one such text.

As the book's subtitle already suggests, Dany Bébel-Gisler's purpose
is to recover the "hidden" or "buried" history of Guadeloupe specifically from the vantage point of one who, like her, is both black and
female. Her *roman-témoignage* is in many ways an oral-history project
that resonates most immediately with a set of texts that form a distinctive genre within the broad category of the contemporary documentary: that of the *testimonio*, or testimonial narrative, a Hispanic-
American (para)literary practice whose Caribbean beginnings, in such
works as *Biografía de un cimarrón*, are both descended from narrative
forms of the sixteenth-century chronicles of the Indies and complexly
intertwined with the birth of socialist Cuba.[19] This, however, is not to
suggest that the production of *testimonios* originated in, and has been
limited to, postrevolutionary Cuba. In fact, one of the classic texts in
this genre, *Juan Pérez Jolote—Biografía de un tzotzil*, was published
as early as 1952 by the Mexican anthropologist Picardo Pozas. In the

Afterword

1960s and 1970s, the idea of documenting the social and cultural histories of marginal groups by narrating the life of a representative individual, which had been pioneered by Pozas, became increasingly popular among many Hispanic American and European writers. One of the best-known recent examples is Elizabeth Burgos-Debray's *Me llamo Rigoberta Menchú y así Me nació la conciencia* (I, Rigoberta Menchú: An Indian woman in Guatemala, 1983).[20]

Exactly what is the *testimonio*? Barnet's remarks about his own writing in "La novela testimonio: Socio-literatura" (Testimonial narrative: Socioliterature, 1983) amounts to a working definition of this new genre. Perhaps most importantly, this form of socioliterature—which, much like the documentary novel in the United States from Truman Capote to Norman Mailer, has roots in contemporary journalism—requires that the self of the writer or sociologist be suppressed or suspended: in other words, that the presence of the author in the text be kept to a minimum. "It is in this depersonalization," Barnet contends, "that art approximates science."[21] The *testimonio,* then, is an articulation of a collectivity, a "we" instead of an "I," a distinction best understood as what Wilson Harris has called the difference between the "human person" and the "individual."[22] As a form of collective memory, the *testimonio* contributes to the knowledge of reality; it invests reality with a sense of history in order to dislodge ingrained biases and prejudices.

The contribution of the *testimonio* or testimonial novel to tradition is the knowledge of a reality through the knowledge of a language. In that sense, it can revitalize literature even as it resists overt literariness. Of course, the fundamental thing about the language of the testimonial novel is that it leans on spoken language without simply being transcription. The informant provides the tone and the anecdotes, whereas the amanuensis (or *gestor*) is responsible for style and structure. According to Barnet, he must use his imagination "to invent from within a real essence."[23]

Leonora shares much with the Cuban *testimonio,* above all its sense of being what Octavio Paz has labeled foundational. Explains Barnet: "The writer of a testimonial novel has a sacred mission, which is to reveal the other side of the coin. . . . Therefore, he has to investigate, to discover the intrinsic nature of the historical event, its real causes and effects. Continents like ours, which lack a cultural definition, need the testimonial novel in order to lend their tradition shape and image."[24] Much like Barnet's *Biografía, Leonora* seeks to fill particular gaps in the official annals of Caribbean history by chronicling the everyday chores and struggles of its black population from the vantage point of a subject whose representativeness resides precisely in his or her lack of social and economic privilege. *Biografía*'s narrator / protagonist Esteban Montejo, former runaway slave, illiterate farmhand, womanizer, veteran of the War of Independence, and 106-year-old resident of a Havana home for senior citizens at the time Barnet interviewed him in the early 1960s,[25] is clearly no more a José Martí or a General Antonio Maceo than Leonora is a female version of the Haitian father of independence Toussaint L'Ouverture or a variation on Guadeloupe's legendary mulatta heroine Solitude.[26] Rather, Leonora, like Montejo and also like the *santero* in Lourdes López's award-winning *Estudio de un babalao* (Study of a Santería priest, 1976), is descended from those blacks who never appear in the French or Cuban history books. Also like Montejo, who becomes more politically aware as the narrative progresses—Barnet calls him a "good example of revolutionary conduct"—and even more so like Rigoberta Menchú and like the cast of Cuban freedom fighters in Marta Rojas's famous account of the attack on the Moncada Barracks in *El que debe vivir* (He who must live, 1978), Leonora undergoes a process of *concientización,* or growing self-awareness, which fosters in her a sense of the need for collective action and which results in her political activism with the labor unions. In this respect, Leonora resembles closely the title character in African-American novelist Ernest J. Gaines's fictional testimony novel, *The Autobiography of Miss Jane Pittman* (1972), who joins the Civil Rights activists in the American South at a rather advanced age.

Despite such broad thematic affinities, however, there appear to be marked differences among *Leonora, Biografía,* and *Rigoberta Menchú.* What obtains in *Leonora* is a textual and ideological situation quite different from the dialogic relationship between chronicler / ethnographer and native informant reenacting the kind of American primal literary scene that has become typical of at least the Cuban *testimonio.* "The formula," Roberto González Echevarría explains in his reading of *Biografía,* "entails a chronicler, possessed of writing, asking the native to unveil his or her secrets, and the native doing so, but only by gradually usurping the chronicler's place and turning the account of this confrontation into something quite different from what was originally intended."[27] This formula may be applicable to *Biografía* and, gender differences notwithstanding, to Rigoberta Menchú's narrative as well, for in neither case is the native informant another myself. Leonora's story, her culture and her history, is also that of Dany Bébel-Gisler in ways, for instance, that neither Montejo's nor Rigoberta Menchú's respective Afro-Cuban and Quiché cultures and histories are those of their white interviewers (even if both Barnet and Burgos-Debray are themselves natives of Latin American and / or the Caribbean). Not by any stretch of the imagination can we see Esteban

Montejo and Rigoberta Menchú as what Barnet and Burgos-Debray used to be.

This is not to obfuscate the differences that do exist between the two Guadeloupean women: on the one hand, Leonora the peasant woman with little formal education who is reminiscent of Bébel-Gisler's own mother; on the other, the French-trained intellectual with degrees in literature, ethnology, sociology, and linguistics from a prestigious French university. Yet, Bébel-Gisler does not fix Leonora, or any of the other Guadeloupean women whom she interviewed during her stay in the island from 1980 to 1986, in the often pernicious role of the native other replete with differences of class, language, and, more often than not, race. If anything, those women are already part of her self, of what she calls another myself, the one who grew up speaking the Creole to which she returns in her conversations with Leonora. To the extent that Bébel-Gisler can be said to have rediscovered herself in Leonora, the book's hybrid language serves as an acknowledgment that identity, hers and Leonora's, exists in both a historical and a linguistic continuum.

Although Martinique's Aimé Césaire, arguably the father of negritude, is not included among those Caribbean writers whose work furnishes epigraphs to several of *Leonora*'s chapters, he might as well have been. For the project of cultural and historical recovery on which this testimony novel embarks, and especially the questions Dany Bébel-Gisler raises in her own Postface, resonate as loudly with the writings of Simone Schwarz-Bart, Jacques Roumain, and Frantz Fanon—all writers who are mentioned in *Leonora*—as they do with Césaire's renowned negritude epic, *Cahier d'un retour au pays natal* (Notebook of a return to the native land), which was first published in 1939. Bébel-Gisler asks: "And what if we stopped seeing ourselves through the eyes of the other, the colonizer? If we tried to rediscover our own history? If the term *Nèg mawon* no longer struck terror into the hearts of children and threatened the virginity of young girls, but referred to a heroic resistance fighter, more alive than Joan of Arc, Schoelcher, or de Gaulle . . . ?"

It may seem entirely too facile to code the obvious differences between Césaire's quite erudite literary diction and Bébel-Gisler's more accessible quotidian prose as masculine and feminine. At the same time, *Leonora* may well be read as a revision of the *Cahier*, one that restores female voices to a literary culture dominated by men, be they of European or of African descent, or both, and by decidedly masculine visions (or versions) of national history, identity, and authenticity.

Afterword

For writers such as Fanon, Roumain, and Césaire (the latter also sponsored the 1946 law that created the Overseas Départements), the achievement of national identity was a significant function of restoring one's literary virility in the face of the emasculating forces of French colonialism. In this sense, poems and novels such as Césaire's *Cahier*, Roumain's *Gouverneurs de la rosée*, and Joseph Zobel's *La rue Cases-Nègres* (Black-shack alley, 1950), which became the basis for an award-winning film by the female Martinican director Euzhan Palcy, are indeed literary monuments to imperiled Antillean masculinity.

Curiously perhaps, Bébel-Gisler's use, in the quoted passage above from *Leonora*, of the Creole *Nèg mawon* (runaway slave) bears affinities to one of Césaire's famous poems, "Le verbe marronner" (The verb "marronner" / for René Depestre, Haitian Poet) (1955; rev. 1976). In an earlier note to her text, Bébel-Gisler mentions "the verb *marronner* (*mawonné*)" (note 50) but does not invoke Césaire, who probably derived his purported neologism from the Creole.[28] To point to this connection is by no means to situate Bébel-Gisler squarely within the macho environment of Césairean negritude (notwithstanding Suzanne Césaire's contributions to the movement). Rather, it is to attribute a possible origin to one of Césaire's most famous neologisms and thus to emphasize what may be involved in revealing the "true" (or unofficial) history of Guadeloupe. In *Leonora*, as in Césaire's poem, *marronnage* is not just about "escaping them" ("marronnons-les"), that is, the French colonizers who, for centuries, have written Antillean blacks out of their history books. It is also, to borrow James Clifford's words about Césaire's poem, "about [self-]reflexive possibility and poesis. Césaire makes rebellion and the making of culture—the historical maroon experience—into a *verb*. A necessary verb names the New World poetics of continuous transgression and cooperative cultural activity ('Marronnerons-*nous* Depestre')."[29] But there is a difference: "They," for Bébel-Gisler and for Leonora, are also the Antillean literary elites who have ignored black women—peasants and intellectuals alike. It is perhaps by virtue of its being the product of an actual collaboration, rather than a literary projection of an imagined and clearly male cultural community, that the text of *Leonora* shows, even more clearly than Césaire's poem could, that continuous transgression and *cooperative* cultural activity has everything to do with language, with the attitudes people adopt before and within language—their own and that of others. And Bébel-Gisler's "taste for the exploration of our roots and words,"[30] her sensitivity both to her own French and to the different cadences of Leonora's Creole, necessarily complicates our sense of what the "hidden" or "buried" history of Guadeloupe, and, for that matter, of the rest of the Caribbean, actually may be. *Leonora* makes us realize that this history, much like its own narrative, is polyvocal and polyphonous, and that it includes black women as cultural producers. Leonora may be an old, uneducated woman, but her language, her perceptions, and her imagination are, to borrow a term from Guyanese novelist Wilson Harris, eminently literate.

We mentioned earlier that literary histories of the French West Indies have, by and large, excluded women writers and continue to neglect them even after the publication of Maryse Condé's *La parole des femmes: Essai sur des romancières des Antilles de langue française* (Women's words: An essay on women novelists of the francophone Antilles) in 1979. Early novels by female authors such as Suzanne Lacascade's *Claire-Solange, âme africaine* (Claire-Solange, African soul, 1924), Mayotte Capécia's *Je suis martiniquaise* (I am a Martinican woman, 1948); Françoise Ega's *Lettres à une noire* (Letters to a black woman, published posthumously in 1978); and the Guadeloupean Michèle Lacrosil's *Sapotille et le serin d'argile* (Sapotille and the clay canary, 1960) and *Cajou* (Cashew, 1961) have been all but forgotten. These novels and their women authors have been eclipsed by the work of their male compatriots, which, as in the case of Césaire and other negritude poets, was readily embraced by French avant-garde intellectuals such as André Breton and Jean-Paul Sartre. To add insult to injury, Antillean women writers were at times harshly criticized for their lack of political decorum. The most notorious and vicious of these attacks, and a clear instance of threatened masculinity, was Fanon's attack on Capécia's novel in *Peau noire, masques blancs*. Fanon's rather literal reading amounted to the indiscriminate accusation that Martinican women were selling out their people by sleeping with white men.

Even more recent writers such as Simone Schwarz-Bart, Maryse Condé, and Miriam Warner-Vieyra, though they are better known than their female predecessors, have not escaped criticism on the part of the male Antillean elite for representing female sexual desire and for their alleged apoliticalness.[31] A case in point here is Simone Schwarz-Bart's first novel, *Pluie et vent sur Télumée Miracle* (The bridge of beyond, 1972), originally shunned as an exoticist folktale but now widely recognized as one of the great Antillean novels.[32] Along with *La rue Cases-Nègres,* it is one of the few Antillean novels to be read in island schools. Some of the criticisms aimed at Simone Schwarz-Bart's work anticipated the way in which *Leonora* has been treated by the Antillean intellectual community. If the history of the fictional Lougandor dynasty of women, which Schwarz-Bart's Guadeloupean narrator Télumée chronicles in *Pluie et vent,* seems to eschew politics, certainly patriarchal politics, *Leonora* appears to be too overtly political in its focus on how the daily life of the protagonist is affected by color and class prejudice, and especially by language issues.

That *Leonora* is very much a book about rebellion and resistance, about, as it were, "running away with language,"[33] renders the tasks of translating it into English a complex challenge. As noted above, the issue of translation is itself very much at the heart of what is, for all intents and purposes, already something of a bilingual text that brings French into contact with Guadeloupean Creole. According to Bébel-Gisler, "translating the other consists in investing onself (body and mind) into his [*sic*] culture, grappling with the two languages to make them disclose their secrets." She also acknowledges that "the theoretical, methodological, linguistic and cultural problems involved in translating the other are multiplied in the French West Indies by the tension between Creole and French and a repressive policy against Creole and Creole speakers."[34] This repression is evident throughout Leonora's story, and Bébel-Gisler's social-scientific work, complemented by her community work in education at the rural Centre Bwadoubout, has been dedicated to establishing the value and validity of Creole and to fighting against discrimination on the basis of language use. On the one hand, her decision to write *Leonora* neither in Creole nor in academic French was clearly a practical decision not to limit the "novel"'s audience. The book has even been approved by the National Secretary of Education as a textbook appropriate for use in secondary education.[35] Given that very few Caribbean writers actually appear in the curricula in Caribbean schools, this is no small feat. Given Bébel-Gisler's proindependence politics, it is also an ironic feat.

On the other hand, does one politically further the cause of Creole by writing a book in what at least appears to be the dominant language, French? Bébel-Gisler clarifies this issue:

> If it is acknowledged that each of these warring languages [French and Creole] has its own concepts, a system of thought which determines what can be thought, that either language imposes upon the reader prohibitions and evidences which are inscribed in its grammar, that the latter is the essence of the language for on it depends the way the individual or group organizes experience, [then] it becomes clear that the problem is not so much to translate Creole into French, as to translate oneself, to translate the other, to translate ourselves, to say what we are. . . . If I take the word "mofwazé," "to metamorphose," used by Léonora to qualify my role, in the sense [of] referring in

Afterword

Caribbean popular culture to some people's ability to
transform themselves by magic at night into a dog or bird,
I realize that it aptly expresses both Leonora's thought
and the role of "double agent" assumed by the translator
of another person's biography.

That the language of *Leonora* itself enacts such transformations is
amply confirmed by the responses of different groups of readers to the
novel's language: "For those who do not master French, *Leonora* is
written in Creole. For others, beyond the French words one can hear
the song of Creole."[36] Multiplicity, metamorphosis, hybridity: these
concepts and processes operate at many different levels in *Leonora* and
place it squarely within both the popular and the literary cultures of a
Caribbean that has moved beyond negritude.

Vera M. Kutzinski
Yale University

Cynthia Mesh-Ferguson
Colorado State University

Notes to Afterword

1. While *Leonora* was reviewed widely both in France and in the Antilles, there have been virtually no critical studies of it to date. In fact, *Leonora* is rarely even mentioned in accounts of francophone Caribbean literature. An example of such neglect is a *Callaloo* special issue on "The Literature of Guadeloupe and Martinique" 15 (1992), in which none of the contributors even make reference to *Leonora*. One exception is A. James Arnold's "Poétique forcée et identité dans la littérature des Antilles francophones" (Forced poetics and identity in the literature of the francophone Caribbean), which contrasts *Leonora* with a "hyperintellectual" text such as Edouard Glissant's *Le discours antillais* (1981) (in *L'Héritage de Caliban / Caliban's Legacy*, ed. Maryse Condé [Pointe-à-Pitre: Editions Jasor, 1992], pp. 20-21).

2. Jean Bernabé, Patrick Chamoiseau, Raphaël Confiant, *Eloge de la Créolité* (Paris: Gallimard / Presses Universitaires Créoles, 1989), 14, translated as "In Praise of Creoleness" by Mohamed B. Taleb Khyar in *Callaloo* 13 (1990): 886. See also Antonio Benítez Rojo's Introduction to his *The Repeating Island: The Caribbean and the Postmodern Condition*, trans. James Maraniss (Durham, N.C.: Duke Univ. Press, 1992).

3. Jack Corzani, *La littérature des Antilles-Guyane françaises*, 6 vols (Fort-de-France: Désormeaux, 1978; Roger Toumson, *La transgression des couleurs: Littérature et langage aux Antilles (XVIIIe; XIXe; XXe siècles)* (Paris: Editions Caribéennes, 1989); Patrick Chamoiseau and Raphaël Confiant, *Lettres créoles: Tracées antillaises et continentales de la littérature, 1635-1975* (Paris: Hatier, 1991); also "2000 titres de littérature des Caraïbes," Special issue of *Notre Librairie*, July-September 1991.

4. Because of the widespread availability of television and radio, almost all children can understand French fairly well by the time they enter school (competence), but a significant number in rural communities have very little speaking ability at that time (performance). In an interview Cynthia Mesh-Ferguson conducted, an educator of primary-school teachers in Guadeloupe estimated that up to 60 percent of all Guadeloupean children entering school can have significant difficulties expressing themselves in French.

5. Marie-Josée Cérol argues for the recognition of the contribution of African languages to Creole in her study *Une introduction au créole guadeloupéen* (An introduction to Guadeloupean Creole) (Pointe-à-Pitre: Editions Jasor, 1991). Also, for a well-documented account of the development of Antillean Creole and a study of attitudes toward this language in the Antilles, especially Martinique, see Lambert-Félix Prudent, *Des baragouins à la langue antillaise* (From gibberish to the Antillean language) (Paris: Editions Caribéennes, 1980).

6. Frantz Fanon, *Black Skin, White Masks*, trans. Charles Lam Markmann (New York: Grove Weidenfeld, 1967), p. 18. Dany Bébel-Gisler, "Who is the Other? What does translating the Other mean?" unpublished typescript of a talk delivered at the Seventh International Conference on Translation at Barnard College, Columbia University, November 16-17, 1990, p. 4.

7. See Corzani, *La Littérature des Antilles-Guyane françaises,* 5:195.

8. See Ellen M. Schnepel, "The Politics of Language in the French Caribbean: The Creole Movement on the Island of Guadeloupe." Ph.D. diss., Columbia University, 1990.

9. Bernabé, Chamoiseau, and Confiant, "In Praise of Creoleness," pp. 896, 891, 890.

10. A note to "In Praise of Creoleness" informs us that "Creole and French cannot be opposed on the generic model of national language / colonizers' language, which does not mean that this precise relation is not a colonial one. But precisely, all colonial relations are not identical. In spite of its dominant characteristic (on the social level), French has acquired a certain *legitimacy* in our countries. If, in many respects, it is a *second language,* French cannot be considered, in Guadeloupe, Guyane, and Martinique, as a foreign language, with all the psychological implications of this notion." This quotation is attributed to the G.E.R.E.C. (Groupe d'Etudes et de Recherches en Espace Créolophone: research group for study of the creolophone region), founded by Jean Bernabé (p. 908 n. 34).

11. Maryse Condé, "Order, Disorder, Freedom, and the West Indian Writer," *Yale French Studies* 83 (1993): 134.

12. For further details see Georges-Henri Léotin's "A Summary Overview of Antillean Literature in Creole, Martinique and Guadeloupe (1960-1980)," *Callaloo* 15 (1992): 190-98.

13. See, for instance, Hector Poullet's *Dictionnaire du créole guadeloupéen* (1984). Léotin points out that "In the case of Creole spelling, the rejection of the etymological solution—reference to the French spelling—beyond the pragmatic reasons, exemplifies a political and ideological choice: independence from the French spelling, refusal of a spelling tutorial, and affirmation of autonomy; in brief, a willingness to constitute Creole into a major language that is adult and sovereign" ("A Summary Overview," p. 191). The inconsistencies in Creole spelling within the text of *Leonora* signal such politics and have been left intact for that reason.

14. Marie-Denise Shelton, "Literature Extracted: A Poetic of Daily Life," *Callaloo* 15 (1992): 171; Jean Bernabé, "Contribution à l'étude de la diglossie littéraire: Le cas de *Pluie et vent sur Télumée Miracle," Textes, Etudes, et Documents,* no. 2 (1979): 103-30. (*Textes, Etudes, et documents* is published by the Groupe d'Etudes et de Recherches en Espace Créolophone (G.E.R.E.C.) at the Université des Antilles et de la Guyane, Fort-de-France, Martinique.)

15. On Ortiz, see Gustavo Pérez Firmat, *The Cuban Condition: Translation and Identity in Modern Cuban Literature* (New York: Cambridge University Press, 1989), chap. 3, and Antonio Benítez Rojo, *The Repeating Island,* chap. 4.

16. Michel Leiris, quoted in Clifford, *The Predicament of Culture,* pp. 255-56; Zora Neale Hurston, *Mules and Men* (1935; rpt. Bloomington: Indiana Univ. Press, 1978), p. 3.

17. Benigno Sánchez-Eppler, "Telling Anthropology: Zora Neale Hurston and Gilberto Freyre Disciplined in Their Field-Home-Work," *American Literary History* 4, no. 3 (1992): 467.

18. Ibid., p. 484.

19. For further information see Roberto González Echevarría, *The Voice of the Masters: Writing and Authority in Modern American Literature* (Austin: Univ. of Texas Press, 1985), chap. 6; Klaus Bunke, *Testimonio-Literatur in Kuba: Ein neues literarisches Genre zur Wirklichkeitsbeschreibung* (Testimony Literature in Cuba: A new literary genre for the description of reality) (Pfaffenweiler, Germany: Centaurus-Verlagsgesellschaft, 1988); and the more broadly conceived volume *Testimonio y literatura,* ed. René Jara and Hernán Vidal (Minneapolis: Society for the Study of Con-

temporary Hispanic and Lusophone Revolutionary Literatures, 1986), which includes a reprint of Miguel Barnet's "La novela testimonio: Socio-literatura" (1983).

20. See also *Mujer y testimonio: Serie documentos* (Woman and testimonial narrative: Documents series) no. 1 (Santiago, Chile: Programa de Estudios y Capacitación de la Mujer Campesina e Indigena, 1983) for an overview of the use of the *testimonio* specifically as a medium for recording women's history. Also, Jorge Narvaez, *El testimonio: 1972-1982 (Transformaciones en el sistema literario)* (Santiago, Chile: CENECA, 1983).

21. Miguel Barnet, "La novela testimonio: Socio-literatura," in his *La Fuente Viva* (La Habana: Editorial Letras Cubanas, 1983), p. 25.

22. See Wilson Harris, *Tradition, the Writer, and Society: Critical Essays* (London: New Beacon Publications, 1967).

23. Ibid., pp. 30, 42.

24. Ibid., pp. 27-33.

25. See Barnet's Introduction to his *Biografía de un cimarrón* (Madrid: Ediciones Alfaguara, 1984), p. 15. The Introduction to both the British and American editions of this text is substantially different from the Spanish original.

26. See André Schwarz-Bart, *La mulâtresse Solitude.*

27. Roberto González Echevarría, *The Voice of the Masters,* p. 123.

28. Clayton Eshleman and Annette Smith, in what is the best English translation of Césaire's poetry to date, translate the verb *marronner* as "running away like a slave" (*Aimé Césaire: The Collected Poetry* [Berkeley: Univ. of California Press, 1983]).

29. James Clifford, *The Predicament of Culture* (Cambridge, Mass.: Harvard Univ. Press, 1988), p. 181.

30. Bébel-Gisler, "Who is the Other?" p. 6.

31. See Simone and André Schwarz-Bart, "Sur les pas de Fanotte (interview)" (In the footsteps of Fanotte), by Héliane and Roger Toumson in *Textes, Etudes, et Documents* 2 (1979): 22.

32. Interviews conducted by Cynthia Mesh-Ferguson in Guadeloupe and Martinique in the spring of 1992 showed that most Antilleans she questioned could name only a few Antillean writers, if any: for instance, Césaire, Glissant, Simone Schwarz-Bart, Condé.

33. Clifford, *The Predicament of Culture,* p. 181.

34. Bébel-Gisler, "Who is the Other?" pp. 2, 4.

35. According to Bébel-Gisler, a group from the Lycée Baimbridge in Pointe-à-Pitre won a national contest with the pedagogical materials they created to accompany *Leonora,* so it can now be taught in high schools. This does not mean, however, that the book is actually widely used. In her interviews with a number of teachers of French in Guadeloupe, Cynthia Mesh-Ferguson did not come across a single one who had included *Leonora* on his / her reading list. Some French teachers explained that they did not consider *Leonora* to be a novel and thus appropriate for literary study, but admitted that it would be valuable for classroom use as a sociohistorical account of Guadeloupean culture.

36. Bébel-Gisler, "Who is the Other?" pp. 8, 9.

Acknowledgments

My thanks go to many people who helped me maneuver through the translation challenges posed by *Leonora*. A. James Arnold and Cynthia H. Foote, respectively General Editor of CARAF Books and manuscript editor at the University Press of Virginia, read and reread the translation for clarity, accuracy, and consistency. Bishop Krister Stendahl found the perfect English equivalents for the (partially Christian, partially pagan) references to church and religious life. Dr. Richard Berlin served as my expert on medical matters. Carrol Coates helped with Creole words and phrases; so did Cynthia Mesh-Ferguson, who also, together with Vera Kutzinski, read early drafts to help me find the proper tone for Leonora. My graduate assistant, Linda Fries, diligently entered revisions to the manuscript and tracked down books and Creole dictionaries. My greatest thanks go to my husband, Tommy Olof Elder, whose ear could always discern the nuances of both the French and English voices of Dany Bébel-Gisler and of Leonora. His help and support were invaluable throughout the work as I searched to faithfully capture the tone of the original *Leonora*.

Leonora herself communicated with Dany Bébel-Gisler in Creole. Her words formed the basis for the French text that was translated into English for this book. My hope is that, despite these multiple transformations, English-speaking Caribbean women can recognize themselves and their lives in *Leonora* just as their Francophone counterparts did in the original book. Insofar as I have succeeded, all of the people above deserve heartfelt thanks.

AL

The authors of the Afterword would like to thank Claudine Romana for her help in translating and explaining Creole words and phrases in the Paris edition of *Léonora*.

VMK and CM-F

284

Acknowledgments

The General Editor greatly appreciates the assistance received from Richard Philcox on difficulties in Creole; from Olivier Mounsamy on the South Indian Hindu rituals practiced in Guadeloupe and described in chapter two; and from Karen Richman on specifics of the *expédition* ceremony in chapter three.

AJA

Caraf Books

Caribbean and African Literature

Translated from French

Serious writing in French in the Caribbean and Africa has developed unique characteristics in this century. Colonialism was its crucible; African independence in the 1960s its liberating force. The struggles of nation-building and even the constraints of neocolonialism have marked the coming of age of literatures that now gradually distance themselves from the common matrix.

CARAF BOOKS is a collection of novels, plays, poetry, and essays from the regions of the Caribbean and the African continent that have shared this linguistic, cultural, and political heritage while working out their new identity against a background of conflict.

An original feature of the CARAF BOOKS collection is the substantial critical essay in which a scholar who knows the literature well sets each book in its cultural context and makes it accessible to the student and the general reader.

Most of the books selected for the CARAF collection are being published in English for the first time; some are important books that have been out of print in English or were first issued in editions with a limited distribution. In all cases CARAF BOOKS offers the discerning reader new wine in new bottles.

The Editorial Board of CARAF BOOKS consists of A. James Arnold, University of Virginia, General Editor; Kandioura Dramé, University of Virginia, Associate Editor; and three Consulting Editors, Abiola Irele of Ohio State University, J. Michael Dash of the University of the West Indies in Mona, Jamaica, and Henry Louis Gates, Jr., of Harvard University.

Caraf Books